THE LIFE LIST

*The Difference Between Doing
Something and Doing Nothing Is Everything*

So Sue!
Can't wait to
find out what you
think of the
book!.
xoxo—
Chrissy
Anderson

BY **CHRISSY ANDERSON**

ISBN: 1482774860
ISBN-13: 978-1-4827-7486-3 (sc)

Abbott Press rev. date: 4/5/2012

THE LIST TRILOGY

The Life List

The Unexpected List

The Hope List

For Scott and Mia…My angels on earth.

TABLE OF CONTENTS

During (preposition) dur*ing:

Throughout a period or event, either continuously or
several times between the beginning and end.

INHALE

FEBRUARY, 2001

I'm standing in front of hundreds of people giving her eulogy. Even though I'm the one doing all the talking, I'm not standing up here all by myself. My two remaining best friends are on either side of me holding firmly onto my hands. For once, I'm the strong one in the middle, and they're counting on me to hold them up. I had three best friends, but one is in the casket behind me. She died when she was only thirty-one years old.

I begin by describing the relationship the four of us had, what each of us offered to the other, how the three of us will never be the same after suffering such a tragic loss, blah, blah, blah. I'm keeping the eulogy lighthearted and short because in the audience sits a scattering of schmucks from my high school days, and I don't want to ruin my makeup in front of them. I haven't seen most of these people for nearly fifteen years, and I know that a few of them are just dying (no pun intended) to get a glimpse of me and my two remaining best friends in all of our pain and agony. You see, back in the day, we were "the shit," and I'm sure there are more than a handful of folks in the pews who we pissed off, humiliated, dissed...you name the crime, and I'm sure we committed it.

I look up and see several of those familiar faces, and relief washes over me as I confirm, one by one, that I look better than all of them. My friend in Heaven is most likely laughing her ass off because this is exactly the kind of moment she and I got the most enjoyment out of. No, we wouldn't enjoy the funeral part, but after the service we would've driven straight to a bar, hunkered down with a bottle of wine, and picked every single person apart. Had our old classmates brought their children, we would've criticized them too. No one would've been off limits. She and I have been each other's best source of gossip and useless information for eighteen years, and the thought of living without that connection suddenly makes me want to launch into full blown tears--exactly what I didn't want to happen in front of these people!

All of the sudden, my eulogy comes to a halt and the grip I have on my two friends' hands tightens as I try to process the questions that are shooting through my brain. Who will I call when my favorite person gets voted off of that new show *Survivor*? Who's going to help me determine the next body part to have surgically altered? Who am I going to call when Angelina Jolie and Billy Bob Thornton expectedly split up? There is no one. I tell myself to breathe, just keep breathing.

I turn slightly to look at her shiny pearl white casket, which I've done an exceptional job of ignoring until this very moment, and I can hear the collective gasp from the crowd in front of me as they anticipate one of my classic meltdowns.

I try to gain control of myself, but it's nearly impossible. She's in that box! How am I breathing and she's not? This is not right. Oh shit, Oh shit, I have to breathe. I feel my facial muscles tighten, and I can't find a drop of moisture in my mouth. What's she wearing? Is her skin shriveling away? Is my letter in there with her? Would it be horrible if I walked over and took a peek?

Choking back tears, my focus turns back to the crowd when, thank God, I notice the one guy from high school I regret not having made out with. Wow, he got really fat. I instantly regain my composure. I'm not about to give him or any of these other people the satisfaction of seeing me flub this moment, her moment...*our moment*. It's what they would expect. I want to be everything they hope I'm not: articulate, admirable, classy. I want to wipe away their confused looks as they wonder why I'm the one speaking. Mostly, I want them to see that despite my seemingly colossal screw ups, I'm extraordinary.

To maintain my composure, I channel Patsy. You know, that glamorous friend of Debra Winger from the movie *Terms of Endearment*.

Debra Winger plays a woman named Emma and she gets cancer. Emma ends up dying from the disease, and it's all very sad, but that's not the point. Emma's best friend, Patsy, is the point. Patsy was beautiful, independent and smart. She fled her stupid small town to go make something of herself in New York, and despite how opposite their lifestyles became, Emma and Patsy managed to stay best friends. I'm a Patsy. Unlike my friend in Heaven, right after high school, I left our crappy city of Fremont, California, or as I refer to it "Freakmont," to live in the more exciting city of Palo Alto. Palo Alto was no New York, but it was a huge step up from Freakmont. There was a bridge separating the two cities, and the water between provided a wide enough gap for me to feel like I was a world away from my roots. Palo Alto is home to smart people, over-priced retail stores, fancy restaurants, and humungous houses that I still dream of living in. Freakmont has row after row of cement grey strip malls housing stores like Beedazzled, TJ Maxx, and Miller's Outpost. It also has more Jack-in-the-Boxes than I can count, *and* it's home to street after street of low income apartment complexes. Okay, okay, I stand corrected. Most of them aren't low income, but any apartment complex outside of Manhattan is low income to me. I used to *love* Freakmont…when I was in high school. Many of my best (although drunk) memories are from those years. But to remain in Freakmont after graduation would have resulted in me becoming either a teacher, a hair stylist, or if I really applied myself, a manager at Albertson's. In retrospect, two out of the three of those careers would've afforded me a comfy retirement package and medical coverage for life, but I would've rather been a homeless, toothless geriatric begging for money and peeing herself while roaming the streets of a cool city than take the safe route and stay in Freakmont post-high school.

I'm about to continue speaking and then uh-oh…I see some of my old high school teachers. There's the one who said I would never amount to anything, the one who recommended I become a flight attendant, and the big asshole who threatened to delay the graduation of our entire senior class because…Well, this is actually a funny story and I'm going to deviate from the eulogy for a moment to tell it to you…

I have a brother who's two years older than I am, and back in high school I would study off of his old exams to prepare for mine. Clever, right? Well I got even cleverer when I decided to sell copies of one of those old tests. And it wasn't just any old test; it was a copy of his senior year economics final. I charged $3 for a copy of the test if I liked you, $5 if I didn't, and $7 if I had never heard of you before. I also created an elaborate system to protect myself in case someone got caught with a copy. I chose two people I trusted with my life to help me. Isn't it amusing how you think you can trust someone with your life when you're in high school? Anyway, those two people, my middlemen, were the only ones who knew I was the originator of the test, and I relied on them to keep my identity a secret. I gave them 20 tests at a time to sell so it was easy for me to track cash flow. Let's be real, I trusted them with my life but not my cash! I let my middlemen choose two of their own people, the distributors, to sell the test and handle all of the cash transactions. I'm not sure how essential the distributors were, but I really enjoyed having a staff. I even promised everyone a bonus of movie theatre tickets if at least 250 tests were sold, because I'm a firm believer in incentives to keep people motivated!

And then something so wonderful, so miraculous, so beyond every senior's imagination happened! The test administered to us was THE EXACT SAME ONE AS THE TEST I SOLD! I was already a popular girl, but in one hour I became a legend, *and* I ended up making over a grand in cold hard cash. The team and I were happy and rich and hundreds of seniors were skipping around in jubilation…for about a week. The jig was up once the economics teacher realized 265 out of 300 seniors got an A on the final. That bastard (who's now sitting four pews back, second from the left) interrogated every single senior one by one; eventually one of my middlemen fell victim to his tactics and narked me out. I was in big trouble, but I fought back. I argued that I shouldn't be blamed because his lazy ass couldn't come up with any new test material in the last two years. I contended that he should've praised me as a savvy young business woman with an entrepreneurial spirit. For fuck's sake, didn't he see the economics in what I was doing? Nope, it became a big to-do. He turned the fate of the entire senior class over to the administration, and they threatened to delay our graduation until the issue got resolved. Didn't they care that we already had graduation parties lined up, relatives flying in, and kegs hiding in the trunks of our cars? Apparently not, because they didn't back down to any of the tizzy-fits I threw. I felt an intense need to protect my staff, my payroll, and my quality customers, so I regrouped and used the proceeds of the sale of the test to distribute fliers and make posters that explained my side of the story. I screamed from my megaphone that it's the work ethic and creativity of clever Americans like me who drive our elite economy, and I warned the economics teacher that he was in for the fight of his pathetic life. After I threatened to take the situation to the media, the administration became eager to do away with the whole mess. The decided punishment was that the senior class had to retake the final. I got a C- on the second test, but who cares. The valuable lesson I learned at a young age was to never back down to a bully. Well…that, and to *always* state in fine print that all sales are final, and no refunds will be provided under any circumstances.

I suddenly feel really good about myself and calm enough to proceed with the eulogy. I stand proud in my three-inch black patent leather Via Spiga's. My perfectly fitting Banana Republic pencil skirt has the cutest black satin stripe down the side. It really accentuates my small hips. My crisp white Calvin Klein blouse clings to my slender 5'6" body, and my pink cable knit sweater is tied loosely around my neck. My pearls are real, my legs have a fake tan, my blond hair is highlighted to perfection, and my skin is flawless, thanks to my overpaid esthetician. My eyes are ice blue and piercing through the faces of my past, and I'm actually enjoying it until they land smack dab on the one man that consumed most of it.

I saw him earlier when he drove up in his Porsche. That damn car. I can't help but wonder if he bought it as some kind of last-ditch effort to get me back. I doubt it, since he hardly tried (at least not the way I wanted him to) when I left him that one, no wait, two… *Jesus how many times did I walk out the door?* So many that I lost count. He called right after my friend died. There's still love there or maybe it's a need to protect. Who knows, the break up is still so fresh. Anyway, our conversation that day wasn't about what we went through over our last three years, but what she went through over her last one. It was bittersweet to *finally* have something else to talk to him about. He didn't mention *the other woman* at all, and he didn't ask about *the other man*. Not out of character for him to ignore the big pink elephants in the room, but I have to admit, for once it was a relief. At the end of the phone call he told me he had some pictures of the gang--the gang being the two of us, my best friends, and their husbands. He thought I might like to have them, and why not look at them together…over coffee. I cautiously accepted his invitation.

Looking at him now, he's dressed too casually for a memorial service and for a second it irritates me. It's as if I had no impact on him during the time we were together. I *never* would've allowed him to show up to something like this wearing jeans. But this is how he is, and people have always found his casual approach to things endearing. I guess I have to admit, now that I don't feel responsible for his actions, I kind of I find him a little endearing too.

He's excessively handsome. I mean, really, one would not think it possible to cram so many striking features onto a man unless you saw it for your own eyes. If looks were all that mattered, I might still be with him. Unfortunately it wasn't long after we moved in together that I couldn't even see what he looked like anymore.

Now that the dust has settled, I can see him again, standing at the back of the memorial hall, dead center between the pews. He's concentrating on every word I say, and it *almost* looks like he's in pain. He should be. She was his friend, too.

I'm at the part of the eulogy where I describe the relationship my deceased friend had with her husband, and my gaze shifts to the poor guy. It's an unbearable sight. He's shifting around in his seat like it's taking all of his self-control not to run to the bathroom and throw up. My friend and her husband were special. At sixteen they formed a bond that was intimate and deep, and from the moment they met I was no longer her closest companion. When we were younger, my other two best friends and I would criticize their relationship. It wasn't until I grew up that I could admit to myself that I was jealous of what they shared for over fifteen years. And right now, especially, it's worth noting; if you're lucky enough to find your soul mate, you should treat them like you would die without them. You never know when either one of you is going to the kick the bucket.

Ahhhh, there's my mom trying to hide in the back of the room. She's clinging tightly to my father and, of course, she's wearing her trademark black sunglasses. I'll let her get away with that look today because, after all, it's a funeral. But normally, rain or shine, indoors or outdoors, day or night, those suckers are glued to her face. She thinks she's hiding from the world when she wears them, but they just draw more attention to her.

Those damn sunglasses have *always* made me sad. They're like her outward symbol of her inward insecurities that none of us--my brother, my dad, or I--have been able to alleviate, no matter how beautiful, smart, and needed we tell her she is. My mom wasn't going to come today. Said it was because she didn't think she could handle the pain of seeing my friend's mother bury her daughter, but I knew it was because she was afraid her sunglasses wouldn't be big enough to hide behind. But, I stood my ground and told her she had to go…for me. And look, she showed up…for me. I will always give my mom first right of refusal for kissing my boo-boos. But on the days when her sunglasses are too small to do it, I have two remaining friends who can. And with that thought, my grip on their hands tightens once again.

I conclude the eulogy and I stand at the podium for a moment longer to take it all in. I turn to look at my friend's casket, and a tiny smile forms on my perfectly-lined lips. I'm overwhelmed with the guiltless knowledge that if it wasn't for her agonizing death and all that it taught me, I wouldn't be as happy as I am today.

UNLOAD

<hr>

FEBRUARY, 2001

We used to call ourselves the A-BOB's. It stood for A Bunch of Bobs because for a brief period of time in high school we all had identical bob-style haircuts. When we went to parties where nobody knew who we were, we made up fake names, names we *really* wished our parents had given us like Vanessa, Charlotte, Tiffany and Ginger…you know, good ol' fashioned slut names. One thing's for sure, we loved to keep people guessing, and my best friends and I rarely used our real names, Chrissy, Courtney, Kelly and Nicole.

After the funeral, ol' Charlotte, Tiffany, and I (a.k.a. Vanessa) spontaneously decided to spend a much needed week of grieving in Cabo San Lucas because the funeral after-party, if that's what you call it, didn't really allow us the opportunity to do that. It was a chaotic blur of entertaining strangers, fake laughing, bad wine, and escaping to our dead friend's bedroom to get away from it. We took turns smelling her clothes, sitting in her empty bathtub, rummaging through her purse, applying her lipstick, and using her hairbrush. We didn't let our emotional guard down in front of the guests because it was her house, and she wouldn't have wanted us to. So we decided to go to Mexico to mourn in our own way: with old pictures, lots of tears, and massive amounts of tequila. We needed to be hysterically angry one minute and hopelessly lost the next. We needed to throw things at the wall, kick and scream deliriously for no reason and every reason, wish out loud that one of us had died instead, and then quickly admit we're thankful we hadn't. We needed to curse God, doubt God, and start believing in God. We needed to refill each other's glass, fear for our own lives, worry out loud about our dead friend's child and curse those that foolishly say she'll be okay. We needed to argue about which one of us was closest to her, laugh at her laugh, talk shit about her stubborn streak, her horrible taste in cars, and her annoying ability to put her own needs ahead of anyone else's, always. We needed to relive every memory shared with her for the last eighteen years, and we needed to do all of it over and over again until we were ready to face the fact that she was gone. For days we stayed up late, woke up swollen, kept our cell phones turned off, and wore no makeup, jewelry or semblance of a coordinating outfit. We sat by the edge of the pool and burst into unprompted fits of rage followed by long streams of silence. But mostly we made endless toasts to the magnificence of our bond, and we spoke as if *all* of us were still alive because her death was just too fresh.

There's Kelly, the voice of reason amongst the four of us. She's the most awesome wife, mother and school teacher in the entire world. She's organized and bitchy just like me. But…Kelly and I are about as opposite as two people can be when it comes to our fashion sense. She's a bargain-hunter and a pack rat. She doesn't live in filth or anything like that, but the chick won't throw away her old clothes…even the ones from high school! She's hell-bent they'll make a comeback and sometimes even throws on something fluorescent to try and convince us of her point.

Kelly's the one to tell you what's on her mind, no matter how painful it is to listen to. She'll tell you your outfit's ugly, to shut up when you talk too much, and to stop whining when you complain too much. She isn't a completely horrible person; she just tells it like it is. She's the one person I've never been able to bullshit, and I've always gone to her when I needed a dose of reality and a good slap in the face. Kelly doesn't wear her heart on her sleeve, and she doesn't really care if you think she has one. Her actions let me know she loves me, but for the life of our friendship, I've never heard her tell me so. *Well, maybe that one time.*

The thing I admire most about Kelly is her confidence, but it's always gotten in the way of her asking for help when I know she's needed it. But lucky for her, I'm damn stubborn! I'm the only one who's had the guts to come to her aid when she's needed it the most. Like when she told me to stay away when her dad died and I showed up at her doorstep with a big bouquet of flowers anyway. Or when she went into labor after enduring a high-risk pregnancy, she said "stay home and I'll call you when it's over." I didn't. I paced outside of her delivery room and to her dismay yelled encouraging words to her through the closed door. I know my big sappy heart has bugged the shit out of Kelly for eighteen years, but I don't care. Even though she's never admitted it, she's the only one of my friends who truly needs me.

Ahhhhhh Nicole, the sarcasm of the group. Whenever things get tense between the four of us, Nicole eases the awkwardness by cracking a joke or poking fun at the person who caused the friction. Her honest cynicism, although frustrating at times, has quickly turned major arguments between the four of us into super fun cocktails at happy hour more times than I can count. Thank God for her humor too, it's gotta be the only thing that makes her fucked-up job as an ER doctor at Highland Hospital in Oakland somewhat tolerable. Yep, gangland baby!

Nicole's the person I *always* go to when I have something uncomfortable to confess. No matter how embarrassing or disgusting my confession is, she always has one of her own to make mine seem silly. She makes me feel sane when I know I'm not, and I've always been scared to death to lose the refuge she provides me. What's she look like you ask? Well, bless her heart, but Nicole's always a mess. You can usually find a stain on her clothes, and her curly hair is constantly disheveled. She's also my only black friend. I wanted more, but she didn't come as a set. She's late to everything and always has to borrow a buck from one of the three of us because she can't remember where she put her purse. She's a total disaster, but at the end of the day, her husband and child are the most perfectly loved and cared for people in the world. She's got an amazing giggle and an enviable happy-go-lucky attitude. Throughout our friendship, Nicole's sarcasm and my sensitivity have caused a lot of drama.

Out of the four of us, we're the ones who have the most theatrical arguments and the most heartfelt reconciliations.

Courtney, Courtney, Courtney. She's the problem solver of the group. She's the rational one who's always tried to talk the rest of us out of doing completely stupid things. But unfortunately for her, it's always been three against one, so she spent the earlier years of our friendship in deep doo-doo with her parents. Courtney was voted most likely to succeed *and* best looking in high school. It's a good thing for her she was my best friend back then or else I would've made her life miserable by slashing her tires or TP'ing her house. She was valedictorian of our high school class, her college under-graduate class, *and* her medical school. Yes, Courtney's a doctor, too, but not the laid back kind like Nicole. Court's a friggin' worka-holic maniac who's all about prestige. For a thirty-one year old, she's got the longest job title in the world, something like:

Assistant Professor of Medicine
Assistant Residency Director
Primary Care Internal Medicine Residency Program
University of California, San Francisco School of Medicine

I don't know what the hell any of that means, but she's really fucking smart. If I ever get arrested, Courtney's the girl I'll use my one free phone call from jail on, because she's completely reliable and entirely non-judgmental. She's everyone's friend, and I've never heard anyone say an unkind word about her. You can believe that if I did, I would've punched the person in the face. Courtney's flaw (although she wouldn't see it that way) is that she has an unhealthy need to help the world. Since high school she's let her beauty fade more than I would've liked it, but stuff like that isn't as important to her as it is to me. Work is what's important to Courtney, and so it shocked the hell out of me that she married very young, at twenty-one. Perhaps she knew she wouldn't have time to do it later. I mean, it wouldn't surprise me if she had the ability to see into the future. She's just that smart. Somewhere in the last few years she even found the time to pop out a kid. Looking back, I wonder if she thinks marriage and a kid were good choices. I'll never ask her because I know she doesn't have the time to second-guess her life, and I don't want to do anything to stress her out. She has enough of that. I'll never get tired of telling Courtney to take care of herself because she's my touchstone, and I love her so much.

Then there's me, Chrissy. It's not hard to figure out that I'm the emotional core of the group. But I'm not just the type of girl who sees a stray animal and bursts into tears. I'm so much more than that. For *most* of the last eighteen years, I haven't let a month go by without talking to my friends, and I've even gone so far as to micro-manage the friendships they have with each other by making sure they call each other on birthdays and what not. Sometime during college, I got tired of being the mommy of our friendships, and I went on strike to see if they would call to check on me, but I only lasted three days before I picked up the phone. I was too afraid to get let down. I've always needed our friendship to be a success, and I have, at times, even created the false impression that we were closer than we really were. What's even more fucked-up is that when, for a brief period, we weren't close at all, it was my fault.

I'm a lot stronger and smarter than I look and these qualities come in handy in all sorts of dealings. I can do thirty boy pushups in a row and kick anyone's ass at poker, *and* I've been known to hustle unsuspecting guys out of their hard-earned money by betting them I couldn't do either of those things. People can be so stereotypical, and I relish the humiliated look on their faces the moment they realize they got outsmarted by someone they thought was weak and dumb. There's nothing better. I get a lot of compliments on my appearance from men and never any from women, so the only thing I derive from that is that I'm pretty. I'm *overly* generous, but at the same time horrifically mean-spirited. I'm the girl who'll pick up something you just dropped, run to give it back to you, and then talk shit about your hair and clothes once you're out of ear-shot.

When I was sixteen, I made a life list that looked like this:

1) Graduate college in 4 years with a Business major and Marketing minor. My parents will be so happy.

2) Get a job in the fashion industry where I can travel and boss people around. I love the GAP!

3) Save money and buy first house with Kurt by 23. Don't move in with him until we're married though! Tee hee.

4) Marry Kurt when I'm 25. I want to get married on the beach!

5) Move into a big giant house (hopefully in Danville) by the time I'm 27.

6) Have first baby when I'm 28. I want a boy first and a girl second.

7) I want my kids to be two years apart so they can be best friends forever! Yay!

And being the control freak that I am, I stuck to the list. Even as a grown-ass woman I chased after stuff written in purple ink, on college rule binder paper, and folded into a fancy little triangle. It never occurred to me that all of my satisfaction came from *crossing* things off the list, not what I was accomplishing! Sticking to the damn list explains why my life was so empty once I had everything I thought I ever wanted and it also explains the total mental breakdown that led me to a therapist's office three years ago. One of my best friends has been stopped by cancer, something totally out of her control, but I was my own disease.

My last appointment with my therapist is set for a week after I return from Mexico. Sure I'll struggle with life after therapy, but who doesn't? There's not one thirty- something year old woman out there who doesn't struggle with men, marriage, wrinkles, cellulite, and money. It's time to grieve the loss of my best friend and the greatest love (and sex) of my life on my own.

REHASH

I wouldn't say Mexico was great, but it was necessary. Coming home was a lot easier than I expected and for the first time in a long time, my eyes aren't puffy. At first I thought I wanted to stay with my two best friends in Mexico forever. There's nothing more soothing than wallowing in misery with the people you know and love the most. But after day three, I started to miss my job, and my job missed me, and I became anxious about coming home to see what that phone call I had with him would lead to.

Today is my first day back to reality. It's a rainy March day just like most of the other March days in Northern California, except the rain here is more beautiful because it's in Danville. I adore it here. It's clean, safe and full of people who look just like me, except with lots of money. I worked my ass off to live in Danville, but sadly for me it was short-lived. I only come back now to see my therapist.

I'm pulling into the parking lot of my miracle worker for the last time. After three years, I still don't know much about her except that her name is Dr. Maria, she's divorced from a pro-baseball player, and the extra box of tissues resides behind the ugly grey couch. Over the last three years, I noticed the diplomas hanging behind her cluttered desk, but I never thought to look at where she was educated. You could say I've been pretty self-absorbed while I've been coming here.

At first, I kept coming back to therapy because I felt like it was the right thing to do. But Dr. Maria always managed to leave a sprinkling of reality on the table that drew me back for clarity and guidance. She knows the lies I've told, the hearts I've broken, the damage I've done, and the damage done to me. This woman knows every morbid detail about me, and all I know is her name. It isn't until today, the day I'll be saying good-bye, that I wish I knew more about her. Too late for that I guess.

I walk into the waiting room and push the buzzer that alerts Dr. Maria of my arrival so she can wrap it up with the loon sitting on her couch. I used to hate it when that happened to me. It always seemed like just when we were getting into the real meat and potatoes of my problems, I'd hear that loud BWAAAAAAAAAAAAAAAAAAAAK sound that told me to write the check and exit immediately. Every single week we'd spend thirty minutes re-capping our last appointment before we could make any progress. Then before I knew it... BWAAAAAAAAAAAAAAAK!

And people wonder why therapy takes so long!

I give a friendly nod to Sad Frumpy Lady. She's the other woman who's always in the waiting room at the same time as me. In all the time I've been coming here, she's never made an attempt to look nice. She wears the same old denim capri pants week after week, carries the same crochet handbag, and pays zero attention to her strands of grey hair that shine like high beams on a dark country road. I always thought she was one of those people who relishes talking about their problems all of the time yet does nothing to find a solution. And for years, I've silently mocked her sad, dead eyes and accused her of being a time waster. Like always, we don't say a word to each other. We just sit in awkward silence until one of us gets invited into the back.

Finally, the door cracks open, and I see Dr. Maria's saintly face. I'm instantly teary eyed.

"Oh Hunny, knock it off!" Slapping me in the rear end and nudging me into her office, she continues to rattle off in her brassy Jersey accent.

"You don't need me anymore! You're happy and happy people certainly shouldn't waste their money on me!"

"I know, I know. It's just that I've been thinking so much about the last three years. Where I ended up is so different than where *I thought* I wanted to be. I think I'm happy. Yeah, I'm happy…I'll probably be okay."

"Oh dear Lord…*Probably*?"

"Don't panic. I'm okay. The only thing that freaks me out now is imagining that I might have called someone else about my little problem three years ago. Do you know how different my life could've turned out?" Faking a shiver, "I get scared just thinking about it."

"What if, what if, what if, Chrissy? Are you trying to get another session out of this? I'll set it up you know. I know how much money that little racket of yours is raking in, and I don't mind taking it."

"*I know, right?* Who would've thought my crazy idea would've worked out! I feel very lucky."

"It wasn't luck; you made it happen. Just remember that, okay?"

And then it hits me: we don't have anything else to talk about.

There aren't any fires to put out or lies to contend with. There are no problems left that I can't handle on my own.

"I'm proud of you, Chrissy. You're so *you* now. It's got to feel good."

"Good and kinda sad."

"Why sad?"

"Just wish I had figured it all out sooner."

"Join the club! Look Hunny, it's been a rough road for you these last few years, and like I already told you, it's going to take a great deal of time to adjust to a life without the people you've lost. But I think you're ready to handle the healthy part of the grieving process on your own. If you get stuck along the way, you can call me. Speaking of calling, have you heard from him again?"

"Not a word since that one phone call after she passed away. I'm sure he forgot about asking me out. He was probably just being nice. It's okay though. I heard he's really happy with his new life. It's all I ever wanted for him."

"Have you thought about reaching out to him?"

"Nah. I've done my fair share of chasing him down. I'm not playing hard to get, it's just that I made my feelings for him known. If he doesn't want to see me, it's only because he's not comfortable reciprocating. Crap, can you blame him? Oh come on, stop looking at me like that. I'm fine…really. There comes a time when you have to stop hoping and start accepting. That time has finally come for the both of us."

I feel so smart for saying that, but then I look at her, exhale and say,

"But I still miss him every day."

"I know you do, Hunny."

"But…I'm excited about my future. I'm so busy right now with the new business and stuff. I don't have the time to be sad."

"How are you managing things? Please tell me it doesn't involve a list of things to do from now until you're a hundred!"

"That's funny. No, I only have daily, *maybe* a weekly list now! Much more realistic, right?"

"Definitely."

"Just so you know, I burned the life list I made when I was sixteen. Yep, had a fun little ceremony with my friends in Mexico. It went up in smoke just like everything I wrote on it."

After sharing a quick giggle, "Geez Dr. Maria, do you remember that January morning when I made that call to you?"

"Remember it? How could I forget? And how about the time of day you called?"

"I was such a mess."

"You know, Hun, I have a copy of that message saved in your file. Would you like to hear it?"

I wasn't sure if she was testing me. Like, if I said yes, would I be displaying some kind of unstable behavior, like a person who can't leave the past behind? Or did she just want me to be proud of my progress? Who cares? I was curious to hear myself as a guilt-laden lunatic charlatan.

"Sure, let's hear how desperate I sound."

Before (preposition) bi*fawr:

A grammatical word indicating that a point in time, event, or situation precedes another in a sequence.

LOST

JANUARY 25, 1998

It's noon when I finally open my eyes. Even though I know I'm alone, and I will be for another couple of days, I totally expect to get caught. So I lay silent and still for as long as I can. After an hour passes and I know the coast is clear, plus I have to pee, I roll onto my side and slowly scan my body. I'm still wearing my jeans and lime green cashmere sweater set. It appears that I had some sense about me to kick off my boots, because there they are on the floor. My eyelashes are stuck together, and as I rub my hands over them, I'm horrified that I still have mascara on. I went to bed with make up on? That's a first. I got home a little after 6am, so I guess I can forgive myself for the dirty face, but certainly not all the other dirty stuff.

What exactly happened again? Think, think, think. Omigod! The bits and pieces are coming back to me and at once, desire is waging war against shame. Why the hell was I even there? Why did he have to be talking about that? *Why did I leave with him*? Disgraced, I cup my hands over my face, and right away I'm hit hard with the intoxicating smell of him. It's sexy and smart and it's clinging to my sweater set like a scarlet letter. It makes me want to do last night one more time. I want to see those eyes and feel his hands on the back of my neck and in my hair. His amazing hands...they were so strong and soft, perfect. And that voice, it was so serious and hypnotic.

My body is trembling with exhilaration as I frantically dig for the phone number that's hidden in my pocket. I want to see his handwriting, touch the paper he touched. I'm like a frenzied drug addict hunting for leftovers. *Pleeeeeease* let there be something on the other side of the paper that'll give me more information about him…a grocery list, a store receipt, something.

The instant I find the scribbled-on piece of paper, I feel heavy with remorse. I go from feeling seventeen and silly to seventy and sucker-punched. Don't even look at it Chrissy, you CAN'T call him! I look. 925-397-08…D'oh! Flip it over. Nothing on the back. I'm such a fool. I wad up the tiny piece of paper and throw it in the garbage like it's a piece of contaminated hospital waste.

I can't understand why he wanted me to call him so badly anyway. I mean, I'm so much older than he is. I was shocked when we revealed our ages, twenty-eight and twenty-two. Oddly, he didn't flinch at the huge gap. Shaking my head as if to magically purge the insanity of all of this, I stumble over to the closet, all the while making sure I don't look at my cheating ass in the bathroom mirror. After delicately removing my sweater set, I sniff it one more time and then shove it as far back in my closet as possible. I'll take it to the dry cleaners to destroy all evidence. But not yet, I want a few more days to inhale it.

I have to do something to take my mind off of last night or else I'm going to go crazy. I'll clean. I scrub my floors, my toilets, refrigerator, anything and everything. I do it all except empty the garbage can, which I casually pass by every few minutes. I want a cocktail real bad but it's only two in the afternoon and I've been conditioned not to drink before 5pm. I can't think of a better time to change that retarded way of thinking, so I slam a beer. Just as I'm about to crack open another one, I impulsively leave the house and head straight for the walking trail at the end of my street.

I look like a crazy person…on a trail…in pouring down, freezing rain. But I don't want to go home. What if he's out here? *Wouldn't that make us meant to be?* Wait, he was there last night, so why can't that make us meant to be? Jesus, cheater, stop thinking so much!

My heart races whenever someone appears in the distance. It stops when I realize it's not him. I point my face up toward the sky and let the rain pound onto it, hoping it will wash away the improper thoughts racing through my mind. I stand motionless for what seems like an eternity.

Friendly people who have already walked past me are now walking past again to return to wherever they came from. Soaking wet, staring up at nothing, they now rush past me and keep their heads down like I might leap at them and stab 'em or something. I can't blame them; I look like a lunatic. I'm wearing nothing but jeans and a t-shirt, and even though I'm totally drenched, I'm not cold. I'm numb. I look like I should be begging for food and, in a way, it feels like I am. But as hungry as I am for him, he'll never find me. He has no idea where I live and even if he knew the city, he would never guess this neighborhood. Only married people live here.

After the fifth "Lady, are you okay?" I make my way home. I kill another hour by taking a bath. I've never been a time waster before. I've always been a super busy girl with super important stuff to do, and a minute wasted is like burning money to me. There have never been enough hours in a day for me to get all of my stuff done, and there's certainly never been enough time for me to lounge around in a bath tub. The last bath I took was the night before my wedding, and that's only because it was on a *Modern Bride* magazine list of ten things you're *supposed* to pamper yourself with the night before you get married. I basically got in, shaved my legs, got out, and promptly crossed it off the list. It felt like a waste of time, but the crossing it off the list part was a very satisfying moment for me.

But at this very moment, all I want to do is waste time. Candles are lit, the bath is extra bubbly, and "Crash Into Me" is repeating on my Discman. When it was on my car radio last night, I told him how much I *looooove* this song. He told me he hated it because everyone *loooooves* it so damn much. "How is a song that ends with the words 'I'm the king of the castle and you're the dirty rascal' even remotely remarkable?" He said it sounded like a five year old wrote it. Ignoring his stubbornness, I explained that the song's about a voyeuristic young guy and an older woman who enjoys giving him the pleasure he craves. He cocked his head and said given the situation at hand, I definitely made the song more likable and he'd give it a chance.

While I'm soaking in the tub, I do two things for the first time in my life: relax and examine my body. I'm a sexually active (or at least I used to be) attractive and physically fit twenty-eight year old woman.

You'd think I would've done plenty of exploring by now. I haven't. My body has never been as interesting to me as it has been to other people. Boobs are just boobs and all the other stuff down below is so hard to make sense out of. Seriously, how can so many nooks and crannies be crammed into such a small area? Anyway, nothing downtown has ever been sexy to me, and I've certainly never wanted to poke around it… until now.

On my way down, I wonder…If I had ever been single, *would I have done more exploring*? I mean, I bet single girls are more inclined to explore their bodies and digitally please themselves because they're not sure if or when the next fling will come along. Or maybe pure boredom drives their curiosity? Both make sense to me. But if you start a long-term relationship with someone when you're still a kid, like I did, the desire to explore just isn't there yet. And for some reason, it never surfaced. Maybe I never got bored enough, or *maybe* it was because I was an idiot who thought my seventeen year old boyfriend knew everything about everything and he could take care of my girl parts *wayyyyyyyyyy* better than I could. And twelve years later…I'm *still* giving him jurisdiction over the area! I'm starting to think I was a dumb girl who handed over the keys to the most precious machine ever created. I had absolutely no idea I wanted them back, until last night.

What happened twenty hours ago, woke something up in me. *Something I never even knew existed.* The dizziness that fills my head when I smell my sweater set, the stirring in my stomach when I imagine his eyes, and the throbbing I feel down below when I think about what we did last night, makes my body impossible to ignore any longer. I've got to reclaim my keys and take myself on some test drives, so that maybe I can do something to change my pathetic sex life.

But hold on! Once I figure out what feels good to me, how do I get motivated to try it with my husband? How do I ignite a spark that's been gone for…wait, *when was the last time I felt a spark like the one I felt last night*? Crap, now I'm sad.

I warm up the tub with hot water and rewind "Crash Into Me." Happy again. I think about last night and how he was seductive enough to tease my senses and even though I begged him to, he was respectful enough not to cross the line. With my new curiosity and thoughts of him, I go on a long, long, long…long…long, long, long test drive. I come precariously close to crossing my own line, but strangely I pull back.

The line eludes me, it always has. The water turns cold again and the bubbles disappear. There's nothing to hide under anymore, and I'm back to feeling ashamed and confused. My pruned up hands reach over to grab a towel, and with an exasperated sigh, I yank myself up.

When I bend down to dry off my legs, I see the crumpled up phone number in the garbage can. "Son of a bitch, I don't want to do this. *I can't do this.*" But it'll feel so good, and it's what my body wants! Is this what an addict feels like? I once read that when you try cocaine for the first time, you're most likely to do it again within the next eight hours. It's been exactly ten hours since I left him, and I'm wondering if I would've been better off doing drugs last night instead of meeting him. Seriously, what's worse, breaking the law or breaking an oath? The law is looking less overwhelming right now.

What to do, what to do. I sit on the toilet and consider all of my options. It takes only two seconds to strike a deal with myself. One phone call and then first thing tomorrow, I'll find the best therapist money can buy and get myself fixed. Deal!

Excited, on my way to my bedroom, I trip and fall flat on my face.

LIAR

After applying Neosporin to my scuffed knees, I dress myself in my most comfortable *and* sexy outfit. Lucky brand jeans, a white tank top, and my super low v-neck merino wool sweater. It's the most beautiful color of lilac, and I just love how it hangs off of my left shoulder. Even though he won't be able to see me through the phone, I still take extra time to pick out my prettiest bra and panty set and, of course, spritz on the same Carolina Herrera perfume I wore last night. The smell makes me woozy with excitement. I light a fire in my obnoxiously massive fireplace and pour my favorite St. Francis Zinfandel into an even more obnoxiously massive wine glass. I'll need it. Before I make the call, I sit on the hearth and wonder how many other women are feeling just like I am right now, struggling with doing the right thing and the thing that feels right. I'll never know, because this is isn't the sort of thing you find a support group for. What a nice idea though. I mean, wouldn't it be great to sit in a circle with other cheaters and ask things like:

"Why'd you do it?"

"Do you ever get over the guilt?"

"Does the desire to do it again intensify or fade with time?"

It would be comforting to surround myself with women who've been at this same crossroad, to question those who have made the same mistake as me and listen to why they're grateful, or not so grateful, that they chose as they did. Unfortunately, it's a free pass from resolution that I'll never have because as far as I know, there is no support group for good girls gone bad wanting to be good again.

Attractively dressed and wine glass full, I'm ready to make the call. But I better not call him from the house phone; he might have that new caller identification thingy that people keep talking about and I can't chance him stalking me when this is done. Dammit, I left my cell phone at work! *I have to call him though*...I gave myself permission, and I can't wait until tomorrow, the suspense will kill me! I'll take my chances that he's not a psycho stalker and use the house phone. It should be okay since *this is the only time I'm ever going to call.*

Right, Chrissy? Right.

My hands are trembling as I dial. What if he thinks I'm crazy for calling him so quickly? My single girlfriends say they always wait a week before even returning a call from a guy. Jesus, there are so many dating games these days. But I guess I shouldn't let that bog me down because it's not like I'm dating or anything. I just want to hear the sound of his voice, feel beautiful one more time, and then forget all of this ever happened.

Ringing, ringing, ringing, and then... oh shit.

"Hello?"

His voice is deep and hopeful. I hear music in the background, but not the youthful angry kind I expected to hear like Rob Zombie or GodSmack. This music is charming.

"Hi, is this...Leo?"

Oh Lordy, here we go.

"Chrissy?"

Am I really doing this?

"I know I told you I wasn't gonna call but..."

Yep...I'm really doing this.

"No, I'm glad you did. I've been dying to hear your voice again."

No games with this guy.

"I guess that's why I'm calling...to hear *your* voice just one more time."

"Explain again... What's up with this one more time business?"

"It's kinda obvious isn't it?"

"No."

"We had a great time last night, but I'm twenty-eight and you're only twenty-two. I have a career and you have…well, you have college."

I was shooting for cute honesty, but I think I sounded condescending.

"So what."

God, this was a mistake.

"Leo, how on earth would I explain you to people…my friends and co-workers? They would think I lost my mind."

"Funny. Last night you didn't strike me as the type of person who gave a shit what anyone else thought."

Actually, it's not as funny as it is sad. I usually *do* care what everyone thinks about me, but not last night, not when I talked to him. I mean, he was just some young guy out with his buddies, and I was a married chick having a cocktail with a co-worker. I didn't think he mattered much. There was nothing I wanted from him and nothing I could give him. But almost immediately after we started talking, I knew something was wrong. I was a version of myself I had never experienced before. A version that felt incredibly natural and dangerously exciting. Oh God, what the hell is happening to me?

"Tell me where you are. I wanna see you."

"*Now?*"

"Why not?"

Think fast, girl.

"Well, for starters, I'm exhausted from last night, and I have a big day at work tomorrow."

"C'mon, I just want to talk to you in person. I promise that's all that'll happen."

He makes me feel dizzy and delightful.

"What's that music from?"

"*Braveheart.* And don't change the subject. What's your address?"

"Leo, there's no way! Besides, isn't it a school night for you?"

"Very funny. Look, I don't know why you're making such a big deal about college. I would've been done a year ago if I wasn't working full time."

It really is admirable. He goes to one of the most expensive private colleges in the Bay Area and he's financing most of his education on his own. What he's overcome to get this far is amazing. I wanted him to tell me more last night but we ran out of time.

"Forget my age and think about our conversation last night. Connections like that are either total luck or made by a higher power. Don't we still have to figure out which one brought us together?"

I kind of do want to get to the bottom of that myself. But there's no friggin' way he's coming to my house. It'd take three hours alone to take down all of the pictures of me in a wedding dress.

"I'm serious. Last night you refused to give me your phone number *and* your last name, and you told me you wouldn't be calling me, which I don't understand at all. But here you are now, and I just want a chance to get to know you better, go on a real date. What's wrong with that?"

There was nothing wrong with that; it's how things are supposed to be. Girl meets boy, girl is crazy for boy, boy asks girl out on date, girl accepts and hopes he's "the one". For the first time, I understand the anxiety my single friends feel when they meet someone new, someone with "husband" potential. They're constantly questioning how much of themselves to give, always scared it's too much and they'll scare the boy away. So, they hold back, never revealing their true heart's desire, only to get short changed in the end. You'd think a twenty-something year old single gal on the hunt for love would lay it all out on the line to get true love. But NOT the ones I know. Instead of speaking to the "husband" potential from the heart, they refer to their cheesy dating books and try to pre-plot his next move so that they can one up his probable lame behavior. I see the same song and dance all the time. No single person I know has the courage to break the cycle. *No one has the guts to be vulnerable*!

Leo thinks I'm a single girl, and right now he's wearing his heart on his sleeve for me to laugh at or to take (no lame behavior with this guy). I wonder, how would I respond to his pleas to date me or his request to come over and talk if I was single? Would I reciprocate and show him my heart or would I doubt his sincerity and play with his? Gosh, I think I would show him my heart but that would be so scary because what if, somewhere down the line, he rejected it. It seems safer to be the one to hold back a bit, to be the one in control of the game. But isn't that why I know so many unhappy single people? Come to think of it, isn't it what my husband has done to me for so many years?

"You there?"

"Yeah, I was thinking about what you just said, and while it's tempting, it's just not that easy."

"I'm not trying to make this hard for you."

Jesus! *Why does his voice have to sound like that?* It makes pretend single girl want to show hot college boy a lot more than her heart! This is insane!

"You know what...I should probably go. I'm sorry...this was a..."

"Okay, okay, okay, since you won't let me come over and you won't commit to a date with me, I'll have to do whatever I can to keep you on the phone for as long as I can."

"Oh yeah...how do you plan on doing that?"

"Tell me what you're wearing."

Before I know it, pants are off and hands are in places never before traveled...since before my bath anyway. He's doing the same, but for some reason I get the feeling he's a frequent flier to his South Pole. *Is this how young guys are these days?* Most guys my age think it's "gay" to masturbate (or at least they pretend it is). But, judging by the sound of things on the other end of this phone, I'd say they're missing out big time! This guy's not shy about what he's doing to his body, and it's the single most erotic thing I've ever been a part of. His breath is steady, not exaggerated, and it's letting me know exactly what he's feeling. When he speaks there's a confidence in his commands that makes me blissfully obedient. I do everything he tells me to do, and for once, I don't fake a single move. He truly wants me to satisfy myself and finally, for the first time in my life, I cross the line. I feel it coming on like a tsunami, and it's so much better than I've read about or heard my friends talk about. In fact, an orgasm is damned amazing, I think my friends have been lying about having as many of them as they say they do. If this happened to me on a regular basis, I'd be Skippin' to my Lou, singing Zippity Do Dah and handing out Fourth of July sparklers to anyone and everyone. I'd be one happy mother-fucker. But regrettably, this has never happened to me before. I'm trembling, and tears are flowing at the realization of having waited twenty-eight years for this feeling. I can barely breathe thinking of a lifetime ahead without it.

"Are you okay?"

"Oh my God yeah, that was amazing Leo."

"Are you sure? It sounds like you're crying."

"Just overwhelmed, I've never done that before."

Obviously, he thinks I'm referring to the phone sex.

"Me neither. I loved it."

And then, out of my euphoria and completely out of my ass, I say the words I'm fairly certain one is never supposed to say to a stranger they just had phone sex with.

"I think I could fall in love with you."

Noooooooooo! I did NOT just say that!

Silence and then, "I don't feel the same way."

Uh-oh there's that humiliated feeling vulnerable people hoping for true love get.

"I *know* I could fall in love with you."

This is a no-win situation for me. I was damned if he said it and damned if he didn't. I have to put a stop to this! But I can't tell him I'm married because then he'll think I'm some suburban trashy whore who got bored one night and picked up a college kid for shits and giggles. That's not who I am, but I won't be able to convince him otherwise. There's no way out of this. I just need to suck it up and tell him the truth.

Finally, after two hours of delaying the inevitable with conversation that does nothing more than confirm the fact that I could fall in love with the guy, I decide it's time to drop the M bomb.

"Leo, I have something to tell you, it's the reason why I can't see you, and I have a feeling you're gonna hang up on me."

"I doubt that."

"No really, listen to me. I didn't expect to meet you last night. I'm not in the position to hang out with a guy at a bar and talk to him until the sun comes up. Not to mention all of the other stuff we did in my car. You were just there last night talking about something fascinating and you drew me in for what should've been a short conversation. But then…"

"What's your point? Because so far I still want to see you again."

"Leo, I'm, I'm, um, I'm… engaged."

Engaged? Did I just say engaged? I was supposed to say married! What the hell is wrong with me? No, no wait, this is good! It's not a total commitment like marriage and although it's sleazy, it's somewhat conceivable that someone could slip up before tying the knot. I may be able to escape this with a morsel of dignity. I proceed to tell him that I'm engaged to be married in July to a guy who I've been dating since high school, and I've never cheated on him, until now. Other than the engagement part, all of the other stuff is true.

"I'm so sorry."

"Sorry for what? For meeting me? I'll admit the timing is bad, but it doesn't take away from the fact that we probably have something better going on than what you have with that other guy."

Leo's claim that my relationship with my husband isn't all that special makes me irritable. I married a good guy, a guy that would *never* do to me what I did to him. All of my energy has to be on repairing the damage done to him and not on this insanity. Right now I need to end this, this game I'm playing alone.

"Leo, regardless of how crappy my relationship with him might look, I have to figure out where to go from here. We've been together a long time, and I have to show some consideration for that right now. Can you understand that?"

"I understand your world turned upside down last night. I understand you never thought you could spend eight amazing hours with a twenty-two year old guy you met at a bar. I understand we have more in common than either of us thought was humanly possible. I understand that you called me tonight to say good-bye but ended up telling me that you think you could fall in love with me. I understand all of that, Chrissy, but don't ask me to UNDERSTAND why you would *ever* consider marrying some other guy."

"I think it's best if I go now."

"Just give me your phone number."

"I can't."

"C'mon, I want a way to reach you."

"You can't."

"*Do you live with him?*"

If he only knew.

"Please stop. On top of feeling terrible, I feel like a fool."

"Chrissy, think about everything that happened last night and tonight. Do you think stuff like that happens every day?"

No. And it's making pretend single girl feel like one fucked-up married woman. This is over…now.

"I meant everything I said to you, Leo. I really hope you believe that."

"Just tell me where you live…please."

Why is this so hard? I don't even know him.

"You have so much to look forward to. So many years of your twenties ahead of you…your last year of college. All of that needs to be your focus right now. You can't get wrapped up in my stupid mistakes."

I made the call. I heard his voice. I felt beautiful one last time. The deal I made with myself is done.

"You're only twenty-eight, Chrissy, not that much older than me. Don't give me the "enjoy your young life" speech. Just give me a chance."

"I'm sorry, I can't."

He says nothing, but he doesn't hang up either. After a few seconds, I press the end call button. Slumped on my Ethan Allen couch, I stare into the perfect fire and sob uncontrollably.

Is Leo a message sent to me to repair a marriage that I didn't even know was broken? Or is he a sign to run as far away from it as possible? I definitely need a therapist! I put my pants back on and scramble for the phone book. After running down the list of family and marriage counselors, I settle on the first woman I find. Like my gynecologist, I gotta have a woman. How the hell is a man supposed to know what I feel, medically or mentally? Never mind that it's the middle of the night, I call her anyway.

"Hi, uh my name is Chrissy. It's, oh geez, its three o'clock, Monday morning. I need some help. I made a horrible mistake. I've been married for three years, and I love my husband *very* much. I, I met someone in a bar on Saturday night and I…I crossed the line.

Jesus, I don't even go to bars! I'm a good person! I *have to* fix the damage I've done. I need help. Can you please help me?"

I leave my contact information on her voicemail and set the tear-encrusted phone back on the charger. I'm so tired but I don't think I'll ever sleep again. I repeat his name over and over again in my mind. Leo, Leo, Leo, Leo, Leo. I reach for my wine glass. It's still full. Apparently he was all the stimulation I needed tonight.

FRAUDSTER

JANUARY, 1998

Kurt arrives home from his tradeshow in thirteen hours. My trusting and unsuspecting husband, who never in a million years would imagine the shame I've bestowed upon our marriage, is going to crawl into bed with me tonight. Until two nights ago, it's a thought that would only irritate me. Now it makes me want to throw up.

Last night, after I left the message for the therapist, I pulled my lime green sweater set out of its hiding place and clung to it like a security blanket. The smell of it lulled me into a few hours of sleep and facilitated restless dreams about Leo. I wonder…will I have those same kinds of dreams when Kurt's sleeping beside me? I also wonder what's going to stop me from calling Leo the next time Kurt goes out of town. Will I be able to act like I did *before* he left?

Since meeting Leo a few days ago, it's been hard to concentrate on anything other than him. I *thought* coming to work this morning would be a nice distraction from my slut-fest of a weekend, but not so. I cancelled all of my meetings, forwarded my calls to voicemail and I've been hiding in my office for the last six hours, staring at my wedding ring and rehashing every second of my time with him, hoping to find a reason to beat myself up. But my thoughts only make me giggly and tingly. I wonder what's going through his mind right now. I want to think he's overwhelmed with heartache about my so-called engagement, but I bet I'm already a thing of the past to him. He's probably laughing with his friends about how he got an older chick to talk dirty to him on the phone. It all seemed so special when it was happening, but right now I feel like such a fool. He's twenty-two, for Christ's sake and I'm sure he's already got a couple of girls lined up to hang out with this week. That's what twenty-two year old guys do right? He seemed different, but I bet he's not.

I leave work early to meet my best friends for one of our monthly girls' night out thingies. We gotta wrap it up earlier than usual because Nicole's working the nightshift and has to be at the hospital by eight. It's a bummer for me because I'd rather arrive home long after Kurt falls asleep. You know…postpone the inevitable lies about what I did while he was away. I'm last to arrive at the restaurant because, as usual, I take extra time touching up my makeup in my car.

"Well don't you look pretty, Miss Chrissy!"

"Thanks Court! You look…shit, you look *really tired*!"

"Get off my back. I came straight from working the last sixteen hours. You're lucky I even made it."

"Right, like you'd rather be home with your screaming baby instead! I know you're hoping Guss puts him to bed before you get home, don't even try to deny it!"

Courtney swings her glass up at me in a silent toast of agreement and takes a swig of her wine.

Shaking her repugnant head, Kelly says, "That's terrible! I feel bad for even being here. My kid was crying 'Mommy, Mommy, Mommy' as I was walking out the door. Craig had this little sourpuss look on his face. Poor guy is hopeless without me."

We all look at Kelly like we want to vomit, but of course, I'm the only one who speaks up. "Well, good for you and your friggin' Hallmark card family life, Kelly."

"Shut up and order guys! I gotta be at work in two hours. We can talk about how perfect Kelly's life is over appetizers, how chaotic my life and Courtney's life are over dinner, and we'll talk about how easy Chrissy's life is over dessert."

"*Easy*? And why do I get dessert? It's the shortest course!"

"Oh puleeez, my charmed girlfriend! You make more money than me and Courtney with NO student loans to pay back. You get to travel to really cool places like New York, Hong Kong, and Yap." Looking at Court and Kel, "And for the record, I still don't think Yap exists." Then, back at me. "You go to fashion shows…boss people around…and get tons of free clothes! You have an awesome house in Danville that gets cleaned once a week by a housekeeper, and *you don't even have kids*! Seriously, how messy can it be? And don't even get me started on that husband of yours. Are you fucking kidding me that you get to go to bed with that man whenever you want? Damn right, you get the shortest course!"

They're lovingly laughing at me and I'm doing my best "don't you wish you were me" dance in my seat. Inside, I'm horrified. I've been questioning my career since the day it started, and since Leo, I wonder if I'm even in the right relationship. The two things that define me are the two things I'm not sure I want anymore. Without them who am I?

The conversation soon moves past my so-called perfect life and onto topics that are more important, from the guy who had a coke bottle stuck up his ass on Nicole's shift a few nights ago to Courtney's urinary tract research grant proposal and Kelly's crusade to make hot school lunches healthier for kids. The coke bottle up the ass story was engaging, but after that my thoughts drifted off to Leo. These women are supposed to be my garbage can for all the shit life dumps on me. So why is it so hard to tell them I screwed up, that I turned my perfect little life into a total clusterfuck? Probably because I've been trying to shed my role of the clusterfuck queen since high school…

MAY, 1985

"C'mon Court, we're cutting fourth period and driving to Nicole's house to watch *One Life to Live*!"

"Uhhhh…Earth to Chrissy! We don't have our driver's licenses yet! Shit, we don't even have a car, you fool!"

"We do now. I told my brother I forgot my bio book in his car."
I take the keys out of my pocket and dangle them in front of
Courtney's face, as Kelly grabs her arm to drag her to the parking lot.

"It's no biggie! Kelly's almost done with drivers-ed, she knows
what to do!"

"No way! Besides, I'm still grounded from the vodka that
CHRISSY put in my hair spray bottle."

"Well, you're the dummy who let your mom borrow your hair
spray!"

"Amen to that Kelly. C'mon though Court…you have to admit
it's a genius way to get buzzed at the movies. A little spritz here and
a little spritz there and voila!"

"Yeah Chrissy, you're a rocket scientist. You and your genius
ideas already have me grounded for the rest of my life. "

"Please come, Courtney, it won't be the same without you.
Please, please, please!"

"No way! Later."

Five minutes later, with Kelly in the driver's seat, we're cruising
down Fremont Blvd. having the time of our lives with hamburgers
and fried zucchini from Carl's Jr. Ten minutes later, we get pulled
over by a cop. An hour later, we're sitting in the principal's office, and
thirty minutes after that our parents arrive to beat the crap out of us.

APRIL, 1986

"I wanna wait outside of Kurt Gibbons's house and follow him
when he goes out."

They're staring at me like I'm a total stalker freak.

"What? You asked what I wanted to do tonight, and that's what
I wanna do! Can you three think of anything better?"

Obviously not, because fifteen minutes later we're filling up
Kelly's tank at the Gas-n-Go in preparation for "Operation KG."
Just as the three of them are piling back into the car, I run out of the
bathroom and breathlessly tell them the greatest news ever.

"Omigod, you guys, there's cases and cases of beer just sitting
in there!"

"So?"

"What do you mean, so? Let's drink some of it! How the hell will they know who took it?"

"Omigod, that's such a good idea, Chrissy!"

Nicole always has my back when it comes to alcohol consumption. And before Courtney can talk us out of the plan, she and I yank her into the bathroom, while Kelly parks the car. Once she arrives, we let her in, lock the door, and immediately get to work on the beer, laughing and burping like sweet little sixteen year olds do. After slamming beer number two, there's a loud bang on the door.

"Hey ladies, you don't think we have cameras in there? When you get out, I want to see some driver's licenses and some cash."

After contemplating making a run for it, we give ourselves up to Aabdar Muhammed Abdallah who, after taking a quick glance at our licenses, calls our parents. That was the end of anyone driving anywhere for a month.

MAY 1987

"Ahhhh...C'mon guys, this could be the last really stupid thing we do together before we go to college."

"Chrissy, I'm NOT hopping on a plane to go to Los Angeles to be on *The Price is Right*! You've had a lot of stupid ideas, but that's the stupidest one by far!"

"Shut up, Court, it'll be fun! Think about it. We'll leave Sunday night and fly home Monday after the taping of the show. We might get caught for skipping school on Monday, but who cares? We graduate in like three weeks! Seriously, what could possibly go wrong?"

It took thirty minutes to talk Courtney into the idea and ten minutes to plot out what we were going to tell our parents. Once we got the logistics worked out, we booked the flight and flew ourselves to Los Angeles. It took seven busses (because none of us had ever been on a bus before or knew how to read a bus schedule) to get to Bob Barker's 'hood.

"This is totally awesome you guys! I can't believe we're in Studio City waiting in line to get into *The Price is Right*!"

"Not awesome at all, Chrissy. That motel we stayed in last night was totally bogus. I swear I heard gun shots. And tell me again why we're all wearing your brother's Santa Clara University sweatshirts?"

Nic, Kelly, and I roll our eyes and shake our heads at Courtney's lack of familiarity with one of the most rudimentary tactics of how to get picked as a contestant on *The Price is Right*. Tediously, I answer her.

"Duh, Court, *everyone* knows Bob Barker likes to pick people wearing college gear. If you'd put down your text books and pick up a remote control every once in a while, you'd know that."

After giving bogus answers to a few basic questions by someone wearing a massive headset, we put our fake name-tags on our fake sweatshirts and take our seats.

"Any of you brainiacs thought about what would happen if one of our names gets called?"

"Right, like that's ever gonna happen, Court."

But then I look at Kelly and mouth the words, "I hope not." She mouths back a very concerned, "Shit."

"Look you guys, it's starting!"

"MILFRED SMITH, COME ON DOWN!"

"THOMAS DANIELS, COME ON DOWN!

"BETSY CLARK, COME ON DOWN! YOU'RE THE NEXT CONTESTANT ON *THE PRICE IS RIGHT*!"

"Holy fucking shit, he just said my name!"

"*Seriously*, Nicole, you picked the name Betsy? That's a really stupid name!"

"God Chrissy, who the hell cares what name she used! Run down there, Nicole! Go! Go! Go!"

"BETSY CLARK, COME ON DOWN!"

"Are you crazy, Kelly? I can't go. MY MOM WATCHES THIS SHOW! What if I win the showcase showdown or something? What happens if I win a friggin' camper? I'm outta here."

Just like that, Nicole runs out of a set of double doors marked EMERGENCY EXIT ONLY and sets off the alarm. The rest of us are immediately asked to leave. As we make our exit, we're hit hard with thunderous boos and hisses of crazy *Price Is Right* fanatics.

Who knew lovers of such wonderful things like Bob Barker, Plinko, and Triple Play could be so mean.

A piece of bread hits me in the face and I'm brought back from the past.

"Hey, blondie, you gonna join in this conversation or what?"

"Yeah Chrissy, what's going on with you? Normally we can't get you to shut up!"

"Yo, Barbie! Tell us what you're thinking."

Now the three of them start to throw bread at me.

"Sorry about that. I've got a lot of work stuff on my mind."

Kelly strokes my hair and gives me one of her famous back-handed compliments. "Look at you, little Miss Responsible! Who woulda thought our little mess of a girl would end up so together?"

As if on cue, Nicole interjects with one of her famous sarcastic sex comments. "Work shmirk! Kurt gets home tonight. Someone's thinkin' about getting lucky!"

Responsible and lucky my ass. The clusterfuck queen is back in business like it's 1987 all over again.

After I promise to love you forever
What happens to us if I fail?
I fear that my heart is a wavering thing and
I'm scared that your heart is frail
Do I give up and just let go
Or remain, I don't know

("About Me," *Keri Noble*)

EXISTING

JANUARY, 1998

It's a somewhat normal Wednesday morning except our separate alarms go off two hours apart. I'm already exercised, showered, and dressed by the time Kurt strolls into the kitchen. He should be curious by this because I'm *never* awake earlier than he is. Yesterday and today I got up at the crack of dawn to run up and down the trail. The funny thing about that is that I'm not a runner! Despite my husband's decade-long suggestion that I take it up, it wasn't until I hung up the phone with Leo that I starting running. I can't figure out if I'm running toward something or away from something. Either way, I kind of like it.

It was awful when Kurt arrived home last night. I had hoped to be asleep before he walked through the door, but he pulled into the driveway a few minutes after I got home from dinner. I've probably kissed Kurt's lips a million times before. He has one of the most beautiful mouths in the world and when he smiles, clouds part in the sky, bluebirds sing, and there's no pain or suffering in the world. It's just that enchanting. But when I kissed his lips last night, they had lost their magic and I wondered, had it been like that for a long time or was it because I had experienced Leo's kiss? We wandered into the kitchen and made small talk about his trip and my weekend. He unpacked, and I changed into my pajamas in the bathroom. Another thing he should've thought was curious, but still he said nothing. We settled in the family room to watch the eleven o'clock news, and I pretended to fall asleep on the couch where fortunately, he left me. Even before Saturday's escapade with Leo, things were tense between us, but not "slept on the couch" tense.

I used to try to talk to Kurt about what's bothering me in the relationship, but he just got annoyed with what he calls my "constant complaining." One day he even went so far as to bring home a bottle of St. John's Wort, in effect, making me the sole owner of turning my frown upside-down. He'd rather I drug my bad attitude, than explain why I have it. But I'm sorry…it's going to take a lot more than a couple of sugar pills to numb my feelings.

A few months ago, Kurt invested ten thousand of *our* dollars in a crap-shoot stock without consulting me. Obviously, when I noticed the money missing from our savings account, I immediately questioned him. Instead of being apologetic, he got defensive and said "If I asked you for permission you would've said no," as if that's justification for not talking to me about it! It's about as insane as me saying, "If I asked you if I could have phone sex with a guy I met in a bar, you would've said no." Give me a break!

The other thing he doesn't want me to "complain" about is all of his business trips that extend into long vacations involving some kind of an extreme sport. Kurt's an adventurous guy, and I've been *mostly* supportive of what I think are totally stupid hobbies. But he's missed a lot of important occasions in my life--friend's weddings and grandparent's funerals--just so he could go motorcycle riding or hang gliding. Often times, okay *all the time*, I find myself making excuses. I say things like "Kurt just couldn't break away from the conference in Vermont," when he's really snowshoeing, or "Kurt wishes so badly he could be with us today, but he's so busy at the office," when he's really indoor rock climbing. Everyone's dopey look of admiration for his imaginary work ethic has slowly taken a toll on me. All the lying makes him seem conscientious and me supportive, but in reality he's super selfish and I'm truly pathetic. What hurts the most though is that Kurt doesn't care that I'm always alone, and he *hates* that I lie about where he is. He's not apologetic or ashamed of how he prefers to spend his time, and it's like a straight shot to my heart. Yeah, I'm *pretty* sure he wants me to pop the St. John's Wort so I don't bring up that stuff anymore. But I'm *mostly* sure it's because he doesn't want me to bring up what happened last October.

Kurt and I have been together twelve years, and we've worked super hard for everything we have together. After college when most of our friends were renting apartments and partying every night of the week, we moved back home to save money to buy a house, which we did when I was only twenty-three. Right on time! I can't remember what felt better, when our agent called to tell us our offer was accepted or when I crossed that accomplishment off of my life list. Whenever Kurt and I do show up somewhere together, we're the couple who gets the party started and the ones who stay to help clean up. We're the friends you call when you need help moving and everyone's first choice to be their first-born's Godparents. If I had a dime for every time someone called us Ken & Barbie, I could've afforded the Range Rover instead of the Land Rover. We hit the ground running the day after college and we've been sprinting ever since. As I stare at him pouring milk into his cereal bowl without taking his eyes off of the newspaper, I wonder when we started going in opposite directions. I *think* it might've been when we bought the *house* we live in now.

Kurt didn't want to move to Danville. He said, "Too white and too rich, are those really the kind of people you want to raise kids around?"

I'm sorry, but when did it become so terrible to be around people who are too white and too rich? Those are the two things I strive to be the very best at, and I'm already fifty-percent of the way toward reaching my goal! But he'd be mortified if I admitted money meant that much to me, so I sold him on the stellar public schools and how much money we'll *save* by sending our kids to one of them instead of the private school they'll have to attend if we move to the miserable city of his choice. In the end, I got what I wanted, and even though he LOVES it here, he reminds me of his sacrifice all the time. If you ask me, I don't think that's how a married Ken & Barbie should act.

Since we moved to Danville six months ago, our relationship has gone from a somewhat harmonious shade of grey, to completely detached smudges of black and white. Given Kurt's sensitivity to the racial demographics of Danville, I'll claim the white smudge and he can be the black one. Either way, it's clear we're different colors moving farther away from each other as each day passes. My complaining has a lot to do with our distance, but I'm also convinced my dreams put too much pressure on Kurt, and it's causing huge rifts in our relationship. For example, and this might seem stupid, but I've always dreamed of owning a Porsche. I would look RIDICULOUS in one of those things! But Kurt, who by the way ohhhhhs and ahhhhhs over every single Porsche he sees, calls me materialistic for wanting one. It's a head-scratcher. He also flips out whenever I mention being a stay-at-home mom once we have kids. He says, "Why should I have to be the *only one* supporting the family?" As if a stay-at-home mom isn't a supporting role! For a while, I tried to tenderly explain to him that I want the white picket fence, the kids, soccer games, and pool parties. But my pretty pictures of domestic bliss were always met with a snicker and a look of repulsion. He'd say things like, "Sounds nice but who's gonna make that happen for me?" I could never find an answer to that, so I stopped "complaining" and started popping St. John's Wort like they were tic-tacs. And I also keep moving my white smudge farther away from his black one.

I can barely look him in the eye, let alone sit across from him right now at the breakfast table and have a conversation. It's not all because of guilt, either. I can't get Leo off of my mind, and I'm scared to death I'm going to say his name out loud. Thank God the therapist was able to squeeze me in for my first appointment tonight. I have an hour to set the record straight with her, come up with an action plan, and begin executing it immediately. I work fast. I hope she does, too.

Kurt finally realizes I'm in the room. Time to grab my crap and haul ass.

"Did you eat yet, Babe?"

"Nah, not hungry, I'm just gonna grab some coffee and head out. I have a sales meeting at 9:00."

I'm not sure if the sweat on my upper lip is because I'm nervous I'll call him Leo or because I know he's going to reprimand me for not eating a healthy breakfast.

"*You have to eat, Chrissy.* Breakfast is the most important meal of the day. Wait a few minutes and I'll make some eggs."

Here we go. I haven't wanted eggs for twenty-eight years. Will he ever stop asking or will I just eventually agree to eat them? I can see him trying to shove pureed eggs down my throat when I'm ninety years old. It'll be a struggle to the bitter end. No! I won't eat them. Never!

"No thanks, I *really* gotta get going. I'll bum a bagel off of some-one at work."

"Nice, is that how it's gonna be when we have a kid? Are you gonna bum a bagel off of someone in the school parking lot because you didn't make time to feed the kid properly at home? You should start taking better care of yourself now so you're more prepared for a family later."

When we were younger I accepted Kurt's obtuse comments as concern for my well-being. It was thoughtful when he suggested I bypass the chips and salsa so the mucho grande burrito would taste *that much better*. Now it just makes me feel fat. It was thrilling when he urged me to try new things like kayaking, but when I wanted to stop at the class three rapids it wasn't good enough for him because "even his ten year old niece could do *that*." As I've become more vocal about things like *loving* chips and salsa and *hating* all water sports, we've started to argue a lot more. But I'm tired of arguing. All I want to do right now is sit in traffic and listen to the *Braveheart* soundtrack.

"Oh, and I have a dinner meeting after work tonight, so I'll be home late."

"Again? Don't they know you have a family? All those long hours over there are getting to be a bit much."

"Kurt, we don't have a family, we have a dog. Look, I joined a start-up company, and I told you it was gonna be like this. I'd appreciate it if you would stop making me feel guilty."

"I'm with a start-up too, but I don't let them take advantage of me…"

I'm not sure how long Kurt continued to ramble after I closed the door to the garage but I really did have to go if I planned on getting everything done before my appointment with Dr. Maria.

As I sit in traffic, I think about the days when I worshipped the ground Kurt walked on. When we were younger, I thought he was so cool. He was the kind of guy who rode his bike through crowded streets with NO HANDS! He would take his dog anywhere and everywhere without a leash. And he had the mad skills to merge onto the freeway going 70 mph, slide over to the fast lane in one fell swoop, and talk a police officer out of a well-deserved speeding ticket. Know what's even crazier? He still does all those things. At sixteen they were wow factors but as an adult they just make you ask, "Why?" I remember the first time I talked to him. It was at his high school graduation party. I was a year younger than he was and it took a lot of nerve for me and my friends to show up somewhere we weren't invited. But there was going to be a lot of beer, so we had to try! The party was at his buddy Tom's house, and Tom had a cool Mom who let you drink alcohol at her house if you gave her your car keys and committed to spending the night.

God Bless the 80's, right?

JUNE, 1986

"Okay guys, play it cool when we get inside. Just drop your keys in the bowl and act like we're invited."

"That's easy, Chrissy. But once we're in, how do we get out? I'm gonna be grounded for life if I don't get home by my curfew. Not to mention the beating you're gonna get from your Marlboro Mama if you don't come home tonight."

Before Courtney and I can finish debating the subject, Nicole and Kelly are on the dance floor with a couple of Miller Lights in their hands.

"Well, Court, it looks like there's no turning back now. Go in and start looking like we belong here."

"Omigod, Chrissy, look! There he is."

For the last three years, I've watched Kurt Gibbons from a safe distance--partly because I felt like he was totally out of my league and partly because he always had a girlfriend. He's captain of the football team, captain of the baseball team, and captain of dating any girl he wants. Since he has his pick of the lot, it surprises me that he dated Debbie Tedaro for the last year. Debbie's a scary-looking girl with huge-ass hair and the longest legs I've ever seen. She looks a good ten years older than anyone else in high school and whenever she holds his hand, it looks like she's hurting him. But the word on the streets of Freakmont is that he broke up with her months ago, even though she's telling people they're still together. Her manipulations are working, because no girl will go near him with a ten-foot pole. As I walk in to the backyard, I surmise that he knows this and is pissed as all hell.

"Debbie, we're not together anymore, so quit telling people we are."

"But can't you see how much I love you?"

"Look, I don't wanna be mean, but I don't feel the same. I'm sorry, just move on."

Wow, harsh. I kind of feel sorry for Debbie until...

"What the hell are you guys looking at? Who let you into this party anyway, you're JUNIORS!"

I wanted to correct her because technically we're seniors because they just graduated, but after looking at the scowl on her face, I opted not to. I stood frozen, as she stormed past us to get to the bathroom, bashing into my shoulder on the way.

"Did you guys see that? She assaulted me!"

"I'm so sure, Chrissy! Like, she even knows who you are! She's big, she's pissed, and she's totally moted right now. Stop making this all about you."

"Nahhhhh, she's right. She bumped into her on purpose."

I whirl around in a state of shock to find Kurt and Tom sipping on a couple of beers, listening to every word we're saying. Looking right at ME, Kurt asks, "Do you guys wanna grab some wine coolers and hang out in the gazebo?"

In unison and sounding like total retards, Court and I answer, "Yeah. Cool. Sounds good. Okie dokie."

It was clear within a matter of minutes that for whatever bizarre reason, Kurt wanted to talk exclusively to me, and after a few Very Berry Bartles & James wine coolers, I let myself go a little bit.

"So it's your big graduation party, that's exciting! But geez, are you sure you wanna spend all your time sitting here with me?"

"Are you kidding? I'm pissed that I didn't do it sooner. We would've had a great time hanging out in high school. You and your friends seem cool."

"I didn't think you even knew who I was."

"I noticed you last year at Cheerleading try-outs. I think every guy noticed you that night."

I think I'm going to shit my pants RIGHT now. Boys noticed me? Kurt Gibbons noticed me?

"Debbie sure is a rough girl."

"She's not so bad. You just have to know her."

"Oh, right. I'm not sure why I said that. Sorry. Why'd you guys break up?"

"We're just different. I either want to be alone or find someone who likes to do the same things as me."

"What kinds of things?"

"I like to go fishing, camping, hike, ride my motorcycle, bike ride. Pretty much anything to do with the outdoors. Oh, and I like to read, too."

"ME TOO! I love to do all of that stuff. I was just gonna buy a new bike. Maybe you could help me pick one out."

Courtney whips her head around and shoots me a look of disgust and pity all mixed together. She knows the closest I ever got to nature was in a lawn chair by the pool and the last I book I read was…no book. I shoot her a look back that says, "Don't say a fucking word!"

"Hey, what are you and Courtney doing tomorrow? Do you guys wanna play some tennis with me and--"

Before he can finish his sentence, Debbie and her motley crew of hair bears stomp into the gazebo. With her finger about an inch from my face, she squeals, "Great! Is this the girl you like now? *Her?*"

"Leave us alone, Debbie. You're embarrassing yourself." As he gently guides her finger away from my face he says, "Chrissy has nothing to do with our break up."

He just said my name! Somebody pinch me.

Debbie's voice escalates to a dog whistle-like pitch; her hands flail all around as she yells at him, Tom, me, Courtney, the world. Kurt stands up, puts his arm on her lower back, and guides her and her friends to an area by the pool. She shoots me a look that says "Ha ha, he still cares for me." My heart sinks. I was so stupid to think that Kurt Gibbons would be interested in me. Just as I'm about to grab Courtney's hand to leave the gazebo, Kurt and Tom push Debbie and her three friends into the water. As he walks back to me he says, "Maybe now she'll cool off."

I'm in love.

And I still do love him. We're Kurt and Chrissy, the super cute couple who's been in love since we were kids. How can a love story like ours turn into a nightmare?

DELUSIONAL

FEBRUARY, 1998

So this is what a therapist's office looks like. It's sparsely decorated with a couple of uncomfortable chairs that look like mauve threw up all over them, a side table stacked with outdated issues of *Time* magazine and, one really sad, frumpy looking lady. I try to make eye contact with her so I can give her the obligatory head nod, but she just glances at my shoes and then back down at the floor. Geez, what a miserable human being. I wasn't prepared to sit amongst people with big problems. Then again, I'm not sure what I expected. *Humph…* I guess I didn't give it much thought; I was too busy working my ass off all day at the office solving other people's problems so I'd get here in time for someone else to solve mine. I arrived right on time and, thank God, because I can't stand to sit in this waiting room of shame for one minute longer than I have to. Just as I bend down to grab something out of my purse to pretend I'm interested in, the door that I assume leads to the individual therapist's offices opens and an official looking woman eyeballs me. She's maternal looking with a classy Bohemian sense of style. Sections of her shoulder-length hair are pulled back in a loose bun held together with a pencil, and her chic tortoise shell glasses are dangling on the very tip of her nose. Judging by the expression on her face, I'm exactly what she expected. Dumb blonde.

"You must be Chrissy."

"Hi! Yes!" Extending my arm out for her to shake, "Sooooo nice to meet you!"

I realized there was way too much glee in my greeting when Sad Frumpy Lady rolled her eyes up and gave me a blank stare.

"Hi Hunny, I'm Dr. Maria. Follow me on back."

Her office is dimly lit. She points to an area on the couch where she wants me to sit. I plop myself down, cross my legs, and immediately start to twirl my hair like I just settled into the best booth at Whiskey Bar. I swear, if we had a couple of martinis, this could be a cocktail party.

"Do you want to tell me why you're here, Chrissy?"

What, no drinks?

"Well, I assume you listened to my voice message and it's all very embarrassing. I don't know why I did what I did, but I certainly don't *ever* plan on doing it again. Mostly I just wanna understand why I did it, figure out how to deal with the guilt, and move on. I've never even dated another guy, never wanted to at all! I love Kurt. That's my husband's name, Kurt. We've been together since high school, just like my parents! We married three years ago and he's amazing! Lights up any room when he walks through the door. Everyone just loves--"

"Why don't you tell me about this other man--the one you spent Saturday evening with?"

I could *really* use that martini right about now.

"Oh, uh…His name is Leo."

Saying his name makes me feel pretty.

"And?"

"And he's just…different."

"Different than what?"

"Different than anyone I've ever met."

"How does it feel to talk about him?"

"Obviously, it's embarrassing and I'm totally confused about all of it."

"Anything else?"

"I guess it's also electrifying, and I don't know why that is. It seems like what I did should have the opposite effect, like I should be depressed, but I'm not. I feel like I have super powers or something."

"Tell me more about Leo."

"I don't really know how to explain him; he's just someone I wish I could get to know better."

"Why?"

God I hate this.

"I guess when I was with him, I felt alive, and I feel alive right now talking about him. And I wanna shout out that I met the most amazing person in the world, but I can't do that. It kinda scares me that he'll have to stay in my mind forever. Feels very *Bridges of Madison County*, ya know?"

Since I'm not a middle aged Iowan woman of Italian decent with two teenage kids and an ol' fart farmer husband, she's obviously having a hard time making the connection.

"I saw that movie a few years ago, and it depressed the hell out of me. The woman, Francesca, had an affair with some traveling photographer dude who rolled into town, and even though she only knew him for a few days, he was the one for her. Did you see the movie?"

"Who didn't?"

"Tell me about it. Anyway, I remember being on the edge of my seat when the photographer…crap, what was his name again?"

"Robert Kincaid."

Yep, she saw the movie.

"Right! Remember that scene when Robert was waiting for Francesca in his beat up old truck at the stop light, and she was in the car behind him with her husband sitting in the driver's seat?"

"Oh I remember. It was pretty heavy."

"Beyond heavy. Robert was giving her one last chance to run away with him, and she sat there totally agonizing over the choice… I agonized with her. I mean, he was the love she'd been waiting for her whole life! I thought…she has to go! But she didn't. The obligation to her husband and kids was greater than the one she had to herself, so after the light turned green, she watched her love drive away forever. I felt like letting him go was more shameful than her affair. Should I be embarrassed for admitting that?"

"Do you think Francesca knew something was missing from her life before she met Robert?"

She ignored my question. Rude!

"I don't think so. I think she was busy living the life she chose. I don't think she knew what was missing until it smacked her in the face."

"Was this Leo guy your smack in the face?"

Afraid of my answer I turn my focus to the ugly picture hanging on her wall, hoping she'll move on to something else.

"Chrissy, do you think Leo is making you second guess the life you chose?"

I guess you get what you pay for around here.

"Not at all."

"Then why does your encounter with Leo remind you of *Bridges of Madison County*?"

This lady's starting to bug me.

"Well, I'm not second-guessing my decision to be married to Kurt, if that's what you think. But I guess I'm having a hard time fighting the feelings that surfaced when I met Leo last Saturday night." I abruptly stop mid hair-twirl and blurt out, "You know what really bothers me about that movie?"

"What's that?"

"It never showed Francesca coping with any guilt, and it never showed how she survived the loss of her true love! The movie cut from when the photographer drove away to like twenty years later when her husband kicked the bucket. *What the hell was she doing all those years in between*? How did she resume her life after her true love disappeared? It sure would help to know where I'm supposed to put all of my feelings so I can go back to the choices I made before Leo. Choices I was happy with, by the way."

"Do you think it's possible to find true love after only knowing someone for a few days?"

"I don't know. But…I think meeting someone so perfect for you can make you question the true love you thought you already had. Hold on, are we talking about me or Francesca?"

She says nothing, and the quiet allows me to ponder the movie a little bit more.

"Remember when Francesca was toying with pulling the car door handle?"

"Big moment, huh?"

"Huge. You *think* she's gonna get out and run. I mean she HAS TO, right? It's her destiny to be with Robert! But then she peels her fingers away from the door handle, slumps back in her seat… crushed by her obligations."

I laugh a little.

"What's so funny?"

"I watched the movie with Kurt, and I remember telling him that I thought she should've pulled the door handle. He looked at me like I was a monster. I quickly explained that I only said that because I imagined *him* as being Robert, he was the one I would have an affair with. Then he got angry that I would even suggest an affair. It became a big argument."

"What happened?"

We had an argument. Duh! I just told you that.

"Well, I *tried* to explain to him that he was my whole world and, married or not, I would escape any situation to be with him. I thought it was sweet, but instead of feeling moved by my confession, he pooh-poohed all of it. I dunno…maybe I didn't explain myself right. Seems like I always have a hard time explaining myself to Kurt."

"Now that you've had this experience with Leo, how do you see yourself in that car scene from the movie?"

It takes me a long time to process her question. When I finally answer, it's slow.

"Kurt and I are in the same car. Leo's waiting for me in the truck ahead of us, and I can see his eyes in the rear view mirror, they're pleading with me to run away with him." Goosebumps pop up all over my arms, and I close my eyes in almost agonizing pain as I envision the scene I'm creating. "And my hand is gripping the door handle."

"Knowing you might not ever see Leo again, do you pull the handle?"

My eyes pop wide open.

"My situation is different than Francesca's…I'm younger… I don't have children."

"Are you saying it makes your choice easier?"

"No…I'm saying that…I'm saying…I don't know what I'm saying! I've never had anyone to compare Kurt to. He's all I've ever known."

"Pretend you're her and you *have to* make a choice. Do you pull it?"

"I never wanted to be Francesca."

"Do you pull it?"

I want to pull that pencil out of your hair and stab you in the face with it!

"Chrissy?"

"Damn it, my obligation tells me no, but the craving for whatever I felt on Saturday night tells me I have to, and I'm scared because craving is kicking obligation's ass."

"Sometimes it's easy to confuse safety with obligation. Do you think that's what Francesca did?"

I'm really starting to regret bringing up this movie.

"You mean, do I think that's what *I'm* doing? Look, maybe obligation was the wrong word. Bottom line is I love Kurt. He's all I've ever loved, but since Saturday, that love feels like some kind of a sacrifice and it's driving me crazy."

"Chrissy, you just traded in the word obligation for sacrifice." For the love of Christ. Coming here was a huge mistake.

"Dr. Maria, I came alive on Saturday night, and all I want to know is how to keep that feeling and go back to my life before I met Leo. Is that possible?"

"Anything's possible. Why don't you tell me more about Saturday and the events leading up to it."

I tell her everything about the night I met Leo and the phone call the day after. I tell her about walking around aimlessly in the rain and my first-ever orgasm. I tell her that I went days without thinking about my husband and that I let the few calls he did make to me go straight to voicemail. But mostly, I tell her about the type of woman I've always been and how that woman is so opposite of what I was the night I met Leo. I thoroughly explain how much men annoy me, and have my whole life. I get furious whenever one of them checks me out, attempts to grab a seat next to me at the airport, just says "hello." I can spot those schmucks a mile away, and my invariable response to them is to flash them my wedding ring, a dirty look, and walk away.

"If that's the case, why didn't you walk away from Leo? What made him so different?"

"There was nothing to walk away from. He never even approached me."

"I see. What made you approach him then?"

"It's so stupid."

"Tell me."

"He was just talking about something I thought was interesting. I guess I wanted to know more."

Please don't ask! Please don't ask!

"What was it?"

Oh, Lordy.

"Ghosts. He was talking about ghosts."

And I thought her *Bridges of Madison County* face was weird.

"I know, I know, it's corny. Kurt thinks my fascination with ghosts is completely silly as well."

"No, not silly at all."

"Sure it is, but hearing Leo talk about them was, I dunno… almost serene. Anyway, I interrupted his conversation to ask him a question and he made me feel stupid, like I was some kind of bar whore or something. It was pretty embarrassing. I was gonna leave it at that, but as he turned back around to continue to talk to his buddy, our eyes met. Frankly, he intimidated me a little bit, and I told him so. I mean, not in a bitchy way just in a sarcastic 'are you always this pleasant' kind of way. Anyway, my comment amused him and now I'm in therapy."

I thought it was her turn to talk, but she's just staring at me, waiting for me to say more.

"A few months ago, I read some stupid article in *Cosmo* about dating. I don't know why really, because well…I'm married and obviously I don't date. But anyway, it said the quickest way to determine true companionship is to interview your date the minute they show up at your door. Just put yourself totally out there and request they do the same. It's supposed to speed up knowing if you should pursue a second date or end the first one on the spot. No sense wasting time right?"

Just a nod.

"Like if during the interview I confessed to being a diehard vegetarian and the guy revealed he loved veal, obviously we would immediately agree that we were totally wrong for each other, no matter what physical attraction originally existed."

"Seems like there would be no shame of rejection with a process like that."

"Exactly! I mean, if a guy didn't want to be with you, chances are you wouldn't want to be with him either and you'd both know exactly why. And there's no embarrassment…no heartbreak. As long as everyone's honest, it seems like a very efficient way to find a true companion, right?"

Another nod, but at least this one shows some positive consideration for what I'm saying.

"Anyway, I know I wasn't technically on a first date with Leo, but I thought it would be fun to try what I had read. Within the first hour of meeting him, we covered politics, abortion, religion, money, dreams, goals, fears, you name it. I honestly answered all of his questions and remarkably, he did the same, and what happened was insane. He liked me. The good, the bad, and the ugly, and I felt the same way about him. It was like every other second one of us was saying 'me too' or 'I totally agree!'"

"Would you say you were 100% you?"

"More like 200%. I told him things I've never admitted to another human being."

"If you don't mind sharing, what was the craziest thing you told him?"

"That I wanted to be a good wife. I know…how twisted is that? There I am, a wife, flirting with a guy I met at a bar and I'm telling him I want to be a good wife. Makes me sick to my stomach."

"What does it mean to be a good wife to you?"

"Being given the freedom to act how I want to act, do the things I want to do, so that I can enjoy my husband and make him happy. You know…I actually told Leo that I *might* want to quit my job and be a housewife one day. Yep, told him that I thought it was a good idea to keep my options open because, who knows what I'll want when I have kids. Crap, I can barely admit that stuff to myself! Who blurts that out to someone they just met?"

"Probably not many. I'm curious, have you ever tried this interview process with Kurt?"

"Nah. It wouldn't go well."

"Explain."

"I used to admit my hopes and dreams to Kurt, but it was clear they put too much pressure on him. So I stopped. The troubling thing about meeting Leo, other than the kissing and orgasm of course…" I wanted her to think that was funny but I got nothing, "Is that I told him all the things I stopped telling Kurt a long time ago. I think that's what's bothering me so much."

"Do you think we can create a safe place in this office for you to tell Kurt your dreams?"

"A week ago, I would've been doing back handsprings for an opportunity like that. But after meeting someone who's so perfect for me, the reinvention of Kurt and Chrissy seems like such a struggle."

"So is that a no?"

"I wouldn't say it's a no. It's more of an uncertain yes."

She stops to tap her pencil on her pad of paper.

"What do you think the best relationships are made of?"

It's funny, or maybe it's sad, but I immediately draw on my short time with Leo for an answer.

"Passion."

"Where do you think passion comes from?"

What is this… a fucking game show?

"I dunno, when you have common ground with someone, when you agree more than you disagree…you get happy, you get connected. You get passion."

"I think so, too."

You do?

"Couples don't always agree, of course. But I think the best relationships are about a shared vision. Shared visions create passion. Passion keeps people together."

Kurt and I don't have a shared vision, we never did. The flood gates are now open.

"Do you need a tissue, Chrissy?"

I grab four.

"For three days I've been crying over what I did to Kurt, but right now I'm crying because of how sad it is that my dreams frustrate my husband to the point that I stopped having any with him. I managed to keep them to myself for a while, but that was totally frustrating. Eventually I just stopped dreaming altogether."

"That's not good."

I blow my nose and think for a minute.

"I always thought that life was just one long list of *mostly* unfulfilled dreams."

"What do you mean?"

"Well, we're constantly dreaming of what we want to accomplish, places we want to go, people we want to meet. Obviously everything we dream about isn't gonna come true, right?"

"Right."

"Well, I think when one dream goes unfulfilled, you create another one to take its place so you always feel like you're working toward something. Along the way, hopefully you can feel intermittent successes. Those little successes are what make life great. And I imagine what makes it even better is when you share the dreams, the old unfulfilled ones and the ones that take their place, with the person you love."

"I couldn't agree more."

Here come the tears again.

"But when you stop talking about your dreams with the person you love because he thinks they're ridiculous, all that's left is nonsense."

"When did you stop?"

"I'm not sure exactly, because for a long time I assumed Kurt's dreams as my own."

"Why?"

"Because it made him happy and it made us look like a team." I take a deep breath before I proceed. "Sometimes I feel like I've sacrificed too much of myself to be with Kurt, and for the life of me I can't figure out why."

"Maybe you had your eye on the prize rather than on what you were actually winning."

"Maybe you're right. But there are wonderful things about Kurt too."

"I'm sure there are plenty of wonderful things about him just like there are plenty of wonderful things about you. And initially all of those wonderful things are what attracted you to each other, but maybe you two were always on separate paths."

"Are you saying we should give up on each other? Because I don't want to give up on him."

"Not at all. Any marriage can be repaired if both people want to fix it and conversely, any marriage can end if both people agree they made a mistake."

"I don't want my marriage to be a mistake. I wanna share my dreams with Kurt and have him share back. I wanna feel close to him. I wanna have the kind of marriage with him that I always dreamt of: intimate, special, nurturing. Can you help me with all of that?"

"I'm going to do my best to help the two of you get what you need."

"Gosh, Dr. Maria, so many thoughts are stacked in my head, I can't make sense out of anything anymore."

"You know what happens when too much gets stacked in our heads?"

"Yeah, we cheat on our husbands."

I got a slight smile out of her on that one.

"Not necessarily, but it's safe to say that one would eventually go nuts if they kept all of their true feelings and thoughts to themselves, never feeling safe from harassment for being authentic. It would make for a very lonely world right?"

"Very lonely."

"Tell me, what do you do for a living?"

"I'm the Vice President of a clothing company."

"Wow, so young to have such a big job."

"Yeah, I get that a lot."

"Do you like your job?"

"On the one hand, I love what I do because I'm good at it. But on the other hand, I resent my career because of how demanding it is. It'll never allow me to be what I'd like to be."

"What's that?"

"A mom. And if time permitted and it didn't take away from my family, I imagined having a job that felt more like a hobby, like an interior decorator or a writer or something. I feel like I have something creative in me that's dying to get out. It sounds very spoiled and stupid, I know."

"It doesn't sound stupid at all. Tell me, what's your relationship like with the people at work?"

"They probably don't like me very much. I'm tough. But they ask for my advice a lot, so I take that as a sign of respect. I enjoy helping them solve their problems, and I think I'm pretty good at it."

"Does Kurt mingle with the people you work with?"

"Oh no, no, no. He wouldn't like who I am around them."

"Explain that to me."

"I don't know if I can. I'm not sure I understand it myself."

"You just got done telling me you're good at what you do and you enjoy helping the people you work with, but *then* you say your husband wouldn't like you in that environment. Why?"

"I guess he would think I was too controlling. He wouldn't like my dark sense of humor, my abrasiveness…uh, my high standards. I don't let people hold me back. He doesn't like those things at home so why would he like them there?"

"Do you think Kurt's holding you back?"

She got me with this one. I want to defend him, *us*, so badly, but after everything I just said, how can I?

"I don't know. Obviously I don't know anything anymore. Why else would I act the way I did on Saturday? I just wanna be a real team with Kurt, not the team everyone thinks we are."

"Does it matter to you what people think?"

"Definitely not at work, but outside of it, I would have to say, yes."

Jesus, solve my current dilemma already! I don't need the full monty life analysis of Chrissy. Just tell me I'm a bad, bad girl for cheating on my husband, then tell me how to bury the guilt and move on with the life I've spent the last twelve fucking years creating!

"How would it feel to be how you are at work around your husband?"

I chuckle a little. "Liberating and impossible all at the same time."

"Why is it impossible?"

"It just is."

"But why do you think that?"

"I'd be too much for him to tolerate. I'd be opinionated and strong-minded. He'd be mad at me ALL THE TIME!"

"He'd be mad at you for being authentic, for being *you*?"

"Yep."

"Chrissy, how can you be on a *real* team with Kurt when you're not *real* with him?"

I hate her. As if she knows, she changes the subject.

"What's your relationship like with your parents?"

"Fine."

"How do you think they'd react to what you did on Saturday?"

"They'd probably expect I'd screw up sooner or later."

"Any close friends?"

"Yeah, my best friends from high school: Courtney, Kelly, and Nicole. Kurt's also good friends with their husbands. We do a lot together."

"How would they react to what you did on Saturday night?"

"They'd be confused because they think Kurt and I are perfect."

"Have you thought about confiding in them?"

"No way."

"Do you think their relationship with him is more important to them than their relationship with you?"

"Of course not, they love me like I'm their sister! I just can't tell them. Nobody can know about this."

She's compassionately nodding her head; she can sense I'm on the brink of a meltdown. I have an overwhelming feeling that I'm fucked.

"Chrissy, you did really well today, but I'd like to set up another appointment for next week. Will that work for you?"

I did really well today? We didn't accomplish a damn thing! I gotta leave here with unresolved issues? *What the hell?*

"Sure, next week sounds good."

I'm such a pathetic pleaser.

"Good. I'd like to talk about your family a little bit more. Would that be alright with you?"

I give her an exasperated "Sure."

"Hunny, therapy's a marathon, not a sprint. I can tell you're a fine young woman and I want to help you, but in order to do that

I have to learn a lot more about you. My hope is that you will also learn a lot about yourself. You *will* find the answers you need in this process and you *will* be okay. Just give it some time."

"I hear what you're saying, Dr. Maria, but what if I slip again? What if I cave into the urge to call Leo? I can't get him off of my mind."

"That's a tough one."

Jesus, what good are you people?

"But what I can tell you is that you should do whatever feels right to you. Yes, you made a vow to your husband, and I know it's killing you that you broke it, but Chrissy, your first commitment is to yourself. If you're not happy you will *never* make another living soul happy. I'm not condoning adultery, but I'm also not condoning a miserable existence. That being said, I would hate to see you compound the guilt you're already feeling. So it would be best to resist the urge to contact Leo until you know what you'd be contacting him for. Do you think you'll be okay until we meet next week?"

What am I thinking? I'm here to fix my marriage; of course I can make it a week. *I have to make it a week.* I nod my head yes like it's no biggie, but the hole in my heart that's flashing a big neon vacancy sign says otherwise.

DAYDREAMER

FEBRUARY, 1998

It's too early to tell if Dr. Maria will be able to help me, but for now it's nice to know that I can say Leo's name out loud to someone. I felt kind of normal for about a day after meeting with her, but then yesterday I was back in la la land, fantasizing about the night I met him and resisting every urge to pick up the phone and call him.

As much as I'd like to sit around and daydream about Leo all day, I've got to put thoughts of him aside for a couple of hours and focus on my job. I have a company to run. Lord knows the owner can't do it. For the first time in a long time I'm grateful for my stress-filled job. The busier I am these days, the better.

Today started off with a 7am conference call with a pissed-off distribution manager from the East Coast. That was fun; nothing like being called a bitch and a liar before I've had my morning coffee. I hung up the phone just in time for the 9am production meeting where I had to break up a fight between the head designer and the production manager. Thank God I got there in time because the New York Jewish American Princess designer was about to get her ass handed to her by the short-tempered Hong King Kong production manager. A typical conversation between the two of them goes something like this:

JAP: Why can't you get my fabwik samples hea by next week?

69

HKK: I tell you million times HELLS NO! They come from China! It not happen on such short notice.

JAP: Well din it's yoa fuggin' fault I can't meet my deadline!

HKK: HELLS NO! It not my fault! It your own damn fault you not give me request on time!

JAP: Chrissy, can't you do somedin bout' this?

I want to say hell's no, but I can't because it's my job to do something about *everything*. I instruct H.K.K. to overnight the samples so that we can get the fall line done in time for March market, but not before I scare the crap out of J.A.P. by telling her I'm deducting the cost of the air shipment from her next paycheck. I end the production meeting just in time to grab a non-fat vanilla latte before my drive out to the most disgusting part of San Francisco. I have an 11am meeting with one of our factory owners. I love Mr. Yee, but I can only understand every other word that comes out of his mouth.

"Ahhhhhh Kwissy, so good meeting today! We always do good wuk fo you, yes?"

It's so hard to not stare at the long wire like hairs protruding out of the mole on his right cheek. Don't even get me started on the long pinky fingernails either. Nasty! Mr. Yee is a sweet man, and I hate to be so critical of him, but doesn't he see what the rest of us see?

"Yeah, yeah, but remember, you have to get those cartons on the truck by 5pm or the shipment's gonna be late...AGAIN! I'm sick and tired of driving over the Bay Bridge to make sure your people are meeting the deadlines. Got that?"

"Yes, yes, yes, Kwissy. You woowy too much! Why you leave so fast? You wan stay fo lun?"

Oh Lordy, I'm going to take a stab at this and guess it's an invitation for lunch...

"Not today Mr. Yee."

Not EVER, for that matter! The sewing ladies are taking a break from their machines, but they don't spend their down time buying mochas at Starbucks or running over to Tower Records to pick up the new Matchbox 20 CD. *Noooooooo*, they're ripping the feathers off of a dead chicken and preparing to plop it into the thousand year old pot that's boiling away in the make-shift kitchen crammed into the back of the factory. It's like this in every factory I've been in, all the way from here to Hong Kong. It's a wonder to me that most articles of clothing hanging in department stores don't smell more like poultry.

"Heh! Heh! Heh! Kwissy you na no what you miss! Do'h woowy bout chipmen. We get on twuck soopa fas!"

I have no fucking idea what he just said, but he's smiling, so I'm smiling. Seriously, I can only say "What?" to this guy so many times.

I hop on the freight elevator and say my usual "Hi, how's it going?" to the sick fuck whose injecting God knows what into his arm. For a brief second I want to ask him what he thinks is worse, drugs or adultery? But I'm pretty sure I know the answer, plus I don't want to die, so I pass on the opportunity and run out to my car, which thankfully is not stolen and still has all of its windows intact.

It's an absolutely beautiful day in San Francisco. One of those freakishly warm winter days when you get a hint of what spring is going to feel like. Instead of cutting over to 5th Street to hop on Interstate 80 for a quick return to the office, I head up Van Ness and tool around California and Bush Streets. It's a longer route to the Bay Bridge, but I like the vibe of the financial district; everyone looks so confident and successful, like they're kicking life's ass. And one day, if everything goes according to his plan, Leo will be walking amongst them.

It takes about thirty minutes to drive three miles, and I savor the respite from the world. I daydream about last Saturday. I was only supposed to grab some sushi with a friend from work who I lovingly refer to as Slutty Co-worker. I've worked with her for years, and she's a great gal with a big ol' heart but trust me, her nickname says it all. I planned on staying in on Saturday night for some much needed rest. Kurt was out of town and I looked forward to a night at home to relax how I want to relax, eat what I want to eat, and just be how I want to be. But after a beyond shitty phone conversation with Kurt, Slutty Co-worker forced me to go out to dinner so she could cheer me up. Then, after that, she begged me to hit up Buckley's, her favorite dive bar. Even though I detest bars, I didn't protest because it's actually pretty entertaining to watch her work a bar crowd. Sure enough, within fifteen minutes, she left me all alone to run off and have a smoke with the first cute guy who approached her. To occupy my time until her return, I ordered a martini and eavesdropped on the odd conversation the guy sitting next to me was having with his lively Korean friend who he lovingly referred to as Ho-Bag.

JANUARY 24, 1998

"I'm telling you ghosts exist, dude. You think all that paranormal shit is made up?"

"Uhhhhhh, yeah man, I do."

"Alright then, what about what happened at my grandparents' house last month? I went to bed with the hallway light off, and the last thought I had before I fell asleep was that my grandfather always kept that *same* light on. It helped him find his way to the kitchen in the middle of the night. How do you explain it being on when I woke up at three o'clock in the morning? Huh? Yeah, that's what I thought you'd say, Ho-bag. Nothin'! What's up my little Korean friend, you didn't eat the cat before it ate your tongue?"

"Dude, how many times do I have to tell you, we don't eat cat! Now dog…that's another story."

I keep listening for another fifteen minutes as the serious guy, who has the most riveting voice I've ever heard, recounts some other ghost stories with the Ho-Bag person. *What does this guy look like?*

I casually turn around to get a peek, but all I see is the top of his head staring down into his brown drink. The Ho-bag dude is smiling right at me though. I zip back around in my barstool. Damn, I really want to see this guy's face. Hold on, why do I care so much?

The serious guy makes another crack about the Ho-Bag's Korean ethnicity, and it makes me giggle. I wonder if he noticed. Turning ever so slowly so that I don't look completely obvious, I catch him… staring into his friggin' glass again! God, are there naked women swimming in it? I look at him a little longer this time. There are signs he's attractive: tall, good hair, strong hands, but I can't be absolutely sure. He passed on the bartender's offer to get him another drink, so I assume he's not staying long, and it bums me out. I kind of want to talk to him, but so far everything I do to get his attention, like sit here and look pretty, isn't working. I think I'm going to have to butt into his conversation and show him just how cute I am. Here goes nothin'.

"Maybe your grandmother turned the light on just to screw with you."

Oopsy, maybe I shouldn't have opened my big mouth. The look on the face of the serious guy, who, by the way has the most amazing green eyes *I have ever seen*, tells me I should mind my own business. The little Korean guy, on the other hand, thinks I'm hilarious.

"Yeah, dude, Blondie's gotta good point! The grandma's the friggin' ghost! She kind of looks like one too, ya know? All pail and frail and shit. Plus, she never liked you anyway, right? I wouldn't put it past her to fuck with your head like that. Whoa, hold up! The hot girl's drink is almost done! Let me get you another one, Hunny. Bartender!"

Keep your pants on, you little Kimchi-eating bar leech! I didn't interrupt to get *your* attention.

"Ah, no thanks, but perhaps your friend, ghost boy over there, could use one. He's a little wound up, don't you think?"

Ghost boy turns his head, looks deep into my eyes, and says "I'm not drinking," then turns his head back down toward his… *is that a Coke?*

Helloooooooo! What's his damn problem? I've been blowing off guys left and right since I sat down on this barstool, and the *one* guy I decide to give the time of day to treats me like I have the word gonorrhea tattooed on my forehead! Geez, I was only trying to make small talk.

"Wow, are you always this serious or are ya gearing up for a spirit sighting tonight?"

I think I see a tiny smirk on his face, but it's hard to tell because he's NOT looking at me!

"Don't waste your time on him, he's *always* this serious! Let me buy you a drink to make you forget about what a dick he is."

"Thanks anyway, but I was kinda hoping the dick would buy me a drink."

Holy crap where did my nerve to say that come from? Before total mortification sets in and I excuse myself to run out of the bar, the dick slowly tilts his head up and to the side and looks right at me, like he's studying me. My heart feels like it just froze.

The little Korean guy hops off of his barstool and says, "Good luck with that, Hunny! I'm gonna go look for that friend of yours. Seems like she has better taste in men than you. Later."

The oddly beautiful green-eyed ghost dick boy is just sitting there cupping his glass with the most well-built hands I've ever seen. He looks back down at his drink and makes no attempt to talk to me. Kind of makes me want the Ho-Bag back. My expectations are low that this is going to develop into an interesting conversation, but since I have a few more minutes until Slutty Co-worker returns (hopefully), I carry on.

"You don't really have to buy me a drink you know, I was just trying to get rid of Long Duck Dong. His eagerness or excitement or whatever you call it was kinda getting on my nerves."

"I call him that too sometimes. It really pisses him off because he's not Chinese." And then he looks directly at me again, "I'd buy you that drink, but I'm a little short on cash these days."

"I guess the cash crunch explains the Coke you're drinking, huh?"

"Something like that."

"Well then, how about if I buy you a drink?"

"No, I'm fine with this. I'm laying off the booze these days."

"What for?"

"Trying to get in better shape. Plus, alcohol's too expensive. I'll have a couple of Olympia's at home if the mood strikes. But that's about it."

"Wow, Olympia…I didn't think they still made that stuff."

"They do."

"Well, if you get the bartender's attention, I'd like another vodka martini, please. It's like you and him are the only two guys who won't pay attention to me."

He's staring at me. I can't tell if this guy's angry, shy, or what. He's totally ambiguous. I really, really want to know what his deal is.

"All right, scary boy…just so we're clear, and you can stop being irritated with me, I thought your ghost story was interesting, and I totally believe everything you said about your grandfather and the light thing. In fact, I'm more of a freak than you; I actually talk out loud to my dead grandfather. Even chatted with him tonight before I came here."

He lets out a little laugh. Why does it make me so happy?

"I'm not irritated with you."

Finally he turns his whole body completely toward me, and our eyes lock. It's like staring into the black and white hypnotic twirly circles you see on old Road Runner cartoons. You know, after Wile E. Coyote's been hit in the head with an ACME anvil.

"Oh, yeah…then why so unfriendly? Your friend, what did you call him? Ho-Bag? He seems to have a liking for the ladies, but what's your deal? Girlfriend?"

Pleeeeeeeeeeease say you don't have a girlfriend. I know I'll never see you again, but I never want to see you again knowing you don't have a girlfriend.

"No, no girlfriend."

Thank you Lord Jesus who I don't believe in! I extend my hand to him and as he takes it, I say, "I'm Chrissy" in the most adorable way possible. It doesn't sound like me, but it sure as hell feels like me.

"Leo."

"So Leo…not into the girls tonight?"

He shakes his head and snickers.

"C'mon, there's plenty to choose from but you're just sitting here with your goofy friend and your scary stories. How come?"

"Actually I noticed you the minute you walked in here, but I'm not the kind of guy to get in line for a girl's attention, no matter how beautiful she is."

Omigod, did he just insinuate that I'm beautiful? Hold it! *Why the hell am I even caring about any of this?*

"Like, look at that guy over there. All night he's been jumping from girl to girl just so he can feel like a cool guy. He's nothing but a tool. And the girls who are flattered when they get their turn with him are even worse."

"Oh I know! They're such cheesedicks!"

Really, Chrissy? You couldn't come up with a better word than cheesedick?

"Yeah, and I've been listening to you blow off a lot of those cheesedicks. Does that mean you have a boyfriend or just good taste?"

Okay…wedding ring is now sliding off the table and into my lap.

"Nope, no boyfriend."

"So you have good taste, then."

"I'd like to think so, but it's more than that. If a guy wants to buy me a drink, I'd rather he talk to me for a while before offering; I prefer the offer is based on my brains, not on my boobs. I can buy my own drink. I don't need some idiot who thinks I'm hot to do it for me."

This is fun! As I lift my drink to my lips, I give him my best seductive sweet girl eye/smile combo stare. And by "my best," I mean my first. He pulls his barstool a little closer to me. My God, he smells like Heaven.

"Maybe I didn't want to talk to you and have you call *me* an idiot."

"What makes you think I'd do that?"

He laughs a little; it's cute. "That's what you did to all those other guys."

"What are you talking about?"

"Every time you told a guy to take a hike after he tried to hit on you, you'd whisper the word 'idiot' as he walked away. Me and Ho-Bag stopped counting the carnage at four. I dared him to buy you a drink and even he was too scared to take a shot. Seriously, it takes a lot for that guy to pass on a dare."

"That's hilarious! But let me clarify…those idiots were offering to buy me a drink and look, I already have one! And like you said, you don't have any money to offer me a drink, all you have to offer me is conversation. Why would I blow that off?"

Still just a sliver of a smile. He's shy, been badly burned in the past, or he's a psychotic killer. Must press on to figure out which one.

"And even if you could buy me twenty drinks, it's obvious you're not a cheesedick, because I haven't seen you take the proverbial lap around the bar to talk to everything in a tight tank top. Nope, you seem content with your ghost stories, while lonely girls whose friends ditch them eavesdrop on you and marvel at your good looks. Hey... wait a minute! This little friendship we have is kind of one-sided, don't you think?"

"How so?"

"Well, I seem to have noticed an awful lot about you, but I don't think you've noticed that I've been sitting here noticing all of it for the last hour. That doesn't seem fair."

My super sweet giggle coupled with the way I'm playing with my martini olive should suggest I'm teasing, but without cracking a smile, he speaks as seriously as if he's giving the pledge of allegiance.

"I just told you I noticed you the minute you walked in."

"Yeah, right."

"Your first drink was a dirty martini with three olives, and you sent it back because it was too dirty. Not in a bitchy way, in a cute way that makes me think you always get what you want. You went to the restroom twice, probably because you've also had two glasses of water. You're here with a co-worker who likes to party, hard. Before she ditched you, you guys talked about clothing and deadlines and shipping problems. Sounds like you work in fashion, and it seems like you're in charge of a lot of people. You've been to New York twice in the last four weeks and you want to get home early tonight because you're tired from some bad phone call you had earlier. I've been watching and listening, and I think you're beautiful and interesting. Seem fair now?"

Focus Chrissy, be cool, stay interesting, channel beautiful.

"So to spare..." Clear your throat you fucking moron! "So to spare being called an idiot, you'd let me walk out of here without taking a shot?"

A shot at *what*? Jesus, I'm such a huge slut right now.

"Yeah, I would."

"That's kinda sad. Doesn't it make you wonder how many good women you've let slip away?"

"You can't miss something you never knew existed."

I see pain in him, or is it anger?

"What are you, too lazy to make the effort, or scared of rejection?" He's laughing.

"Come on! What then? Shy?"

"Nah, I think you meet people when you least expect it, when you're not trying. I think it's just meant to happen…" He's staring at me like he thinks it's happening right now, and it causes me to swallow so hard that I think the entire bar can hear the gulp. "Besides, I'd say it's a bad idea to hit on a woman when you can't even afford to buy her a drink."

He's good looking *and* profound.

"You know…your eyes are amazing. I've never seen eyes that green before."

Jesus, who's the cheesedick now? Fix it, Chrissy!

"Trust me, though, I wouldn't have interrupted your conversation to tell you that. I interrupted it because I liked what you were talking about. You don't meet many interesting people in bars."

"Speaking of interesting…take a look at that."

Funny little Korean guy is now drunk little Korean guy and he's barreling right toward us with a cigarette tucked behind his ear and his arm slung over Slutty Co-worker's shoulder.

"Hey Blondie, looks like you got the serious dickhead out of his shell! That's a first!"

Looking into the beautiful eyes of the serious dickhead I say, "I don't know, did I?"

AWAKENING

FEBRUARY, 1998

"It's been a week since we last met. How are you doing?"

"Fine, I guess."

"Any contact with Leo?"

"I wanted to call him but what would the point of all this be if I did that?"

She ignores my sardonic question and plugs on.

"How has it been with Kurt?"

"Same as usual: work, exercise, dinner, sleep."

"No talking?"

"About what? Sorry, I don't mean to be rude. I'm just frustrated."

"It's understandable. Has Kurt noticed a difference in you?"

"Nah, he's been busy with work, and he left this morning for *another* backpacking trip."

I thought she'd want to tackle my bitchy backpacking comment, but for some reason she sticks with the agenda she set last week.

"Chrissy, I'd like to talk a little about your family today. How's your relationship with your folks?"

I don't understand the point of this direction and it's annoying because it's costing me seventy-five bucks an hour. But she's the pro. I'll let her do her thing for a while; maybe I am more fucked-up than I thought.

"I had a normal childhood; the stay-at-home-mom, the hard_ working dad, the loving brother. Everyone used to call us the Brady Bunch. I used to think we were even better than that."

"Used to?"

"I don't remember a lot about my childhood, but what I do remember was pretty good. You know, the block parties, Halloween parades at school…Christmas pageants. It was all good."

"Did the fun come to an end?"

"That's an understatement."

"Did your folks divorce?"

"Oh, God no!"

"Why are you laughing?"

"Oh it's just funny that I would say that with such intensity."

"Why?"

"Because looking back, I can't believe they didn't get a divorce. My parents went through a pretty rough patch in their marriage, so I guess you could say the whole family went through a rough patch. Anyway, they got through it and since then they've been stronger than ever. They're the poster parents for never giving up, and I guess they're the main reason why I wanna make things work with Kurt."

"How old were you when the rough patch hit?"

"Let's see…thirteen. It was right after we moved back from Japan."

"Wow, Japan. That's very interesting. Tell me more."

"Not much to tell, really. When I was in the eighth grade my family moved back from a three year stint in Asia. My dad's position in the wonderful world of semi-conductors, whatever the hell those are, made him an ideal candidate to uproot our family from our tranquil little town of Amherst, New Hampshire and relocate us to Tokyo."

"But what a great opportunity, huh?"

"In some ways, yes. But while I was busy living a completely sheltered life in Japan, most kids my age in the United States were spending their time learning how to dress like Madonna, break dance, smoke pot, and form cliques. I had no clue how to do any of those things, and it was stuff like that that made moving back to the U.S. one of the worst ordeals of my life. And apparently it proved to be just as difficult for my mother."

"What do you mean?"

"We lived large in Tokyo. Country clubs, maids, drivers to take us wherever we wanted to go. But then we were relocated to California with its ridiculous cost of living and 15% mortgage rates. In order to buy a home that was remotely similar to the ones we had always lived in, my mom had to get a job, her first, and I had to go to public school, my first. Neither one of us were prepared for the transition."

"What happened?"

"I didn't have a mom at a time in my life when I needed one the most, that's what happened. I hated her, she hated my dad, and my brother hid in his room with his Thompson Twins records to avoid all the hate. We went from being the Brady Bunch to The Bundy's."

Clearly she's never watched *Married with Children* because she didn't get how funny that was.

"You were thirteen, you say? That must've been hard."

"It was confusing. I don't feel like my mom tried hard enough to help me adjust to life in the United States. In Japan I was sheltered from normal American kid things and then, WHAMO! On my first day of school here, I was introduced to all of it. I had no ability to relate to those kids--it was total culture shock. For months, I ate lunch by myself in a freezing cold portable classroom. No one talked to me, and I had tears in my eyes every single day when my mom picked me up."

"What did she say about the tears?"

"She was too preoccupied with her own problems to pay attention to mine. Luckily, I met my friend Courtney and she saved me. Court and her mom took me shopping, drove me to football games, and to cheerleading practice."

"Well that's good, isn't it?"

"I guess so, but the more Courtney's mom did for me, the angrier my mom got, and she took most of that anger out on me."

"How so?"

"She yelled a lot, hit me...a lot. She was pissed all of the time. Our relationship was pretty tense until I went to college. I've tried really hard to leave all that stuff behind but every so often, I'll think back to those days and it hurts all over again. I'll never understand why my mom was so damn angry and self-absorbed."

"Would you say Kurt's an angry and self-absorbed person?"

Wait, are we shifting the subject?

"He's not angry, but I'd say he's self-absorbed. It's all about what he wants to do all of the time. He rarely asks me for my opinion or advice."

"Do you have a tense relationship with your mom now?"

I guess we're not shifting the subject.

"Not really. Look, I don't want to make my mom out to be some kind of monster. I have to believe she did the best she could."

"Explain her."

"Let's see…she's a beautiful woman who does everything she can to cover up whatever beauty she possesses, usually by wearing baggy black clothes and dark sunglasses. She was super strict about the way I dressed as a teenager--no black clothes or makeup until I turned sixteen. She said only white trash wore black." I think back to a time when I saw my mother dressed up and it unveils emotions I've tried very hard to bury. I clear my throat and continue. "I thought she was very pretty. I would've liked to tell her but I didn't."

"That could've been due to resentment."

"I guess so." And then I pick up on something. "It's funny…Kurt criticizes my clothes a lot like my mom used to."

"He tells you what to wear?"

"*Allllllll the time*! I'm either over-dressed or under-dressed with that guy. He's so critical of whatever I have on or what type of shoes I'm wearing. *He's obsessed with me wearing comfortable shoes*! It's like he thinks he knows what's best for me or something."

"Continue describing your mother, Chrissy."

Son of a bitch.

"How she is now or how she was back then?"

"Whatever comes to your mind."

"Alright…she had an incredibly dysfunctional childhood that she was *always* quick to remind me of whenever I got mad at her. She had a psychotic mother; literally, she was locked up in an asylum for a while. Her father was a drunk and wasn't fit to raise my mom, so she was sent away to live with relatives. When my Grandma got sane, as if that can magically happen, my mom was sent back home. She always talks about how awful it was, which is why I don't understand why she allowed me to be around my Grandparents so much when I was a kid. I mean, really, how can she complain about being damaged by those people yet allow me to spend the night at their house? It never made sense to me."

"How did it make you feel?"

"Unprotected, confused, kinda unloved, I guess."

"Chrissy, how does Kurt make you feel?"

Aha, I finally see where this is going and without hesitation I say, "Unprotected, confused, kinda…unloved. Dr. Maria what's this all about?"

Taking her glasses off and addressing me like she's not sure I'm going to be able to handle what she's about to say, "Well, certain studies show that our choices of marital partners, *the relationships we have with them*, are determined by relationships with parents or important persons in one's childhood. Meaning, marital relationships can be repetitions of relationships with parental patterns from childhood."

I'm looking at her like, *yeah, so?*

"And the assumption is that you'd gravitate toward a partner that resembled a parental figure that made you feel loved, protected, say…maybe your father?"

I'm apprehensively nodding my head.

"Okay, and while I'm sure it was always your intention to marry a man just like your father, it seems that in your case, you may have married someone more like your mother."

A loud chortle slips past my lips as I belt out, "C'mon! Why the hell would I do that? I love my mom, but trust me, one of her is enough. Why would I have chosen a relationship, no wait, *a pattern of behavior*, that I so badly wanted to be rescued from?"

"That's just it, Chrissy, I don't think you wanted to be rescued from it. I think you wanted to fix it."

A few seconds ago my face screamed indifference. Now my forehead is crunched up tightly and my eyes are darting around the floor in an obvious state of distress. Dr. Maria just insinuated that I'm with Kurt because apparently I wanted to fix some kind of residual pain I had toward my mother through him.

"Do you *really* think I'm trying to get from him what I always wanted from her?"

"It's a theory I'd like to delve into more."

No need to delve. I think she nailed it.

"You know…when we first met, everything was fun with Kurt. I felt so protected and loved by him. But when I got older, his, shall we say *limitations* when it comes to matters of the heart became obvious. I tried to help him feel emotions that came naturally to me. But over time, he started to get annoyed with me and I started to get frustrated, and it caused all kinds of trouble between us."

"You married when you were very young--twenty-five, right?"

"Yes."

"Well, usually it's not until much later in life that one realizes they can't possibly change another human being. I'm sure you tried and tried to get what you needed out of Kurt, but eventually you realized it was like shoveling shit against the tide."

My head is hanging low and unwittingly shaking from side to side.

"But you had invested so much time and hope into the relationship, so you slowly let more of his unsettling behaviors slide by without raising a red flag. His assumption was that things were just fine but you…"

"…Married him and signed on to a lifetime of neediness I had hoped to escape when I met him."

Did I say that because I want her to think I'm absorbing what she's saying or because it's true? Both are shitty suppositions.

"This is so sad."

"Tell me, what?"

"Everything we're talking about. All of it makes me feel so pathetic."

"How so?"

Pausing for a really long time because it hurts so much to say out loud the thoughts that are racing through my mind.

"I used to…I used to beg Kurt to love me like Romeo loved Juliet, just like I *wanted* to beg my mom to love me like Carol Brady loved her daughters. I never did that, of course, because I was too afraid she'd tell me she couldn't and, *oh my God*, that would've been the worst. Anyway, when I'd beg Kurt to love me more, he'd scream that he gives me all the love he has." My head hangs back toward the floor, and my voice is merely a whisper. "I wanted him to tell me stuff like he'd die without me and I'm the most important thing in the world to him, but he just said stuff like that is stupid and excessive." I clear my throat and look up at her. "This hurts Dr. Maria...a lot."

"I know, Hunny."

"Do you think I was clinging so tightly to the *idea* of Kurt that it made it impossible to see he's incapable of loving me?"

"I'm sure he loves you very much. If we can--"

"*If we can what*? Make him love me in a way he thinks is stupid and excessive?"

Man, I actually stumped her with that question.

"I've been so fortunate to have Courtney, Kelly, and Nicole feed me the maternal love my mother couldn't. It's probably the only reason why I can be close to my mom. But my friends can't possibly fill the emotional void that exists in my marriage. That probably explains the screw up with Leo."

"Let's assume it's the case that you became so emotionally neglected, it caused you to have an indiscretion with another man. Our best shot at preventing that from happening again depends on getting your needs met by your husband."

She ignores my loud defeated sigh.

"We have to work together with Kurt and hope that he willingly responds to your needs. We're not going to try to change him, but we're going to educate him on who you are and what you need to be happy. We want him to be more emotionally available to you, so you feel satisfied within the relationship. Satisfied married folks don't cheat!"

"You're saying the only way my marriage stands a chance is if I tell Kurt what I need and he responds with a willingness to make things better?"

"That's correct."

"And we can only work if I'm free to be the real me and he validates my feelings?"

"That's what I'm saying."

I don't know whether to laugh or cry.

"It seems so simple, and so impossible, all at the same time."

"It won't be simple and it *is* possible and it will be well worth it if it's what the both of you want. Chrissy…what is it? What's wrong?"

"I'm disgusted with myself. It's been easy to blame Kurt for this whole mess, but it's really my fault. I started letting him off the hook for stuff right before college. If I hadn't, we would've most likely broken up."

"Was letting him off the hook a conscious decision?"

"I'd like to think it was unconscious because how pathetic would I be if I fought so hard to be with someone that never made me feel good enough?"

I reach for a couple of tissues, and I think I see Dr. Maria prepare herself.

"Back in high school, every girl I knew would've sold their soul to be Kurt's girlfriend, and I knew once he started college the number of girls throwing themselves at him would multiply. To keep us together, I started acting how he wanted me to act and I stopped pestering him to love me more. I didn't pitch a fit when he went away to college and I didn't complain when he asked me *not to do* the same for myself."

"*He told you not to go to college?*"

"He convinced me not to go to the one I wanted to go to. He made me feel like I wouldn't be able to handle it."

"It didn't make you feel controlled?"

"Nope, it actually made me feel loved. But it wasn't long before I became very jealous of his college experiences and we fought constantly. I became suspicious of what he was doing all the time and I freaked out. I mean, I went ape-shit crazy. Anyway, mid-way through college he couldn't handle my 'neediness' anymore and broke up with me."

"Oh boy."

"Exactly. It was the most horrific heartache I had ever experienced. I *honestly* didn't think I could live without him. I begged him to give me another chance, and he did. But from then on, I began to believe I was the one with the problem. I was afraid to make him mad, so I tried to act tough and not as needy. I did whatever it took so that I didn't have to be alone."

It's quiet for a minute and Dr. Maria's letting me absorb the enormity of how appalling my responsibility is for what's happened.

"Shortly before we got engaged, Kurt had a big talk with me about how important it was for him to be with someone who liked the same recreational activities as him. It was a warning that I had better buck up or we wouldn't make it. I hated every minute of it, but I did every stupid activity he asked me to do. Like an idiot, I convinced the both of us I was exactly what he wanted so he would marry me, and he did. We had a big, beautiful Barbie dream wedding, and I was the envy of every girl I knew."

"How long did their envy sustain your happiness?"

"Until our first dance."

"Wow, that soon huh?"

"I kept waiting for those special words a new husband is supposed to whisper in his new bride's ear. I kept trying to get him to look deep into my eyes and create some kind of magical unspoken happiness between us. But it just felt like any other dance we had danced in the past. I started crying and the crowd *ohhhhh'd* and *awwww'd* at what they thought were tears of joy. It only made me cry more."

"What was going through your mind?"

"That a handsome husband, a big diamond ring, and a fifty thousand dollar wedding can make you look special, but they can't make you feel special. The more I swayed from side to side, the more lost I felt, and it's like I never stopped swaying. I don't like the woman Kurt fell in love with. She's not the woman I was meant to be, she's not the wife I dreamed of being, and she's certainly not going to be the kind of mother I have to be."

"Do you still do the kinds of activities Kurt wants you to do?"

"Not really. Last year I decided I had enough and I put my foot down on all the extreme sports he guilted me into doing. I started watching more TV, drinking more wine, eating Lucky Charms for dinner, working longer hours at the office. All of it has made him incredibly angry, and we fight more. But instead of going back to how he wants me to be in order to stop the fighting, I've just shut down. Now I think I'm too lost to try and find my way back to who I'm even supposed to be."

She lets it remain quiet again.

"You know what hurts the most?"

"What, Hun?"

"That I have so much love to give to both Kurt and my mom, but I'm cut off from giving it because they're incapable of receiving it. It's painful to hug...*really* hug someone and not feel them reciprocate. It's painful to say *I love you* and get a 'love ya too' in return. Over time, you just stop giving up those parts of yourself because it's not appreciated. I pay a heartbreaking price for my mom's limitations every time I see her, and I'll continue to do it because she's my mom. But am I supposed to pay that kind of price in my marriage? Am I supposed to be cut off from giving my husband the kind of affection that comes natural to me?"

"Absolutely not, and my hope is that Kurt learns to be receptive to your offerings, but without having met him, it's tough for me to know if he's capable. It's very important for you to realize that all individuals own the responsibility of whether or not they want to change. Your responsibility is to be honest and consistent in what you need. The rest is up to him. Remember, a person who tries to change another human being is a person fighting a losing battle--a person who's wasting precious time and energy. And know this too: even if he is receptive to your needs, there are certain behaviors in him that you will just have to accept. Once we know what you *have to* accept, you can work on being healthy, as opposed to resentful, with your decision to be with him. I'd like to see you alone again next week, but why don't you talk to Kurt about coming to therapy with you the week after next?"

"I think that's a good idea."

Just as I'm getting ready to leave the appointment, I turn back to Dr. Maria who's primping the pillows for the next nut job.

"Dr. Maria?"

"Yes, Dear?"

"I understand when you're married you're supposed to forsake all others and I know I broke that vow. But if I understand the meaning behind today's session, didn't I break something even bigger years earlier when I decided to forsake myself? Isn't that what's gotten me into this mess today?"

"Yes, Chrissy. I believe that to be true."

After leaving therapy, I sit in my car with the seat reclined and stare at the stars through my sun-roof and think. I've been fighting for Kurt to love me a certain way since the day we met and I'm tired now. What remains is a choice. Stay and accept the emotional limits of our relationship or leave in search of some kind of love that may or may not exist. I'm glad he's on a two-day backpacking trip, because I don't have the heart to look at him right now. Jesus, he doesn't even know I'm seeing a therapist. He's really going to hate the thought of that. But not as much as he's going to hate the suggestion that he see her too. I stop at the liquor store to grab a bottle of wine before heading home. I feel like I could drink a couple of bottles, but Kurt doesn't like it when I drink during the week. He's concerned it will dehydrate me and cause me to have less energy. It's just another one of those things I thought was sweet when we first met. Now it annoys the hell out me. As I'm mulling over the Cabernets, I wonder *why didn't I tell my girlfriends about my problems with Kurt*? Why the hell is it so important to me that they think I have it all together? Stupid therapy! It's making me question way more than I ever intended. Fuck it, I grab two bottles of wine and a six pack of beer and head home.

LEERY

FEBRUARY, 1998

Until I see Dr. Maria again, the plan is to immerse myself in work. At work I don't lie, cheat, or break hearts. I'm safe there. And it's just another day in my safety net as I drive back to my office. I just left a lovely ass-ripping meeting with a slimy San Francisco fabric vendor, and thinking about that jerk makes me so completely angry that I turn on the radio to redirect my thoughts. That's when my safety net breaks. On the radio is none other than Dave Matthew's *Crash Into Me*. Morsels of the night I met Leo begin to flash through my mind…naughty, naughty morsels. It makes me want him real bad. Then again, this song makes me want to hump a tree. Damn it, Dave!

As if I'm on auto-pilot, I skip the exit to my office and drive toward Moraga, home to Leo's college and his apartment. I promised Dr. Maria I would stay away, but I also promised my husband a lifetime of love and fidelity and look how that turned out. Obviously my word means nothing.

Fifteen minutes later, I'm roaming the streets of Moraga looking for I have absolutely no idea what. To be quite honest, I don't exactly remember what Leo looks like. Sure, there are the eyes, the hands, the voice…I can see and hear stuff in pieces but his entire life form is a total blur to me and it's weird because we spent eight hours together in my car. Maybe I'm suffering from the same shock as a witness to a horrific crime. It all happened right in front of my face, but it was so scandalous, so unimaginable that I can't put it all together in my head.

Ten minutes into my search for bits and pieces of Leo's body parts in a town that I'm unfamiliar with, I decide to end the fruitless search and head back to my office. *But of course*, I make a wrong turn and my car spills out onto Mt. Diablo Boulevard…right in front of the Lafayette Reservoir.

Leo told me about this place the night we met, and it's even more beautiful than I imagined. How have I lived twenty minutes from here and never known about it? Maybe I can call him real quick, just to tell him I finally saw the reservoir. It would be nice if I forgot his phone number so that I could stay on course with what I promised Dr. Maria, but since I made it my fucking computer password, all hope of that is gone. I swear I'm my own worst enemy. I think I'm going to call. No I'm not! Yes I am! Ohhhh I hate myself so much right now! I'm sure he won't be home though, its late afternoon on a Thursday; he's gotta be busy…and he is. There's no answer and, thank God, because I should NOT be doing this. I throw the car into reverse and slowly make my way to the exit of the overpriced parking lot. What was I thinking paying $5.00 for an all-day space? Was I hoping for some kind of Saturday night slut-fest repeat? Kind of. And with that admission, I tip the scale of total unbalance and start to laugh and cry at the same time. Good Lord, I'm like Diane Lane in any one of the million cheating wife movies she stars in that can be seen seven days a week on the Lifetime channel.

An emergency work call from Slutty Co-worker pulls me back into my safety net, and by the end of the conversation I'm ready to leave the reservoir nonsense behind. As I'm touching up my lipstick in preparation to go back to the office, I notice a tall guy get out of a dingy red jeep. The kind of jeep you see in cool beer commercials with people driving around in bikinis and stuff. It's definitely not one of those perfectly cared for jeeps that gets washed and waxed every week. This one's used, dirty, and sexy as all hell. I squint my eyes to get a better look at the guy who's dropping a few quarters in the meter and my focus zooms in on his perfect hands. Could that be… *is that*…it can't be him! He did mention he likes to come here to be alone with his thoughts, and that *does* look like the jacket he wore the other night, but it doesn't make any sense that it would be him. Then again, it makes all the sense in the world that it would be.

I back up, park, and watch the guy as he walks to a bench on the edge of the reservoir. He sits, rests his elbows on his knees, leans his chin into his fists and stares at the water. *Is that him*? The bits and pieces look right, but it's so hard to tell. Maybe I should go look. Nah, whoever he is, he's come here to think and I should leave him alone. I'm outta here. WAIT, no I'm not! Okay, wait a fucking minute, Chrissy! You made the ridiculous attempt to call him, so why not make one more final effort to see if the guy on the bench is Leo. I get out of my car and slowly walk up behind the man. Even though I know he can hear the crunch of the rocks under my boots, he doesn't turn my way. It reminds me of the night I met Leo when no matter what, I couldn't get him to look at me.

"Leo?"

His head slowly lifts up, but instead of turning my way, it tilts slightly to the left and faintly shakes from side to side in a "this cannot be happening" kind of way. I'm about ten feet away when I notice the familiar grey shirt peeking out from under the very familiar green jacket. I recognize the shiny black hair and I smell the smell that's still hiding in my closet at home.

"Oh my God, it is you."

He turns around, and his green eyes pierce right through me. Wow, he looks *much* older than twenty-two. He has the blackest of black eyebrows that make his eyes pop out at you like dart boards. He has stubble on his chin, but not the overly groomed kind, the kind that doesn't give a fuck. In fact, everything about him screams, "I don't give a fuck." He walks toward my stiff as a board body which feels cemented to the ground. My heart is pounding, and I hear loud swishing sounds in my ears. I feel like I could faint, but I remember what happened the last time I fainted, and I'll do whatever I can not to repeat that humiliation.

He puts his hands in his jacket pockets as he approaches me. He's leery of me. He should be.

"I had a feeling you'd show up here eventually."

"You actually come here and wait for me?"

"No, not like a freak or something. I do have a job and school--I'm busy. But I don't have your number or your address. Shit, I don't even know your last name."

And there's a mighty good reason why.

"So in between work and school I hang out here sometimes and hope you might show up before it's too late."

"Too late for what?"

He lowers his eyes at me in a "don't make me fucking say it" kind of way, and then it hits me. He's talking about my imaginary wedding.

"It's Anderson."

"What is?"

"My last name."

Well, my maiden name anyway, but at least it's some kind of truth.

I invite him back to my car, and as the rain pours down, we spend the next three hours talking. Our conversation picks up right where it left off early that Sunday morning, just before he kissed me. He talks about college, and I talk about my career. I'm fascinated that's he's going to achieve great things, and he's fascinated that I already have. Things are feeling as magical as the night I met him, and just as he's leaning in to get a better look at my necklace and *I think* kiss me, the park ranger bangs on my window and notifies us that the reservoir is closing. We have to vacate the premises immediately or be locked in all night. Not a bad thought, but definitely a bad idea.

"I'd offer to buy you dinner, but you know my situation…my *temporary* situation."

Man, we're at such different stages of our lives.

"I'll buy."

Over sushi and several sakes, Leo describes his life to me. He was adopted when he was one day old from Eureka, and all he knows is that he's part German, Irish and Native American. He has two older brothers who were also adopted; none of them are biologi-cally related and he has nothing in common with either of them. His parents divorced when he was sixteen, and after they sent his two brothers to college, he was told there was no money left to send him. As if that wasn't hard enough to deal with, the home he had lived in his entire life was facing foreclosure.

He never felt like he fit in with his family and describes his relationship with his best friend, Taddeo, as his only real close one. After high school, he went to Cal Poly, San Luis Obispo and majored in Construction Management. Not his first choice as a college or a major but he thought his Dad would pony up some of the tuition if he followed in his footprints. Sadly, his Dad never stepped up, and survival soon became a problem, so he left to be closer to his grandparents who offered to help him with half of his tuition at the college he always wanted to attend, St. Mary's College in Moraga. He moved to Moraga but went to a junior college for a year before attending St. Mary's so he could work full time and stock-pile some money. He's been at St. Mary's for five months now.

He works part time in a rock yard to finance his rent and the other half of his tuition that his grandparents aren't covering. He's doing everything he possibly can to finish school quickly so he can pursue a career as an investment banker, which by the way, his brothers think is a silly pipe dream. They call him a Gordon Gecko wanna-be. What a bunch of assholes.

He's had one girlfriend and said that he didn't care much for her. She joined a sorority and, that being one of the stupidest things in the world to him, he dumped her and hasn't talked to her since. He makes it very clear that once he cuts you out of his life, it's permanent, and I believe him. He's a genuine guy and a true friend, but only to a select few. He's been known to punch guys who disrespect women, and he hates the word "tits." He likes drinking beer, *a lot of beer*, but under no circumstances will he play a lame drinking game. The only money he justifies spending is on his gym membership, which as far as I can tell, is money well spent. He hates going to the movies because he can't stand being that close to strangers. He's a total germaphobe. He's been in way too many fist-fights in the last couple of years, but he's working on his rage because he feels like he's old enough to get sued for it. He will NOT own a cell phone until the day an employer requires him to, and he hates anyone who talks on one while driving their car. He's opinionated, confident, and brutally honest and makes no apology for any of it. He tells me that he hardly ever smiles, until recently, and it's all due to meeting me. After everything he just told me, I believe him.

During dinner, the subject of my engagement didn't come up once. It makes me wonder if he assumes it's broken off or if he decided not to care one way or the other. It also makes me wonder if all he's really looking for is a piece of ass, and then *that* makes me wonder why I didn't bolt after dinner when he asked me if I wanted to come to his apartment. Actually he didn't ask me. He just said, "Come to my apartment." Right away I thought of three things that *should've* made me run home as fast as possible:

1) I'm a married woman.

2) I'll seduce him if I go there, and I have *all night* to do it because Kurt's still backpacking in God-knows-where USA.

3) Leo could actually be a psychotic killer who wants to get me to his apartment and do really bad things to me.

Because I've apparently lost my mind, I decide to abandon any and all logic and go with half of number two. I *may* seduce him, but I definitely won't stay the night. I have to draw the line somewhere. Isn't that what Diane Lane would do?

We arrive at his place and walk up the outdoor stairs to his floor. It feels like my heart is going to pop out of my chest. We pass a trio of girls leaving the apartment next door to his, and in unison they chime "*Hiiiiiiiiii Leooooooooo.*" Man, are they ever checking me out! I love it! He gives them a quick, "Hey," unlocks the door, and places his hand on the small of my back to guide me inside. His touch releases a thousand butterflies into my body. This is the most exciting thing I have EVER done in my life. I can't believe there are single people out there who get to do this whenever they want and they complain about it! Are they high?

His apartment looks exactly like I thought it would. College text-books piled high on a dreadful looking brown tiled coffee table, a couple of frayed chairs, a mattress on the floor of the bedroom, empty beer bottles lined up on the kitchen counter, and the most massive television I've ever seen. There are miles of wire spread across the floor going from the TV to a couple of video game joy-sticks. Is that...*Nintendo*? Seeing the look of horror in my eyes, he quickly kicks the joysticks under the curtain.

"That would be stress relief for the poor man. Wanna beer?"

He seems nervous. Surprisingly, I'm wildly in control. He hands me a beer and then sits in one of the broken chairs and takes a swig. God, he even makes drinking out of a bottle look sexy.

"Don't you want to know if I'm still engaged?"

"I decided not to care about it. Once you get to know me, you'll do the right thing."

His confidence is a total turn on. I place my beer on his shitty table and kneel down in front of him, nudging myself between his legs. I don't know where all of my courage is coming from but I don't question it. I extend my neck up and grab the back of his, pulling his lips toward mine. The kiss is slow and long and the best one I've ever had. After a few minutes, he leaves my lips and eagerly travels to my right ear. Everything is loud, wet, and wonderful. No part of me wants to go home. I want to move into this four hundred square foot piece of crap apartment and live the rest of my life feeling like this. As my hands start to rub his thighs, I feel him tremble, so I pull away.

"You're shaking."

"Stuff like this doesn't happen every day. Goddamn, I ran into you TWICE! It's gotta be fate because I'm not a lucky guy."

I hope I'm long gone before he finds out just how unlucky he is.

"Chrissy, I've been dreaming about you for two weeks, and to actually find you is scary."

"Scary?"

"You could go away, and what are the chances of finding you again?"

"I don't think I can go away Leo and *that* scares me."

"You don't have to go anywhere. Get to know me."

"I don't want to talk anymore, kiss me"

"Come to my bedroom."

SHEDDING

MARCH, 1998

The only things I'm good at lately are yelling at people at work and avoiding my husband and friends. The plus side about being a bitch at work is that I'm giving every asshole we do business with a run for their money and my boss is giving me kudos for my tenacity. I smell a raise on the horizon. Courtney's called a few times wondering where I am, but those calls have gone unreturned. Since Dr. Maria made me start wondering why I don't talk to my best friends about my problems, I feel uptight talking to them about anything. It hasn't been hard to avoid Kurt, though. In fact, I think we've been avoiding each other for years. He's been busy planning a kayaking trip for the two of us. You know…because I love kayaking so damn much. To prepare me for the trip, he bought me the most ridiculous looking shoes I've ever seen. They're called Uggs and they're *UGG*ly as all hell. They might be on the cover of Outdoor Idiot Magazine but they'll *never* make it into mainstream fashion or onto my feet. Seriously, where does he find this stuff?

The last time I saw Leo was at his apartment, six days ago. We didn't have sex that night. At first it seemed like it was certain we would, but after all of my clothes came off and he started to explore my body, I broke down in tears. Sure, I had already committed adultery in every sense of the word, but there was no absolution from having sexual intercourse with another man. Once I did that, there was no going back, and up until that moment on Leo's bed, all of my sanity rested on the hope that I could put him behind me, forgive myself for my one and only mistake, and move on with my life with Kurt. I knew if I had sex with Leo, every single thing I had worked for in the last twelve years would come to a crashing halt. My much admired wedding ring would feel like nothing more than costume jewelry; my dream home would become a house of cards, and my fifty thousand dollar wedding vows would make about as much sense as jibber jabber. Everything I thought to be precious would really be shit. Maybe it's already shit, but until I determine the full extent of its shittyness, I owe it to Kurt to put a lid on my libido. Plus, even more disturbing than blowing up my shitty world with adulterous sex is that it would officially make me a total failure. And the thought of that was more overwhelming than the desire to have sex with Leo. So he held me tightly while I cried uncontrollably.

For a few hours, I felt safe in his arms, a fraud sheltered from my fraudulent life. When he finally walked me out to my car, I told him I probably wouldn't see him again because I needed time to sort my life out.

He grabbed both of my wrists, stared deep into my eyes and said "You have to." And I do. As much as I want to be done with him, I can't be. I'm addicted now. The next day, I gave him my phone number. Okay, not really, it's just the phone number to my voicemail account.

There's no way I can give him my real cell phone number!

Because of work and obligations at home…like ones that require me to act like a wife, I haven't been able to talk to Leo for days. And as I listen to his latest message on my way home from work, I can tell he isn't happy about it.

"You're worrying me, Chrissy. If you don't want to see me anymore, then at least have the guts to tell me. Don't leave me hanging like this."

Just as I'm about to pull into my driveway, I maneuver the car straight and drive to the end of my street. Am I crying because it really is over or because I don't want it to be and I don't know what to do about it? How come the only time I've felt sane in the last twelve years has been in the last few insane weeks? Jesus, I'm so exhausted from asking myself questions like this. I start to cry harder than I ever have; it's truly an academy award-winning performance. I can't go home until the redness in my eyes goes away because Kurt will want to know "what's wrong now" and I can't lie to him anymore. I park next to the trailhead that I've come to know and love as the start of my morning jogs and give myself time to calm down.

I tend to make very quick decisions about things. Whether it's about upping my 401k contribution amount, changing my political party affiliation, or lasering a mole off of my body, when I decide on something, I do it immediately. No decision is ever kept in limbo long with me, and what to do with my marriage shouldn't be an exception. So if I don't plan on divorcing Kurt, and I don't, at least I don't think, I cannot continue to see Leo. No good can come out of what I'm doing to those men and eventually I'm going to get caught. Plus, if I end up on Leo's bed again, I'm screwed, literally. The best way to end the charade, *and my addiction*, is to tell Leo I'm going forward with my so-called wedding in July and say good-bye to him once and for all. I pick up my cell phone and slowly dial his number.

"*What the hell are you talking about*? Tell me one good reason why you're gonna marry that guy."

"For starters, we've been together a really long time."

"That's a stupid reason and you know it."

He's right, it is a stupid reason, but this is also a stupid lie. This whole charade makes me look and sound like a stupid idiot.

"I'd be hurting a lot of people if I backed out of the engagement. I guess I'm too scared to do that."

"Then you aren't the same person I've been talking to."

That's an understatement.

"So you're gonna go through with a wedding to a guy you cheated on because you feel *obligated* to?"

Nope, I'm going to stay *married* to a guy because I feel obligated to.

"Leo I don't know how to explain all of this to you…"

"Why don't you try explaining the connection you guys have. If you can convince me it's more powerful than the one we have, I'll send you a fucking wedding present."

"It's not. It's just--"

"*THEN WHAT THE FUCK ARE YOU DOING?*"

I wish I knew.

"Christ, end it with both of us. At least that might make a shred of sense to me."

"Leo, it doesn't make sense to me that a twenty-eight year old woman can be with a twenty-two year old guy. It would never work."

"The age thing is bullshit. I'm sick of it, and it's not the reason we wouldn't work out."

But I wonder…just how much of my decision to end it with him *is* based on that very insecurity?

"But say you did give us a chance and it didn't work out; at least you wouldn't be married to a guy you cheated on. He's not the one for you, I am."

"How do you know?"

"You wouldn't cheat on me!"

Shut up, shut up, shut up! I have been cheating on you, but not because I want to, because I'm obligated to.

"I think you're confused and making a huge mistake, but I'm not gonna talk you out of it anymore."

Confused is putting it mildly.

"Ya know, Chrissy, when you told me you were engaged, I didn't give a shit about the guy you were gonna marry. I was like, fuck him! My philosophy's always been, if you don't take care of business, you go outta business, and his loss was my gain. But now that you're actually gonna marry the guy, I feel sorry for him."

That stung a little.

"Because I cheated on him?"

"No, because you don't love him as much as he probably loves you. Nobody deserves to be in a marriage like that."

His assertion that nobody deserves to be in a marriage like that is correct, but I feel like he has the order all wrong. And, what about what I deserve? *I feel like I deserve Leo.* This call was a mistake. I don't want to end it with him.

"I gotta go, Chrissy. Ho-Bag's waiting for me outside to go to the gym."

"I don't want to end it like this. Can I--"

"No. I'm done. This...whatever it is, is over. Don't call me anymore."

I know I called to say a final good-bye, but I thought he would talk me into seeing him one more time. I'd refuse. He'd convince. We'd be back to square one. But nope, he's quick to get off the phone. I'm panicking. If I hang up, he's gone forever. His eyes open to look into someone else's, his hand available to hold another's. His voice will be able to tell someone else "I love you." I'm stunned at his quickness to dismiss me. By the time I'm finally able to speak, "Leo, wait..." he's gone.

The sky is purple like a bruise
I lie beneath it counting
All the dreams I fear I'll lose...
And I just want something for the pain

("Something for the Pain," *Leslie Nuchow*)

PAIN

MARCH, 1998

It's been two weeks since I've seen Dr. Maria. I cancelled last week because I needed a reprieve from facing the fact that my life is a freaking mess. I've been a total wreck since I called Leo and told him I decided to go forward with my big fat fake wedding. I can't focus on anything, I can't sleep, I can't eat. Since that phone call, I've lost about three pounds and quite frankly, I didn't have three pounds to lose. As I make my way to Dr. Maria's office, I try to remember what I ate today. Oh yeah...a bag of Ruffles and a stick of gum, same as yesterday. I walk into the office and buzz the thingy to let Dr. Maria know I'm here. I glance over at Sad Frumpy Lady, and I finally see that we have something in common--pain. Pain is so much worse than the guilt I had when I first started this process. The guilt was somewhat tolerable, and I bet with therapy, it would've faded with time. But the pain in my heart, although good for the waistline, is debilitating and gets more intense every day. And I think it's going to be around for a while.

I haven't tried to contact Leo. I came close about a hundred times, but he made himself perfectly clear, and I can't stand the thought of him rejecting me like that again. Besides, if I did call him, it would have to be for a significant reason, like that I wasn't getting married anymore, and telling him that would be like falling off the wagon. Instead I've immersed myself in work and my new love, jogging.

And then when I'm home, I don't talk. Until Kurt comes with me to therapy, I feel like it's pointless to say anything. I spend a lot of my quiet time thinking about my girl Francesca from *Bridges of Madison County*. Now that I'm officially her, I get her choice, *I get the obligation*. And now I finally know what the hell she did all those years after she watched her love affair drive away. She spent time wondering what her life would've been like if she got out of the damn car and ran. She had a miserable, fucking existence is what she had! This is the declaration I make when I plop down on Dr. Maria's couch.

"When you put it like that, Chrissy, it sounds like you're giving yourself a death sentence."

Dr. Maria's being facetious, but my heavy sigh lets her know I'm in no mood.

"Bad week? Tell me what's on your mind, Hunny."

I think I'm finally about to get my seventy-five bucks worth! I feel like I've been in detox for the last week and a half and I'm friggin' pissed that I can't have the only thing that's ever made me feel normal IN MY ENTIRE LIFE! Without my Leo drug to keep my mood elevated to super-euphoric-sex-kitten-queen-of-the-I-could-give-a-shit-about-the-world levels, I've been freed up to evaluate why my marriage is in shambles. And what I've unearthed is maddening.

"I love Kurt."

"Okayyyyy."

"I *never* would've married him if there was any doubt about it. I mean, if there was doubt I *doubt* all of this would be hurting so bad, right?"

"Right, and you're not alone there. Few people go through with a marriage they have doubts about. But that doesn't do much to keep the divorce rate low in this country. Even marriages that start off with the best of intentions sometimes aren't strong enough to support all of the changes people go through."

"I NEVER CHANGED!"

"I disagree. Pretending to be someone you're not so that Kurt would fall in love with you and marry you. Then, deciding all of a sudden that you don't really want to be that person anymore. That kind of qualifies as a change."

Rolling my eyes, I think…whatever.

"It might not seem like it to you, but it sure as heck will to him."

This is exactly what I want to help the two of you with. I want to help you become more authentic with Kurt and help the both of you accept and cherish who you really are as individuals. I want to help the both of you transition and grow in the relationship in a positive and loving way."

"Easy for him."

"How so?"

"Kurt's always known that I love him because I *showed* him and he has that base to build upon. But I don't know if I can forgive him or even be in love with him anymore for the things he did, or shall I say *didn't* do for me."

"What are some of those things?"

Here we go.

"For starters, the way he reacts toward his family's idiotic behavior."

I thought if I were ever given the opportunity to complain about this stuff, it would feel good. Nothing about this feels good.

"You want to elaborate on that?"

"His dad's a drunk jerk, and his mom is the classic submissive co-dependent spouse. He has four older siblings and every one of them is a wreck. They're all divorced, a couple of 'em are really bad single parents, one's an out-of-work piece of crap, blah, blah, blah. If you ask the mom about any one of them, she'll say they're perfect and when they're clearly not perfect, it's someone else's fault. God forbid any of them are held accountable for how screwed up they are."

"What's this got to do with what he *didn't* do for you?"

"Kurt's a lot like his mom. If you ask him how his siblings are, well…everyone's always GREAT! Never a negative thing to say about any one of them! Everyone in that family says great, great, great all the damn time. No one acknowledges the dysfunction, and no one EVER has a negative thought. It's disturbing."

"How is not being negative an unforgivable thing to you?"

"Because to me, not being negative about some things is the same as accepting them. And some things that Kurt's *not* been negative about have been pretty disturbing."

"You want to give me some examples?"

"Kurt's dad gets vulgar and intimidating when he drinks. I've voiced my concern to Kurt...told him it scares the crap outta me."

"What did he do?"

"He made excuses for his dad, told me to mind my own business."

"Did it make you mad?"

"Quite the opposite. I became very concerned for him."

"*For him?*"

"Yeah, it seemed so strange to me that we weren't on the same side of such an obvious issue. I felt like I needed to protect him from his family, like he needed my help or something."

"And it would seem strange to anyone who's not the child of an alcoholic."

"Okay fine, but how much is someone who's *not* the child of an alcoholic supposed to pretend she doesn't see? And look, it's not like he just ignores his dad's inappropriate behavior. He ignores his whole family's! Kurt was the first person in his family to graduate from college and not one of those people showed up to the graduation ceremony!"

"That's horrible."

"My heart ached for Kurt that day. But you know who he got mad at? Me. He told me that my expectations are always too high and if I wasn't so narcissistic, I would realize that sometimes people have more important things going on in their lives. You'd think the guy would've clung to me for dear life after being treated like that. But that wasn't the first time his family acted inappropriately, and it wasn't the last time Kurt reprimanded me for telling him so."

Sad just officially turned into mad. I pound my fists on the couch and let it rip.

"Damn it, I've hurt for that man since the day I met him. From the start, I wanted to show him unconditional love and protect him from those people. I thought, no *I still think*, I'm the only one who can help him when the anger and pain about his dysfunctional family surfaces. But you know what? It's not going to surface. Trust me, it's had plenty of opportunity to. I've tried and tried to talk to him about the dysfunction, hold him, be his confidant. But the more I tried, the more he pushed me away and made me feel like I was the

108

crazy person. Eventually I stopped questioning everything I thought was right and wrong and he thought was wrong and right and, like a dumbass, I stopped doing it long before we got married."

I'm on a roll now. Inhale. Continue.

"You know, I *thought* Kurt and I were happy together, but after our last session, it occurred to me that the only one that's been truly happy in the relationship is him. Whatever ounce of happiness I've experienced since knowing him was derived from doing things that made *him* happy."

"How so?"

"Like when I hike to the top of a stupid mountain because he wants me to or when I camp at places without bathrooms. He's proud of me when I do things outside of my comfort zone and, for a long time, I thought it made me happy, too. But it didn't. Over time it just pissed me off."

"I can see that happening."

"And I stopped wondering a long time ago if the reciprocal of all my ridiculous effort was ever gonna show up. Ya know, like if he would go to a wedding or birthday party with me without complaining…but it didn't."

I take a deep breath as I stare out of the window for a moment. "I suppose I could deal with all of that garbage if he would stop controlling what little I do to make myself happy."

"What are you talking about?"

My head is now aimed at the floor because what I'm about to admit is so humiliating that I can't bear to look her in the eye. It's everything I've tried to hide from family and friends and up until now, has never been mentioned to a single soul.

"You have to understand that no one would believe the stuff I'm about to tell you. I've even convinced myself that none of it is as bad as I think it is. But after meeting Leo and coming here a few times, I don't think the stuff I've put up with is normal. But maybe I'm just crazy. My God, I'm so tired of thinking I'm crazy."

"I don't think you're crazy, Chrissy. Tell me how you think Kurt controls you. Just start with the first thing that comes to your mind."

"Okay, whenever I take a much needed day off of work, he pesters me about how I should spend my free time. If I'm not doing something he deems relaxing, like bike riding or hiking, *which I loathe*, he lays in on me and calls me lazy for wasting a perfectly good day doing nothing. I guess it doesn't sound like a big deal, but it is to me."

"It's a very big deal. You work hard and deserve to spend your downtime however you see fit."

"I can also forget about sleeping in late on the weekends. If I'm not raring to go by 8am, he'll open the shades and make comments like, 'I can't believe you're wasting the day away like this.' He acts like I'm ruining his weekend. I work sixty hours a week, and I'm on a plane every other fucking day. I'm tired! Shouldn't he be content with my much needed rest? Shouldn't he *want* to take care of me like that?"

"Why, yes he--"

"Oh! And he expects me to become an expert at whatever type of exercise I pursue. Now that I'm jogging, he encourages me to bring a stop watch so I know if I'm improving my time, and he'll even ride his bike along side of me and cheer me on. I don't want to get faster! I run to escape, not win a medal. I want to burn my bike, my roller blades, my TWO goose down sleeping bags, hiking shoes, and all of the other bullshit gear he's pushed on me. None of that stuff is enjoyable to me because I have to be *all extreme* ALL THE TIME!"

I can't tell if Dr. Maria's looking at me like I should've known what I was signing up for or if she feels sorry for me. But if she doesn't think I'm a stupid ass idiot yet, she will after I tell her this one.

"Here's a good one. If Kurt cooks a meal and I don't eat it because *I'm simply not hungry*, he gets mad that he went to all that work to do something nice for me. Worse even, he requests that I eat a certain amount of bites of each food group before I can--"

"Whoa, Chrissy, you've got to be kidding me."

"Not kidding. 'Two more bites of broccoli and one more bite of fish, then you can be done Chrissy.' Like I'm a three year old."

"How do you react when he does that?"

"I eat it all up so he'll stop scolding me."

"Do you think that's the right thing to do?"

"Of course not! It's just easier. Do you know how fucked in the head it is for an adult to argue with another adult about how many bites of food she should eat? IT'S PSYCHOTIC! I'm sorry. I didn't mean to--"

"No, no, go ahead."

"Since we're on the subject of food; I love cooking and I think I'm pretty good at it. But whenever I cook a meal, he has the audacity to suggest ways that I can make it better next time…even when he likes it! Don't you think it's clever that he finds a way to insult me when he's complimenting me? I don't even want to cook anymore. I'm not inspired to do a Goddamn thing because nothing's ever good enough."

I'm quite for a second before another example of Kurt's control pops into my head.

"Oh, and here's a sick one…ready to hear this?"

"I am, Chrissy, but are you okay? Do you want to take a break?"

"*Are you kidding me?* Isn't this what you people call a break-through?"

"Does it feel like a break-through?"

"More like a break down, if you ask me."

"Well, I'm ready whenever you are."

"It's a doozy…He hassles me to give birth naturally."

She's truly shocked.

"I mean, he doesn't preach it from the hilltops, but the few times we've had the conversation about childbirth, he gets appalled that I would even *consider* having drugs. He tells me I should tough it out like women did in the old days. What the friggin' hell does that mean? Am I supposed to forget about all the modern day medical advances that are available and suffer through labor and delivery like a pilgrim? Christ, he's already made me feel like a failure over something I haven't even attempted yet!"

"I should say so."

"I'm so frustrated! I can't complain about work because then I'm a grouch. I can't justly criticize a friend or a family member because then I'm too negative. I can't condemn a perfectly healthy able-bodied homeless person or disapprove of an overly obese child without being called cruel. I have to be happy all the fucking time or else I'm a bad person! Tell me this, where's the motivation to be a good wife when you're always made to feel like a stupid, lazy, mean one?"

Just as she's about to tackle that question, I furiously interject, "I'll tell you where the motivation is: it's at a bar seducing the first nice man it meets." Exhale.

"Are you okay, Chrissy?"

"No, I'm not okay! I came here because I thought I was a shitty person for cheating. But that's not where the shittyness started. It started when I pretended to be someone I'm not so Kurt would marry me. And yeah that's pretty shitty, but does my shittyness justify his? Shit! Shit! Shit! How could I have allowed for this to be my life, my marriage?"

I'm devastated and disgraced and my voice is cracking like a log on a wet fire.

"You know, I've lost ten pounds in four weeks because I'm a total stress case."

"I noticed."

"My co-workers think I've become anorexic, and my boss pulled me aside and asked me if I've been doing blow. You wanna know what Kurt's said about it? Nothing! *He's said absolutely nothing about it.* Why would he ignore me like that? He's crazy. No! I'm crazy for letting him get away with all of it."

"Chrissy, maybe we should--"

"I'm so tired of hurting and hoping. God, I'm so tired. I've known Kurt my entire adult life and I can't think of a day I felt cherished by him. You know, once I even asked him why he doesn't tell me I'm beautiful and he said it's because he doesn't want me to get too full of myself. I don't even know what to make of that."

I detect a note of pity on Dr. Maria's face, and it feels like a stab wound to my heart because despite all of the other bullshit, not feeling cherished is what hurts the most.

"I can't think of a time when Kurt's paused long enough to tell me how much he loves me, and that includes our wedding day. I met Leo all of three months ago, and he made me believe his world would fall apart without me in it. *I just want Kurt to love me like that, Dr. Maria! Why is it so hard for him to think I'm special just the way I am?*"

"Chrissy, I think we need to ask him those questions. Did you ask him if--"

Lifting my head from the tissue I'm ferociously blowing my nose into, I interrupt again.

"Lately I've been thinking really hard about what triggered my weird behavior in January when I met Leo. I think it goes back to something that happened three months prior, in October. Yeah, sure there was all of that other dysfunctional crap going on in my marriage, but something so bizarre happened and I think it immediately severed whatever tiny connection there was holding me and Kurt together."

The timer alerts us that the session is over, and Dr. Maria motions for me to stay seated while she walks out of her office. I presume to tell the next whack job that she needs a few more minutes with the one she's currently with. It gives me a second to reconsider what I'm about to tell her.

"All right Hunny, continue."

"If you have to go…"

"Please. Continue."

"Last October, I had a miscarriage, and Kurt wouldn't talk to me about it."

"Did he…hold on…did you *try* to talk to him?" I knew it was unbelievable.

"A little bit."

"Why not a lot?"

"You just heard me describe him to you. What's the point?"

"What happened exactly?"

"I wasn't planning on getting pregnant, and we barely even have enough sex to make it possible but it happened."

"How did Kurt react to the news?"

"Like he needed proof."

"What do you mean?"

"I told him I took a test and it came out positive. He said, "Wow" and that was about it. We didn't talk about it again."

"How long was it until the miscarriage?"

"I guess about two weeks after that. I asked Kurt if he wanted to talk about what happened and, without even a hug, he said it's not worth agonizing over since we didn't know for sure if I was even pregnant." Staring out of the window and into the dark night,

I continue. "The illusion of me and Kurt being the perfect couple, *the illusion I had been living every single day for the last twelve years,* was shattered the moment he doubted the pregnancy."

Dr. Maria looks repulsed. I wonder if she thinks I'm lying.

"So, he had no reaction to either the pregnancy or the miscarriage?"

"Nope. Not one day during the pregnancy did he ask me how I felt or touch my tummy. He never asked if I called a doctor or asked to take a pregnancy test with me. Then, after the miscarriage, he just rejected the idea that we even lost anything. Kinda like when we were younger."

Oh crap. I didn't mean to bring that up.

"What happened when you were younger?"

"You're gonna think I'm a total mess."

"Trust me, you're not the messiest."

"Kurt and I had a pregnancy situation when I was seventeen."

"How horrible for you guys."

Looking back out into the darkness, "I terminated it. That was supposed to be that, except it wasn't."

"It was pretty bad?"

"The worst."

"And Kurt?"

"We were both in pain, but of course we handled it differently. I tried so hard to talk to him, but he completely shut me out, told me what's done is done, so move on. I wanted the tragedy to bring us closer and he wanted it to disappear. But I never let it disappear. I just buried it."

"And that's not a healthy thing to do is it?"

"Nope, because all these years later, it still hurts. The disappointment is as fresh today as it was then. The sad thing is I know it's the same for him, but he won't talk about it."

"Do you think that experience compelled you to stay with Kurt? You know…ignore the things he did that made you feel bad because you felt the need to right a wrong with him?"

"I'm beginning to think there were a lot of naive reasons we stayed together. I'm not sure which one to put at the top of the list."

"What was *your* reaction to the miscarriage in October?"

"It was the opposite of the abortion. I didn't beg for attention. I didn't cry. I didn't force Kurt to feel something that wasn't there.

I even remember being in awe of his disconnection from the experience. Not in a distraught way, more like a, 'so this is who you really are,' kinda way."

I address Dr. Maria like I'm the one in charge.

"So now I know. The miscarriage was the knife in the back of my illusion; it was the thing that killed us."

"Regardless of your responsibility for how things are in your marriage, it's not normal that a married woman would have to give proof of a pregnancy to her husband. Her word alone should be cause enough for celebration, or in your case of loss, compassion. That must have been a very difficult time for you."

"*Loss?* Call me heartless, Dr. Maria, but I never mourned the loss of that baby. That child would've only perpetuated my illusion for God knows how much longer. Shit was gonna hit the fan eventually, no need for a child to be a part of the pain. That experience was my wake-up call. I feel like Kurt's commanded control of nearly every aspect of my life. I eat what that man wants me to eat, I wear the shoes he wants me to wear, I go on the vacations he wants me to go on, and the list goes on and on. But when he made me doubt what I had experienced, I totally checked out of the marriage."

I don't think I've been this true to myself since I was sixteen years old. It feels awkward, like a crippled person who stands up from a wheelchair and takes a few miraculous steps. *Don't fall, Chrissy.*

"You have to figure out why you let him control you. That's something you and I will work on together. In the meantime, I'd like you to put your foot down on some of his demands about the food you eat and other personal choices like that."

"I already have, and it's created a pretty turbulent environment. I don't want to live like this anymore, Dr. Maria. I love him, I really do, but I'm afraid there's too much space between us to ever have what I need out of my marriage."

"Hun, it's critical for your sanity and your marriage to get Kurt in here right away. Can you make that happen next week?"

"Yeah. And by the way...you're gonna love him. Everybody does."

SINKING

APRIL, 1998

"You've been going to therapy without telling me? What's wrong with the St. John's Wort I gave you?"

I roll my eyes up from my computer screen and attempt to ridicule his inquiry, but he cuts me off at the pass.

"Here's an idea. Instead of spending money on a therapist, maybe you should take up something like yoga. It'll relax you, plus it's cheaper and you'll get in great shape."

Okay, first of all yoga is "gay" and second of all…I want to rip my clothes off and show him that I'm already in great shape, but it'll just make him want me and I can't even go there.

"I dunno Kurt, guess I'm unhappy. Actually…she wants to see us both next week."

Judging by my tone, he can't possibly think I'm hopeful his presence will amount to anything.

"Why me? This has nothing to do with me. I'm happy."

"*Really?* You're happy, Kurt? As my husband, I wonder how you can be happy when I just told you I'm not. Seriously, if you told me you were unhappy, I'd walk over hot coals if I thought it would help you." Well…maybe a year ago I would have. "And I'm not talking about torturing you with therapy either." But I kind of am. "I hope you'll go willingly because you love me and you want me to be happy. But of course, if you have a problem with any of that, I'll just continue to go alone and talk about you and all our problems."

"Geez babe, you know I love you. What day and time? I'll have to let the softball team know I'll be missing practice."

"Wednesday at 5:30pm."

"Great, that's game night."

"Great, I'll tell Dr. Maria that."

"Man, Chrissy. Calm down. I'll be there for you."

"For us."

"What?"

"Nothing."

I grab my coat and yell, "Be back soon," as I make my way out to my car to meet my best friends for dinner. I'm not going willingly though. Courtney threatened to cut me off for good if I didn't show up. She knows something's wrong. On my way to the restaurant, I purposely pass the spot where Leo and I sat in my car and talked until the sun came up on the night we met. It's been weeks since that last phone call with him, and I haven't stopped thinking about him or stopped doing stupid stuff like this. In fact, I've driven to the reservoir three times, but there was no sign of him. Maybe he knew I'd go looking, so he deliberately stayed away. I pass Dr. Maria's office and see her light on. Busy lady. I try to feel an iota of optimism about Kurt going to therapy with me, but there's none. I'm scared to death that it's pointless and I'm going to spend the rest of my life wishing it wasn't my life…just like Francesca. I park my car at the restaurant and schlep my way to the door, wondering if I can pull myself together long enough to convince my friends that "everything's perfect!" As I'm entering, a girl with hair blonder than mine and eyes even bluer than my own, grabs my arm. I hated her the minute I saw her.

"Hey! Is your name Chrissy?"

"Do I know you?"

"Oh, I'm sorry, no! My name's Megan. I saw your picture at my friend Leo's house."

"*You did?*"

"Yeah, I wondered why he still had it up. You know…being that you two aren't seeing each other anymore. Poor guy, seemed so sad at first, but a bunch of us set him straight, and he's real good now. In fact, we just partied at his place last night."

Megan, Megan, Megan...*OH, MEGAN*! Leo told me about this chick. She has some classes with him at St. Mary's, but he said she also takes night classes at The Fashion Institute of Design and Merchandising. She wants to design her own label and run her own business one day. Get in line, bitch! Anyway, she's always flirting with him and showing up at his apartment without invitation. Obviously she's in love with him. It didn't bother me while I was seeing him because...well, I'm me and she's just a kid. But seeing her now makes me want to stab her in her childlike eyes. That'll have to wait though, because my three best friends are walking-toward-me-right-NOW!

"There was a picture of me?"

"Oh don't worry, it's cute! You're sitting by a pool or something."

Ah yes, I remember now that I conveniently left that picture, along with my bra, at his apartment. I looked amazing in it, and I hoped by leaving it behind, he would show it to his friends. I'm so fucked in the head.

"So when are you getting married?"

I can't believe Leo told her I was getting married!

"Um...well I haven't figured that out yet. Hey, I gotta run, I'm meeting some friends and..."

Oh shit, here they come. As I walk away from her, I yell out, "Tell Leo I said hello and I hope he's doing well." I didn't have time to think about how lame that sounded because I was too preoccupied with my rapidly approaching friends. I hope to hell she doesn't tell him I hope he's "*doing well.*" It dilutes the magnitude of pain I feel without him. But I'm in shock right now! Leo's people are infiltrating my city, my restaurants! This CANNOT happen! Omigod, what if I was with Kurt? My two worlds could've just collided! Jesus, I'm going to have to look over my shoulder the rest of my life! I can actually feel another pound melt away from my body.

"Hey, girly!"

It's Courtney, and as I get closer, she reaches her hand out to me.

"Geez woman, why so pale? Are you okay?"

I look up at the three of them, and just as I'm about to lie about having the flu, Nicole blurts out, "Who was that girl with the great hair and who's Leo?"

The jig is up.

"No, I'm not okay. Girls, I have some stuff to tell you. First, we need cocktails."

After the head-on collision with Megan, I desperately wanted to tell my friends about Leo. Being recognized by that girl scared the shit out of me, and I wanted them to comfort me. Then on the way to our table, my fear turned into anger, and I wanted them to help me beat Megan up in the parking lot. But once we were seated and I had my martini in my hand, I wimped out of saying or doing anything about Megan or Leo. If I end up staying with Kurt, which for some reason seems to be my goal right now, I can't have my shame belonging to anyone other than me. Besides, who am I kidding? My friends are the types to *run away* from a fight, not instigate one. Buncha pansies. Instead, I gently introduce the three of them to my soap opera by finally telling them how screwed up my marriage is. After an hour of non-stop talking, I pause long enough to take a swig of my now very warm martini.

"I knew it. I never thought you two had much in common."

"Thanks Courtney, maybe you could've mentioned that like I dunno…ten years ago!"

"Right, like you would've listened to me anyway. You were gonna marry Kurt whether I told you it was a bad idea or not. You're too damn stubborn, Chrissy." Kind of chuckling she adds, "Besides, the man's so damn good looking, I guess we all sorta thought it wouldn't matter what you guys had in common."

Not chuckling and staring at my drink, "I can't even see his beauty anymore."

"Really, it's that bad?"

"It's that bad."

"I'd be a wreck if my marriage was a mess like that."

"Wow, Kel, you just made me feel about ten million times worse than I already felt. But hey, as long as your marriage is great, that's all that matters, right?"

"I didn't mean to make you feel worse. God, I was just saying this must be really hard for you."

"THEN SAY THAT, THEN!"

"Okay, everybody calm the fuck down! Chrissy's marriage sucks, Kelly's is great, mine and Courtney's are so-so. Honestly, they're all gonna suck at some point. Chrissy's just sucks first. Let's help her through this the best we can so she doesn't abandon us when we're in her shoes."

Thank God for Nicole. You can always count on her to diffuse a sticky situation with a shot of humor. She puts her arm around my shoulder and speaks softly.

"So, when did you realize your marriage sucked so bad, Hun?"

Then again, her humor can also make a crappy situation seem even crappier.

I roll my eyes over to Courtney to plead her to take this seriously.

"What Nicole *meant* to ask is when did you notice things were falling apart?"

"I'm not sure if things were ever together. But I guess my breaking point was after the miscarriage when he acted like it never even happened."

"Sounds familiar."

The three of us snap our heads in Kelly's direction.

"What's she talking about?"

"Yeah, what sounds familiar?"

Kelly's looking at me like she's *sort of* sorry she let the cat out of the bag.

"I'm sorry, Chrissy, I thought you would've told them by now."

"Nope. Kurt wanted it to go away so I let it…sort of."

"He wanted *what* to go away?"

Right before their very eyes, I morph back into my long lost role as the 1987 clusterfuck queen.

"Uh, I've been pregnant before, but I…we…didn't keep it."

In unison, Courtney and Nicole whip their heads in my direction and loudly whisper, "*You had an abortion?*"

Now Kelly's looking at me like she's *really* sorry she let the cat of the bag.

"Hold on, Kelly knew about this?"

"What's up with that? I thought we knew everything about each other. Any other secrets you two are keeping from me and Courtney?"

Crossing my fingers under the table, "I don't know about Kelly, but I promise that's the only one I've been keeping from you."

"When did it happen?"

"Geez, Nic I can't even deal with talking about that right now. It'd be like going back to *Titanic* and I don't think I can."

"I don't care if it's like reliving the friggin' spiral perm you got three hours before our junior prom." Turning to Courtney and Kelly like all of the sudden I'm invisible, "Remember that mess? She looked like Dee Snider from Twisted Sister, but with a fucking bob haircut! What the hell was she thinking?"

"Hello…Nicole! I told you to NEVER bring that up!"

"Well then, speak! Now!"

"Okay, fine. It happened when I was seventeen."

"*IN HIGH SCHOOL?*"

"Yep, told you it was like going back to *Titanic*."

NOVEMBER 1986

"For fuck's sake, Chrissy, get up! We only have three weeks until Nationals and you aren't trying!"

"I am trying, Kelly! I don't know what's wrong with me. I keep getting dizzy, and I don't have the energy to get through the routine."

"Then go sit on the bleachers so you're not in the way!"

"Fine. I'll be in the bath…"

"Chrissy! Omigod! Someone call 911!"

Twenty-five minutes later, with Kelly by my side, I'm on an emergency room table.

"Do you have a history of fainting?"

"No, and I didn't faint. I got really dizzy."

"Are you experiencing any flu like symptoms?"

"No."

"Are you more tired than usual?"

"Yes."

"Are you sexually active?"

Giggles. "I guess".

"It says here you're seventeen. Is that correct?"

"Yes."

"Are you taking precautions to protect yourself during intercourse?"

More giggles. "Yeah, condoms."

"Every single time?"

"Yes."

That's not the case, there was that one time, but I can't admit that to this guy.

"Is there any chance you could be pregnant?"

"NO! No way. Gosh, I'm too young!"

"Miss, if you menstruate, you can get pregnant. You can be as young as twelve, even younger.

"Gross. But no I'm not. I feel better now. Let's go, Kelly."

"Miss, I would feel better if we did a pregnancy test before you left. Don't worry, it's completely confidential. Your parents won't find out about any of this."

I'm looking at him like he's fucking nuts. I barely even know how to get pregnant, so how can I actually *be* pregnant?

Hopping off of the exam table, "No thank you. I'm fine. I just wanna go."

"I'll tell you what, let's do the test, and if it's negative, which I'm sure it will be, I'll give you a three month supply of birth control pills. Does that sound like a good idea?"

I can get birth control pills without my mom knowing? That does sound like a good idea! Kelly's looking at me like I'm the luckiest girl in the world.

"Sure."

After a quick pee in a cup and a trip to the vending machine for a Dr. Pepper and a Snickers, my test comes back negative. Kelly and I head back to cheerleading practice with my little bag of birth control gold.

For the next four weeks I continue to suffer through practice, and even though I'm incredibly tired and lightheaded, I force myself to hide it from my squad. Nationals are a big deal. No squad from American High School, let alone any squad in Northern California, has ever qualified for this competition. One hundred of the best cheer squads from across the country are heading to Disneyland to compete and it's being televised on ESPN. Granted, it'll air at 2:30am on a Wednesday, but who cares! My squad has worked on our routine for three hours a day for the last six months, and I can't let whatever the hell is wrong with me ruin this opportunity of a lifetime. It'll have to wait until the competition is over. And that it did. The minute we got off the stage, I ran to the bathroom and threw up.

"Hurry, Chrissy! They're about to announce the winners. What the heck…are you throwing up?"

"Kelly, what's wrong with me?"

"I dunno. Maybe you're getting sick from those birth control pills."

"That's impossible, I haven't started taking them yet."

"Why not?"

"The doctor told me not to start until the first Sunday after my next period. I haven't had it yet."

"Chrissy, that was like, four weeks ago! When was your last period?"

"I guess like a month and a half ago. Maybe longer. I don't keep track of that stuff."

"Jesus, Chrissy, I think you might be pregnant after all. You should take another test."

We ended up finishing fourth place at Nationals, which was pretty good considering it was our first ever appearance. I'm finally back home and back to reality. Time to tell Kurt the news.

"Kurt, I think I screwed up on something."

"What's that?"

"Well, I haven't started my period yet."

"Okay…"

"And I know the pregnancy test I took at the hospital turned out negative, but I'm scared, Kurt. With all of my dizziness, throwing up and stuff, I think I might be anyway."

"Like you said, the test came out negative. Just give it another weekd and stop worrying so much."

"Kurt, I haven't had a period in seven weeks."

All of a sudden he looks scared.

"You probably forgot you had one or something."

"Kurt, I feel like I'm pregnant." And then I lose it. "Oh God, but I can't be! I'm a good girl, a fucking all-American cheerleader for Christ sake! My parents are gonna die! What will happen to college? Oh my God, this can't be happening!"

"Chrissy! Calm down! What do you want to do?"

Fifteen minutes later, we arrive at Planned Parenthood. He parks and doesn't ask to join me inside. I'm alone.

Head down and speaking softly, I explain my situation to the man nurse person. He tells me it's best to administer a blood test so we can get to the bottom of thingsd and like a jerk off he says, "Don't worry, you'll be fine. It's best to remember how you're feeling right now and do everything you can to prevent this situation in the future."

I want to say, "no shit," but I keep my mouth shut. At least he doesn't make me feel like a total slut, and for a minute I'm calm. The minute is over when he confirms that I am, in fact, pregnant.

"But when I took a test six weeks ago it was negative!"

"Well, sometimes when a pregnancy test is taken too close to conception it can't detect enough hCG. That's the substance produced by placental tissue, and it needs to be present in order to give you a positive result. Seems to me this is what happened to you."

Hc… Placental…*What the*?

"So you're telling me I have a baby… growing inside of me… RIGHT NOW?"

"That's right, and if your calculations are correct, you're probably about eight weeks pregnant."

Doing the math in my head. Eight divided by four is…

"OH MY GOD!"

With my head buried in my hands and barely able to speak, he asks me what I plan to do about it. I don't even know how to make dinner for myself yet. I turn every load of laundry pink, and I can still only manage to get a tampon half-way in. I'm just that inexperienced in life! Oh no! What about my prom? Will Kurt break up with me? How will my father explain this to his co-workers? My Mom will blame me for ruining her life. I'll have to quit the squad! No! No! No!

"I have to get it out. Oh my God...I'm gonna have an abortion, aren't I?"

"Well, that's one option, but you can also give this baby up for adoption."

"No, I can't let anyone know I'm pregnant."

About thirty minutes later, I walk out to Kurt who's standing outside of the car. He takes one look at my smudged mascara and the large pamphlet of papers I'm carrying and mouths the words "oh shit." Then once I'm in front of him he asks, "Are you okay?"

"I will be next week when this is over with."

"Whoa, we didn't even talk about it yet."

"*Talk about what*? Is this what you want with your life, to be an eighteen year old dad?"

"I'd be nineteen by the time you had it."

"Big fucking deal, Kurt! Look, I'm not some loser high school slut girl. Do you know how many people will laugh at me and get sick satisfaction over this happening? They'll be like, "There's prego Chrissy! She thought she was so cool being a cheerleader and dating Kurt Gibbons. What a loser!"

"Why do you care so much what people think about you?"

"BECAUSE I DO! PLUS, THAT'S EXACTLY WHAT I WOULD SAY ABOUT THEM!"

"Okay, okay calm down. It's gonna be okay. I promise it'll be okay. If this is your decision, then I'll help you with it. When is it, and how much does it cost?"

Slightly hyperventilating, I tell him it's next Saturday, and it will cost $400 with a local anesthetic and $300 without.

"I, I, I d-d-d-d-don't have a-a-a-a-any money, Kurt!"

"Don't worry. I think I can get about $300."

Don't worry? I've never had minor surgery, not even a cavity in my entire life and now I'm about to have a human being sucked out of my body without a local anesthetic! Jesus, sometimes I wonder how tough Kurt expects me to be. I've endured really scary four-wheeling trips with him and been water skiing even though I'm more afraid of fish than anything in the world. I've run through fields of bulls, and I've fallen off of my bike about a thousand times because he wanted me to push myself to the extreme. And I did it all for love. But I wonder…in the name of love, *am I supposed to settle for the cheapie abortion*?

On Thursday night, two days before the abortion, I call Kelly.

"Hey, Kelly, what's goin' on?"

"Nothing, just watching Knott's Landing and looking for something to wear to Joe's party on Friday night. What are you gonna wear?"

"I'm not going."

"What are you talking about? It's gonna be killer!"

"I'm pregnant."

"Oh, shit. I knew it. What are you gonna do?"

"I'm having a you-know-what on Saturday. I'm telling my mom that I'm staying the night at your house on Friday night, but Kurt and I are really staying at a motel near the place because we have to be there really early in the morning. Can you make sure you cover for me in case my mom calls your house to check if I'm really there?"

"What if I'm at Joe's party when she calls?"

"God, Kelly, don't go to the party!"

"Oh man, his parents are out of town, and it's supposed to be totally rad but yeah, you're right, I should probably stay home."

"Probably or you will?"

After a longer than I'm comfortable with pause, "Fine, I'll stay home."

"I need another favor. I don't want anyone to know, not even Nicole and Courtney."

"Why?"

"You know Nicole will just crack some sick joke to try and cheer me up and Courtney will want to get her mom involved so that I get the best abortion money can buy. As if there can be one."

"This really sucks, Chrissy. Who would've thought this could happen to you?"

Through my tears…"No one."

Two days later, on January 2nd, instead of ringing in 1987, my high school graduation year, I'm on my way to the abortion clinic. I'm wearing my cheerleading sweat suit and a Minnie Mouse sweatshirt that I bought last month at Disneyland. Strange choice of clothing, but it makes me feel somewhat official. I want the people at the clinic to think I'm a respectable girl, not one of those stoner chicks who cuts class to hang out by the bleachers and smokes. Just as Kurt parks the car, we notice the protestors.

"Jesus, this is the kinda thing after school specials are made of."

"I'm so sorry you have to go through this, Chrissy."

On the one hand, I hate his guts for this, but on the other, I realize I'm the one who allowed it to happen and I only have myself to blame. I put so much faith in his eighteen years of experience, but really he's just another dumb guy and I'm just another dumb girl who didn't realize it until it was too late.

"Here's the money. I'm sorry I couldn't get more than $300. I feel terrible about all of this."

My trembling hands carefully take the money. I'm glad this is almost over with because the last five days have been torture. I wanted to talk about every single aspect of the pregnancy since I found out about it. Kurt's been totally incapable of talking about any of it. I asked him to go to the library with me to get more information about abortions and the stages of pregnancy. He told me that I was only making things harder on myself. I wanted to talk about what it might be like if we did have it. Would it be a boy or a girl? What would we name it? I wondered out loud about what the abortion would feel like. Would I see the baby afterwards? Would they be able to determine the sex? The more I pressed on, the angrier he got with me. I know I was clear from the start that I didn't want to keep the baby, but that didn't mean I was numb to the fact that I was getting rid of it. I know Kurt holds himself to a higher standard than to do something like this. But so do I, and if he has any heart at all he'll put his frustrations aside to support me and that's my hope for after this thing is over.

"Do you want me to go with you, you know…inside?"

To say "yes" means I'm asking him to do something he clearly doesn't feel comfortable doing. I feel so let down, and I can hardly look at him. I'm quivering with emotions that I'm too young to describe. I want my mom. Sure she would make me feel like I ruined her life, but she wouldn't let me walk into that scary place by myself and when it was all over, she would feed me soup and put warm washcloths on my forehead. Tears are streaming down my face, and in my mind I'm pleading for him to insist that he comes with me. But I stay tough.

"I think I'll be okay."

"I'll be waiting for you."

I wonder if he can hear our two little hearts breaking.

"I'm not sure how long this will take. They said it could be as long as five or six hours depending on how many other girls need one today."

Please see how scared I am and come inside with me. Please want to protect me from the scary people who are yelling obscenities and carrying picket signs with pictures of shredded up fetuses on them.

"It's not too late to change your mind. We can keep it."

"No. I can't."

I take a deep breath and step out of the car to go do what I think I'm supposed to. The second my feet hit the ground, I'm swooped up by two men. I hope to God they're not some crazy Pro Life freaks trying to kidnap me to make me have my baby in some abandoned warehouse or something.

"It's okay, kiddo, we're here to get you safely inside. Just keep your head down and walk fast."

Yep, that's me. The kidd-o-with the baby-o-in her stomach-o-. I turn back to glance at Kurt, but before I'm able to zoom in on him, the bodyguards open the door, shove me inside, and then slam it to go out and protect the next irresponsible slut. I look up and I'm shocked to see about fifteen other women crammed in the tiny overheated waiting room. I'm younger than all of them by at least five years and the ones I have eye contact with give me half smiles and nods of support that say, "It'll be okay, honey." I was hot in Kurt's car, but I'm really hot now, and I'm sweating buckets through every single pore on my body. I'm also starving to death because I was instructed not to eat, which is odd since I'm not getting any FUCKING anesthetic. This place is underground seedy gross and it smells like burnt rubber and sweat. What's that noise? Sounds like a vacuum cleaner. Oh my God, that's not a vacuum cleaner…it's the killing machine! On, off, on, off, on, off. Jesus, how many girls are back there? Oh my gosh, I have to sit down. Can't see so well. What's *that* sound? BOOM! BOOM! BOOM! Is it…my heart? Oh God, what if it's the baby's heart! I can't see. I close my eyes tightly and I *see* the sound. Swirling around in my mind is one of those scary toy monkeys banging its symbols together. It's laughing at me. It's getting louder! I'm so thirsty. Need water NOW. I reach out to the person in front of me and try as hard as I can to focus, but all I see and hear is the evil monkey.

"Sweetie, are you okay?"

"I can't…can't stand."

"What's that? I can barely hear you."

I extend my hand out to the lady for support but before it reaches her, my knees crumble and the entire room turns into the color of a bruise. The only things I'm aware of are the evil monkey and the enormous fart exploding out of my body. My last conscious thought before I hit the floor is, could my life possibly get any worse?

"Well hi there, Minnie. We we're worried about you there for a minute. Here, drink some of this water."

I take little sips and stare at her from above the lip of the cup. *Minnie*?

"What happened to me?"

"You fainted. Don't worry, you're not the first. They keep that waiting room so darn hot! Now, let's sit you up and start filling out some paperwork." She points to my Disneyland sweatshirt and says, "Can't keep calling you Minnie forever."

I like her.

The rest of the day is a nightmare I don't wish on any girl, woman, slut, whore, whoever. I'm shoved into a room with three pieces of white trash who are way too proud of their gang affiliation. We're expected to watch hours of videos of our options: keep the baby, put the baby up for adoption, or abort the baby. But truthfully it's hard to focus with all their gang talk, looks of intimidation, and fake farting noises. It doesn't matter though. I know my only choice is to have an abortion and that's exactly what I tell the head of the baby-killing department at my last pit stop before finally being guided to the room where they do the procedure. It's a horrible room, and it makes me sad…like Anne Frank sad. The walls are grey and artless; the air is stale and smells like death. I'm tired, I'm hungry, and even though I just want to get this over with and forget it ever happened, I don't feel like it's fair to the thing growing inside of me to do that.

I have to find a price to pay for my irresponsibility. As I walk to the exam table, I notice a pale blue dish-washing bucket strategically placed underneath. Great, my baby will end up in a bucket. Is that sanitary? As instructed, I take off my clothes and slip into the paper gown to wait for the murderers. It makes me scared…Anne Frank scared. Should I run? If I do, will we stand a chance of surviving? *Did I just say we?* Am I considering its feelings? I can hear the murderers marching down the hall and panic attacks me…Anne Frank panic. Without even a courtesy knock, they barge through the bookshelf, I mean door, and without introduction they instruct me to lie down. How can all these people allow this to happen? Oh Anne, is that what you thought too? Jesus, they're about to stop a heartbeat! But wait… I'm the one who gave them the command! Who am I, Anne or Hitler? Am I good or evil? Is this the thing that forevermore makes me one or the other? The gravity of the situation didn't hit me until this very moment. Seriously, no video outlining my options could prepare me for how morbid this is. If they wanted me to *really* consider my options, they should've made me watch a video of an actual abortion, given me a tour of this very room, and then made me sit alone in it with the bucket and my Anne Frank thoughts. Oh God, I'm torn between wanting them to save the baby's life and making it easier for me to go back to mine. My eyes are darting around the room pleading for someone to question my choice just one more time. Somebody give me an honorable command! PLEASE! Where's my nice nurse? I need my nice nurse!

The only guy in the room flicks on a machine and *commands* me to lie still. No honor there. He pries my legs apart and instructs me that his job will be a lot easier if I just relax. *Relax?* The fucker's shoving a Hoover vacuum cleaner inside of me and he wants me to relax? I'M ONLY SEVENTEEN, AND I HAVEN'T BEEN SEDATED!

"Young lady, you're going to have to lie still so I can finish."

"I don't think I…wait, it started? I DON'T WANT TO DO THIS! STOP!"

"Nurse, get a handle on this girl! We can't stop now."

"Minnie, I need to you relax, sweetheart. I'm sorry you have to go through this, but right now the worst thing you can do is tense up. Look at me sweetie. Look in my eyes. We're almost done. A few more minutes and we're done. Shhhhhh, it's gonna be fine. Shhhhhhhh. There we go, Minnie, it's over."

Nice as my nurse was, she had to run off and kill another baby, so she left me alone on the table, naked from the waist down, bleeding, and terrified to move. I just killed the first thing I've ever known to have died. The persecuted side of me wants to burst into tears but the executioner side of me says I have no right to be melodramatic, so I lay traumatized on the cold table until the person pounding on the other side of the door tells me my time is up. Next to me, I find a pad as big as a queen size mattress. I scoot off the table and with trembling hands remove the adhesive tape and put it on my underwear. As I bend down to pull it up from my ankles, I see the bucket. My price to pay. Looking at the carnage of my irresponsibility, I know I'll carry the pain of my poor choice around with me the rest of my life.

"I'm so sorry, Chrissy."

"Nothing for you to be sorry for, Courtney. I'm the stupid idiot."

"I still can't believe you didn't let Nicole and me in on this. We would've wanted to help you through it, too."

"Well, no offense to Kelly, but it's not like she helped me through anything. In fact, this is the first time she's ever heard me talk about it."

"I didn't know you needed to."

"I did. But I really needed to talk about it with Kurt and he wanted nothing to do with the subject, so I let it go."

"Are you angry?"

"Of course I am."

"Who are you angry at though, yourself or him?"

"I'm trying to figure that out, Court." Finally chuckling a little, I ask, "Do you guys realize you probably know Kurt just as well as I do?"

They're looking at me like I'm nuts.

"Seriously. There's no behind closed doors Kurt and Chrissy. What you see is what you get and it's not enough anymore. I want a deeper connection to the man I'm married to. I'm gonna try to get it by taking him to my therapist, but deep down, I think it's pointless."

"You have to try."

"For how long, Kelly? How long am I supposed to feel ignored? What if Craig blew off your pain, told you to quit bringing up stuff that bothered you?"

"He wouldn't."

"Exactly. And I want my happiness, my sadness, my joy, my pain to be the most important things in the world to Kurt, just like yours are to Craig. I want to dream out loud with him without it turning into an argument. I want to show up to weddings, parties, and funerals *with* him instead of alone."

"*Hey, that's right*! That bastard didn't go to my wedding, did he? He was at some bullshit tradeshow!"

"No, Nicole, he was surfing."

"Then why did you--"

"Because it's Goddamn humiliating, that's why!"

Courtney moves toward me and places a drink in my hand as if she's giving me pain medication. It's cute until she says something logical.

"Just keep your expectations of therapy and marriage realistic, Chrissy. Life's not supposed to be a fairytale all the time."

Oh yeah? Well mine is.

SURRENDER

APRIL, 1998

Leaving the restaurant, I feel proud of my peculiarly productive day. I told Kurt about my therapy, and I finally told my friends how shitty my marriage is. That's what I call progress! My growth even makes running into Leo's trampy little friend, Megan, seem less daunting. Man, it's nice to have a little conviction, a little power, back in my life. I used to have so much conviction when I was younger. In fact, if there was a 'Most Likely To Exhibit Conviction' award in high school, I would've won it hands down. Whether I was convincing my friends to cut class or sneak into an R-rated movie, nobody did anything with as much fervor as I did. But gradually I let Kurt suck all the conviction outta me and somewhere along the line, I got soft. I didn't start getting hard again until about three weeks after I met Leo.

I remember I was running late for my morning meeting at work, and I was stuck in a long line at Starbucks. In a move never before attempted by me, I made eye contact with the guy at the front of the line, tapped my watch and bestowed upon him the cutest smile imaginable. I was thinking, what the hell are you doing, Chrissy? But something in me said, just try it, everyone else does. He motioned for me to walk up to him, asked me what I wanted and...not only did I get my latte lickity-split, the dude paid for it! I left feeling like the guy got the satisfaction of helping a pretty girl in distress and I got my coffee in a hurry. Not a bad way for either of us to start our day! I immediately took my win-win act on tour. Later that day, I got my toll paid for on the bridge. The following week, I was let out of a speeding ticket and a week after that I got my dinner paid for by a bunch of Japanese business-men. None of it cost me more than a smile or a "Hi how are ya." Overnight my new motto became--

Take everything that's offered to you but NEVER accept stuff that makes you feel like a cheap slut.

I cringe thinking back at how much time and money I could've saved if I had lived by that motto sooner. FINALLY, at the age of twenty-eight, I'm starting to figure out how to get my needs met and it's empowering. Today was the start of being true to the people I love in the hopes of getting what I need. It's up to them to decide if they like it or not.

I feel way too good to go home to potentially feel bad again, so I hop in my car, open up the sun roof, blast the radio, and set out on a drive that peculiarly leads me back to the bar where I met Leo. Once there, I settle into the familiar parking space where he and I spent all of those glorious hours talking on that rainy January night, and I watch as carefree boys and girls go in and out of the place that changed my life. Whenever the door opens, I catch a glimpse of the barstools Leo and I sat on and I envision the two of us on them again. Conviction tells me to make this the first day of the rest of my life and go inside for a celebratory drink to the new and improved Chrissy.

Once inside, I walk toward Leo's empty bar-stool, and I can almost feel my drug rushing through my veins. Just as I'm about to plop down on it, I see her again…Megan, my nemesis! On the one hand, I'm mortified that I keep running into her in my home-town, but on the other hand, it does give me the perfect excuse to call Leo. *Someone* needs to tattle on the girl's ballsy behavior at the restaurant! I'm going to do it! I'm going to call Leo! With all the conviction I can muster up, I raise my glass to Megan, slam my drink, and hightail it back to my car to make the call. I'm literally as excited as a crack addict on her last day of court-ordered rehab.

Subconsciously, I knew I'd find a way back to my addiction. I just didn't know it was going to be some twenty-one year old college girl who paved the way for me. I pause midway through dialing his number. But…what about the fact that he told me not to call him ever again? No! Go away doubt! Seriously, Chrissy, he *could* make you feel like an idiot for going against his wishes. Maybe you should reconsider. Ah screw that, I bet a million dollars he told Megan not to mention my so-called engagement to a single soul, and a betrayal of his trust is not something he would take lightly. All right, all right, never mind that I've betrayed his trust in the most despicable way imaginable by not telling him I'm married. I'll deprecate myself later. Right now I need to tell him what that awful, awful girl did to me…I mean him.

"Hello."

Dizziness is setting in. Heaven.

"It's me, Chrissy."

I'm scared of what might come out of his mouth. Rejection and disrespect will break me. This was a mistake. Hell.

"Are you okay?"

He still cares. Back in Heaven.

"I'm all right. How are you doing, Leo?"

I'm saying his name…out loud…to him! I don't want this conversation to end… ever.

"I've been better, but I know breaking things off with you was the best thing to do. You're not the right one for me."

He's not rude, just his brutally honest self. I brace myself for an ass-kicking.

"Who is the right one for you?"

"Someone who's willing to give me 100% of her heart. I wanted it to be you, but you made your choice, so I'm dealing with it."

This guy's got a lot of self-control. Even though I'm fairly certain he wants me, I'm a bad deal for him and that's why he hung up on me last month. He'll reject anyone who offers him less than he's worth. *Anyone who makes him feel like a cheap slut.* I have nothing but respect for him; it's my new motto he's practicing after all.

"Are you there?"

"Yeah, sorry."

"What were you thinking about just then?"

"That you have my heart, but things are just complicated."

"Let me get this straight. I have your heart but you're marrying someone else? That makes a lot of sense."

He's starting to get angry. I should hang up.

"Look, I did run into a little situation tonight but you know what...it's my problem. I'm sorry I called."

"I'm on the phone, tell me what it is."

He's super irritated. My drugs are laced with some yucky shit tonight!

"It's about your friend, Megan. She approached me in the parking lot of a restaurant, just as I was about to meet my friends. Apparently she recognized me from a picture you showed her. I'm sorry though, I shouldn't have called--"

"Are you fucking kidding me?"

Kidding that I called to tell him that or kidding that Megan did that? Damn! *I don't know what to say*!

"What the hell did she say to you?"

Oh good, it's the Megan one.

"She asked me why we stopped seeing each other and went on and on about how well you're doing without me. It could have been a disaster, Leo! My friends were ten feet away! What if I was with my parents or...him?"

"HOLD ON! First, I could give two shits about HIM, so don't mention HIM to me ever again."

"I'm sorry, I--"

"And second, I'm not doing well without you, so don't believe the bullshit she's spewing."

He's not doing well without me! He's not doing well without me! Why does his heartache give me hope? There should be no hope! And dammit, I think I was even getting close to being sort of okay without the hope, too. They say it takes 21 days to break a bad habit and it's been about that long since I last spoke to Leo. In fact, just yesterday I was praising myself for getting close to some kind of Leo detox finish line and then I make this call. He says he's not doing well without me and BAM! I'm back to where I started. Crazy in love and confused. My heart's pounding, my fists are sweaty, and there's a fluttering in my lower abdominal region that I haven't felt since the last time I heard his voice. I need him, and I'm powerless to stop needing him. Yep, last time I checked, that's called an addiction. But ho ho *hooooold* on…maybe he's not the toxic addiction I need to shed. Let's think about this for a minute. Here's a guy who adores my dark sense of humor, my psychotic work ethic, my weird appetite, my love of unpractical footwear, my silly dreams, my everything! What Kurt thinks are flaws, Leo considers magnificent. I've down-played, even hidden, so many wonderful things about me because I knew Kurt wouldn't marry me, he wouldn't think I was perfect for him. And I thought by doing that, I'd get something really good in the end, like happiness and true love. But all I really ended up getting was a fabulous-looking husband, a killer house and a whole lotta useless sporting gear.

Maybe my true bad habit, *my toxic addiction*, isn't Leo at all! Maybe it's my need to be perfect for Kurt and everyone else. But I'm scared! If I shed my perfection addiction, maybe I'll find the only reason to stay married is because I made a vow. A vow sure doesn't seem worth sacrificing my happiness over, and Leo *does* make me happy…Stop Chrissy! Talk to Dr. Maria about all of this before you do something stupid! Stay focused on the reason why you called.

"Leo, you told me you would keep us a secret. I was afraid of something like this happening and now I'm scared to walk around in my own town and--"

"CHRISSY, I TOLD HER BECAUSE I'M A FUCKING MESS OVER HERE!"

That makes two of us.

"Christ, I barely know you, but I can't get you outta my head. It's driving me crazy."

Ditto.

"I miss talking to you about all the stuff I can't talk to anyone else about. I miss holding you and smelling your neck. I miss your laugh and your pretty face, and in a weak moment I confided in her. I made her promise not to breathe a word of your engagement to any-one, and I'm pissed that she would walk right up to you and embar-rass you like that. Trust me, I would love for that asshole to find out you cheated on him, but I would *never* do anything to intentionally hurt you. You know that, right?"

God, I hate it when Kurt's name, in this case it's "asshole," gets dragged into all of this. The only asshole in this whole mess is me.

"I just know how much you must hate me and then when she mentioned how much time she's been spending with you and--"

"I don't hate you. Jesus, Chrissy, I want to give you everything you told me you wanted the night we met, and it's tearing me up that you're making such a stupid mistake by marrying that guy."

"Leo, stop."

"No, I'm serious. I don't think you realize how hard it is to find someone like you, and that guy gets to have all of it. It makes me fucking crazy."

Duh, I know it's hard to find someone like me. Until me, he's only been shopping the early twenties market, the whole package doesn't exist there. Chicks in their early twenties would NEVER tell a guy their hopes and dreams, out of fear it'd scare him away. I know because I was one of them. Most guys like 'em young and dumb, but that's what makes Leo different from most guys. Stupid appeasing girls annoy him. And on that one January night we crossed paths at a rare moment in time when I was not the appeasing girl everyone else knows me to be. I was the girl I needed to be. I'm sure Leo wanted to get into my pants the night we met, but first he wanted to get into my mind and once he was there, he adored me. That he wanted to get there made me adore him. It's simple, really. True love is all about adoration! For a relationship to thrive, you've got to adore each other's dreams, personality, *shoe selection*! And when you're adored, you're unstoppable. You're prettier, funnier…smarter! You become Superwoman!

I feel all of those amazing things and more when Leo is present in my life. Okay, I know what you're thinking. You're like, "Give me a break, you *just* met this guy, and *EVERY* girl feels all tingly inside when she first meets a cute guy and he compliments her." You're saying, "Just wait, those superwoman qualities will fade when the compliments fade!" And you know what? I have to agree with those allegations because I had those initial Superwoman (or since I was just sixteen, we'll call them Supergirl) qualities when

I first met Kurt. But I'm not talking about *complimenting* each other; I'm talking about sharing dreams with each other and having those dreams mesh. They're two totally different things and they MIGHT be the difference between a great relationship and a laborious one.

"Leo, can I see you?"

"You're killing me. Please don't ask me that. I'm not like most guys who would say yes, sleep with you, and then go on with their lives like it's no big deal. I want you, but not like that."

"You can have me."

Just then I hear the knock at his door.

"What are you talking about?"

"Don't you need to answer your door?"

"They'll go away. What the hell do you mean by saying I can have you?"

"*You can have me, Leo*. I'm not getting married. I've had a lot of time to think these last few weeks, and I know that right now I need you in my life more than I need anything else."

When I set out to make the phone call, I didn't plan on telling Leo about a broken engagement, but I had my little adoration epiphany and then he went and made me feel all drugged up by telling me he still wants me. And like a drug addict who lies, cheats, and steals to get her fix, I'm doing whatever I have to do to score. I'll figure out the details of how to manage this lie later. Right now, I need this.

I hear the knock through the phone again.

"Are you serious?"

"As serious as that knock at your door. You should see who it is."

He's pissed at the interruption, and I can hear him mumble expletives as he marches to the door. His mood shifts when he opens it and finds me standing there. Sometime during the phone call, I changed my direction and drove to his apartment. He grabs my arm, pulls me close, and slams the door. I've read about moments like this in books and I've seen it on TV and in the movies, but my real life moment of torrid passion is more primal than I ever could've imagined. For the first time in my life, my body is acting out on its own, completely separate from my brain and any form of logic or common sense. It must be how men feel most of the time. My keys and purse float away as Leo takes hold of my neck and cradles me to the ground.

The smell of his soapy clean skin, the pressure of his mouth on mine, and the brute force he uses to tear off my clothes triggers my addiction and makes me act like an absolute maniac. When I reach down to unzip his pants he pulls my hand up to his heart so I can feel its rapid beat. I try to tug it away to finish what I started, but he yanks it back to the place that houses his true love for me.

Never in my life could I have imagined receiving such a raw and tender gesture from a man. Lost in the haze of his heartbeat, I have no idea how his clothes came off, and I do absolutely nothing to stop him as he slowly pulls his naked body on top of mine. He looks down at me and a tear drops onto my face. Like a woman is supposed to love a man, I love him.

"Please, Leo. I need you."

Still he waits. He kisses my neck, my ear and my mouth again. My legs are squirming like I'm a fish out of water, and I can feel the rug burn on my back from having traveled half way across his living room floor with him on top of me.

"I'm not scared anymore, Leo. I want this. Please."

I hear him murmur "Oh my, God," and it tells me this means just as much to him as it does to me. I feel no guilt that Kurt's at home, possibly wondering where I am and at long last no sadness that he's probably not even wondering about me at all. My inner voice that's been muzzled for so long is singing and it's telling me I'm exactly where I'm supposed to be. It's ironic that I'm a married woman about to commit the ultimate sin and this is the closest I've come in my entire life to believing in God.

"Once this happens, I'm not letting you out of my life."

I look deep into his eyes and slowly nod.

"I'm serious, Chrissy, I'm telling my friends and family about you. There's no more hiding. Can you handle that?"

"Yes."

I just made it official. I'm a twenty-eight year old married woman with a twenty-two year old boyfriend who lives twenty minutes from a husband who he doesn't know exists. That God I started believing in a few minutes ago is sending me straight to Hell.

When you look at me I start to blush and all that I can see is you and us...

I wanna be in love with only you

("Blush," *Plumb*)

SPELLBOUND

APRIL, 1998

Two nights ago, after I sealed the deal with Leo, I wasn't sure what I was going to walk into when I arrived home. It had been at least seven hours since I left the house to have dinner with my friends. I had no idea if Kurt had left me several panicked messages, or if he had called the police, my friends, or my parents, because once I arrived at Leo's apartment, I turned my cell phone off. I wanted to hide from my life, my obligation. When I was with Leo, I didn't care about search parties or missing person reports. All I wanted was to concentrate on the magnitude of what I was giving him. But when I pulled into my driveway and saw the lights on inside of my house, the magnitude of what I just took away from Kurt hit me like a brick of cocaine. I became paralyzed with what I gather are the most common emotions that plague adulterers: fear and shame.

I opened the garage door, inched my car inside, and waited nervously for Kurt to come barreling out demanding to know where the hell I had been. But he didn't. I unlocked the door to the house and tiptoed inside. All I wanted to do was make it to the shower before he saw me, and it looked like I was going to get my wish because miraculously, the dog was the only one to greet me, and discernibly, my crotch. But instead of high tailing it to the bathroom, I became paranoid of my luck. Just like the stupid curious chick in a horror movie who decides to leave her bedroom after having been chased into it by a mask-wearing, knife-wielding lunatic, I called out Kurt's name. No answer. I ran to the window to look for his car, it wasn't there. I assumed he had gone out to search for me, so I hurried to the shower and scrubbed off the proof of where I had been.

The story that I decided to tell Kurt was that I stopped by my office after dinner with my friends to catch up on some work and fell asleep at my desk. I know, it's a totally lame excuse, but it was all I could come up with. But he never came home for me to try it out and, as the clock ticked away, I became very worried about him being very worried. And despite enjoying the various forms of worship Leo and I shared earlier, with every minute that passed, I became very sorry for my conduct unbecoming of a married woman. During the hour of waiting and pacing, I became re-committed to therapy and to figuring out why I'm making such a mess of things. At three o'clock in the morning, I finally decided to call Kurt and tell him to come home. That's when I remembered my cell phone was still turned off. I ran to it, turned it on, and fretfully waited to confront the plethora of anxious and angry messages, but there was only one.

"Hey babe, Geoff from work wants to go on a last minute fishing trip up to Hat Creek, so I'm on my way to pick him up. Gonna stay for the weekend. The dog's been fed. Probably won't have cell phone reception where we're going, so don't expect to hear from me. See ya Sunday."

Not that I deserved it, but there was no "I love you," no "call me when you get home so I know you're okay." NADA! Just a "see ya" and a click. My God, I could've been car jacked, dead in a ditch somewhere, or worse, *having sex with another man who I was falling in love with.* But thoughts like that don't cross Kurt's mind. Nope, everything's *always* great. That's how it's always been, and it'll never change.

Since Kurt didn't care where I was, what I was doing or who I was doing it with from Friday until Sunday, I decided to finally put love for *my* recreational activities ahead of my love for him and spend every single minute of my free time with Leo. On Friday morning, I called in sick to work, asked my neighbor to babysit my dog, and surprised Leo at his apartment with bagels and coffee. He blew off his classes, told the rock yard to fuck off, and we hopped into his jeep and headed west to Mill Valley, where I was certain nobody would recognize me.

Once we got to Mill Valley, we held hands while we window-shopped. We ducked into every alcove and alley-way and made out like sex-starved maniacs. We looked at real estate fliers while sharing our thoughts of living together one day. We drank a bottle of wine and ate a late lunch at Piatti's while we ripped on every single person who walked by, except our waiter of course, because doing that would be service suicide. Then, after lunch, we hit up all the stores. While I was looking at rings at Banana Republic, Leo slipped one on my finger and made a comment about the huge rock he planned on buying me one day. He said he wanted the diamond to "shine from a mile away to keep guys from even *trying* to make a move." I thought about the huge one I had on the night I met him and how size doesn't matter if you hide the damn thing. Leo bought the little metal ring for me and told me not to take it off until he can replace it with the real thing.

After lunch, we walked to the famous Sweetwater Saloon where musicians like Bonnie Raitt, Santana, and Boz Scaggs have been known for their impromptu performances. We found a cozy table in the corner and sat there for hours drinking Corona's, eating popcorn, and overtly adoring each other.

Too tipsy to make the drive home, we checked into the Mill Valley Inn where we made love, lots and lots of love, until we fell asleep in each other's arms. Well, Leo fell asleep, and I dozed in and out of consciousness. Sometimes I woke feeling blessed, and some-times I woke feeling cursed, always wondering which I would end up feeling for life and overwhelmed with the responsibility of the looming choice. The next day I returned home to pack a fresh bag of clothes, pat the dog on the head and check the answering machine. It was empty.

Two hours after leaving Leo, I arrived back at his apartment where he had dinner waiting for me. He spent whatever amount of money he had on a couple of chicken breasts, some prosciutto, fontina cheese, red wine, and candles, and we ate our meal on a blanket on the floor. I've eaten in the finest restaurants in Tokyo and Hong Kong, the best steak houses in New York and Chicago, and watched Kurt incessantly curse at the stove, at me, and at the world to make a perfect meal, but the simple, no spice, no utensil, no nothing meal Leo made for me was the best I've ever had. After dinner, just as we were getting cozy on the couch for some bwamp chicka bwamp bwamp, the phone rang.

"Aren't you gonna get that?"

"You're the only one I want to hear from and you're here."

I thought that was sweet, but I really wanted to know if a girl was calling him. Granted he's done nothing to make me think he's fooling around behind my back, but *he* thinks *I'm* genuine and LOOK AT WHAT I'M DOING TO HIM!

"Answer it."

"Why?"

"Just answer it. I wanna know who it is."

"No! Come here."

Just as he was about to put his arm around me, I jumped up from the couch, picked up the receiver, and handed it to him. If I wasn't his dream girl, I'd be scared shitless of the glare he gave me as I placed the phone in his hand.

"Hello? Yeah, I was meaning to call you. No, not about that. Did you run into Chrissy a while back?"

Holy shit! It's Megan!

"Uh-huh. Interesting, that's not what she told me."

Oh boy.

"And I believe her, so that means you're lying to me. I don't like liars…"

Uh oh.

"Look, I really don't care, and don't call me anymore. Stay out of Chrissy's life, too. I mean it." And then he hung up on her. I sat there astonished at Leo's ruthless ability to cut someone out of his life.

"Are you really never gonna talk to her again?"

"That's what I said."

"You'd do that for me?"

"I'd do anything for you, but I did that mostly for myself. I might've cut her some slack if she told me the truth, but she lied, and I don't want that in my life."

His words repeated over and over again in my mind after I left his apartment. What in *THEEEEEE* hell is the guy going to do to me when he finds out the lies I've told?

Three nights ago I thought going home to Kurt after having sex with Leo was the most despicable thing I had ever done, but I'm not so sure anymore. Let me see…I just spent the last three days talking about a future with a guy who's falling in love with me, and oh yeah, he doesn't know I'm married. I'm four days away from attending a marriage-saving therapy session with a husband who's only going with me to pacify what he thinks is a bump in the road of our relationship. My therapist believes me when I tell her I love Kurt and that I haven't spoken to Leo since the day after I met him four months ago. I'm fairly certain that every day, with every lie, my life gets more and more despicable.

SHAM

APRIL, 1998

As despicable as it is, I've created some kind of weird normalcy out of my revolting life. I exercise early in the morning, have a quick cup of coffee with Kurt, and then call Leo on my way to work to tell him I miss him. Sometimes when I call, I tell him I'm on a business trip so there's no pressure to see him right away. Trust me, I want to spend every waking minute of every day with him, but it's just not feasible. Whenever it is possible to see him, we meet at The Marriott after work for a quick drink and some flirting, and then I rush off to a make-believe work function when, in reality, I'm getting home just in time for Kurt to force-feed me dinner. Every so often I shake things up a bit and tell Kurt I have to work late so I can surprise Leo at his apartment. But no matter what lie I'm living, all my days end with a long bath (*huge* fan of those now) or I work on the computer until Kurt falls asleep. Eventually I slip into bed, careful not to wake him, and dream about Leo until I wake up and repeat the vicious cycle. But every so often, before my thoughts turn to Leo, I stare at Kurt in his peaceful slumber and I cry for us.

I remember at one of my very first sessions with Dr. Maria, she mentioned how easy it would be for someone to go nuts if they kept all of their thoughts and true feelings to themselves. And no doubt, I went coo-coo for cocoa puffs by not being authentic with Kurt for so many years. I mean look…being a fake drove me all the way into the arms of a twenty-two year old guy! But the multifarious lies I'm telling to Kurt and Leo make my old days of hiding my hatred of sky diving and well balanced meals seem like a walk in the park. I'm seriously going CRAZY! I feel like I need to be strapped to a table and have an intravenous drip of truth serum jammed into my arm to shake me out of my love coma and stop any and all future damage I might cause to these men. A rehab, so to speak.

So yes, at that session, Dr. Maria did an excellent job of rationalizing my one little slip up with Leo when she explained the side effects of not being authentic. But obviously she did it in the context of me working on a relationship with one man, my husband. For pity's sake, that's what I told her I wanted to do after all. But I've become a pathological liar so that I can work on a relationship with Leo. I know I could easily get snapped out of my love coma if I came clean to either Dr. Maria or my best friends. You know, check myself into rehab. But they would only force me to choose a man and I'm not ready to do that yet. *I can't strap myself to the table*!

Desperately needing to share my dirty little secrets, but not with my therapist or my best friends, I confided in Slutty Co-worker. She's was with me the night I met Leo. The hooker even saw how much fun I was having talking to him and convinced me to keep on doing it! Of course telling *her* about my life as an adulterer is like a heroin addict consulting a meth addict for guidance, but I had to tell someone about my affair before I exploded. And as a woman who sleeps with married men and makes no qualms about accepting expensive tokens of their appreciation, Slutty Co-worker was completely non-judgmental and totally supportive of my situation. In fact, she said I could use her as an alibi *and* use her apartment to rendezvous with Leo until I sorted out my life. It's ironic how I used to think she was a complete whore, but in one conversation she went from being Linda Lovelace to my Mother Theresa. Funny how fast things can change. Slutty Co-worker's doing the opposite of what those who love me would advise me to do. But like I said, I'm an addict, and right now I'll use anyone that'll help me get what I need.

I'm just finishing up listening to a message from Leo when I pull into Dr. Maria's parking lot. Tonight's the big therapy session with Kurt…and there he is.

"Hey, Babe! So this is where you come to talk about how unhappy you are? Ahhh, stop looking at me like that. I'm kidding!"

I almost feel bad about what I'm about to put him through. That is, until he starts cracking jokes about what a waste of time and money this is going to be.

Sad Frumpy Lady is sitting in her usual spot but instead of keeping her head buried in her book like she usually does, she lifts it up to get a good look at Kurt. Holy moly, she *almost* looks delighted.

After we're beeped in and introductions have been made, Dr. Maria invites us to sit down, but not directly next to each other. She has an L shaped sectional couch that we sit on in the middle, near the part with the crack that forms the actual L, so our knees are almost touching. I'm tense. I'm not sure if I want Kurt here to work on the marriage or if I want him here to understand my reasons for ending it. Until I'm clear on which one, should he even be here at all? I look up at him; he has a big ol' smile on his face.

"It's nice to finally meet you, Kurt. I'm glad you could join us. As I'm sure you know, Chrissy's been feeling sad for some time now."

His hand moves to my knee. It's a move I would've craved seven months ago. Now it bothers me.

"We've discussed her sadness in some detail, and…well…seems like a lot of it is about you."

Smile's gone.

"Can you tell me why you reacted the way you did to Chrissy's miscarriage?"

Oh no she didn't! I DID NOT think she was going to drop that bomb! Oh my God, he must be so uncomfortable. I'm uncomfortable! I can't bear to watch him stumble through this. I want to save him! Should I save him? No, no, no I can't. I have to see where this goes. I have to see what Kurt does when he's forced to feel, or worse…realize he's incapable.

He clears his throat.

"I'm not sure what you're talking about."

"Didn't Chrissy tell you she had a miscarriage in October?"

"She said she did."

"You don't believe her?"

"I believe her but…how can we really know for sure?"

"Well, she took a pregnancy test at home and told you it was positive and you never had a baby."

"Those things can be wrong."

"Sure they can, but I believe her and she's not even my wife."

I think that was meant to shake him up, but it was me who felt the punch in the stomach. After a long look at her notepad and a noticeably irritable shift in her mood, she finally looks up.

"Was the test she took when she was seventeen wrong?"

I can feel Kurt's eyes fixated on me like I'm in big trouble, so I keep my head down. He answers, his voice contemptuous.

"No, it was right."

"But how do you know for sure?"

"Well, she had…" He clears his throat, "an abortion."

I've never heard him say that horrible word before. It sounded like he was speaking a foreign language. Like, as if the word handschuh-schneeballwerfer just came flying out of his mouth. Coincidentally, handschuhschneeballwerfer is a word my grandpa used to throw around. It's German and it means coward. Seems appropriate to use that word at the moment.

"But what made you believe her and drive her to get the abortion?"

"I don't know."

"Really? I mean, there has to be *something* that made that experience different than the one you had in October to have made you act on it."

Wowza, he looks wayyyyyy pissed right now.

"*I don't know*…I guess it's because she took the pregnancy test at a clinic and the person said it was positive."

He's getting awfully shifty over there on that couch.

"What if a technician never administered the test, would Chrissy's word have been enough or would she have had to drive herself to have the abortion?"

"That's ridiculous, of course not! I'm not sure what she told you but we got through that ordeal just fine. We've been together for twelve years, we got married didn't we? I can't be doing everything wrong."

"I'm not implying you're the only reason we're sitting here today. But I do think Chrissy needs to understand why it's so hard for you to talk about the miscarriage."

"I guess I'm someone who needs proof before I get overwrought with happiness or sadness."

"Kurt, I peed on a stick; a monkey could read the results. What more proof did you need?"

Dr. Maria puts her hand in the air to silence me.

"Let me ask you this, Kurt. If last October, Chrissy took a test in her doctor's office and the pregnancy was confirmed right in front of you, would that have made the loss of the baby something you would've wanted to talk to Chrissy about?"

Kurt's never been emotionally challenged like this before. I want to save him.

"I don't see what the point of all this is. It's in the past, and I don't think it's healthy to relive painful experiences over and over again."

He doesn't see the point of all of this? Save yourself.

"It's understandable that you wouldn't want to rehash the same tragedy over and over again, but can you tell me what you initially felt? You know, right after Chrissy told you what happened."

He's smiling. He's actually smiling. It's not a funny smile, and it's not a disrespectful smile, it's just a smile meant to inform Dr. Maria that he will not be answering the question. I've seen it a million times before, and I'm curious to see how a professional responds to it.

"Okay then. Did you try to talk to Chrissy about the pain *she* might have been feeling?"

Hold on a minute! HE DIDN'T TALK ABOUT *HIS* PAIN! I WANT TO HEAR ABOUT *HIS* PAIN!

"No."

And then he turns to me in his typical fatherly fashion.

"But you never tried to talk to me about it, so I let it go just like you did. How am I supposed to know when something bothers you if you don't tell me?"

He makes me psychotic. My head shakes back and forth, my eyes roll back in my head, and my voice gets lost in my throat. I learned a long time ago to walk away from Kurt when he gets like this because I can't win, but Dr. Maria nods her head at me to answer him.

"What would've been the point of talking to you about *that* pain when your response to all of my other pain has been 'stop complaining' or 'get over it'? Sorry Kurt, but that miscarriage was the straw that broke the camel's back of things I tried to talk to you about."

He completely ignores me and turns to Dr. Maria.

"For the record, I did talk to her about what happened when we were younger. I never felt like it was the right thing to do, and she knew that."

Excuse me? Someone hold me back!

"I needed support, not judgment!"

"Hey, I supported your choice! Why do I have to make you feel better about it for the rest of your life? Jesus, what we did was wrong, and I don't know if I'll ever forgive myself. But just like we got over what happened to us eleven years ago, we'll get over what happened in October."

"*We*? We didn't get over anything. You did!"

Dr. Maria shushes me again with her hand in the air.

"Maybe it's easy for you to move past things without talking, but your wife can't. She needs to talk about her heartache and pain, and she needs you to do the same. Doing so will help you both have a more intimate connection. Isn't that something you want?"

His elbows are resting on his legs and his fingers are like spider webs covering his eyes. It looks like he's being tortured.

"Something created by the two of you was destroyed…twice. The most healing way to move past that is together. My goal in working with you is to help you feel everything, the good and the bad, *together*. Are you interested in that?"

"Hold on, I feel! I FEEL like I've been made out to be some evil, uncaring husband. Chrissy knows I love her and I don't like it when she's sad. But I can only be sad with her for so long. After a while, I don't see the point in crying over the same thing."

"How does she know you love her?"

"I tell her."

"You tell her?"

"Yeah, that's what I said. I tell her."

"Would you believe Chrissy loved you if she didn't eat what you wanted her to eat?"

Holy shit. I want to crawl under the table.

"What are you talking about?"

"What if she refused to do the recreational activities you ask her to do or wake up as early as you ask her too? Would telling you she loved you be enough for you to feel it?"

Wow, she's really going for it.

"I don't do all of that stuff. I don't *make her* do anything."

"Yes, you do, and you make me feel bad if I don't do it! You compare me to other people, and you constantly remind me that all you ever wanted was an adventurous wife. And if that's not bad enough, you even criticize the things that I like to do for fun. I'm tired of feeling like I'm not good enough, Kurt!"

"Chrissy, let's give Kurt an opportunity to speak without being attacked."

What the? Whose f'ing side is she on here?

"Kurt, Chrissy feels like she's done an awful lot of things for you that are outside of her comfort zone. She did them because she loves you and she wants you to be happy. However, she feels like the relationship has been one-sided in that way. Perhaps you've started to notice her reluctance to do things with you that normally she would."

Surprisingly, he nods his head yes.

"It's resentment that's causing the reluctance, and resentment is *very dangerous* territory in a marriage."

"What's that supposed to mean?"

I didn't think I had to remind her to keep Leo top secret but I also didn't think she would drop that miscarriage bomb. She's making me nervous.

"Resentment can lead to all sorts of things…adultery, separation, divorce. So before things potentially get out of control, I suggest you reach across the aisle a little, do some of the things your wife likes to do. To achieve some balance in the relationship, would you consider eating what Chrissy wants to eat or maybe lounge by the side of a pool and do nothing but talk to her for hours? How about sleeping in until noon on the weekends, just for the heck of it?"

Kurt's chuckling like this is all one big joke.

"This is ridiculous. First of all, I resent the suggestion that divorce is where we're headed. And second, I made it pretty apparent who I was before we got married and she was okay with all of it then. I don't know where this is coming from."

Omigod! I can't take it anymore!

"No, Kurt! I *pretended* to be okay with all of it because I wanted you to love me! I was naïve and stupid, but I don't wanna be those things anymore. And I'm not sixteen anymore, but for some sick reason in this relationship, I still am. I'm a twenty-eight year old woman who loves impractical shoes, cocktails on a Saturday afternoon, and coffee late at night, and *sometimes* all I want for dinner is Cheetos! I love working long hours at the office and sleeping in late on the weekends and NEITHER of those things will make me a bad mother one day. I hate bike riding and camping and water sports and I *really* hate the stupid outfits you make me wear to do it all. I swear to God if I get one more pair of Gortex socks for Christmas, I'm gonna scream. I want you to buy me something you think I want, not what you want me to want. And sometimes, I want you to do things that I like to do without adding your little sarcastic comments that suck the fun out of it. *Do you see where all of this is coming from now?"*

Kurt's staring at me with dragon nostrils and heavy breathing. He's fucking pissed. For a second, I'm scared, but then relief sets in. I'm glad we're cracking this marriage open. Let's see what we really have when we're exposed.

"Are you two okay? Does anyone need a break?"

In unison, "No."

"Kurt, do you understand what Chrissy's telling you?"

"Yeah."

He does? Shit, now I'm nervous that he's actually going to try to do something to make me happy. It's all I ever wanted until…I met Leo. Now I'm in too deep with him to let any man, even my husband, win over my heart. I screwed Kurt over by making him think I loved the real him, and now I'm screwing him all over again by making him think I ever could.

"Let's move on a bit, guys. Kurt, what's your relationship like with your family?"

Boy, if looks could kill.

"Why, did Chrissy tell you they're evil or something?"

"No, but she mentioned they make her feel confused and a bit scared at times."

"That's ridiculous, scared of what?"

"Come on, Kurt, please don't act like you've never heard me complain. I'm always put on the defense with those people, and you take their side all the time. I walk away from every encounter with them feeling like I'm going crazy."

Kurt slowly takes his gaze from me to Dr. Maria, and in a tone that implies I'm somewhat of a lunatic, "Chrissy comes from a very small family. She's not used to the pandemonium that ensues in large families like mine."

"Oh yeah, Kurt…what kind of pandemonium was ensuing the day of your college graduation? Seriously, I gotta know…what was so chaotic that kept all ninety-nine people in your family from celebrating your accomplishment?"

He smirks and shakes his head like I've lost my mind.

"How's that funny, Kurt? *They shit on you!*" Turning to Dr. Maria, "Please tell me how we can have children when he thinks it's perfectly acceptable to have them around those people and I think it would be child abuse?"

"Your concern is valid, and I'm not neglecting it. But I'd like to cover a few other things before our time is up so I can give you some recommendations on what to work on before our next meeting. Is that okay?"

No it's not okay! An answer to that question could be a clear-cut reason to end this marriage. It wouldn't have to be about my mistakes. It could be about our differences.

"How's your sex life?"

Oh boy, here we go…

"What sex life? She's always working or tired."

"No I'm not. I just don't want to."

He's looking at me like I just shot his dick off.

"Then why do you tell me you're tired all the time?"

"I'm *tired* of you telling me what to do. Really Kurt, do you expect me to get on all fours and DO IT after you just got done telling me to take three more bites of chicken? It'd be like having sex with my dad."

Or like cheating on Leo, but let's stay focused on today's agenda.

"Jesus Christ, Chrissy, what's wrong with you?"

"*What's wrong with me*? Did you hear what I just told you? It's no wonder I've never been able to have an orgasm with you."

I stand corrected. *That's* the look of having your dick shot off.

"That's a fucking lie and you know it!"

Dr. Maria throws her hands in the air and interrupts with, "Hold on, Kurt."

Thank God she butted in because I feel like I'm about to open up a twelve-year-old can of whoop-ass on this guy.

"A woman has to feel cherished, *admired*, for her to want intimacy with a man."

See, admiration! I knew it!

"Let's start with some effort to address a few of Chrissy's wants and needs, and we'll see where the intimacy goes from there."

Kurt's screwed and not in the way he wants to be. There's no way I'm having sex with him *and* Leo. I might be a lying, cheating, adulterous bitch, but I'm no skank and there will be NO double dipping! But let's be real, there's no point in worrying about fighting off Kurt just yet because what are the chances he's actually going to try to address my wants and needs?

We wrap up the session with Dr. Maria's request to see each of us individually for a few months and then we'll re-group after that. Kurt's like "whatever," and I'm like "sounds fine to me."

I'm glad we drove separate cars to the appointment, because I need a few minutes alone to prepare myself for the war that's going to break out when we get home.

"I guess I'll see you at home, Kurt. Should be a blast."

"Wait, Chrissy. You know…you might've been right about some of that stuff in there."

Whooooooda huh? Never in a million years did I expect him to say that.

"Do you wanna grab a beer and some of those appetizers you're always talking about before we go home?"

Apparently the chances of him addressing my needs aren't as low as I thought.

As I look into the eyes of the man I once thought of as my knight in shining armor, I want to be happy with the little bit of effort he just mustered up. But I'm not. And the joylessness filling my soul helps me to answer all of the questions I had surrounding my motive for bringing Kurt to therapy. I didn't bring him with me to save the marriage; I brought him with me to end it. I don't want appetizers. I want my freedom. I've been forcing myself, Kurt, and Dr. Maria to believe it was things like eating cupcakes for lunch and sleeping in late on the weekends that would make me happy, but if I choose to settle for things like that...well, that'd make me the handschuh-schneeballwerfer. What I want is so much bigger than that stuff. I want an intimate hand on the heart kind of connection with a man, and it's time to confess to everyone, mostly myself, that I'll never have it with Kurt.

But freedom's going to come with a hefty price...I'll be called a failure, a cheater, and the bad guy. *The big three I never wanted to be.* The big three that scare me so much that I've considered living an unfulfilling Francesca-like life instead of confronting them. But dammit, I don't want to die feeling obligated, unfulfilled, and heart-broken like she did! Those three things kick the big three's ass! And so there you have it; the big three are my price for freedom. And the sooner I get over what everyone else thinks of the cost, the better. Only I know my life's true worth.

At tonight's therapy session I learned that I don't want the evening to end with jalapeño poppers and garlic cheese fries. I want it to end with Kurt realizing we're a hopeless cause. I want him to throw his hands in the air and suggest we go our separate ways because he can't possibly love me the way I need to be loved. I want him to make this easy for me. But that'll never happen because no matter how fractured we are, Kurt will *never* divorce me. You see, when he starts something, he finishes it. No matter if he's lost for days without water on a remote hiking trail or starving because a bear ate his food two days into a five-day expedition, the dude never asks for help and he NEVER gives up. Regardless of how exhausting and completely idiotic his actions might seem, he's committed to the bitter end of whatever it is he starts…unless, of course, there's adultery involved. But let's see if I can end this marriage without being exposed as the devil incarnate. I'm going to look bad enough already.

Yep, tonight's therapy session taught me one thing. Ending this marriage will be my responsibility, and staying in it will be my sacrifice. I still don't know which is more daunting.

GOOD TIMES

APRIL, 1998

Tonight's my eleven year high school reunion. Why an eleven-year reunion and not a ten-year reunion like most normal classes have? Easy, everyone from my graduating class is a fucking moron, especially the dude we left in charge to plan this kind of stuff. Oh… he *tried* to have the reunion on time; he set the date for June 16, 1997, exactly ten years to the date of our high school graduation day.

I was at work when I opened the invitation. It was printed in black and white on a piece of crappy printer paper, and it was inviting the class of '87 to "get crazy" at the Stargaze arcade located in the heart of Freakmont. *An arcade*? What the fuck kind of fun are we going to have there, and what kind of cute outfit would fit in at a place like that? It's not like cleavage and high heels would work! But most importantly, I want Patron tequila, not Pacman! I promptly called our so-called reunion coordinator and told him he was a douche and that if he didn't immediately send out a notice cancelling the reunion and notifying the class that I would be taking over to plan a more respectable affair, I'd show up to that arcade and make his life hell. He did as he was told. It felt like high school all over again! Good times.

It took a year to finalize all of the details and give our class the glamorous reunion it deserved. Aside from my wedding, it was the most fun I'd ever had planning an event…and I kept it completely hidden from Kurt. Not because I didn't want him to attend the event with me! Are you kidding? That was the thing I was looking forward to the very most! I couldn't wait to show up with him *and* my huge wedding ring and then brag about our new house in Danville. High school Ken and Barbie were definitely going to show up in full force!

The reason I didn't tell Kurt I was planning the reunion was because he would've just criticized my involvement. He'd go on and on about all the time the planning was taking away from him and my job, all the ways I'd probably lose money on the event, and he'd ridicule my need to always be the center of attention. Okay, so he probably would've been right to ridicule me about that last one, but as far as everything else goes, there was no time lost at work to pull off the reunion, and all of the planning I did at home was done long after he went to bed. And Kurt was *way* off on the money thing. I price- gauged the hell out of everyone and actually profited on the event. I considered it money owed to me after the great economics test fiasco of 1987.

I got the harebrained idea to plan my high school reunion a year ago, back when I *thought* Kurt and I were happy. There's NO WAY I would've propelled myself to the front and center of all of the faces of my past if I thought for one minute I'd have to show up without him. But it's a year later and a lot has happened…Leo has happened. I take the freedom revelations I had from my last therapy session very seriously, and if I ask Kurt to attend my class reunion with me, he won't think we're a hopeless cause. This reunion has to be my first attempt at facing my fear of failure--just one of the big three roadblocks to my freedom, and I have to go alone.

Courtney, Nicole, Kelly and I are getting ready in one of the rooms at the hotel where the reunion is, and their husbands, all ex-football buddies of Kurt's, are pounding beers in the room next to us. It doesn't take a rocket scientist to figure out that none of them are very happy with me. I hear Craig say something about, "It won't be the same without him," and Kyle chimes in with "Even though he wasn't in our class, he's the one everyone wants to see." Then fuck-ing Guss raises his beer bottle and says, "Here's to Kurt." Assholes.

"Just ignore them, Chrissy, they don't know what they're saying, they're drunk."

I take a sip of my wine while I glare at Nicole. She knows full well those guys know exactly what they're saying. Then I walk into the bathroom and close the door. I look down at my hand for a really long time before I slip my Banana Republic ring off of my finger. For weeks, I've been wearing it lieu of my wedding ring. It's been easy to use my weight loss as an excuse for the substitute, but the truth is not many people noticed. Not even Kurt. I carefully place the ring on the counter and then take my wedding ring out of my purse. I stare at it, too, for a really long time before I slip it into place. Then I ask myself, which ring gets me closer to my freedom goal? Knowing the answer, I take my wedding ring off. But which one will spare me total embarrassment? Good Lord, what are those Freakmontians going to say when I walk in there without my ring *and* without Kurt? I can't do this fear-facing bullshit! Why is this happening to me? WHY NOW?

"Chrissy, you ready to go?"

"Be right out."

Staring at my jewelry for a minute longer, and feeling the pressure to hurry up and pick a piece, I gently place the rings on a towel and close my eyes. I wrap them up, shake them, and then unfold the towel. Without opening my eyes I tell myself the first one I touch is the one I wear.

"Shit."

Other than Kyle's burp, it's silent on the elevator ride down to the ballroom. I can tell that half of the gang is nervous for me and the other half is bitter that their evening won't be half as much fun as it would be if Kurt were here. I tightly wrap my right hand over my left hand to touch *and* conceal my ring. I'm looking straight ahead at the shiny metal elevator doors and the reflection I see of all of us in our fancy clothes makes me think back to my senior prom. My heart and mind were a mess way back then, too, but for entirely different reasons than they are right now.

MAY, 1987

"Omigod, you guys! I'm gonna wear peach!"

"Like you're gonna look hella good in that color, Chrissy! You're totally gonna dye your shoes to match, right?"

"Fer sure, Nicole! Like, I'm not an animal, I know how to merchandise myself!"

The fashion events leading up to my senior prom were supremely fabulous. Courtney, Nicole, Kelly and I color-coordinated our prom dresses so that we wouldn't color clash in any group photos. We knew we'd be splattered all over the year book, and no stone was left unturned to make sure every shot would be *Seventeen* magazine-worthy. Everything down to our rhinestone earrings and dyed-to-match bow ties for our boyfriends were ready to go weeks before the prom. I *wish* the same degree of fabulosity could be said about my relationship events leading up to the big event. Truth be told, I wasn't even sure if Kurt was going with me. He had graduated a year earlier and felt like one prom was enough in his lifetime. He was having trouble choosing between the most important event to date in my life and the college softball world series. Yep, that's my competition.

Ever since I met him a year ago, I haven't felt like I stood at the top of his fun list. Unless, of course, if I agreed to go along with whatever activity he planned for himself, then I made the cut. But I feel like my prom should be different, it should be something that he's able to separate his feelings about and go along with because it's important to me. Isn't that what all normal guys do? I mean, other than the four gay guys in our class, what guy *really* wants to put on a tux, pay for a limo, and attend a prom? Exactly… none! But they do it anyway for the special girl in their life who they hope to bang in the back of that limo at the end of the night. Why can't Kurt be that sweet? I want to ask him but I learned that he doesn't like to be pestered about things he doesn't care about. He wouldn't get angry at me, he'd just flat out refuse to go to my prom out of contempt for being questioned and then I'd really be screwed. My only hope is that Craig, Guss, and Kyle convince him to go or the college softball world series is a close-out. But since I haven't told my girlfriends about Kurt's potential no-show, because it's shameful, I can forget about their boyfriends helping me out. Time to start watching college softball so I can track the fate of my future.

And…my future doesn't look so bright. The softball series is tied 3-3, with the tie breaking game set for, of course, tonight…prom night. Staring at myself in my bedroom mirror, covered in peach from head to toe, I curse myself! *Oh, why couldn't I have befriended one of those four gay guys?*

"What time does the limo show up?"

Looking at the Hello Kitty clock on my nightstand, I let out a heavy sigh and tell Courtney, "In about five minutes."

"Why so sad, Chrissy? I mean, you look mega cute."

And I do. My strapless form-fitted floor-length peach taffeta creation turned out way better than I expected. My shoes and purse are dyed to match to perfection, and I could NOT have asked for a better hair day. Total redemption from junior prom! All that being said…it makes perfect sense that Kurt won't show up and I won't be able to rub my splendor in everyone's face. This sucks.

Just as I'm about to confess my horrible secret to the girls my mom bursts into my room, cigarette dangling from her lower lip, and pissed that she had to walk away from Phil Donahue to tell us, "Limo's here girls. Don't be too late tonight. Doors lock at 1am. You come home any later and you sleep on the porch. Capish?"

In unison we let out a patronizing, "*Caaaaaaapiiiiish*"

On the way down the long hallway, which feels more like a walk to death row, I'm wondering how I'm going to pay for my portion of the limo.

"You guys, stop. I can't go! I feel totally moted!"

Peering out the front door, Nicole belts out, "Like no way! I'm the one that's moted!"

"What are you talking about?"

"The corsage that Kurt's holding…it's the one I wanted, but Kyle's such a fucking cheapskate he wouldn't pop for it! I'm so hating you right now, Chrissy Anderson."

Almost knocking down the hundred and twenty-five pounds of taffeta that exists between the three of my friends, I whiz out the front door and run into the arms of my knight and shining armor.

"You're here!"

"I was always gonna come, Babe."

"Then why couldn't you just tell me that, why put me through all of this torture?"

"I dunno, I guess I just don't like it when you put so much emphasis into trying to impress other people. I wanted you to focus on something else."

A lesson? Kurt used my prom to teach me a lesson? Shouldn't I react according to how fucked up that is? He put me through hell for the last four weeks! He sucked whatever morsel of pre-prom fun I've dreamed of experiencing for the last four years of high school! He made me think I wasn't special! I have to react accordingly! But… he looks so handsome. Everything about us is so perfect right now. I can't be the one to spoil this night for everyone…mostly myself. And after all, he may have a point. He just wants me to be a better person. What's not to love about that?

"I guess you're right."

After a sweet kiss on my lips and a look that tells me he's always right, he yells out, "Limo's on me guys! Now let's party!"

Another obnoxious burp from Kyle knocks me back into my present dilemma. The one where I either stake out the nearest emergency exit and make a run for it before the idiots from the class of 1987 notice I'm solo or face them head-on and admit my marriage failure. Like the snake I am, I slither my way to the back of the elevator to give myself more time to make a choice. My heart is about to pop out of my skin. What was I thinking by choosing my high school class reunion as my coming out alone party? Sure I was full of all kinds of freedom conviction when I left Dr. Maria's office last time, but that was like a whole entire week ago! More than enough time to turn back into the fear-infested Francesca that I am.

Think, think, think, think, think. I know! I'll make up a story about Kurt arriving later and then I'll call him and beg him to show up. Nah, he's most likely off on some kind of hiking or biking excursion. Maybe I can tell everyone he had to go out of town on business! Shit, that won't work. It'll only be a matter of minutes before his drunk meathead football buddies throw me under the bus. Who am I kidding, at least half of my graduating class showed up at this thing to see Kurt Gibbons. They're going to demand answers. It'll be a mere matter of minutes before I'm laughed at and people start asking me for refunds…again. I'm so screwed. The elevator makes its crash landing and the doors open a lot faster than I want them to. Fuck me.

Almost instantly I hear like seventy-five "Dude's!" and about thirty-three "Bro's!" and I'm wondering what the hell has Kyle, Craig, and Guss so excited. And then I hear him.

"I'll catch up with you guys later." Walking toward me, Kurt says, "I need a minute to talk to this beautiful woman."

I should be mad…furious really. But I'm not. I'm so relieved I could die.

"How did you--"

"The catering company left a message at the house about the balance due on the account, said they'd take a check tonight at the reunion. Babe, why didn't you tell me this was tonight?"

"I wanted to see what it would be like to choose to be alone for once. You know, instead of listening to you complain or wondering if you'd bail at the last minute because the fish were biting in some far off location."

"Chrissy, I'm so sorry for all the stupid shit I put you though over the years. I'm an idiot." Extending his hand to me, "Can you forgive me?"

And then I see them. All the girls from my past, staring and salivating over my husband. It makes me sick. But not quite as sick as I make myself when I cave in to all of my fears and take Kurt's hand. As painful as the man makes my life, he really does show up when I need him the most. Then, like being rushed by a bull at Pamplona, some chick from the class of '87 runs up to me.

"Oh my God, Chrissy, you're ring is *totally* amazing!"

Looking down at my ginormous diamond wedding ring, I think to myself: not quite as amazing as the ring I left upstairs, and *not even close* to how amazing of a coward I am.

PANIC

MAY, 1998

Well I certainly won't be winning any conviction awards any time soon. And I probably won't be getting any freedom anytime soon, either. My weak moment at the reunion triggered all kinds of optimism. Optimism amongst my friends that Kurt and I are going to work things out, and optimism in Kurt that we're not nearly as damaged as I portrayed us to be at our therapy session.

I miss Leo so much. It's been weeks since I've seen him because Kurt's been ON FIRE with optimism and planned all kinds of fun little activities to keep me nice and busy. He took me on a gondola ride at Lake Merritt in Oakland. That fucking sucked. He took me on a boat ride to Alcatraz in San Francisco. That fucking sucked. He took me to an outdoor bizarre in Berkley. That *really* fucking sucked. But the thing that sucked the most about all of it was my inability to tell him it all sucked. Tell me, how do you tell someone who's trying their very best to please you to stop? No seriously…tell me!

No matter what activity Kurt drags me off to, I'm always on the lookout for Leo, and my hand is always on the car door handle. I put myself in these imaginary heart- wrenching scenarios where Kurt and I stumble into Leo as we're holding hands, pretending to be happy. Leo demands answers, Kurt starts swinging punches, Leo starts kicking the shit out of Kurt. Both of them are expecting me to side with one or the other but there's no way I can root for or against either of them. I love them both. Sometimes, on the way to the activities, I feel like pulling the car door handle when we're on the freeway going 70mph so I don't have to put myself through the torture.

I told Leo I was in Chicago last week to give myself some breathing room, but I was really in Dallas. Why, you might ask? Because two weeks ago, when I couldn't see him due to obligations with Kurt, I lied and told him I had to go to Dallas for work. Then, when I *really* did have to go to Dallas, I told him I was in Chicago because he'd probably think it was strange that I was in Dallas two weeks in a row. Or maybe he wouldn't, but do you see the paranoia I'm dealing with here? I don't even need to lie about some of the things I lie about, but I can't keep track of which of the honest bits of my days I tell to either of them, so I keep on making stuff up. And when my stories don't add up, I play dumb. Or worse, I make them feel like they're the ones losing their mind. Note to anyone considering the arduous task of adultery and the mini-tasks associated with it like lying and manipulating: It's not the cheating that makes you a sicko. What makes you a sicko are the lies you deliberately tell without regard for how insane you might make other people.

And the lying is just the tip of the iceberg. Try managing a boyfriend and a husband who live twenty minutes apart! It's much more difficult than I ever could've imagined, and I don't recommend it for the faint of heart. Yesterday was Cinco de Mayo and Kurt took me disco bowling in Danville with Nicole and her husband, Kyle. Let's pause for a moment and reflect on Kurt's poignant effort. I don't like disco, and I don't like bowling, and I HATE the shoes you have to wear to do it, and he should know ALL of that after twelve years together. I can't wait for our next therapy session together when Dr. Maria gives him two snaps for his effort and then I dive bomb him with all of the reasons why taking me bowling was the stupidest idea in the world. I digress…sorry about that. Anyway, I suppose the bright side of the evening was that I got to spend some time with Nicole. At first Kurt suggested we go on "the date" alone, but I convinced him to bring along another couple and there were two big reasons why.

1) I can't be alone with Kurt. He might try and get romantic, and I can't have that. I'm already cheating enough.
2) If we run into Leo or one of his cronies, I'll DEFINITELY need someone to help me diffuse the situation. Nic's the best person to do that.

Out of my three best friends, Nicole's the *only one* I'd consider telling the secret of my affair to. She's the only one who can sort of relate to what I'm doing. You see, pre-nuptial Nic and her husband Kyle screwed around with other people and were involved in enough overly dramatic break-ups to put Alison and Billy from *Melrose Place* to shame! If I ever got caught, or God forbid, had to confess to having an affair, she has her own prior experiences to draw from to try and make mine not seem so bad. Okay, obviously I'm a much bigger pig than her, but I know she'd at least try to make me feel better. That's what makes her so great. And, thank God, I insisted that my little swine friend go bowling, because #2 on my list of reasons to have her with me crept up and smacked me real hard on the ass and not in a good way like you see on the Spice Channel.

"You guys want another Corona? Me and Kyle are gonna get another round."

"Si, dos por favor."

"God, Nicole, you're so stupid."

"Geez girl, why such a bitch these days?"

I wait to respond until I'm sure the guys are out of earshot.

"Sorry, I just have a lot on my mind these days. There's all that weird stuff going on between Kurt and me, and work is really stressing me out. I'm always on edge."

"Just chill and try to have some fun. It's Cinco de Mayo, Baby! Besides, you and Kurt just hit a rough patch. You guys will work it all out."

"I'm not so--"

Like a shot of lightning, Nicole hits my arm and points to the bar.

"Hey look, isn't that the girl you were talking to at the restaurant a few months ago? The one with the really great hair?"

"WHAT? WHERE?"

"Talking to Kurt and Kyle! Look, she and her friends are... WAIT!

Are they hitting on our husbands?"

"Holy crap, that's that Megan chick!"

"How do you know her?"

"She's the reason why I'm always on edge these days. Well not her exactly, but kinda her."

"What the F are you talking about, Chrissy?"

"Omigod, omigod, omigod! I can't let her see me! I'm going to the bathroom! When the guys get back with the beers, meet me in there. Hurry!"

Five minutes later Nicole bursts into my stall.

"Spill it!"

"Okay, don't freak. I cheated on Kurt."

"Chrissy, noooooooooo!"

"I know, I know, I'm going to Hell. But listen to me, Nic, I need your help right now. My life is already knee deep in doo-doo, but if that girl sees me here with Kurt, I'm gonna be covered in it."

"Who the hell is she?"

"Leo's friend."

"Who's Leo?"

"Leonardo DiCaprio."

"Are you serious?"

"No dumbass, just LEO! The guy I've been..."

"Oh, that's his name? Is he cute?"

"Not the time, Nic!"

"Shit, sorry. When did all of this start?"

I explain to Nicole how I met Leo at a bar, and it was never my intention to continue to see him past that one night, but for reasons that I don't have time to explain, I keep getting lured back to him. I tell her that I still love Kurt, but I've fallen in love with Leo, and that Megan also loves Leo, but Leo told her to take a hike to protect me, and now I bet she'll do whatever she can to ruin my engagement.

"I'm confused. What engagement?"

"Oi vey, Leo doesn't know I'm married. He thinks I'm engaged. Actually, he thinks I *was* engaged, but I broke off the engagement so that he'd see me again, but she doesn't know that and...Jesus, this is the first time I've said it all out loud and it all sounds ridiculous."

"No, you sound like a fucking freak. I get the slip up okay, shit happens, divorce happens. But all that other stuff is just plain crazy, girl."

"Crucify me later, Nic. Right now we need to figure out what we're gonna do."

"What *we're* gonna do?"

"Nicole! Are you seriously gonna let my marriage implode IN A BOWLING ALLY?"

"All right, all right! What do you want me to do?"

"Once we go back out there, spill all of the beers on the floor. You would've done it anyway."

"*All of them?*"

"Yeah, knock 'em all down. The bigger the mess, the better. Break shit if you have to."

She's looking at me like I've lost my ever-lovin' mind.

"Okay Einstein, and then what?"

"You preoccupy the guys with the mess, and I'll run to the bar to get napkins. I have to tell that girl to get outta here before she ruins everything for me!"

After a few minutes of strategizing, followed by some bottle breaking, I sneak over to Megan and tap her on the shoulder.

"Hi. Remember me?"

Twirling around and faking shock, Megan's beady little blue eyes glare at me like she knows she's got me by the balls.

"Of course I remember you, Chrissy. You're the one that's completely mind fucking my friend." Peering over my shoulder, she groans. "Wow, just how many guys are you dating...or marrying?"

"It's not what it looks like."

"It's exactly what it looks like. I might be young, but I'm not stupid."

Who is he?"

"My brother."

Turning to her friends, "Any of you guys ever kiss your brother when you bowl a strike?"

Fuck. I wanted this to go peacefully, but it looks like the bowling gloves are going to have to come off.

"Megan, I need you and your friends to leave. Now."

"You leave. No, even better, let's call Leo right now and tell him what's going on."

Fuck! Fuck!

"I'm pretty sure he told you never to call him again."

"Oh, I'm pretty sure he'd appreciate this call."

Fuck! Fuck! Fuck!

"Before you do something really stupid, Megan, I think you should consider what I do for a living."

It's a stretch, but I'm backed into a corner here.

"Oh, puleez!"

"From what I hear, you're quite the aspiring little fashion designer!"

"Like, what's that got to do with anything?"

"*Like*, unless you wanna use that hundred thousand dollar college education of yours to *like* sew sample garments in *like* Laos or some fucked off place like that, then I'd think long and hard about what your gonna do right now. I know people, Megan. Lots and lots of people, and I'll make the first few years of that little career of yours a freaking shit show if you don't leave, NOW!"

I dodged a huge bullet last night. I never would've had the cover to run Megan out of the bowling alley if Nicole didn't make the most obnoxious mess all over lane seven. I cancelled my therapy session tonight and invited Nicole over for wine so we could rehash the events of last night, and we laughed until we got side cramps. But before she left my house, she got serious and told me she's not comfortable carrying around my big secret, and she made me swear to tell Courtney and Kelly about it. I begged her for some time to come clean, but she said she'd only give me till next week when we meet them for lunch. As much as I dread telling my judge and jury, I need help strapping myself to the table. So before Nicole leaves, I assure her that I'll spill the beans about my affair. It'll be an ass kicking but one I deserve. I want to call Leo the second she's gone, but I can't. There's not enough time before Kurt gets home. I'm just going to have to miss him instead. And I do. I miss him all the time.

Kurt's supposed to arrive home any minute from having spent the afternoon kayaking with clients. I take a break from missing Leo to roll my eyes about that. Does *everything* have to be *so outdoorsy* all the time? I plop down on my bed and stare at a picture of him surfing. I suppose a lot of women might find Kurt's escapades sexy, but they do nothing for me. I'm almost scared of the day he finds the woman who truly appreciates him for who he is. It'll be the day he realizes he wasted the last twelve years on me. I put the picture down, walk to the window to look for his car, and sigh. I'm pre-frustrated about having to fake interest in his day in order to avoid an argument, and I'm pre-irritated that he's going to make me feel like I wasted a perfectly good night farting around with Nicole. He'll tell me I should've gone for a brisk evening walk or stained an end table or some bullshit thing like that.

I daydream for a minute about what it would be like if Leo was my husband and he was the one about to walk through the door. He'd hug me and kiss my neck before he even put his keys down. I'd have something grilling away on the BBQ and a glass of wine waiting for him and we'd compare notes about how much we missed each other during the day as we made our way to the couch. He'd lift my feet onto his lap and rub them while he re-capped his day and I'd *ohhh* and *ahhh* over his investment banker sexiness. He'd marvel at how pretty the house and I look, and he'd convince me to quit my job because, what the heck, I'm going to do it anyway once we have kids. Then his hand would travel up my thigh, underneath my skirt…

The dog barks, and it snaps me out of dreamland and into pissed-off-ville. In order for any of that stuff to happen, I have to do a lot of really confusing and unpardonable shit to Kurt and I have to admit a lot of really confusing and unpardonable crap to Leo. How can I possibly? Where will I find the courage? I mean, I literally have to destroy lives to get what I want, and I'll have to admit so many mistakes. Most days it seems easier to live like Francesca than do all of that. I don't have the answers to anything anymore. The only thing I know how to do is continue to lie until hopefully, God willing, the answers to all of my questions come to me or…my friends inject me with a huge dose of truth serum when I strap myself to the table next week.

I start to pace the house like a caged zoo animal because I'm overwhelmed with the barrage of questions that constantly fire away in my head. The what-ifs and the what-happens-nexts…they never go away and they never get answered. On the outside, I look like I'm in complete control, but really I live in a state of perpetual confusion. I decide to do the only thing I can think of to prevent myself from having a nervous breakdown. I start a journal. I must really be losing my mind because I always thought journals were for total pansies and whackos. I guess I'm both of those things now.

I start writing about the lies. Out of all the horrible things penetrating my brain, the lies are what cause me the most angst. A journal documenting all of them might help me see the error of my ways. If not that, it will definitely help me remember what I tell everybody.

There's the most recent Dallas/Chicago lie. There's the lie to Kurt about staying the night at Slutty Co-workers apartment in San Francisco when I was really hanging out with Leo. I try to keep Slutty Co-worker up to speed with all of my stories and itinerary modifications just in case she crosses paths with Kurt or Leo. But I tell so many fibs it's hard enough for me to remember where I was supposed to be half the time, let alone keep her informed. Then there are the stories I tell Dr. Maria. I have to try to keep those consistent with what I tell Kurt in case my whereabouts come up at one of their sessions. It's a grind.

As I put pen to paper I realize this journal is the one place I can be honest, something I haven't been in a very long time. At first I have difficulty getting the truth down. I write a sentence, read it, get sick to my stomach, and then pace a bit before I make my way back to the journal. After a few sentences and a few laps around the house, the flood gates of my fraudulent life are released and I can't write fast enough. Before I know it, I have fifteen pages of honesty. Shit, I guess I had enough time to call Leo after all.

I take a few minutes to re-read my reality and there's no denying it, it's gross and painfully obvious I need therapy. Real therapy, not the fake kind I've been getting. The sound of the garage door opening jolts me out of my condemnation, and I quickly stash the journal in my work bag. As I make my way down the hall to greet Kurt, it crosses my mind that by now Megan has probably told Leo what she saw last night. I'm sure she used her run-in with me as an excuse to call him, just like I used my run-in with her as an excuse to call him. I haven't had the nerve to listen to my voicemail yet. I'm sure he'll demand that I see him right away and that's not possible until *next* Thursday when Kurt goes out of town. I'm in for a shitty seven days.

SURVIVING

MAY, 1998

The day after the bowling alley shit show, I only had one message from Leo.

"We need to talk."

I knew I was in trouble, so I didn't call him back.

Nothing for three days and then, "It's total bullshit that I can never reach you."

Yep, I'm in big trouble!

Then nothing until the message I received today.

"I was mad. Now I'm worried. Call me today or I'm gonna wander the streets of Danville calling out your name. Someone will tell me where I can find you."

Time to make the call.

"Hey, it's me."

"That took long enough."

"I'm sorry, Leo. I have so much going on right now. We're getting ready to launch a new line and I've been working non-stop."

"Right, so I guess it's a good thing you were able to take a break from all the chaos at the office and bowl a few games."

Uh-oh.

"So Megan told you she saw me?"

"You knew she would. Who's the guy?"

"Hey, I thought you told her never to call you again."

"Don't change the subject. Who's the guy?"

"Kurt."

Silence.

"Leo, we're breaking things off slowly. We have lots of friends together, and we're still settling things with the house and cars and--"

"You guys own the house together?"

"Well, yeah. I assumed you knew that."

"This is fucking ridiculous, Chrissy. End it with him now."

"It's not that easy. We have history and I want this break up to be as amicable as possible."

"*Are you saying you wanna be friends with him?*"

"How can I make you understand any of this?"

You know…without telling you the truth!

"You can't, and I'm getting sick of you trying to make me."

"What are you saying?"

"I'm saying this is bullshit. For months you've gone in and out of my life. You go days without calling me and you NEVER pick up the phone when I call you. I *always* have to wait for a call back. What's up with that?"

"That's totally not true!"

It's totally true.

"Bullshit! Tell me Chrissy…*why do I always have to wait for a call back?*"

"Dammit Leo, can't you just try to put yourself in my position for one minute?"

"No."

"Then we're gonna have a problem because I can't cut Kurt out of my life, not right now."

Finally some truth.

"Honestly, I don't know what my relationship with him will look like in the future. But right now, I can't imagine not knowing him, and I hope you can live with that."

Wow, another truth. I'm on a roll.

"I won't live with that."

"So that's it then? I have to cut off all communication with him in order to have a relationship with you?"

"That's what I'm saying. Look, settle the stuff with the house but when that's over, I don't want him hanging around. He had his chance and he blew it. Why the fuck should he have the privilege of still knowing you?"

Given the lying and cheating, I hardly think anyone would consider it a privilege to know me let alone be married to me. But I cannot fathom *never* talking to Kurt ever again. Every memorable experience I've had in the last twelve years has been with that man. If he goes, will my memories have to go with him? Will over a decade of my life become taboo to talk about? Will Kurt have to be dead to me? Worse, will I have to be dead to him? My God, I can't have any of that. There has to be a way for me to have my wedding cake and eat it too.

"Leo, I love that you want me all to yourself and if I were you, I would be demanding the same thing. But I really need you to give me time to handle this my way. If I told you anything else, I'd be lying to you."

And a lot more than I already have.

"Don't talk to me about him ever again. Okay?"

"Okay."

"Don't do anything with him ever again. Okay?"

Gulp. "Okay."

"Give me your phone number, Chrissy. *The real one*, not some voicemail account."

"What are you talking about? It is real! It's my work cell phone, so I don't always answer it."

"Then give me your personal cell number."

As if things weren't complicated enough, I give him my real cell number, hang up, and then promptly turn off my phone.

If Leo and I met under honest circumstances, there would be no need for demands. I'd give him whatever he wanted, whenever he wanted it. That's what adoration gets you.

And self-deprecation is what adultery gets you. I hate myself for manipulating how much Leo cares about me by keeping the most important thing about me a secret. But there's no way he can ever know I'm married because, if he did, all of his love for me would turn to hate. The guy HATES liars, he said it himself! For that reason, I'm eventually going to have to disappear from Leo's life. The thought of that makes me sick, but not quite as sick as when I plop down on the waiting room chair across from Sad Frumpy Lady who's wearing the same damn outfit she wore two weeks ago and the week before that and the week before that.

"Come on back, Hun."

I've been looking forward to this session. Kurt's solo appointment was earlier today and I'm eager to hear how it went.

"Tell me, Chrissy, how were things with Kurt after the session we had together?"

I bet she asked him the same question and she's going to see how my answer stacks up to his.

"So-so. He took me out to a dinner that consisted mostly of food he hates and he didn't scoff when I ordered three beers. Oh, and he apologized for not coming to my defense with his family as often as he should've and that was nice. I appreciated all the effort, but to be honest with you, those things didn't make me feel good."

"How did it feel?"

"Like he was pretending to be someone he's not, just like I did for all those years. Eventually, he'll get sick of it and he'll go back to how he was before. Or, and this is doubtful, he'll continue to do things he doesn't like just to make me happy and he'll end up feeling like I do now, and that can't be good. How did he say it went when you met with him earlier today?"

"He didn't show up."

"*What are you talking about?*"

I came here today to tell Dr. Maria about wanting freedom… to get help with an exit strategy. But this news totally blows me off course. This news blows. Period.

"Not even a call to cancel. Do you think he forgot?"

Kurt just took a big crap on the life preserver I threw out to him. He just rejected my sadness. He just rejected my anger. He just flat out rejected me.

"I don't think so. We talked about it last night. Gee, something must have come up at work. I'm so sorry he didn't call to cancel."

"Chrissy, you've got to stop making excuses and apologizing for that man. He's a big boy and just like he was conscious of missing many significant events in your life, he's conscious of his decision not to come to therapy today."

The rejection that Kurt just punched me in the stomach with and Dr. Maria's claim that he's *fully* aware of this punch and the *million* before it, made me crumble on her couch. Through my jagged breaths and runny nose, I say what I should've said a long time ago.

"But…if…I…stop…making excuses…I'll have…to…admit…the truth."

"What do you think that truth is?"

"That…I…married a man…who doesn't…love me."

After a few minutes of nose blowing and mascara mopping, Dr. Maria tenderly looks at me and says, "Actually, I disagree. I believe he loves you more than anything in the whole world."

Oh, great. Is she crazy now, too?

"Then why would he reject me like this?"

"I don't think he's rejecting you; I think he's rejecting any type of self-examination that may expose his imperfections."

"But nobody's perfect. What's there to fear about learning about yourself and maybe becoming a better person?"

"I didn't get a chance to spend much time with him but my guess is that he's the type of person who's incapable of tolerating the pain that goes with self-examination."

"Why? I mean, he's such a tough guy with all of his extreme sports and what not. He basically risks his life every time he leaves the house. How can it be any more demanding for him to risk his heart?"

"Oh, it's much more demanding. The pain of a broken heart is a million times worse than a broken arm."

I should know that better than anyone.

"In Kurt's subconscious mind, the pain of self-examination far outweighs the benefit. Let's take his family for instance. He's come to believe the way his family operates, *the way he was raised*, is in good health and, if I'm to take you at your word, it was not. You even said he reprimands you for pointing out their imperfections and hurtful actions. Well, it's quite common for someone who thinks they're perfect or someone who thinks life is perfect to lash out at anyone who admonishes those beliefs. For you to be right about his family or for me to question them is too risky for him. It would break his heart and he won't allow it. He feels safe where he is."

"Can't he see how toxic they are?"

"Chrissy, your realities are so very different. Whether he realizes it or not, he probably didn't come to therapy this afternoon because he knew I would question things he thinks are perfectly fine and his instinct would be to get defensive. You've permitted him to react that way, but he knows it would be inappropriate to lash out at someone he hardly knows. Doing so would make your reasons for coming to therapy legitimate and he's afraid of that. Even if he were to surprisingly acknowledge the imperfections of his family, it would open the floodgates to all the other imperfections that may exist in his life and I just don't think he can do that."

"So he'd choose them over me?"

"He's not even aware of there being a choice, that would be indicative of an imperfect situation and he just can't go there."

"So what's someone like me supposed to do in a situation like this? *Keep on going crazy?"*

"It's probably not what you want to hear, but if you stay with him, you'll have to try to accept the relationship he has with his family. You'll also have to accept that he struggles with feeling misery in the face of tragedies like miscarriages and such. And Chrissy, you'll have to accept that he'll always choose to see the good in things, even when they might not be so good to you."

"Right...keep on going crazy."

"I can see why you'd feel that way. Feeling confused...or crazy... are normal responses to the dynamics going on in your relationship. I remember, in a prior session, you mentioned feeling confused by Kurt very early on in your relationship, and confusion can go one of two ways. You can make it go away by getting away from whatever it is that's causing it *or* it can turn into revulsion if you stay attached to it. Since you stayed with Kurt without correcting the things that caused you so much confusion, my bet is that it turned into revulsion right around the time of the miscarriage. And I *think* revulsion is what ultimately led to certain behaviors that once seemed outlandish and inappropriate to you, like cheating. I'm not saying Kurt's a bad person who deserved what he got; I'm saying nothing about your reaction to his behavior is abnormal and unhealthy."

Somewhat amused by her claim, "I'm not healthy at all. I'm a liar and a cheater."

"Actually, admitting you are those things is what makes you healthy. Hunny, facing the facts about things is always better than ignoring them. Feeling emotions, both good and bad is a healthier way to live. It allows for healthier relationships."

"Like how facing the facts about my mom changed my relationship with her?"

"Exactly. Your acceptance of her limitations is what allows you to have a satisfying relationship with her now."

"True, but I'm able to have a relationship with my mom because I don't expect anything from her. But I do expect a lot from a husband. Accepting Kurt just the way he is won't make my relationship with him better! I have needs! Look at what not getting them met did!"

"Okay then. But you have to understand that you play a key role in getting what you need. You have to stop caving into his control and his emotional neglect. You have to fight for what you want. And what you want will either be there or it won't, but the only way you'll know for sure is if you stop letting him get away with everything that makes you feel crazy and start asserting yourself. You definitely haven't been helping your cause."

"Because I cheated on him?"

"No, because you stopped fighting for your right to feel, to dream, to be happy with him! You gave up!"

"I didn't give up! I brought him to you. You were supposed to teach him how to let me be me."

"I can't force him to do anything, Chrissy. I mean look, he didn't show up today did he? I'm sorry, Hunny, but whether or not you want it, you're the one in control of this relationship, not Kurt, not me."

And what's a person who's afraid of taking control do?

"Sometimes I think it would be easier to give him an ultimatum."

"What kind of ultimatum?"

"Like, go to therapy or I'm divorcing you. But I can't really do that can I? He has no clue we're anywhere near that sort of line."

"But aren't you? You barely talk, you don't sleep together, you obviously resent the hell out of him--"

"And, yet, he's fine...life's perfect for him. *How can Kurt be so unaware of the line?*"

"It's just how he's wired."

Our marriage has been in shambles since October and yet... he's fine. Dr. Maria's right. Why on earth would he sit on this couch and listen to someone tell him everything's *not* fine? He won't. Perhaps taking the cowardly approach and giving him an ultimatum is a way out of the marriage. I won't have to be the sacrificial lamb *and* it will allow me to keep my adultery a secret. I certainly deserve the humiliation of it becoming public knowledge, but he doesn't. An ultimatum might be the only way to protect us both.

"Chrissy, this might hurt, but it's very important for you to hear if you're going to dangle divorce in his face. If you two split up, you're the one who's going to be a mess, but Kurt will appear to be okay. He'll always find a way to be fine."

"But I don't want him to be fine without me. Just for once I'd like to feel what it's like to have him miss me."

"Are you willing to *not be* fine with him, to prevent the heartache of seeing him *be* fine without you?"

"That's a horrible question."

"Answer it."

"I want the best for both of us."

"Right now, it's bad for you and seemingly good for him, right?"

"Right."

"The only way to make it good for the both of you is to assertively go after what you need from him."

"But then it might be good for me but bad for him."

"We're going in circles here, Hun. Look, you *thought* you were in this office because you committed an indiscretion with another man, but I think you're in this office because of Kurt's inability to accept any responsibility for your unhappiness AND because you haven't forced him to. And I'm sorry to say, your marriage will continue to deteriorate unless…"

"...Unless I decide to aggressively fight for what I need and I get it or I decide to accept he's incapable of giving me what I need and I leave."

"Yes, and if the latter happens, you also need to be *okay* with it. You can't accept any behavior and *not be* okay with it. You'll be back at square one with your problems and you'll still be unhappy."

Leaving her office, I think of how weird it is that Kurt's unhealthy, albeit subconscious, necessity to live in La-La land rivals my own noxious efforts over the years to make it look like we did. We are both so incredibly fucked in the head.

SCOOP

JUNE, 1998

I thought for sure I would've told Dr. Maria about seeing Leo by now and that she would've helped me figure out a way to tell Courtney and Kelly about him. But my plan to ask her for advice was derailed at my last therapy session. She actually made me feel semi-healthy and I just didn't have the heart to prove her otherwise by admitting to an ongoing affair. So I never told her, and I left her office with my little secret. Suffice it to say, I bailed on meeting my friends for lunch two weeks ago. Nicole wasn't too happy about that. She threatened that if I didn't meet them this Saturday, *she* would tell them about Leo, and she would be sure to suck all of the romance out of the relationship and make me look like a herpes-infected slut. She won.

"I thought we were meeting at Faz. What's up with this place?"

"I thought it would be fun to meet here for a quick drink. Is that all right, Kel?"

"What's fun about this place? Look, it's filled with a bunch of twelve year olds."

"They're in college Kelly. Geez, can't you just try and have some fun?"

"College people, huh? Is this where you met Leo?"

"Thanks Nicole, way to let me handle this on my own."

Nicole shrugs her shoulders and says, "It needed to be done, my love."

"What needed to be done? Who's Leo?"

"Well Courtney…our little Chrissy here has got herself a boyfriend."

"OKAY, NICOLE, ENOUGH!"

Kelly looks like she just got hit by a truck and the ever-so-calm Courtney asks me if Nicole's joking.

"Sadly, no. It's true, and sadly yes, this is where I met him."

An hour and several awful drinks later, I finish telling them everything about Leo. With my hands flailing all about, I yell at the three of them.

"For fuck's sake, would one of you say SOMETHING?" Then, in unison they blurt out:

"Tell me you have a good therapist."

"It's over, right?"

"Is the sex good? I'm dying to hear about the sex!"

"Yes, Court, I have a good therapist, and yes, Kelly, it's over. Nicole…you're a bigger pig than I thought you were."

I desperately want to tell them the truth: that I'm still seeing Leo, because I need their help strapping myself to the table. I need one of my friends to inject me with some truth serum! But after seeing the look of total disgust on Kelly's face, I changed my mind. She can't handle this.

"The sex, Chrissy! Spill it!"

I'm not sure what stunned me more, Nicole's question or the punch in the arm Kelly gave her for asking it.

"Jesus Nicole, let's not disrespect her marriage any more than it already has been. Chrissy screwed up and she's undoubtedly remorseful. Don't make her rehash the raunchy details of her mistake."

"Actually, I'm not as remorseful as you might think, Kelly."

If looks could kill, hers would. It's the very reason I didn't tell any of them about Leo months ago. Their opinion of me matters more than anything in the world.

"Of course I feel like a failure for not being true to Kurt. He doesn't deserve what I've done. But if I didn't meet Leo that night, I might've been stuck in a really bad place for a really long time. Worse, I probably would've brought kids into the picture. And, for the record, Kelly…nothing about my time spent with Leo could be classified as raunchy. Yeah, I'm beating myself up for so many things, but not so much for my time spent with him. I dunno guys, I feel like he was the jump start on life I needed."

"Jesus, how would you feel if Kurt did this to you?"

"That's a funny question, Kel. Okay, it's not as funny as it is sad really. Kurt *never* would've cheated on me because for the last twelve years I told him every single day how much I loved him and that I'd be lost without him. He got the love that kept him from doing what I did."

"And you didn't?"

"No. I was lost all along and didn't even know it."

None of them look moved by what I'm telling them. Time for some convincing.

"The bottom line is Kurt's had security in knowing how appreciated he was in our relationship. But me, I've been like a dog begging for attention, and I even pretended to be someone I'm not to get it. Everything about the last twelve years has been a lie, I don't even recognize who I am anymore. For God's sake, haven't any of you noticed how much I changed after high school?"

"We just thought you grew up."

"Yeah, we thought you were happy."

"Nope, I was a fraud."

I totally appreciate Nicole and Courtney's concerned nods. Kelly though, she looks like she needs more convincing that I haven't lost my mind.

"Geez, Kelly, you gotta give me a break. I didn't do this because I'm a whore. You have no idea what it's like to be married to someone who never makes you feel good enough, won't talk to you about the things that are important to you…makes you feel lazy."

"Kurt's a good guy, though. He didn't do all of that stuff intentionally."

"I know that. That's what makes what I did so awful. But I didn't plan for it to happen…it just happened."

"So you had *no* clue you wanted another man until the very moment this Leo person sat down next to you?"

"Not a clue, Kel. I know it sounds crazy, but it's true. Look, I wanted what you guys had, and I created such a false sense of reality that I fooled everyone for the longest time, even me. But reality caught up to me and I'm trying to do the right thing now, whatever the right thing is."

We finally make our way over to the restaurant, and during dinner I tell them everything I told Dr. Maria a few sessions ago. I tell them about Kurt's control over my free time, my food choices, my wardrobe, and the tremendous amount of guilt he lays on me when I try to have a say about any of it. I also tell them that he bailed on therapy. They reacted exactly how I thought they would. Nicole believed my every word and while sad for my pain, she told me she was excited for what my future may hold. It was cop-out encouragement. Courtney told me that every marriage has peaks and valleys and that she'll pray for Kurt and me to get through our troubles as better, more loving people. Whatever the hell that means. And as expected, Kelly said nothing. She grabbed the check to divide it by four and went on and on about getting home before her kid went to sleep. At first I was mad, but she was right to say nothing. What can you say about something you don't understand? One thing's for certain though, none of these chicks are going to strap me to a table and inject me with truth serum anytime soon. What's going on with me is so much bigger than their ho-hum lives, and they're going to make sure their hands stay clean of my mess to keep them as ho-hum as possible. Like I said before, buncha pansies.

"Wait, Kel, I have one more thing to say before you leave. In a lot of ways, I know I'm messing up your lives, too. The four of us plus our husbands have shared a lot together. I'm upsetting the balance and I so badly want to apologize for that, but I have to stop taking responsibility for other people's happiness and concentrate on my own. We were close before our husbands came along and we will be when they're gone."

In true Nicole style she adds, "Statistics say that one out of every four marriages ends up in divorce, so I guess we should be thanking Chrissy. It looks like the rest of our marriages are safe!"

Laughing for the first time in a long time, I tell them I'm glad I could help out. Then I add, "You know I heard the same statistic about cancer."

STONED

JUNE, 1998

Thank God for my journal writing. That book has become my at-a-glance life-saver at least ten times in the last week alone. Yesterday, just as I was wrapping up a meeting with Slutty Co-worker, Kurt pulled into the parking lot to surprise me with Taco Bell. I guess to him nothing says "I love you" and "I'm trying" better than a chalupa. Anyway, just as Slutty Co-worker was scrambling to run away, I said, "No worries!" and handed her the last two pages of my journal. In a jiffy she was up to date with my fraudulent life and she was able to have a stress-free conversation with Kurt. Everything was moving along quite nicely until she started flirting with him and then I had to ask her to leave. So yes, thank God for my journal. Not only is it a place to write about and reflect on the horrible things I've done, it's also makes it easier for me to get away with my deviant behavior until I figure out how to stop it.

Despite Kurt's valiant effort to supply me with a diet that consists mostly of disgustingly yummy things like high fructose corn syrup, MSG, and salt, things have become tenser than ever at home. We got into it pretty good when I grilled him about not showing up to his therapy session. His reason for not showing up was...drum roll please...he doesn't think he's the one with the problem. That's it, case closed, have some French fries and figure it out on your own, Chrissy. Then he was off to climb Mt. Everest or something. Dr. Maria was 100% right when she said everything will always being fine for Kurt. It's been about three weeks since that argument and I think three weeks since we've spoken a word to each other.

Regardless of Kurt's nonattendance, *my* therapy sessions having been moving along quite nicely. There hasn't been any mention of saving my marriage or of Kurt's happy-go-lucky attitude. I decided to leave it all behind and focus on why it matters so much to me what people think. Dr. Maria thinks it stems from trying to please Kurt so much when I was a teenager and that eventually it became second nature to me to bend over backwards for everyone. But Kurt and I don't share relationships with my professional contacts, and so work is the only place where I'm authentic Chrissy and it's no wonder I'm happiest when I'm there. No one at work knows the people in my private life, and no one in my private life knows my people at work. If they were to ever cross paths, there would be total confusion in both camps. My work people would be flabbergasted to see me act like a pushover and my personal relationships would be shocked to see me act like an unwavering leader. My work life is my last salvation.

Focusing on just me in therapy has been an eye-opening luxury and with every session I move farther away from feeling like a bad person and closer to feeling like a good person who makes bad choices. Some days, I even feel normal. Well, as normal as a married woman who's contemplating divorce and a break up with her twenty-two year old boyfriend can be, I guess. As crazy as it seems, in spite of my imminent break up with Leo, our relationship has gone to the next level. He started referring to me as his girlfriend, and we even say "I love you" whenever we get off the phone. He worries about my safety when I travel to New York, and I worry about how much money he has in his wallet. He fills up my gas tank when it's down to a quarter of a tank, and I buy him groceries when his fridge is empty. He leaves me affectionate voicemail messages in the middle of the night, and I always call him to tell him I got home safely after leaving his apartment. Aside from the insanity of it, it's all very sane and natural.

The things I fear losing without Leo in my life are very different than the things I fear losing without Kurt. They break my heart in polar-opposite ways. One loss causes my heart to break for what it's never going to have the opportunity to fully experience and the other for what it's giving up on. The reality is, Leo and I are a couple, and I feel like I need just as much therapy dealing with the loss of him as I do with the loss of Kurt.

One thing's for sure, both losses are imminent. But until the one with Leo happens, I do whatever I can to be with him. And I mean WHATEVER. Ready for this…lately I've been sneaking out of the house after Kurt falls asleep so I can meet up with him. I know, I know, it's repulsive! Trust me, if I stopped long enough to think about how fucking disgusting I am, I'd want to kill myself. But I'm having too much fun to die, so I try not to think about it. I go a million miles an hour in a million different directions to keep my latest shenanigan from entering my mind. The only time the disgust creeps in is when I'm doing the actual sneaking out of the house, but by the time I make it to my car, the drug has taken over my body and has effectively kicked disgust's ass. I can't win! I call the sneaking out my "fake freedom," like the kind you get when you escape from prison. I'm out there and I'm doing what I *want* to be doing, but I'm constantly looking over my shoulder expecting to get caught at any moment. It's one more reason why the pounds are shedding off of my body. But sneaking out makes me feel drunk on life and love and I doubt I'll ever be able to stop. Every rendezvous with Leo renews my spirit and makes me feel like I'm the woman I was meant to be. No, not a slut…a free spirited, sexy girl with a boyfriend who adores the hell out of her! Nonetheless, by the time I return home, the drug has worn off and my superwoman powers disintegrate. All that's left is a love-struck adulteress.

Once home, I quietly crawl into bed and stare at Kurt through my tears as I agonize about the unimaginable things that will happen to my soul if I let Leo go, and I hurt all over thinking about losing Kurt as my friend. And then I cry myself to sleep contemplating the only three possible outcomes to the nightmare I've created.

1) If I chicken-shit out of my quest for freedom and stay married to Kurt, *obviously* I have to completely break things off with Leo. Breaking up with Leo is a gut-wrenching option and it'll have to be done cold turkey. It'll be excruciating, like quitting smoking or crack. It can't be slow and drawn out.
2) If I decide to get a divorce, so that I can be with Leo, I *still* have to tell him the truth about having been married. I can't cover it up forever. Hiding my marriage from Leo is unforgivable and he'll react accordingly. For so many reasons this option is worse than the first one because he'll resent me for manipulating him and end up dumping me.
3) Divorce Kurt *and* break up with Leo. The most sensible of the three options. I'm still waiting for the courage to pull this one off.

No matter which way I look at it, my time with Leo is fleeting. Given my appalling behavior over the last six months, you might find it hard to sympathize with me, but you have to admit, it's a little tragic. Oh, to hell with what you think. For now, I'm trying my best to block out everybody's opinion so I can enjoy every minute of my transitory time with him. Obviously this is the stuff I should be talking about in therapy, but instead, I'm still lying to Dr. Maria about having semi-normal nights of dinner, television, and bedtime with my husband. But in reality I've made a habit out of sliding out of bed shortly after Kurt falls asleep and tonight I do the same thing.

Just like all the other times, I sneak out to a car pre-packed with all of the essentials: cute outfit, makeup, bottle of wine. I open the garage door and wait a minute to see if Kurt wakes up. I pull out of the garage and sit idly in the driveway for a few more minutes to see if he rushes out to see where I'm going. I drive to the nearest intersection and pull over to see if he's following me. Every time the coast is clear. Every time I feel a wave of guilt as I imagine him sleeping soundly in our bed, the bed he still keeps trying to convince me to have sex in. Like a drug addict who knows she's hurting herself and everyone who loves her, I don't care. I have to have my drug.

Tonight Leo has some old high school buddies over and excluding Ho-Bag, it's going to be my first time meeting any of his friends. My reason for showing up late tonight is that I've been out with work associates. It's my usual excuse and Leo never questions it. He operates like that's just how twenty-eight year old women are supposed to run around, in their garter belts and matching bra and panty sets showing up in the middle of the night after long business dinners.

As usual, my heart's pounding as I park my car. I change my clothes in the front seat. As I clasp a choker around my neck, I peer into the window of Leo's place, and I can see him and a few other guys standing around drinking beer. It looks like his friends are teasing him about something, probably me. I'm sure they've been giving him a shit-load of crap for dating a woman who's six years older than he is, but he says it's quite the opposite. He says they're jealous. One guy punches Leo in his massive arm and he smiles, shakes his head, and runs his fingers through his beautiful hair. I can tell he's as excited for me to walk through the door as I am.

After one last look at myself in the side view mirror, I pick my thong underwear out of my butt crack and make my way to the door. Deep breath. Here goes nothing. I knock. It instantly gets quiet inside. As he opens the door, Leo tells someone to go fuck himself. Boy talk is so hot. He looks blue collar handsome. Frayed cargo shorts, an old white tee-shirt, and flip flops. Before he lets me in, he places his hands on my waist and kisses me sweetly on the lips. He whispers, "Hey, Baby."

He's never called me *Baby* before. I like it. I like it *a lot*. I like it so much that I wish like hell his friends weren't here.

"You ready to meet these bastards?"

"Of course."

There's the best friend, Taddeo, who's a newbie investment banker with Goldman Sachs in New York. He's got more money than he knows what do with, and he flew home this weekend just to meet me. Leo and Taddeo have been friends since they were two years old, and they're closer than two brothers can be. He's a nice looking Italian boy who's legitimately sizing me up, and I wish I had a friend to set him up with. *How fun would that be?* There's his buddy, James, who's also a newbie investment banker but with Robertson Stephens in San Francisco. He's acting way too excited to meet me, and I want to tell him to calm down, that I'm not here to strip. Then there's the Korean behind-the-ear-cigarette-wearing-rock-yard-worker-roommate whose name I just found out is Billy Ho, a.k.a The Ho-Bag.

After the handshakes and nice-to-meet-you's are over, I hold up a bottle of red and tell Leo I'll be in the kitchen for a minute. I want to give them time alone to react. As I turn to ask where the bottle opener is, I catch James back handing Leo on the head and mouth *"Are you fucking kidding me?"*

Exactly the reaction I was hoping for! So far, so good…and it looks like it's about to get even better. As I open the drawer to find the corkscrew, my eyes zoom in on the mother lode that's taped to the side of his refrigerator. There they are! The four little numbers that will either confirm Leo's commitment to me or negate it and they're as precious to me as the pass code to access the Hope Diamond. I'm staring at Leo's voicemail access code. Just punch in #8855 when he doesn't answer his phone and I'm in. I'll be able to hear what his friends are saying about me and more importantly, I'll be able to find out if he's seeing other girls behind my back. I've wanted to believe Leo's assurances that he's not a player, that he's madly in love with me, that he's different from every other twenty-two year old guy out there, and now I have a way to find out for sure. Is it seedy? Yes. Is it an invasion of privacy? Yes. Is hacking into his voicemail any worse than lying to him about being engaged, becoming unengaged, actually being married, and living with my husband in a town twenty minutes away? Nope, and that's why I'm going to dial into it the first chance I get.

If Leo's voicemail messages prove that he's been misleading me, I'll *have to* end it with him, and in a sense, that makes my life a lot easier. Painful…but definitely easier. I tuck the code numbers into the back of my brain as Leo fills my glass and then kisses me. I close my eyes and get a little dizzy as the drug seeps into my skin.

Green Day is blaring on the stereo and the guys are pounding beers and laughing about the last fight Ho-Bag got into. It's a surreal moment. Everything I'm experiencing is so natural, like it's the life I *should've* been living all along. It beats the hell out of well-balanced dinners, the Discovery Channel, and bed by midnight so I'm fresh for my morning hike. I shiver at the thought of that life, the life I technically still live.

"Cold?"

"No, I'm good."

Leo grabs my legs and tosses them over his lap. It's his way of saying "back off guys, she's all mine."

I reciprocate by rubbing the back of his neck. I don't know what I love more, the power of seduction or making his friends uncomfortable.

The five of us continue to drink and talk and laugh for hours. There are no super big questions about my life, mostly just questions about the night Leo and I met, which continually get interrupted by Ho-Bag's eye rolls. We talk about where I went to college and what my job is like. I tell Taddeo that I'm in New York quite a bit for work and that I'll call him for drinks next time I'm in town. Leo says "Not a chance unless I'm there with you," so I suggest that Leo should come with me next time. Taddeo just nods like he ain't buying what I'm selling. I can't tell if he thinks I'm full of shit or if he's overly protective of Leo. Either way, he's right not to give me the benefit of the doubt. The guys finally leave around 2am. It leaves Leo and me with a few hours alone together before I have to go. Like a vampire, I have to be home before the sun comes up.

"Did I do okay?"

"Baby, you did great. Besides, I already told you, I don't give a shit what anyone thinks about you. Whoever doesn't like you can go to Hell."

"I'm loving this whole 'Baby' thing."

"Good, because that's what I'm gonna call you for the rest of your life. Now get over here…Baby."

He pulls my waist toward him and together we fall to the couch where we kiss like two of the most affection-deprived people on the planet. I swear, if we could take bites out of each other, we would. Like it's vital, he rips the choker off of my neck and the pants off of my legs. I pull him into me, and no matter how out of breath I get while we make love, he won't let my mouth leave his. After a few hours and several failed attempts to get me to spend whatever's left of the night he reluctantly walks me to my car. It's getting harder and harder to come up with excuses why I can't sleep over, and once again I'm reminded of our fleeting time together. My three options are looming over me like a big, crappy cloud. Unless, of course, his voicemail reveals another cloud that might just make the choice for me.

"Come on, just stay with me."

"I can't. I'm leaving for Chicago in about five hours, and I still have to pack."

"So get a few hours of sleep here and then go home to pack."

Think damn it! Think!

"I can't, I have to let the dog out."

"You have a dog?"

"Uh yeah, I kind of share custody of the dog with *him*."

"Jesus. Just let him have the dog."

"No way! I love my dog."

"Then tell Numb Nuts that you want the dog."

"*Numb Nuts?* Is that the name we're calling him now?"

He's not having any of my witty questioning.

"I guess that means you see him when you exchange the dog."

"Um, yeah."

"What the Hell, Chrissy? My parents are divorced after twenty years and three kids and *they* don't even talk. What's going on?"

"I'm falling in love with you, that's what's going on. Can't that be enough for right now?"

"Not when he's in the picture."

"I'm sorry Leo, but I need more time to sort through my stuff with Kurt."

"DAMN IT, I don't want to hear his name! I swear to God I'll punch the fucking car window out if you say it one more time!"

He's mad. I mean *really, really* mad. So I do the only thing I know that will calm him down. I wrap my hands around his neck, pull him to my lips, and kiss him until he calms down.

"I'm running out of patience with all of this, Chrissy."

Even in the off chance that Leo decided to be cool with the fact that I'm married, it takes *at least* eight months to get a divorce in California. We'd never make it with his short fuse.

"I know, I'm sorry about my big mess. Really, I am. Look, I'm back from Chicago in a few days. Do you wanna get together next weekend?"

"I won't be here."

"Where are you going?"

"I leave on Friday to go work for my Dad in Monterey. I can make more money working with him than I can at the rock yard, so I'll be there until school starts in September."

"Why didn't you tell me?"

"I tried to call you, but you never picked up and I'm tired of leaving you messages."

Be cool, Chrissy. He has a point, plus a little time and distance to listen to his voicemail and decide on one of those options will do you good.

"I guess I'll see you in Monterey."

So much for time and distance. Damn the drug!

SILENT

JUNE, 1998

I can't believe it's almost July, a month of reprehensible celebrations. In just a few weeks, it'll be six months since I met Leo and three years since I married Kurt. All of it sickens me. Slutty Co-worker told me to look on the bright side though; I'll be getting two presents instead of one. But since I'm just a misguided girl and truly not a whore at heart, I refuse to get excited about that.

Kurt decided to give me my anniversary gift early because he said I needed time to plan. Just hearing that made me exhausted. Ever since our argument about him bailing on therapy, we hardly speak, and I silently hoped he forgot about the anniversary altogether. Wishful thinking. He made reservations at a Bed & Breakfast in Napa! Hell yeah, I need time to plan! I have to plan how the hell I'm NOT going to sleep with him, because I know that's what this little trip is all about!

But hold on a second, I'd like to take a moment to interrupt the topic of sex and comment on the whole B&B thing. Kurt knows I hate them. Any place without a TV is *not* relaxing and should *not* be called a vacation. And on top of missing my shows, I'm going to have to sit at a breakfast table full of carbs and make small talk with a bunch of needy losers who, on a normal day, would be the target of my overly judgmental criticisms. I mean, who are these people who feel the need to pay for meaningless breakfast conversation? Like, do they expect to learn something of great importance from the stranger sitting across the table wearing pajamas who most likely hasn't brushed his teeth yet? I can barely tolerate myself in the morning, and yet Kurt thinks sending me to a B&B to nosh with total strangers is going to be some kind of cathartic experience. A cathartic experience would be a legal separation. But of course, I didn't tell him that. How could I? He looked so excited about the gift, as he waved a winery bike tour map in my face. All I could say was "Thanks, looks fun!" Then I ran into the bathroom and cried.

Okay, back to the sex. Kurt hasn't pestered me once about it since I started therapy, but I can tell he's getting to the end of his rope. It's literally been seven months since we've been together, and in guy time that's gotta be like ten years. At first he bothered me about sex ALL THE TIME. But now, he's too afraid that I'll throw the topic of therapy at him if he touches me, so he stays away. But I have a hunch that he thinks getting me plastered in Napa will make me forget about "my problems" and I'll put out. Well that ain't gonna happen. It can't happen!

Leo left for Monterey a little over a week ago and before he went, he gave me the key to his apartment so I could bring his mail inside and as he said, still be a part of him. It was a huge gesture and one that *should've* convinced me that I'm the only girl in his life. But it didn't. The first thing I did when I was alone in his apartment was snoop through his drawers, and whenever the phone rang, I let it go to voicemail and then immediately called in to listen to the message. Like a handschuhschneeballwerfer, I'm still looking for unintentional reasons, like girls calling, to break things off with him. But so far every message has been from a friend or a family member. Damn his nice gestures and good intentions!

Leo's apartment is quiet, uncluttered, and cut off from everything that gets in my way of thinking. It makes my head hurt. The first few days, after I finished ransacking the place looking for evidence of some kind of unfaithfulness, I bolted as fast as I could because the silence was painful. For months, I've been running as fast as I can to escape choices, responsibility, blame, and pain and my Leo drug made it easy to do that. When he was constantly at my disposal, there was never any silence in my head. I was either with him or plotting and scheming to find a way to be with him. But now that he's hours away and working ten hours a day, there's hardly any contact, and there's too much silence. As I was jotting those thoughts down in my journal the other day, I decided to take a moment to read over earlier entries. What an eye opener. I thought my secret journal was going to be my place to find answers, you know…get some fucking clarity on my life. But the only thing it's been good for is tracking lies. Flipping through the pages, it became evident that the last six months have been nothing more than a non-stop blur of semi-fake therapy, pretend marriage and compulsive cheating. The only thing my damn journal's been good at is helping me keep up with all of it. I filled up every free minute of my life with something so that I didn't have to think about anything. Just as I was about to rip out all of the incriminating pages and burn them, a teeny tiny light bulb went on in my teeny tiny brain. Duh…I don't need a journal for clarity, I need silence!

So yesterday, I forced myself to be alone in Leo's apartment for some much needed silence. I snuck out of work early, curled up in his bed, and waited for silence to sort out my problems. I lasted about five minutes before the pain kicked in. I quickly hopped up and looked for something to take my mind off of the mess I've created. I tried on his gigantic shirts, smelled his cologne, and drank something purple from his refrigerator. Then I paced around his bed like I didn't trust it before I crawled back in to give silence another try. I only lasted five minutes again. The second I started thinking about telling Kurt I want a separation or telling Leo I can't see him anymore, I'd spring out of bed and make my laps. I put myself through two hours of torture and packed on a massive headache from all the cologne-sniffing before I finally acknowledged to myself that there's no better time like the present to tell Dr. Maria about Leo. Slutty Co-worker is only enabling my addiction, my best friends want to stay as far away from it as possible, and obviously I'm incapable of curing myself. Time to call in the big guns. On my way out of Leo's apartment, I called Dr. Maria and asked to see her right away. I had something huge to get off my chest.

It would've been better if I could've gone straight from Leo's apartment to Dr. Maria's office but she was booked solid. I had to wait an entire twenty-two hours to get a spot on her couch. Almost enough time to wimp out of asking her for help. I shake my head in disgust the entire drive to her office, and the closer I get, the more I decide to minimize my fanatical involvement with Leo. If she knew everything, she'd freak. I pass the apartment complex that I dropped Leo off in front of that fateful January night. I shiver as I remember the exact moment I crossed the line of inappropriate marital behavior, the moment my life got side-tracked. It was when I took off my wedding ring.

JANUARY 24, 1998

"Well, it's been fun talking to you, but I have to run to the bathroom. I guess I'll see ya around."

About ten minutes after I started talking to Leo, I sensibly decided to make my bladder the fun referee. I decided that when it got uncomfortably full, my fun had to end because I feared our conversation could go on all night. Thirty minutes after meeting him, as the buttons on my jeans are about to burst, I concede that it's time to say good-bye and go back to real life.

"Aren't you coming back?"

I hadn't counted on that.

"Do you *want* me to come back?"

"What do you think?"

I guess a few more minutes with him can't hurt.

"Will you keep an eye on my drink then? There's crazies out there who will do sick things to a girl's drink."

"How do you know I'm not one of them?"

"Good point. I'll ask my friend. Where do you think she and that Ho-Bag dude ran off to?"

"I'm only kidding. Your drink will be safe with me."

"Yeah right, I know you want to slip me a drug and do unspeakable things to me."

Good Lord, *who am I right now?* I slam what's left of my martini and strut my way to the bathroom, hoping to God he's staring at me the entire time *and* thanking God I wore my cute butt jeans. Once inside, I lock the door, turn around, put my hands on the wet vanity, and ask myself, what the hell do you think you're doing?

No answer.

No, really Chrissy, this is nuts. What the fuck are you doing?

I don't know, but it's fun.

No, it's wrong. Leave now! If you go now, you can chalk this up to innocent flirting and go back to your perfect little life. No, no, stop looking at your wedding ring. You love what that ring represents! Taking it off means you're hiding your outward symbol of your inward love, and why would you do that?

Okay, you're doing that. Shit, why are you putting it in your pocket?

I just want to see where this goes.

Where what goes?

I want to talk to him a while longer.

But the bar's closing soon. Where do you plan on continuing your little conversation?

In my car, I guess.

Oh, that's disgraceful!

Okay, wait a Goddamn minute; am I literally having an argument with myself?

Yes, you are and I think you lost…or won…or maybe it's a tie, you big fat whore.

After a quick pee, a lipgloss refresher and a spritz of perfume, I bounce back to my barstool, leaving responsible Chrissy behind.

"Hey, I'm back. Any luck locating my friend?"

"Yeah, I saw her and Ho-Bag leave about five minutes ago. It sucks, too because he was my ride."

"Funny, I was hers."

If there was ever an awkward pause, this was it.

"So Leo, if I offer to take you to wherever your car is, you're not gonna kill me or anything are you?"

"I was gonna ask you the same thing."

Then, like a bodyguard, he grabs hold of my hand and leads me out of the crowded bar.

I wonder how far he thinks things are going to go. More than that, I wonder how far I'm going to let things go. I feel intermittent twinges of guilt that almost prompt me to run but they're immediately overridden by blows of excitement that compel me to stay. And I do. Right there in the Buckley's parking lot, all cozy in my car, we talk about all the taboo things people typically don't discuss when they first meet. Stuff like how many kids we want, our political party affiliation, religion, places we want to visit, people we hate…the list goes on and on. It's like we can't get enough of each other's mind. It scares me to think of what we're capable of doing to each other's body.

"Wow, this is a match made in Heaven, Leo. I don't think there are many people outside of this car we can admit this stuff to!"

"It's a match as long as you don't have any tattoos."

"Come on! Do I look like a girl who would get a tramp stamp? Please tell me you don't have one either."

"Hell no. A few of my brothers have them, they're all a result of some drunken night. They're like old girlfriend's names or frat symbols or something disturbing like that. They wear them like they're some kind of badge of honor. I can't wait to see how those things look twenty years from now."

"Do you see your brothers often?"

"I saw them a few weeks ago on Christmas. Man, I hate the holidays."

"C'mon, who doesn't love Christmas?"

"You're looking at him."

"Wow, the first thing we disagree on. But you know what? I bet you'd like Christmas with me."

Why did I just say that? I can't celebrate tomorrow with him let alone next Christmas.

"Holidays with my family used to be somewhat tolerable because my Grandpa was such an awesome guy to be around. But since he died, I come up with every excuse possible to avoid them. My family drives me crazy."

As refreshing as it is to hear Leo acknowledge the one thing I've wanted my husband to acknowledge for over a decade, and as much as I want him to tell me more, I can't help but notice the sky going from black to a blurry shade of yellow.

"Did we actually talk all night long?"

"Went fast, didn't it?"

"I guess I should take you to your car, huh?"

"Oh yeah…right, it's at my buddy's apartment."

I'm never going to see this guy again, and it doesn't seem fair after the night we shared together. I wish his car was fifty miles away, but it's not. It's more like two. After exchanging a few awkward sentences, spoken only to mask the fact that neither one of us wants the night to come to an end, he asks the very question I hoped he wouldn't.

"Can I have your phone number?"

I wish. But absolutely not! This charade ends now.

"Sorry, it's a rule of mine to never give out my number. It's a control thing."

I thought it was a corny excuse, but he thinks it's adorable and totally responsible. I can do no wrong with this guy!

"Do you have a pen?"

I give him one, and he hands me a piece of paper and says "Here's mine. I really hope you call me."

I can't.

His door is now open; one leg is hanging out on the street while the rest of his body is lingering in the car. He's stalling.

"I had a really good time tonight, Leo. You're an amazing guy."

And then out of nowhere I turn into Heather Locklear. No, Tawny Kitaen! No wait…I'm one of those smokin' hot chicks on a Budweiser poster who's licking the side of a dripping wet beer bottle! Whoever the hell I am, I'm NOT Chrissy Anderson. She would never have the guts to look deep into a beautiful stranger's eyes and say, "Do you want to kiss me?"

Before I can get a hold of myself and take back the insane question, he extends his arm behind my head and dives in.

Our full on make out extravaganza lasts forever and while it's happening, I forget who I am. All disgust of my behavior is shoved aside. I'm floored by the domination I possess as I grab his hair and force his lips onto my neck and ear and then back to my lips. I put his hand on my breast that he would have left alone without an invitation, and I'm blown away with my bravery as I toy with his belt buckle. If we weren't interrupted by the people getting into their cars to go to work or church or wherever they had to be early on a Sunday morning, I'm not really sure how far I would've let things go.

"So Chrissy, do you want to drive to Vegas right now and make this official? I have all the proof I need that we're a match."

If I wasn't already married, I probably would.

"You're joking, right?"

"No, actually I'm not."

"Obviously at the moment, I'm in no state of mind to be making major life decisions."

Or for that matter, bear in mind the ones I've made prior to this whole fiasco.

The sun is now totally up, and I suddenly realize that after a night of steady drinking, overlooking the importance of hourly lipstick maintenance and getting pounced on in the front seat of my car, I must look like a total hag. I promptly put my sunglasses on and feel an overwhelming urge to hide from the world.

"So…okay then, I guess I'll be going now."

"But you'll call, right?"

"I…things are…life's just kinda crazy and…"

Wait, if I totally blow him off, he might think I do this all the time AND I DON'T! Plus, *I don't want to blow him off*! He's so wonderful, and I wish so badly I could see him again. But dammit, I can't! Get him out of the car now, Chrissy!

"Look, I'm not really sure what's going on here, and it's completely taken me by surprise. I think right now I need to go home, get some sleep and have some really good dreams about what just happened. After that, I can start thinking about a phone call."

God, did that even make any sense?

"You have to call me because we still have to get to the bottom of why we met."

"What do you mean?"

"Well, was it pure luck or was it divine intervention instigated by some really bored, dead grandfathers?"

"I'm gonna go with pure luck because I don't believe in God."

"That's priceless!"

"*What?* Why are you laughing?"

"Explain how you can believe in ghosts *but not* believe in God."

"Well now, that would take us into tomorrow."

"I'm cool with that. There's a coffee shop around the corner, how about we start our conversation there."

"You're sweet, Leo, you know that?"

He's chuckling. "I don't think many people would call me that and I bet you didn't think I was very sweet when you sat next to me tonight."

"You mean *last night*! And yeah, you were quite the bastard!"

"Now that's a name I'm used to being called!"

"Are you implying I know a side of you that no one else knows?"

Looking fiercely into my sunglasses, "Without a doubt."

I'm struck by the curiosity of his claim that after spending roughly eight hours with him, I could know him better than anyone else, and then I'm struck even harder when I realize I could probably say the same thing about him. Holy shit, I just met my soul mate! I just met my twenty-two year old, college attending, rock yard working soul mate!

I snap back to the present and a warm feeling, *my drug*, slithers through my body and settles in my belly. He's in me. He's so deep inside of me and no amount of time, distance, therapy or alcohol will ever rid my body of him. I can't possibly stay with Kurt with these feelings. I pull into the parking space where Leo and I shared our first kiss and I close my eyes and replay the events of that night until my mind and body can't take it anymore. By the time my eyes reopen, I reclaim the courage to tell Dr. Maria *everything*. She has to help me figure out a way to be alone because I can't be with Kurt the rest of my life with a belly full of Leo.

KABOOM!

JUNE, 1998

When I get to Dr. Maria's office, the lobby is empty. Sad Frumpy Lady isn't sitting in her usual spot, and surprisingly, I'm a little worried about her. She doesn't look like she's in any shape to miss a therapy session. I want to ask Dr. Maria if she's alright, but that would be kind of weird, and she's going to think I'm weird enough when I tell her about my mischief with Leo.

"Well, you seem awfully happy today, Chrissy."

"Yeah, I guess I am."

"Things going well at home?"

Here we go.

"Actually no, but things *are* going well with Leo."

"I don't understand."

"Me neither. First, I want to tell you that I'm very sorry I kept this from you but I was scared you'd be mad."

"It's not my place to be mad or judge you, but I am concerned that you might have taken the therapy you received here and mistakenly applied it to a life you weren't being honest about living. You're most likely making things much more complicated, and might I say…expensive for yourself."

"I know I've wasted a lot of money in here. But just so you know, I'm not delusional about the double life I have going on, *and*

I realize I've been asking for advice on how to save a marriage I've been sabotaging."

"You've been doing much more than that; you're most likely making Kurt a little crazy."

"Whoaaaaaaaaaa, I don't think Kurt has any clue about what's going on, and trust me, I'm not bragging about that, but as you very well know, the guy is *way* too self-involved to notice I'm having an affair."

"He might not say anything to you, Chrissy, but deep down he knows; you're his wife. Internally he's probably struggling with what he thinks is going on and what he doesn't believe could ever happen."

I didn't think I could possibly feel any worse than I did before I came in here. But I do.

"Think about it. I'm sure you exercise more; that's a sign. I'm sure you have way more late nights at the office; that's a sign. I'm sure you pay more attention to your wardrobe, accessories, perfume…these are all signs. But I bet the biggest sign of all is how you'll do everything you possibly can to avoid having sex with him. Any of this stuff sound accurate?"

"So now I know why you cost so much; you know what the hell you're talking about."

"I do. For Pete's sake, tell me what's really going on with Leo so we can actually make some progress here."

I rehash all the dirty details of my time spent with Leo. I even tell her about sneaking out in the middle of the night. I tell her about coming clean to Courtney, Nicole, and Kelly, and since doing that I've virtually cut off all communication with them because deep down I know they want me to stay married and it bugs me. I tell her about my three options and that my heart is breaking because I know it's only a matter of time until I have to choose one.

"I think that about covers it. So, what should I do?"

"What do you want to do?"

Why did I know she was going to ask that?

"For starters, I want to go back in time and choose a different bar to have a drink at that night."

"Not possible."

No shit.

"I want Kurt to be Leo but still be Kurt."

"Can't happen."

Bitch.

"I don't want to hurt Leo."

"If your only options are to disappear or tell him you're married, you'll hurt him. But eventually he'll be fine."

That hurts.

"I don't want to hurt Kurt."

"You will if you decide to leave him or if he finds out you cheated on him, but like I told you before, he'll be fine too."

That pisses me off.

"Okay then...*I* don't want to hurt anymore."

Dr. Maria sits up, takes her glasses off, and stares at me for a second before she speaks. I think she just officially got tired of me.

"Understand something, Chrissy. If you decide to break up with Leo and stay married, you will hurt. If you decide to leave Kurt and still break up with Leo to avoid the shame of lying to him, you will hurt. If you decide to leave Kurt and come clean with Leo about being a married woman, you will hurt."

I throw my hands up in the air and whine, "Well shit, I guess the good news is there are only two options now, because I can't stay married to Kurt, not with the feelings I have for Leo!"

"What I'm trying to tell you is that no one in this charade will be able to avoid getting hurt, you especially. I say 'you especially' because you're the only one in this mess who knows the whole truth. I know you're not an adulterous person at heart, and you're grappling with choices that might expose you as one. But Chrissy, your choice should *not* be one that you think will hurt less; it has to be the right choice."

"So you're saying I should risk telling Leo about my marriage?"

"Does that feel like the right choice?"

"Yeah, if I thought he wouldn't hate me. But...no, no, no, I can never tell him! He thinks I'm special...perfect."

"Well he's an idiot then."

"*Excuse me?*"

"You might be the perfect fit *for* him, my dear, but no one's perfect. Trust me, if he's with you long enough, there will be plenty of things about you that bug the crap out of him, and vice versa.

Chrissy, when you go from one relationship to another, you just trade in one set of problems for another. Of course, the hope is that you're with someone you can actually solve them with. You two might even stand a chance if you realized that."

Wowie, she's actually frustrated with me.

"Did you ever think he might not hate you if you told him you're married? He might even be relieved for knowing the real reason he can't spend more time with you. Lord, you're probably making him a little crazy too."

"He can't know! No one else can ever find out that I cheated!"

"Chrissy, everyone makes mistakes."

"It's shameful."

"Sure it is, but what do you think is more shameful, leaving an unhappy marriage or staying in one?"

"I just told you I don't want to stay in the marriage! I can't turn into Francesca!"

"Okay, and I'll help you with that. But do you *really* think you can give up Leo without exploring the possibilities with him, especially once you're a single woman?"

She's saying everything I didn't want to hear. Now I know why it took me so long to come clean with her. Fucking table, fucking straps, fucking truth serum.

"Hunny, if I told you breaking up with Leo was the right thing to do and I recommended you do it tonight, you'd find a reason to put it off. And even if you told me it was over, you'd probably be lying to me. Don't you see, you have to stop lying to yourself so you can stop lying to everyone else."

She knows I'm an addict, too.

"I know and right after I stop lying to myself, I have to stop lying to Kurt. We're not gonna live happily ever after and the sooner he knows the better, because he deserves a chance at happiness with someone else. Problem is, I'm not strong enough to admit to him and everyone else that I'm a failure."

"Forget about everyone else. Public opinion and the pain associated with it is short lived in our culture. And besides, whoever wants to convict you of breaking some kind of moral code is either guilty of something worse or not worth your friendship, so screw 'em."

"I wish you could understand how hard this is for me. I don't know what it's like to be without Kurt. I've never been alone! What about all of our stuff, our dog, our house? I'll have to take ten steps back in my financial security and the thought of that makes me FREAK OUT like you have no idea."

"Come on, Chrissy! Don't you think what you're doing now with the sneaking out of the house and the lying and the cheating requires a hell of a lot more balls than being on your own?"

Shit, when you put it like that…

"Tell me, what's more overwhelming, admitting you made a mistake or being on your own?"

"I guess admitting I made a mistake."

"Are you willing to hand over your life to judgmental people, people who most likely have just as many problems as you, because you're scared of admitting a mistake? Because that's what you're doing; you're giving other people control of your happiness."

"What if I end things too soon, like right before Kurt decides to get therapy or confess his undying love for me or something? Maybe, like you said, he gets the sense I'm straying and decides to do whatever he can to make me happy."

"First…" She starts laughing. "Men very rarely do whatever they can to make a cheating spouse happy. And second, Kurt hasn't done any of that stuff so far, so what makes you think he will now?"

I hate her so much right now.

"But all right, Chrissy, let's say Kurt did do all of those things. What if he poured himself into therapy and professed his undying love to you? Would it change your opinion of the marriage or do you think it would prolong the agony of it?"

I sit in frustrated silence.

After a long pause Dr. Maria starts back in on me.

"Want to know what I think? I don't think you're as afraid of admitting your own failures and mistakes as you are of exposing Kurt to his."

Where's that fucking box of tissue.

"Yep, I think you're still trying to protect him from stuff you think will hurt him."

"Maybe you're right, but you have to understand, he's never failed at anything! I've never even seen him hurt before. I always wanted to be the one to help him when those things happened, not be the one who caused them!"

"But Hunny…if this marriage falls apart, he won't think he failed and he won't show hurt, not the way you'd expect him to anyway. Just like it's always been with the two of you, the failure and the hurt are the things you're going to own and feel, not him."

"But I need him to understand why all of this is happening. I want him to admit some responsibility for all of this and be sorry we ended up this way, but I don't know how to make him do that."

"It's not your job to force him to admit anything. It's your job to take responsibility for your happiness."

"No one will ever believe me when I tell them he failed me."

"Why do you have to tell people anything?"

"I don't want to be the bad guy."

"There's no bad guy here, Chrissy. What you're experiencing *happens all the time*. In fact it happened to me, and yes, it's painful, but it's not tragic. The real tragedy is when folks don't face the facts but instead turn their cheek to them and pretend everything's okay. You see those people every day, and they're the ones you look at with pity and hope to God you never become one of them."

I think about Kurt's family, the people he reveres, and the hair on the back of my neck stands straight up.

"The people I'm talking about aren't bad people, but they're pitiful because they're unable to notice when they're at a cross-roads and have to decide something really important, something life changing. They're completely oblivious when life asks them a question, much like the tough questions being thrown at you now. They don't make decisions. They forge on, and with each day it becomes more and more difficult to admit they screwed up because it's too painful to go all the way back to the *first wrong choice*; the space between then and now is too great. It becomes too hard to accept the fact that they've wasted precious time and energy. So they either keep on pretending that everything's okay or they become bitter, sad, uninterested, depressed. You name it and you don't want to be it."

"Dr. Maria, can I tell you something kind of ridiculous?"

She's got to be thinking, what could possibly be more ridiculous than everything you've already told me? She nods her head.

"You just mentioned something about being oblivious when life asks you a question and it reminded me of something that happened the night I met Leo."

"Go ahead."

"It's weird."

"It's okay."

"I talk to my dead grandfather a lot--my dad's dad. We were really close when he was alive. I used to talk to him about work stuff and junk like that, but after the miscarriage, when things felt very wrong between Kurt and me, I started asking him for signs that we were meant to be together. One night, when Kurt was away for work, I got down by the edge of my bed and begged my grandfather for some kind of hint that things would get better...I was so lonely, and I was scared I was gonna feel like that the rest of my life. In the middle of my chat with him, if that's what you want to call it, Kurt called. I thought the call was some kind of positive sign from my grandfather, and I lunged at the phone with happiness and optimism I hadn't felt for a long time. I said 'Hi Babe! You're never gonna believe what I was just thinking about!' Do you know what he said?"

"What, Hun?"

"He said the call had to be quick because he was running late for a dinner thing; that he was only calling because I told him to. He didn't even say 'hello.' I thought, what kind of fucked-up sign is this? And then it hit me: this *is* my sign! It's my sign that I'll never get what I need from him. I'll never get my 'hunny, baby, sweetie, I'll always take care of you, you can count on me' thoughtfulness."

"What happened next?"

"The revelation shocked me and I became silent. Kurt asked 'What's wrong *this* time?' And...well, that just sent me over the edge. For the first time since knowing him I wanted to tell him how disgusted I was with him. Then I wanted to tell him how sad the disgust made me, but when I opened my mouth to talk all that came out was, 'I feel dead inside,' and I kept saying it over and over again. The more I said it, the louder I got and the louder I got, the more crazy I became. He got mad, told me to take St. John's Wort, and hung up. But I couldn't stop. The words kept pouring out of my mouth long after he was gone, 'I feel dead inside, I feel dead inside, I FEEL DEAD INSIDE.' I was hysterical. Eventually, I calmed down and cleaned myself up. In an effort to cheer me up, my friend convinced me to hit the town with her. Four hours later I was sitting next to Leo at a bar where I overheard him talking about ghosts."

Clearly, she's not following me.

"You know how you just spoke about the importance of being aware when life asks you a question?"

"Yes."

"Well, I didn't feel like life was asking me a question when I sat next to Leo, but I sure felt like death was answering one. When I looked into Leo's eyes that night, I felt like I was looking into the eyes of my grandfather and he was answering all my questions. I felt like my grandfather was giving me a gift. The gift of Leo. Have I totally lost my mind to put so much faith in that way of thinking?"

"Sounds to me like you're putting faith in faith, and that takes a lot of courage."

"That's the funny thing. I don't have a lot of faith. I don't even believe in God."

"Sounds like you believe in something. I think when we start asking meaningful questions to any kind of higher power, ghosts included, we subconsciously start to look for the answers ourselves. If you never asked your grandfather for a sign, you probably would've been oblivious to Leo's presence. Instead, you were more aware of your senses and your surroundings that night. I think you were on the lookout for answers. Do you think Leo was an answer?"

"I do."

"Well then, what happened was magical and dare I say... spiritual."

"It makes perfect sense to me, but I wouldn't even know how to explain that to anyone."

"You sure are pent up on what everyone else thinks aren't you? Let me tell you this--once there's some space between you and Kurt, you won't care what anyone thinks. I imagine you'll be how you are at work in every area of your life, and won't that be refreshing?"

I slump back into the couch because it all seems so overwhelming. She just lost me, and she knows it.

"Chrissy, do you want children?"

"Very much. I'm almost twenty-nine. What if I never meet someone to start a family with?"

"So you don't think it'll work out with Leo?"

"Nope."

"Because it's too good to be true or because you're too afraid to be honest with him?"

"Both."

After a long glance down at her notes she looks back up at me over her glasses.

"You're adamant that you don't want to be Francesca, right?"

"Right."

"And you believe Kurt deserves a chance to find happiness with a woman who loves him for who he is."

"Yes."

"Okay, but let's say your fear of failure, your fear of being exposed as a cheater, your fear of not meeting another man to have a baby with wins over and you decide to accept a life like Francesca's. Let's say you decide your happiness and Kurt's happiness isn't as important as confronting your fears, and you decide to stay married."

My mouth is literally gapping wide open.

"It's a real possibility you know…I mean…those are big fears you have to get over so that everyone can get on with their life. And since eventually you want to have children, I guess Kurt will be your only chance at having them, right?"

Why have I not considered that?

"At what point do you think you'll be ready to have children with him?"

I haven't thought about having a family with Kurt since…I don't even know when. I'm staring at her as if a pilot just said, "Brace for impact."

"Hunny…*if you were to stay married to Kurt, at what point do you think you'd be ready to have children?*"

"I don't…I…I don't want to have kids with him."

"And why not?"

"I won't be a good mother."

"Why?"

"Because I'll never be able to be myself and…"

"*And?*"

"And I'm in love with someone else."

Dr. Maria leans back in her chair in a "my work here is done" kind of way, and I sigh heavily, because my work is just beginning.

GAME OVER

JULY, 1998

When I started therapy, I compared myself to Francesca because of my affair, but I think it was a subconscious fear of being stuck in an unsatisfying marriage for the sake of my yet-to-be-born children that made me connect with her the most. I truly believe Francesca would've followed her heart...her love, even if it meant leaving a man who most considered to be a perfectly good husband, if it wasn't for her children. I believe she would've found a way to correct the mistakes of her past and allowed herself to have a more fulfilling future...if it wasn't for her children. But Francesca didn't do either of those things and I think her choices probably reflect a majority of married women out there and it makes me very, very sad. For a long time I thought I was in a relationship that set me apart from the Francesca's of the world, but, I'm not, and I didn't become aware of it until the miscarriage. I know now why I wasn't sad when it happened. Subconsciously I knew if I had kids with Kurt, my life would be over.

That's why I was grateful for the miscarriage, *the reprieve*. I guess I thought it would give me a chance to fix whatever was wrong with us. But Leo came around before I got a chance to wrap my head around it all. And after meeting him, the only way my marriage could be fixed was if Kurt became him, something I closed my eyes and wished for everyday. But when Dr. Maria looked at me like I was a fucking moron for wishing something so retarded, I decided it was time to get my head out of my ass.

Yes, I had an affair just like Francesca did, but if I decide *not* to have kids with Kurt, I can be unlike Francesca in more ways than I'm like her. And I immediately wanted to start celebrating all our differences instead of condemning our similarities, but instead I went to a B&B in Napa to celebrate my wedding anniversary. I guess my head is only partially out of my ass.

"Chrissy, what the hell is the matter with you? You won't hold my hand, you won't talk to me…Jesus, you barely even look at me. Do you realize what I've done to make this trip fun for you? I got a massage *from a guy*, went window shopping for TWO HOURS, and I just spent a hundred and sixty bucks on a dinner that consisted of about two ounces of beef, four carrots, and a potato the size of my big toe! I'm trying as hard as I can to be patient, but c'mon, you gotta throw me a bone."

But I couldn't. I'd been throwing him bones for too long and I simply ran out. So right there, as he was trying to bust a move on the canopy bed at the B&B, I said, "down boy."

"I can't do this Kurt."

I remember a time when all I wanted was to have sex with him: sneaking into his bedroom in high school, checking into sleazy motels when they were all we could afford. Doing it at youth hostels in Europe and on the beach the day we got engaged. I'd do it with him whenever I could. But I can't do it with him anymore.

"But I'm your husband."

"I don't feel like you are."

"God, I'm so sick of this! *What the fuck do you want from me?* You say you want me to do things that I *think* you might like, so I give you this trip to Napa and this is what I get in return! Seriously, tell me because I'm going crazy…*what the fuck do you want from me?*"

"Nothing."

"You said doing nothing is what caused all our problems!"

"I know and I was wrong."

"You're going freaking crazy, you know that?"

"I'm not crazy. Don't you see? It wasn't what you or I *did or didn't* do for each other that caused all of our problems; it's that *everything* we do for each other is a compromise. We're too different! We've been a 'if you do this for me, then I'll do that for you' couple since the beginning and it's exhausting. I'm sorry Kurt, but I'm not gonna compromise my happiness for yours anymore."

"What's your point?"

"If I sleep with you now, I'll be making a huge compromise, and I can't go there anymore."

"So we're gonna be a sexless married couple then? That's priceless, Chrissy! What other brilliant ideas do you have that will make the rest of our lives together more enjoyable?"

As I sat in the chair by the side of the bed crying about what had become of us, Kurt continued to rant and rave about sex. He actually thought my refusal to sleep with him was negotiable, like if we continued to discuss the matter, the end result would be furniture-breaking sex. It wasn't. The end result was an early departure from the B&B and a very quiet ride home. And when we got there, I packed my bags and went to my parent's house.

Now that my head is completely removed from my ass and I made my stance with Kurt, I cannot let anything distract me from finishing what I started. Right now everything has to be about me, him, a separation, and therapy. I can't be running off in the middle of the night to jump in the sack with Leo. Like Dr. Maria said, I have to feel it and be okay with it so it doesn't come back to haunt me later.

I'm totally incapable of feeling sorrow when the drug is in my life so I *have to* end it with Leo. Yeah, it sounds so logical when I say it, but actions speak louder than words. I have to keep reminding myself that being alone is better than being in an unsatisfying marriage and that's why I want out of it. And I have to keep reminding myself that being alone is better than telling Leo I'm married…and that's why I'm making a trip to Monterey, to tell him we're through. I suppose I could do it over the phone, but he deserves to be told in person. Ahhh, who am I kidding? I'm going to Monterey to shoot up one last time before I quit cold turkey.

Leo's been in Monterey for about three weeks and during that time I've been acting like a jealous girlfriend by hacking into his voicemail. He's given me no reason to think he's disingenuous, yet I still find it incredibly hard to believe he could adore me as much as he does. Is it my own lying that's made me distrustful, or is it that Kurt's made me feel so unlovable that it's impossible to believe Leo could feel the way he does about me? I have no idea, but the only thing that convinces me of Leo's sincerity is his voicemail account, his only messages continue to be from friends and they're all completely innocent. Even at the eleventh hour of our relationship, I'm still waiting for him to do something horribly wrong to justify breaking up with him.

Now that I'm out of my house and splitting time between my parent's house and Slutty Co-workers apartment, it's hard for Kurt to keep track of me and easier to go missing for a few days at a time. So after work on Friday, I pack my prettiest lingerie and all of the courage I have and head to Monterey to end it with Leo. Twenty minutes after I arrive at The Plaza Hotel, he shows up with flowers and a box from Victoria's Secret. We have two nights together before I have to tell him the news, and I want to enjoy every minute of it. And I do.

I've never visited Monterey without furiously biking my way through it or waiting in stupid lines to get into the stupid aquarium. I imagine it's torture enough to have to take your kids to an aquarium but why on earth would anyone go who doesn't even have children? It's that very subject that sends Leo and me into drunken tears of laughter as we sit in the outdoor patio of a French restaurant.

Yes, this Monterey trip is way different than any of my others. We stay up late, order in-room movies, and kiss the entire way through them. We sleep until noon, eat greasy bar food overlooking the Monterey Bay, and drink Bloody Marys until it's time to drink real drinks. I watch Leo whenever he's preoccupied doing something else, and I'm mesmerized by every move he makes. Everything he does is intense and deliberate and it's electrifying that he has the same degree of passion when he speaks to me.

Last night in the middle of dinner when a very pretty pregnant woman sat at the table next to us, he reached his hands across the table to hold mine and said, "I can't wait until you look like that."

It took my breath away. There were a million other wonderful things he said to me over the weekend, and when he wasn't looking, I wiped away the tears that formed in the corners of my eyes. I didn't set out on this farewell trip to tell Leo I was married, but after spending the best forty-eight hours of my life with him, I knew I had to give him exactly what's he's given me--intense and deliberate honesty. By the time Sunday rolled around, I decided it was time to do the honorable thing and tell him I was married.

"Good morning."

"Hey, Baby, wow you look pretty. How long have you been up?"

"Couple of hours. I've been watching you sleep."

"Are you okay?"

"Not really."

He rolls his feet onto the floor, rests his elbows on his knees and apprehensively stares up at me.

"I have to tell you something."

Two little words are all it'll take to set me free of this lie...I'm married. Just say the words, Chrissy, and you can leave here knowing you did the honorable thing.

"Leo I...uh, I..."

But what if, after everything we did and said to each other for the past six months, he told me *he* was married? How would I react to find out that after every sexcapade and tender moment shared with me, he went home to another woman? I would die. And I wouldn't believe him if he told me he never had sex with his wife. I wouldn't believe him if he told me it was over with her. I would feel like second fiddle, and every beautiful moment we shared together I would now consider immoral and gross. I would hate him. Mission honorable is now aborted.

"I've been doing a lot of thinking and...I need some time to myself."

"Why?"

"Things are complicated."

"Like what?"

"Settling twelve years of business with K...him, selling the house, the stress of my job and JUST EVERYTHING! I'm over-whelmed and I'm freaking out that I'm not giving myself enough time between that relationship and this one. I have to clean up my messes."

"How many times are you gonna do this? Here's a better question, what if I'm not available when you want to come back next time?"

With the proper detox program, there shouldn't be a next time.

"I'm sorry…I have to be alone for a while."

It sounds believable, but it's not how I feel! I want to spend every waking minute of the rest of my life with him, but I can't. I have to finish what I started with Kurt. The part of option #1 where I break up with Leo cold turkey is coming to life, and I can already feel the cold sweat and shakes coming on.

"How does being with me get in the way of all the stuff you have to take care of? We already go days without talking, and since I'm living down here, we hardly see each other anyway." Shaking his head like all of this is something he can talk me out, of he says, "This doesn't make any sense."

"It's an obligation I don't have the capacity to make room for right now."

I'm a monster! I'm making him out to be a pain in my ass when he's really the only thing in the world that makes me feel good. I have to get out of here. Now.

"Take this."

I hand him the pewter ring he bought me in Mill Valley. The only time I took it off was the night of my class reunion. Which right now, I regret doing.

"Maybe, if I ever get my act together, you can give it back to me."

Leo takes the ring, stares at the cheap and beautiful symbol of our relationship, and then gently kneels down in front of me. I can barely hold myself together.

"It's not the ring I want you to have for the rest of your life, but I'm asking you now. Marry me, Chrissy."

"Leo…I can't say *yes*."

"But I know you want to."

"Please don't do this."

"Baby, I don't have to date a hundred girls to know you're the one. Look, take however much time you need for yourself but just say 'yes' to me so I know you're coming back."

If I don't walk out of here immediately, I fear I'll say 'yes' and then I'll be engaged. Next step, *The Jerry Springer Show*.

I pull his arms up so that he's standing in front of me and then I reach up to cup his face. With tears streaming down mine, we kiss for an eternity. It's almost impossible for me to let him go. He tries to pull me back into bed but using all of my self-control, I pull away and stare into the eyes that if all goes according to plan I'll never see again.

"Baby…Baby. Please don't do this. I need you in my life, and I know you need me. Why are you gonna walk away from that?"

Finally, through breaths that are borderline hyperventilation I try to talk.

"Please don't call me. Every time I see or hear from you it makes what I have to deal with that much harder. I don't expect you to understand, I just need you to honor my request."

"No."

"Dammit, Leo, you have to!"

"God, why are you doing this?"

Because I have to go home and settle things with my husband, that's why! What if I just blurt it out? Maybe he could forgive me… maybe we could work. His eyes are telling me it's possible! But don't be a selfish fool, Chrissy! He's *finally* just one year away from finishing six years of college. He's so close to starting a career. He's on the precipice of living a very fulfilling life, and telling him you're married will only spoil all the happiness he deserves right now. But what if it's selfish not to tell him? What if he wants me any way he can get me and by abandoning him I'm making all those great things in his life less great? Dammit, I don't know! The only thing I do know is that I can't chance him hating me. It always comes down to that, and that's why I have to stick to the plan and leave. That's why I have to continue begging.

"Leo, you *have* to let me go."

"No, I don't. I won't."

"If you care for me as much as you say you do, you have to let me do this."

"You're really doing this to take care of selling your house and to focus on work stuff, right?"

"Yes."

"You told me it was over with him, and I believed you. You're not gonna do anything stupid are you? "

"Actually, quite the opposite."

And just like that, I walk out the door and down the hall to the elevator without pausing to look back. If I turn, I'll run back to him. And if I run back to him, I'll have to tell him I'm married because I'll never get the courage to do what I just did to him ever again. The elevator takes too long to arrive, and just as the urge to sprint back to him hits me like a tidal wave, I burst into the stairwell and race down four flights of stairs to my car.

I just quit the best thing to ever happen to me. Only a drug addict could possibly understand the pain I'm going through.

WHAT THE?

Leaving Leo behind in Monterey was torture. I barely made it to my car before the tears started pouring down my face, and when I looked at the room that he and I had shared for the last forty-eight hours, I saw him staring down at me with tears of his own. He mouthed the words "Come back to me," and even though it was another lie, I mouthed back, "I will. I promise."

On the drive home from Monterey, I had grand visions of contacting a divorce attorney, of telling Kurt I want to sell the house, and getting on with my life…alone. But instead, I drove straight to Slutty Co-workers apartment, collapsed on her couch and cried myself silly. And I've been crying for two weeks straight. Whenever she asks me why I can't just end it with Kurt, I tell her that I need more time to prepare him for it, that I don't have the heart to hurt him quite yet. She just shakes her head and says, "Yeah…right…I guess it makes more sense that you and Leo should be the ones to suffer and not him." I know her sarcastic heart is in the right place.

I thought I was a wreck before I put my foot down in Napa and ripped my heart out in Monterey but nothing compares to the fucking mess I am now. Without my drug, I definitely look like I'm coming off of something. My clothes don't match, and I don't care to put on makeup most mornings. I haven't laughed or seemed interested in anything going on around me for weeks. My door is always closed at work, and my window coverings are always down at my parent's house and at Slutty Co-workers apartment, wherever I decide to spend the night. Hiding from the world has become my new obsession. Well, that and calling into Leo's messages. Yes, to make everything a zillion times worse than it already is, I can't stop frolicking with masochism! Fortunately for me, there are no girls calling yet, just one really supportive best friend.

"Dude! Fuck her anyway. You'll find someone better."

And then…

"Dude! She has too much baggage, and she's not the only 5'6, blond girl out there you know."

And my favorite…

"Dude! She'll be like forty when you're only thirty-four. Who wants that?"

With messages like that from Taddeo, it's only a matter of time before Leo moves on. The thought makes me want to gain seventy-five pounds and become a librarian, but there's no time, as I too have my own abundance of messages to contend with these days. My friends have been calling me off the hook and their messages have gone from worry to full on rage that I haven't called them back.

"Chrissy, this is Nic. I'm so fucking pissed that you're ignoring us. I went out on a limb to protect your ass at that bowling alley and this is how you repay me? I swear I'm gonna call Kurt and tell him about you and your little--BEEEEEEEEEEEEEEEEEEEEEEEEEEE EEEP"

"It's me again. Your freaking voicemail cut me off. Okay, so I was kidding about telling Kurt, but call me TODAY! I want to know what the hell is going on with you."

"Hey, it's Court. We missed you at dinner last week and the week before that. You know I don't get mad at much, but I'm frustrated that you dumped all of that Kurt dirt on us and won't give us a chance to help you. I keep calling the house, but it seems like Kurt's making up reasons why you can't come to the phone. Please call me. I won't let you hide forever."

"Hey Chrissy, It's Kel. Courtney and Nicole are making me call you to tell you to get off your skinny little ass and meet us Thursday night. We'll be at Chili's at 7pm."

I just love how Kelly said she called because Courtney and Nicole made her, not because she wanted to. But not as much as I'm lovin' Kelly's restaurant choice. What self-respecting, almost twenty-nine year old with a decent disposable income wants to get caught dead at a Chili's? It's like the aquarium to me, why go if you don't have kids with you? There's no cool scene there, just fat people who want to eat cheap food and get fatter. Regardless of hating the thought of driving all the way to Freakmont to eat at Chili's, it's been weeks since I've seen my friends, and I should tell them I semi-moved out of my house in Danville. So I go.

"Well, well, well, look who decided to show her disgraceful face...*and disgraceful outfit!*"

"Yeah, what's this look all about Chrissy? You look like homeless Barbie!"

"Hey, back off, Nic! We *all* look disgraceful here!"

"C'mon, what's wrong with Chili's?"

"Ahhhh gee, nothing, Kelly if you're celebrating a five-year-old's birthday party or have a hankering for an awesome blossom."

"Nice to see that the attitude matches the outfit, doesn't it girls?"

Kelly looks annoyed, so I do what I know will annoy her even more and give her a big ol' hug and kiss on the cheek.

"I love Chili's because *you* love Chili's, Kel."

"I don't looooooove Chili's. It's just close to my house! I'm sick of driving to all those fancy shmancy places in Danville. It's my pick tonight and I pick economical!"

"Fine with me. The med school payments, the house payment, the car payment...it's all killing Kyle and me these days. What about you, Courtney, making a dent in your student loans?"

"Not even a spec. They'll *always* be there!"

Then it gets quiet. So quiet, you can actually hear the people at the table next to us getting fatter. I can tell my friends have a million questions for me but no one wants to be the first to dive in for fear of getting their ass handed to them. Watching them squirm is the most fun I've had in weeks.

"So, do they have hard alcohol here or just the wimpy stuff like beer and wine?"

"Yeah, they have all the gross stuff you like, Chrissy. Just remember you have a long drive home, so take it easy."

"Not that long, Kel. I'm staying in Pleasanton."

There! It's out. Have at it girls. All three of them tilt their heads and do the, "I feel so sorry for you" pouty face. As usual, Courtney takes the lead in all serious conversations. She gives Nicole and Kelly the "I've got this" look.

"Staying with your folks?"

"Yep, it was only a matter of time."

"Is there any hope for you guys?"

"I don't think so...but then again, maybe. But not maybe because we're gonna magically turn into super happy married couple; it's because I don't have the guts to do anything other than spend the night at my parent's house or my co-workers house in the city. It's weird, guys. Every week I go home to pick up more clothes and it's like Kurt's totally oblivious to what's happening right in front of his face."

"Hasn't that always been your problem with him, though?"

"Among other things."

"Has he gone to therapy like you asked him to?"

"Nope."

"Do you want me to talk to him?"

"Would anyone have to convince *your* husband to go to marriage-saving therapy?"

Courtney sympathetically shakes her head.

"I didn't think so. Please, I'd rather die than have my friend convince my husband to love me."

"Do you still love him?"

"I do. But I'm not *in love* with him anymore. I think I feel for him how he's always felt for me, except for me, it's not enough. I want truly, madly, deeply love, something he could never comprehend."

"Well, you *seem* okay."

"Maybe you just want me to be okay, Kelly."

"What are you talking about?"

"I dunno, it just seems like all of this is just a little too much for you."

"Jesus, calm down. I didn't mean to…"

"I can't calm down! I'M NOT OKAY! If I leave, everyone's gonna think I rejected him, but I feel like I'm the one who got rejected. If I leave, no one's gonna feel sorry for me. No one's gonna think I need support. I'll be alone, Kelly. Do you know how bad all of this makes me feel? If I stay, I'll feel bad. If I leave, I'll feel bad! Everything makes me feel so bad that I wonder if I'll ever be okay. I need a drink! Where's the fucking waiter?"

Kelly knows better than to say another word, so she retreats back into the red pleather booth and keeps her mouth shut. Courtney though, she can't help herself.

"It's like a death. Studies show it takes six months for every year you were together to get on with your life after the death of a loved one. I imagine the same will be true with your breakup with Kurt."

"So you're talking six years before I can get on with my life?"

"Yeah, but the pain fades over time, Chrissy. At first you might think about Kurt every minute of every day but soon it'll turn into every other day, and then every other week and then one day you'll realize it's been months since you've thought about him."

"So eventually he'll be dead to me? Lovely, Courtney, that's just what I wanted to hear."

"Hey, I don't want you guys to break up, but this isn't about me, it's about you, and from what I can tell, *YOU* don't want to be with *HIM*. I'm just trying to be a friend and sometimes friends have to deliver bad news."

Courtney's always right. She bugs me.

"For fuck's sake, where's my drink?"

"We didn't order any yet."

"See! This is why I don't like this place!"

"You're stressing her out, Courtney, let me in on this. Have you seen Leo?"

I want to beat Nicole over the head with the stale bread sticks for asking me that question.

"What? Look, we can either talk about boring stuff like our kids or we can talk about your boyfriend. Pick."

"*Ex*-boyfriend. I haven't seen him in months."

That was a lie, but since it's really over this time, they don't need to know how far things went, and I certainly don't need Kelly's infamous eye roll to further degrade my time with him.

"I wonder if he ever ended up with that Megan girl."

"Jesus, Nicole, you might as well punch me in the stomach or better yet, why don't you throw the drink *THAT I STILL DON'T HAVE* in my face!"

"Geez, I'm sorry, Chrissy. I didn't know he was *that* special to you."

"It's nothing vodka can't fix."

The girls' eyes are darting back and forth at each other. They're too afraid to talk. They're smart to keep their mouths shut until I have some alcohol in me. Oh! Finally the waiter!

"Hey, dude, I'm not talking to these women until you get me a double shot of vodka on the rocks with a lime twist."

"Uh, like, what kind of vodka?"

"Ketel one."

"Uh, I don't think we have that."

"*THEN WHY DID YOU ASK*? Just give me whatever."

"Great Chrissy, now he's gonna spit in our food."

"Puleez! Look where we are. Like it wasn't gonna happen already!"

Silence again. I've scared the begeezees out of all of them and now no one has the guts to speak. I want to feel bad about it, but I don't care about anything anymore. After a few minutes of pretending to look at the laminated seventeen-page food-splattered menu, I roll my head up in disgust and see Courtney staring at me.

"Something you want to say?"

"Were you in love with him?"

It was so much bigger than love. It was belonging, it was sanity, it was bottomless and reciprocal. One by one, my tears fall on the dirty menu. Nicole reaches her hand across the table to take mine, while Kelly and Courtney exchange concerned glances. I've always been the crier of the group, but these tears were different from all the others they've seen me shed over the years. They weren't like the ones I splattered all over the place when I didn't get voted homecoming queen. They weren't like the ones I spewed out when someone else wore almost the exact same dress to my senior prom as me. They weren't phony like the ones I squeezed out when I held their newborn babies. These tears were coming out of makeup-less eyes, they were unrehearsed, and they didn't care who saw them.

"Yeah, I was. I am."

"Do you think you'll ever see him again?"

"Not if I can help it, because I NEVER want him to know I was married...I mean *am* married."

"Why? I mean, it's a part of who you are, and if he feels the same way about you that you feel about him, he'll understand."

"How could he possibly understand, Courtney? What I've done to him is sick. I lied to him and manipulated him for six months."

"But you love him. How do you ignore that?"

"Not easily. Christ, sometimes it even feels like I'm interfering with destiny by breaking it off with him."

"Only time will tell."

I look up at Courtney with hopeful eyes.

"What do you mean?"

"When things are meant to be, there's nothing you can do to prevent it from being so."

"She's right. If you're so crazy about him, why don't you get on with the divorce? Free yourself up to see what the possibilities are with him?"

"Because I'm a chickenshit, Nicole, and I want Kurt to be the one to end it."

"That's never gonna happen...unless he finds out about Leo."

"Right, and according to my therapist, that makes me a pretty pathetic person."

Our drinks finally arrive, and Nicole makes a toast.

"Here's to Chrissy, who's not only wasting precious time and energy but also her good looks that she naively thinks will last forever. You're gonna need those to find yourself a new husband, Hunny! Get the fuck on with it."

After what some people might call dinner, I excuse myself to go to the bathroom to throw it all up. Kidding! I wish I possessed that skill; it would've saved me many, many hours in the gym. I pee, wash my hands and out of habit, search for my favorite Mac lipgloss. By the time I find it, I remember I don't care how I look anymore and throw it back in my bag. I get back to the table just as Kelly's getting up to leave.

"You outta here?"

"Yeah, I promised Craig I'd be home in time to tuck everyone in."

Good Lord, she only has one kid. Does that mean she tucks Craig in, too?

"Well, I didn't drive all the way out here for that crappy drink. You two wanna find somewhere to get a real drink?"

After making Kelly promise me she'll never make me eat at a place where half of our high school graduating class works, I spank her on the butt and receive my final eye roll of the evening. She sets off to her blessed home, getting there just in time to snuggle in next to Craig and catch the last twenty minutes of *Dateline*, making it the perfect ending to her day.

After driving around for thirty minutes, Court, Nic, and I realize there *is* no place to get a real drink in Freakmont, so we buy a bottle of vodka, a bag of ice, plastic cups, and a lime and drive to our old stomping ground, the house in the Mission Hills that MC Hammer used to live in.

Sitting on the grassy hillside bordering the compound, we roll around in laughter as we exchange stupid stories from our past. As it turns out, I'm the only one of the four of us who didn't lose her virginity here.

"God, look at this place! How do you go from all this to declaring bankruptcy in like five years?"

"I know, Chrissy! Wasn't he supposed to be too legit to quit?" I abruptly sit up.

"Omigod you guys, I'm like MC Hammer! I was supposed to be too legit to quit! But now I'm a fraud just like him. I'm a big, baggy-pant wearing, washed-up black-rapper fraud!"

"Okay Nic, time to cut her off."

"I'm serious, guys. Did you see how Kelly looked at me tonight? WAIT, how she *wouldn't* look at me."

"It wasn't that bad, Chrissy."

"My ass it wasn't. It's like she forgot about the sister pact the four of us made at high school graduation. You know…to always be there for each other no matter how stupid the reason. But *where's* Kelly now? Not here! And you know what? We're all close, but she and I should be even closer. Oops, sorry. I spit a little when I said that. Hey! Are you guys even listening to me?"

"Yeah, yeah, we're lis--"

"I mean, didn't those years that Kelly and I lived together in college mean anything to her?"

"Sure, they--"

"God, those were good times. We were so excited when we moved into that apartment…decorated the whole place in turquoise and peach. It looked like Miami Vice vomited all over it. We felt so grown up cooking dinner for our boyfriends and paying bills. Did you know we had the exact same class schedule and worked part time at the same bank? We were always together…"

"Chrissy, I'm not saying you guys aren't close anymore, but all that stuff was like ten years ago. Life gets busy after college."

"No duh, Nicole, I GOT BUSY TOO! But busy doesn't mean you grow apart. For Christ sake, *we were each other's maid of honor at our weddings*! I picked out her wedding dress and she picked out mine. Okay, shhhhhh don't tell her, but I *hated* mine! You know… I kinda feel like she convinced me to get an ugly one so she would look better!"

"Jesus, how drunk are you?"

"I'm not drunk…I'm pissed!"

"Well, did you guys ever talk?"

"What do you mean?"

"You and Kelly. All those years you were together…did you talk?"

"Of course we fucking talked Courtney. Hard to do all that stuff I just told you about without talking."

"One more sarcastic outburst and we're leaving you here. Got that?"

"Fine."

"What I mean is, did you two ever talk about serious stuff? You lived with her and did some fun stuff, but think about it, who were you on the phone with night after night when you and Kurt broke up for that one week?"

"You and Nic."

"And when your dad had the heart attack, who drove home from college and spent five days with you at the hospital?"

"You and Nic."

"And who did you call when you were crying your eyes out after Kurt's parents bailed on his college graduation?"

"You and Nic."

"Right, because Kelly can't talk about the bad stuff, Chrissy. You knew it back then, so why don't you know it now?"

"I guess I don't feel like I can make all these really hard choices without everyone's support."

"Well, you're gonna have to because not everyone's gonna agree with your choices. Chrissy, you can't let everyone else's opinion dictate your life."

"You sound like Dr. Maria, and I know you're both right, but I can't help but be offended that Kelly's treating me like a loser. Soon that's how everyone's gonna treat me. I'm the big letdown, the big cheater quitter! That's all everyone will be thinking!"

"God, you're so full of yourself to think everyone's thinking about you all the time."

I'm usually good at being defensive, but Nic's comment left me speechless.

"People do have their own shit going on, you know. Besides, did you ever think that maybe people will think you're the strong one?"

"What are you talking about?"

"Realizing your marriage isn't good for you and taking a stand about it takes courage. You shouldn't confuse people's reactions with thinking poorly of you."

"Nicole's right. People might act weird, but maybe it's because your divorce will cause them to feel vulnerable in their own marriage. People might think if it can happen to Kurt and Chrissy, it could happen to me. I know I've thought that."

"It has? But you and Guss seem fine."

"We're all right, but it's not glamorous by any stretch of the imagination. I mean, there's no sex on the coffee table or blow jobs anymore, that's for sure. And since Baby Jack came along, Guss certainly doesn't want to go down--"

"WHOA! STOP THERE! I GET IT ALREADY!"

"What I mean is, when things get routine in a relationship, and they *always* do, there's got to be something in it to fall back on. Something special that makes all the boring bullshit not so boring. You made me double-check my relationship with Guss to make sure something special was there and you know what? It is. And because I feel secure in my marriage, I can tell you that I think you're smart for realizing that certain something special isn't there for you and Kurt and that you're incredibly courageous to do something about it. All those less secure people might think differently, but you shouldn't let them guide your choices."

"She's right, Chrissy. Look, I love Kurt, Court loves Kurt, the whole friggin' world loves Kurt. He's a great guy, but we're not married to him, you are."

"I really wish Kelly would talk to me like you guys are."

"She can't."

"But this is a big deal. She can't crawl out of her shell for me?"

"Nope. But she'll always stand by your side in it."

"Court, do you think what's going on with me is making Kelly reevaluate her relationship with Craig?"

"No, not at all. Kelly thinks her life is perfect, and she loves Craig. But maybe she's afraid it'll make Craig reevaluate the one he has with her."

"I never thought of that."

"Yeah, Kyle's afraid you're gonna rub off on me! Like I'm gonna go have an affair or something."

"YOU TOLD KYLE ABOUT MY AFFAIR?"

"Oh, shit…yeah, sorry about that. That's what happily married people do though, they tell their spouses everything. I promise he won't say a word though. Courtney, didn't you tell Guss?"

"Nope, Chrissy told us not to say anything, so I didn't. AND THAT DOESN'T MEAN I'M UNHAPPILY MARRIED! It means I can keep my big mouth shut."

After I sobered up and kissed my two friends goodbye, I set off to spend another night at my parent's house. When I showed up on their doorstep a few weeks ago and told them about my troubles, I was surprised my mom greeted me with open arms, a glass of wine, and a comfy bed. My whole life, she told me that after I got married, I could only come home if I was bleeding. I guess it was supposed to instill some kind of work ethic in me. Mostly it just made me feel unloved. But the older I get, the more I realize that a lot of my mom's threats were empty ones and that maybe I wouldn't be as strong as I am today if it wasn't for her toughness. She might not have wanted me to quit a good marriage, but I sure as hell know she wouldn't want me to stay in a bad one, and something about my mom's reaction when I showed up on her doorstep told me she wants me to leave Kurt.

I give the security guard at the gate of my parents' golf community my name for the hundredth time and sarcastically remind him that I'll be coming and going for a while, so he might as well give me my own clicker so that I can let myself in. He keeps both eyes on Jay Leno and grunts. I'll steal my mom's in the morning…payback for making me feel unloved. I gaze up at the full moon through my sunroof and wonder if Leo's looking at it too. God I miss…woopsy, curb! Geez, so much for taking a moment to reflect. With my newly flat tire, I round the corner of my parent's street and see Kurt leaning against his car. Cautiously, I pull into the driveway. Partly because of the tire, partly because I'm wondering what the hell is going on.

"Where have you been?"

"In Freakmont, with the girls."

"Wow, you actually went to Fremont?"

"I know, can you believe it?"

"About as much as I can believe you moved out of our house."

"So you finally get that I moved out, huh?"

"I get it, Chrissy and I want you to come home, tonight."

"I think we have a lot to talk about, Kurt--"

"Hold on, I've had a lot of time to think about things. I understand why you're upset with me and the way things are. I'm gonna try really hard to make things right, Chrissy. I promise. Just come home and give me a chance to show you."

"Kurt, I'm not ready to go back."

Don't wimp out Chrissy! Tell him you want a divorce right now! Two-thirds of your best friends support you, just get on with it.

"Then I'll stay here with you."

"That kinda defeats the purpose of the whole time-away concept, don't you think?"

"We can't fix things if you're away."

Tell him you're done trying to fix things! Tell him now.

"Kurt, it's after midnight. I can't pack my things up right now, I'll wake my parents."

Hey dumbass, that's giving him hope.

"Just grab what you need, and we'll come back tomorrow and get the rest of your things. Come on, the dog misses you."

"*The dog misses me?*"

"Okay, I miss you."

Am I at one of those crossroads Dr. Maria talked about? But wasn't I already at this one? Why am I being asked all this stuff again? *Grandpa, you there?*

"Why are you staring at the sky?"

"Just looking for answers, I guess."

"Answers to what? Look, you have to come home eventually. What's the difference if it's tonight or next Tuesday?"

He really has no clue that we're on the verge of divorce.

GRANDPA?

"Kurt, I don't know if I ever want to come home."

"What are you talking about?"

Tell him!

"I'm just...I need more time and...things are peaceful for me here and..."

"But Chrissy, we're married, and you don't live here. Come home so we can work on us."

"Do you want me to come home because you're afraid of what people are starting to think?"

"There's nothing to think. Married people have problems, and so what, we're having some."

"So you think what we're experiencing is some kind of bump in the road?"

"Yeah, it's not always gonna be perfect. Those old people you see walking down the street, you know the cute ones holding hands and looking like it's been so perfect all those years. They've had tons of problems like this but they battled through all of them to earn that look."

"Or maybe they're just holding onto each other so they don't fall over."

"Chrissy, I'm serious. This is what marriage is."

I don't know what's worse, that he actually believes this is what marriage is or that I packed up my belongings and went back home.

Every dream that had been shattered
Disappears without a trace
Now that I've found what really matters...
There's a world behind these walls
That I just need to see, believe in me

("Believe in Me," ATB)

BAR HOPPING GUTTER SLUT(S)

AUGUST, 1998

I took one step forward by moving out and ten steps backward by moving back home last month. Whatever ounce of progress I made by alerting Kurt to our problems was all but buried when I got in the car to go home with him that night.

He was giddy as we drove home, talking about normal things like mowing the lawn and giving the dog a bath. I also got a ten-minute tough love speech about how damaging it is to your car to drive around with a flat tire. With my hand on the door handle I sat silent in the passenger seat thinking about Francesca and prison. And I was silent three weeks ago when he came home with the most beautiful diamond necklace for me. That thing must have cost a thousand bucks, and it's the first thing he ever bought me that didn't belong anywhere near a campground. Even so, I barely muttered a word when he clasped it around my neck. And almost immediately after I moved back home, he started praising the long hours I put in at work, *and* he hasn't said a word about the chips and salsa I eat for dinner almost every night. It seems like Kurt's really, really trying, and I wish so badly his efforts would win over my heart, but they're only breaking it even more…and making it more silent. The whole shit show has Dr. Maria totally confused.

"So let me get this straight, you finally got the nerve to move out, you cut off all communication with Leo so you can have time to sort out your affairs with Kurt, *and* you tell your friends you're heading for divorce, but in one five-minute conversation with Kurt you're living at home as if nothing ever happened?"

"Ah…yep, that's correct. Oh except…it's as if nothing ever happened for Kurt. I'm totally aware it all happened."

"Apparently you're not, because you're back at home. You're the one in the driver's seat, Chrissy! Don't you see that?"

"I know I am, but how do I drive someone who's completely unaware there are major problems?"

"You tell him."

"It's not that easy! It makes me think I'm wrong."

After a few seconds of silence, Dr. Maria gets up and starts pacing the floor like an attorney in a courtroom.

"Have you ever fired someone at work?"

"Yeah."

"Did you give them warnings ahead of time?"

"Of course."

"So, after you explained the problems to them on multiple occasions, did you feel any guilt, or second guess your decision to fire them in any way?"

"No.

"Did any of them plead to keep their job?"

"Yes."

"Did you let them keep it?"

"No."

"Why?"

"Business is business, and I have a company to run. I can't have slack holding me back. Plus, if I changed my mind after presenting clear evidence of poor performance, I'd look like a weak fool. I'd lose the respect of my staff."

"Haven't you given Kurt warnings that you're at the end of your rope?"

"You know I have."

"Even though you decided to move back home, have you second guessed your decision to divorce Kurt?"

"No."

"Well, don't you feel like a weak fool in terms of your decision to be with him then?"

"It's different!"

"How so?"

"I've *always* been in control at work and I've *never* been in control at home. Kurt's always been the decision maker, so I'm not only stripping him of a wife; I'm stripping him of his power. I might as well kill the man."

"*Whoa*! Are you saying his power over you is more important than your happiness?"

"No! I'm saying I don't have the heart to hurt and confuse him!"

"We've been over this a million times, Chrissy. Kurt will be fine."

"That doesn't change the fact that I don't want him to be."

"Is that why you're not getting on with your life? So you don't have to endure another one of his emotionally-detached episodes? Because I know those can be painful."

The rest of the session is like déjà vu, and my next session after that is exactly the same. I've become stuck in a vacuum with zero ability to escape; the expression "I suck" totally works. On top of everything else I haven't seen or heard from Leo in five weeks, and the messages on his answering machine have become unbearable to listen to. Not because Taddeo has been throwing me under the bus either. It's because there has been zero mention of me. The last two messages he left for Leo sent me straight to my medicine cabinet to numb the pain. I finally decided to confess to Slutty Co-worker that I've been hacking into Leo's voicemail, hoping she'd help me stop. Wishful thinking.

"Hold on a minute, you've been listening to his messages? That's unreal!"

"Yeah, about as unreal as that bracelet dangling from your wrist that a married father of three gave you."

"Hey, I'm not judging. I'm admiring your work."

"It's not work, it's an addiction that might just kill me before my actual marriage does."

Clapping like a three-year-old she yells out, "Play some for me!"

"Hey Bastard, I'm flying up for the weekend. I'm staying at my buddy's place in San Francisco, and we're going to the Red Devil Lounge on Saturday night. His girlfriend has some chicks she wants to set us up with. I know it's not your scene, but drive down and hang out with us anyway."

"Don't worry too much about it, Hun. You told me before that Leo's not the club scene kinda guy."

"Oh yeah? Apparently he is now. Listen to Taddeo's next message."

"Hey, got your message! I'll pick you up at your apartment in Moraga, and we'll drive to the city together. It's gonna be a good time. Blehhhhh."

"What's *Blehhhh*?"

"Some sort of grunting noise they do when they talk. I used to think it was cute, now I hate it. Damn it! I know he's gonna hook up with a girl!"

"Not necessarily."

"What do you mean?"

"What if you and I decide to go to the Red Devil on Saturday?"

"Oh that's just ridiculous! I can't do that...*can* I?"

"Of course you can! Plus, I want to meet that Italian *Blehhhhh* boy. He sounds cute. What's his name again?"

Two days and two pounds lighter later, Slutty Co-worker and I are in line to pay the cover charge at The Red Devil Lounge. The street is vibrating from the chaos inside, and I'm swaying back and forth to the beat trying to work off some of my nervous energy. She's pissed.

"What the fuck is taking so long?"

"Obviously the place is packed. They can only let as many in that come out. Hey, where are you going?"

I don't mind waiting our turn to get inside, but Slutty Co-worker thinks it's totally beneath her. I'm not sure if it was her slightly exposed left boob that got us in fast and free or if she promised the guy at the door a little something special if he let us through, but within two seconds of her whispering into his ear, we walk through the red rope as ugly jealous girls snicker at us.

"NICE JOB GETTING US IN! I'M GONNA GRAB A DRINK AND HEAD UPSTAIRS TO THE BALCONY TO GET A BIRDSEYE VIEW OF THE PLACE. YOU STAYING DOWN HERE?"

I swirl around to try to hear Slutty Co-worker's answer and then feel slightly embarrassed that I was talking to myself. I glance back toward the entrance and see the door guy put his hand on her waist and walk her to the dance floor. Man, she doesn't waste any time. I order a vodka tonic, pay for whatever the bartender just handed me, and squeeze my way through the crowd and up the spiral staircase to do what I came here for. Once I find my spot on the edge of the balcony I ask myself, "What *did* I come here for?" Am I here to torture myself, get back together with Leo, or make him as jealous as he's unknowingly made me? I have no fucking clue, and I almost hope he and his friends decided to go somewhere else so I don't have to find out the answer. Just when I'm in the middle of figuring out my life, one of the things that annoys me more than anything in the world happens.

"How can a girl like you be all alone?"

God, get a little closer, why don't you!

"Oh, I'm not alone. My friend's down there somewhere, I'm waiting for her."

"Want some company while you wait?"

My first instinct is to tell this guy to screw off, but after giving him a quick inspection and confirming the following:

1) He's over six feet tall
2) He has all his hair
3) He's got on expensive shoes

I'm satisfied that he's fit to be standing next to me as a roadblock against anyone else that might have the audacity to speak to me.

"Sure."

"Great! I'm Josh."

"Hey Josh, I'm Prudence."

I like to give really hideous names to guys who hit on me so they don't have the retarded need to repeat it every five seconds as if it's some kind of hot turn on. You know, when they say stuff like, "So, tell me what you do for a living, *Prudence*," and "That's a really nice shirt you're wearing, *Prudence*." It bugs the hell out of me. Suffice it to say, Josh didn't say my fake name once, but he sure had a lot of other stuff to gab about. I nod every so often, so he thinks I'm listening, but I keep my focus on the real reason I'm here. I scan every person's face who's upstairs leaning against the railing of the balcony. No Leo. I scan the dance floor below and look at every person's face that isn't stuck to another person's face. No Leo. I look at the groups of people smashed at the tiny cocktail tables distributed around the club. No Leo. I run my eyes down the long line of people sitting on barstools, starting on the far left and making my way all the way to the end and then…I see him. In the very darkest corner of the club, standing with Taddeo and two horrid, okay, semi-good looking girls, is my beautiful Leo. He's tan and much stronger than the last time I saw him; probably from working long hours doing construction in the hot Monterey sun. I can no longer hear John or Joe or whatever the hell his name is, and I can't hear the thunderous music. All I can hear is my heartbeat. All I can smell is Leo. All I can feel is pretty. Predictably, the answer to my question of what I planned on doing if I saw Leo isn't immediately answered. I just stand and stare.

Nothing, nothing, nothing and then…*What the hell does she think she's doing?* I watch as the sluttier-looking of the two chicks wraps her arms around Leo's neck and throws her head back in a fit of pathetic fake laughter. *Does he like it?* Before I have a chance to check out Leo's reaction, I react by accidently dropping my glass over the rail of the balcony, straight down two stories, and directly onto the dance floor. It crashes into a million pieces, people scream, the music abruptly stops, and a zillion hands point up toward the direction of where the wreckage came from. I'm already half way down the staircase when I turn around to see two really big dudes grab John/Joe/Josh's arms and lead him out a back door. Sorry about that, dude!

Fortunately, the place is back to full force by the time I hit the ground floor, and I easily blend into the crowd. I head straight toward the door but then suddenly remember that I don't have keys to Slutty Co-worker's apartment. Chances are that if I walk out of the club I won't get back in and I won't have anywhere to go until she decides to leave. And God knows how long she plans on paying that guy back for doing us a favor! I could be standing outside for hours! I whirl around to look for her and, as fate would have it, I slam chest-first into Leo, who happens to be leaving with Taddeo and the two bar hopping gutter sluts.

"*Chrissy?*"

I hear Taddeo murmur, "Shit."

The girl standing beside Leo is sizing me up, and she looks really unhappy. There's no "Hello" from Leo. Just a really pissed off, "Who are you here with?"

He must think I'm here with Kurt because his eyes are darting around, and he looks kind of ready to fight. I want to do what I always used to do to calm him down: wrap my arms around his neck and kiss him, but something tells me that would be a bad idea.

"My friend from work, you know… the one who lives on Clay Street."

Now Leo's bar hopping gutter slut knows we have history. Take that! Glancing at the girls, and not wanting to look like the pitiable trolls they are, I extend my hand toward them and introduce myself. They're so clueless and classless, they don't even know WHAT to make of my handshake. I raise my eyebrows and give Leo and Taddeo a look of disgusting sympathy. I look calm, cool, and collected but it's taking all of my self-control to keep from falling to the ground, curling up in a fetal position, and bawling my brains out.

"It's good to see you again, Taddeo."

Just a grunt.

Leo's eyes are piercing into mine and out the back of my skull. His voice is even more stabbing.

"You never called."

"I thought it would be for the better."

"For me or for you?"

"For you."

"You should've let me be the judge of that."

He's standing inches away and staring at me like he's one angry mother-fucker. I wonder what would happen if I dove in for a kiss. I feel like if I lean...in...just a... smidge...he might...follow...my lead. Just as I'm about to give it a shot, one of the bar hopping gutter sluts says, "Like, are we gonna go to that other place or what, you guys?"

"We are. Come on, Leo."

Fucking Taddeo! I shake my head at Leo's friend's obvious contempt for me, but at the same time, I know I deserve every ounce of it. Then I watch Leo's gutter slut grab his hand and wonder how much longer I can take the beating. My eyes are pleading with his not to leave. They're trying to tell him I have more to say. But after Taddeo nudges him in the back, he leans in close enough for me to smell him and whispers, "See ya, Chrissy." I want to turn around and watch him walk away, will him to come back, DO SOMETHING, but I can't seem to move. The music in the club suddenly intensifies, and people start bashing into my shoulders as they violently dance around. I want to get out of their way, but I can't. My feet are totally stuck.

"HEY CHRISSY, WHAT'S WRONG WITH YOU? YOU GOTTA MOVE!"

Slutty Co-worker, with smudged lipstick and all, finds me just as the tears are starting to drop.

"Hunny, you're gonna get the shit kicked out of that tiny little body if you don't get outta the way."

I baby step to her and lay my head on her shoulder.

"You saw him?"

"He left with a girl."

Then, after stroking my hair for a second, she abruptly stops.

"Well apparently he didn't come back with her."

"What are you talking about?"

Pointing to someone behind me, "Uhhhhh girlfriend, is that the *Blehhhh* boy with him? Damn, he's hot!"

I turn around, and there's Leo walking right toward me with a very unhappy Taddeo trailing behind.

"Leo, what are you..."

"I don't know why you keep running away and it kills me every time you do but I'll *always* be where I know you are."

And just like that, Leo pulls me toward him and kisses me. The drug that I've craved for almost two months slowly seeps back into my body.

For the next hour we don't move from that spot. When we aren't kissing, he whispers things in my ear like, "You look amazing," and "I don't like the thought of you in a place like this." He asks me if I've taken care of my break-up business with Numb Nuts, and like an addict who hasn't scored in months I hungrily tell him, "Yes," before I start kissing him again.

He tries to convince me to go back to his apartment, but not wanting to have a serious conversation with him about the state of my affairs, I convince him and Taddeo to hang out with Slutty Co-worker and me at her apartment instead. Two hours after I stumble into Leo at The Red Devil Lounge, we're hanging out on my friend's deck with vodka tonics as Third Eye Blind blares on the stereo. It's an extremely warm evening in the city and Slutty Co-worker suggests we grill late-night snacks. Everyone's comfortably pitching in, and as it's all happening I think to myself, this is one of those stand-out moments in life. The smell of the food, the sound of the ice cubes clinking away in our glasses, the sultry temperature, the loud music, the indiscriminate company…it's absolute perfection. No matter where I end up in life, thoughts of this night will send chills down the back of my neck, and I'll forever want to go back in time and re-live it.

As everyone's laughing it up at one of Slutty's slutty jokes, I reflect on two months ago in Monterey and the morning I came close to telling Leo about my marriage. As he slept, I lightly traced his eyebrows with my finger and watched his eyes dart around behind his closed lids. I studied his strong hands and tried to memorize the location of every scar on them. I stared at his lips, but occasionally had to look away in woozy astonishment as I recounted all the places they had traveled on my body. I thought of all the secrets and painful accounts of his life he had shared with me and that I owed it to him to share back. If it was at all possible, I fell deeper in love with him that morning. But once his eyes were open, his hands were moving, and his lips were talking, I got scared, took away his options and decided what was best for him. I didn't give him the choice of what to do about my marriage because I thought there would be less pain if I stayed in control. Well, two hours ago at The Red Devil Lounge, he told me I should let him be the judge of his decisions, and he's right. I have to stop playing puppeteer with his life. It gets us nowhere.

For so long I thought it would be best to end it with Leo, get a divorce, get through my sadness, and get on with my life. I guess I kind of felt like losing him was the price I had to pay for my immorality, *and* I foolishly thought that once he was gone, I would press on with a divorce a lot quicker. But as I demonstrated after the Monterey break-up, I still come up with every excuse in the book to suspend divorce when he's not around. And as I demonstrated by stalking him at The Red Devil Lounge, I can't get on with my life without him. Nothing changes. It's starting to look like the only choice I have is to tell Leo my ugly truth and let the chips fall where they may. Nothing changes when I try to strategically position them. Besides, Leo *knows* something's going on. He *knows* I'm scared to tell him something, but even so, he's right here with me right now. He's in love with me, and I'm pretty sure he's strong enough to handle my ugly truth. But…I better double check all that with Taddeo before I do something stupid like let him be the judge of his own life.

"Where's the bathroom?"

"Down the hall, to the left."

"You're not gonna disappear while I'm gone are you?"

"Ha-ha very funny."

The minute Leo walks away, Taddeo looks extremely uncomfortable.

"Geez, relax, I'm not gonna hurt you!"

No grunt this time, just a glare.

"I know it may not seem like it, but I really am crazy about him."

Still glaring.

"And I'm not mad at you for trying to set him up with someone else. You're only trying to be a good friend."

"Yep, boys will be boys."

I do a quick head shake at Slutty Co-worker to tell her to shut up and then an eye roll in the direction of the kitchen to tell her to leave for a minute.

"Right…refills! I'll be right back."

Once she's gone, I turn to Taddeo.

"Okay look, I know you're only trying to protect him, but please try to cut me some slack. I'm not a completely horrible person, just a slightly confused one."

"No, you look. He's had it rough these last few years. His parents screwed up a lot of shit for him, and he's had to scratch and claw for everything he has. I can't even say for sure I've seen him smile since high school. Then he meets you and he's like the old Leo again. He's smiling and laughing and making plans. For seven months, you were all he could talk about, and then you left for something like the tenth, and what we both thought was the final time, and he went back to how he was before, but worse. I spent the last month trying to cheer him up, and tonight I finally succeeded and then BOOM, here you are again. I dunno, it seems fishy to me."

Uh-oh, this guy's intuitive.

"Leo's never cared about *anyone* before, so if you're gonna leave again, make it for good because I don't want to see him get hurt anymore."

"How strong is Leo?"

"What do you mean?"

"There's a little more to my life than I've told him, and I'm not sure he can handle the truth."

"Christ, do you have a kid?"

"No!"

"AIDS?"

"God no!"

"Then whatever it is, he can handle it. He's the toughest guy I know, and the asshole's crazy about you. Man, I don't care how good looking you are, I sure as hell wouldn't put up with your shit."

Slutty Co-worker returned with fresh drinks and Leo returned from the bathroom and with every drink, Taddeo cut me more and more slack. I think he even gave Slutty Co-worker a little lovin' when I wasn't looking. The night ended with breakfast and plans to see

Leo the following Friday, my twenty-ninth birthday. The question I asked myself at the beginning of the evening had been answered. I went to the Red Devil Lounge to get back together with Leo.

The question now, is when do I tell him about my secret life? It needs to be soon because this lifestyle is starting to take its toll on me. My weight is more Ethiopian than sexy, and my once flawless skin is now wearing bags under its eyes *and* has an occasional zit. It's not easy being me.

SURPRISE!

AUGUST, 1998

Every single year, without fail, Kurt goes to the same trade show on my birthday. And every single year, without fail, it bugs the crap out of me…until this year. Sure I feel icky about what I'm going to do in his absence, but watching him load up the car without an iota of guilt for leaving me alone on yet another birthday and not asking me how I'm going to spend yet another birthday alone, made the ick disappear pretty quickly. I waved goodbye from the driveway, and once the car was out of sight, I skipped into the house and dedicated the rest of the morning to picking out the most perfect outfit for my date with Leo. I settled on my red Asian-inspired skinny pants and a black satin chemise that looks more like lingerie than a shirt, and I paired it all up with the highest black heels I could find in my closet. Leo's driving up from Monterey tonight, and I'm meeting him at a restaurant near the Berkeley Marina. Who knows where we'll end up after that. I can hardly contain my excitement at work, and Slutty Co-worker literally has to slap the smile off my face at least once an hour. Five o'clock finally rolls around, and just as I'm about to head home to shower and make myself pretty, my cell phone rings.

"Hello?"

"Hey girl, it's Courtney. I'm in Danville! I just got done shopping with my mom and I thought we could meet for a quick drink before I head home."

"Can't tonight. Sorry."

"Oh come on! We never get a chance to be alone. Nic and Kel are *always* with us. Besides, I need to talk to you about some stuff."

"What stuff?"

"Just some stuff that's going on between Guss and me. I need to pick your brain. Plus, I want to know what the hell is going on with you and Kurt."

"What do you mean?"

"Well, you went from throwing in the towel three weeks ago at MC Hammer's house to moving back home the same night. That's what I mean."

"I'll be at the Faz bar in fifteen minutes."

It's only five-fifteen, and I'm not meeting Leo until nine. Plenty of time. Plus, Courtney's been there for me more times than I can count. If she needs to talk to me about something, then I want to listen. And after twenty-two glances at my watch, I *finally* get to stop listening. I stare at her in disbelief.

"So, that's it?"

"Well, yeah! I'm sick and tired of the damn Nintendo games. It's like Madden football this and Killer Instinct that. He's thirty-one years old and we have a baby for Christ sake! So what should I do?"

"Uhhhhh, I don't know…throw the damn thing out?"

"Right, I'll throw it out. Good idea. Thanks."

What the hell's going on? This girl has like a zillion years of college under her belt. She's a Goddamn doctor! It's not like her to act this stupid.

"So, why'd you move back home, Chrissy?"

This must be the real reason why she wanted to talk to me and I would've obliged in the conversation if she didn't blow her time on Guss's ridiculous video game obsession, but I have to get going. I don't want to keep Leo waiting.

"I dunno, I guess I was still buzzed when he asked me to. Look, Court, I've gotta run. I have this work thing at nine…a conference call…with a factory in Hong Kong. Sorry."

"Oh, right, sure! Hey, can I stop at your house real quick and borrow a dress? I have a wedding to go to, and I've got NOTHING to wear."

Another glance at my watch. Six forty-five. I'm still okay for time.

"Sure."

I was super annoyed when I left the bar with Courtney. She seriously wasted a lot of my precious get ready time! But on the short drive to my house I started feeling light and happy again as thoughts of the evening ahead played in my mind and any annoyance I had toward Courtney floated away. But half way to my front door, light and happy come to a screeching halt, and I stop dead in my tracks. My head darts to the left, then to the right. I notice Kelly's car, then Nicole's car, and then I recognize several of the other cars parked along the street belonging to Kurt's sisters and brothers, his parents and my parents.

"Courtney, what the hell's going on?"

"What are you talking about?"

"THESE CARS! THEY BELONG TO PEOPLE I KNOW!"

"Okay, shhhhhhhh, don't freak out!"

"Why on earth would I freak out, Courtney?"

"Kurt's throwing a surprise party for you."

"Kurt's in Utah!"

"No he's not. He's been planning this for weeks, since you moved back home, really. I was the decoy to keep you away while everyone set up. Should I be sorry?"

My mind is reeling. Leo's on his way to a restaurant in Berkeley, I have no way to contact him. He refuses to get a cell phone. Oh my God, he's going to think I stood him up! I can't bear the thought of him sitting at the table all alone wondering where I am. He's going to be worried sick, not to mention, Taddeo's going to kick my ass!

"I have to go!"

"Go where? There are forty-five people in your house right now! Chrissy, stop and listen to me! I called Kurt on the way here, and he expects us to walk through the door any second now. Listen…see it's quiet in there! They're all hiding behind your fucking couches 'n shit!"

I look at my watch and pace around my porch. It's seven o'clock, two hours until I'm supposed to meet Leo. It leaves me with an hour and a half to think of a clever excuse to leave my party in a sassy outfit and meet my lover for dinner. Jesus, I'm a creative mother-fucker, but I don't think I'm that creative.

"Let's get this over with."

"Over with? I'm confused. You're astrological sign is Leo! You people are supposed to love the attention, the parties, the... *Ohhhhhhhhhhhhh my God*, you were planning on meeting Leo tonight, weren't you?"

I don't even fucking care what anyone thinks anymore! These people are ruining my night!

"Guilty."

"CHRISSY! I THOUGHT THAT WAS OVER WITH!"

"It was...until last weekend when I ran into him. I'm sorry, I can't stop, Courtney!"

"What you're doing is so unfair, do you realize that?"

"*Helloooooooo,* Doctor, I have an *addiction*! Just open the Goddamn door! I have to meet him at nine, let's hurry this up."

Once inside, I'm hit hard with a very annoying "SURPRISE!" and I stare at the faces of all the people I know. All the people I had hoped to avoid on this day. And for the first time ever since knowing me, my face isn't giving them what they expect. Eventually their triumphant clapping trails off in confusion, and they stand and stare at my sour puss of a reaction to their presence. As much as I'm predisposed to sing and dance for them...inclined to give them everything they expect in order to avoid this awkward moment, I can't. That part of me died about five minutes ago. With arms wide open, Kurt comes barreling toward me and with the lips I had hoped to avoid on this day, he plants a big kiss on my forehead.

"Well that's one of the unhappiest faces I've ever seen! Aren't you surprised?"

"Sure am. Who would've ever suspected a *twenty-ninth* birthday surprise party?"

Never one to entertain one of my bad moods, Kurt moves along to visit with his friends and family. I don't see Courtney, Nicole, and Kelly. It's safe to assume they're locked in the bathroom, where Courtney's telling them about my filthy plans for the evening. As soon as people scatter about, I duck back out to my car to grab my cell phone. Once Leo gets to the restaurant, he'll be calling. Frantically tapping my phone against my outer thigh, I start mulling over a list of lies and excuses to explain why I'm not there. Then I imagine him in his car, looking good, smelling good, listening to loud music, and feeling excited about seeing me and my heart breaks. I can't lie to that image.

I do my best to avoid the party and it hasn't been that hard really. I haven't seen Kurt since I walked through the door. He must be busy manning the grill or recycling something. My parents left about twenty minutes into the spectacle. They're in my camp and enjoy Kurt's family about as much as they enjoy their annual colonoscopies. After I give fake hugs and kisses to the Gibbons clan (which by the way, they would recognize as fake if they were sane), I pour myself a ginormous glass of vodka and head to my room to resent them. I'm reminded of how different I am from them as I walk down the hall and listen to their blank laughter and worthless conversation. Why can't they talk about something interesting, like how to dispose of a corpse without getting caught or how Clinton destroyed whatever moral fiber that existed amongst today's youth by saying a blow job isn't sex? But no, I hear someone mention something about a beer can chicken recipe and someone else overstressing the importance of vitamin D. I hate them. They're so empty.

A glass breaks and the house gets quiet for a moment. My first instinct is to find the broom and clean up the mess, but I resist the impulse to do exactly what they expect me to do. Suddenly my anger about everything turns into vengeance, and I ask myself, "What does Chrissy want for her birthday?" The answer is evident by my trip to the shower. Within an hour, I'm looking at myself in the mirror, dressed up in my outfit as if my night is going along as planned. Why shouldn't it? No one's come to look for me. This party wasn't for me, it was for them. I open the shutters and look into my beautiful backyard. The tiki torches, the fire pit, the shish-ka-bobs, the big ice filled bucket of beer and wine, the laughter. It all looks so pretty, but it isn't. I walk over to my vanity and one by one pick up the years of framed pictures set up just so. They all look so beautiful, but they're not. I gently place the picture of Kurt and me from our wedding day back down and decide to go get my real birthday present before guilt gets the best of me.

"Fancy outfit, lady. Got a date?"

Startled, I turn around and face my judge and jury.

"Gosh, I'm surprised at you, Courtney, usually you can keep your mouth shut."

"I had to tell them, this is too big."

I'm trapped. I have two choices. I can knock them over and make a run for it or I can plead my case and hope they cover for me when I ditch the party for my date. I walk back to the window as I mull over my two options.

"Stop shaking your head, Kelly, I feel bad enough as it is."

"How did you…"

As I whip around to address Kelly, I catch a glimpse of myself in the mirror. The ridiculousness of my outfit against the backdrop of the surprise party shit show going on around me literally turns me into a lunatic.

"You've been shaking your head at me since the moment you found out about all of this!"

"You said it was over with him! You made Kurt and all of us believe you were gonna try, and that outfit sure as hell doesn't look like you're trying!"

"Kelly's right. If I knew it was still going on with Leo, I wouldn't have shelled out a few hundred for this spread."

"I'll pay you back, Nic. I'll pay all of you back! Just leave me alone so I can figure out what I'm gonna do!"

The three of them shoot back in rapid succession.

"You can't leave the party, Chrissy!"

"Yeah, what's Kurt gonna think?"

"And don't expect me to lie to him anymore!"

"No shit, Courtney, and I have you to thank for bringing me here in the first place! And Nicole, I don't care what Kurt thinks anymore! If I did, do you think I'd be standing here wearing *THIS*? And you know what, Kelly? I never asked you to lie to anyone, so say and do whatever the hell you want! I don't care about *anyone* anymore and if you don't like what I'm telling you, then GET THE FUCK OUT OF MY LIFE!"

Never in all the years that I've been friends with these women have I yelled at them like this. I'm not sure which one of us is more shocked. With wide eyes and hands covering all our mouths, Kurt comes stumbling into the room.

"A little dressed up for the party aren't ya, Hun?"

And then, surprise-surprise, my phone rings. It jolts me and my friends back to the crisis at hand. Ring after ring, we just stand there and stare at my hand holding the phone.

"What's the problem, Babe, aren't you gonna answer that?"

"Ummmm, yeah. I was supposed to, ummmmm, meet some people from work…you know, before I knew about all of this and… well, uhhhhh, this must be them wondering where I am. Excuse me for a minute."

"Cool, tell them to come to the party! Plenty of food, and 'bout time I met those people!"

All disgust aside, my best friends do what they're predisposed to do. They come to my rescue and engage Kurt in meaningless conversation so I can have an important one with Leo. I rush to the bathroom and lock the door.

"Leo?"

"Where are you? Are you okay?"

"No, I'm not okay." Then I start crying uncontrollably.

"Baby, what's wrong? Were you in an accident? Tell me where you are so I can come and get you."

"I'm, I'm…I'm at home and there are all these people…and I can't leave, and I didn't know… I'm so mad and…"

"What are you talking about?"

"You're gonna freak out, Leo."

"Just tell me what's going on."

"Kurt threw me a surprise party."

Not the way I wanted to start being truthful with Leo but I'm backed into a corner here. He's gotta see how upset I am and show me some compassion.

"WHAT THE FUCK ARE YOU TALKING ABOUT?"

Or maybe he doesn't. I hear someone in the background say, "Sir, please keep your voice down."

"Leo, please listen to me, I came home from work to shower and change, and this is what I walked into. I'm so sorry, but you have to believe me, I didn't know anything about this."

"What the hell makes that guy think he can throw you a party? Tell me, Chrissy, TELL ME NOW!"

And then I hear it again: "Sir, I'm going to have to ask you to leave the restaurant if you don't keep your voice down."

Leo shoots back, "Fuck you! I was leaving anyway." Without even a pause, he turns his attention back to me. "ANSWER ME CHRISSY! WHAT MAKES HIM THINK HE CAN THROW YOU A PARTY?"

"I...don't...know."

"YES YOU DO. YOU'RE FUCKING LYING TO ME!"

"Leo, please calm down."

The pounding on the bathroom door startles me.

"Chrissy, who are you talking to in there?"

"I'll be out in a minute."

"That doesn't sound like a work call."

"I SAID I'LL BE OUT IN A MINUTE!"

Leo then furiously interjects with, "Who the hell are you talking to? *IS THAT HIM?*"

"Leo, stop. Let me ex--"

"NO! I WORKED DOUBLE SHIFTS ALL WEEK SO I COULD AFFORD TO GIVE YOU A NICE BIRTHDAY. I WORKED TEN HOURS DIGGING A DITCH TODAY AND THEN DROVE THREE HOURS IN TRAFFIC TO BE HERE IN TIME, AND FOR WHAT? TO HEAR THAT FUCKING ASSHOLE'S NAME; TO GET STOOD UP BECAUSE OF *HIM?* WHO THE HELL DO YOU THINK YOU ARE?"

"I...I don't know."

"WHAT?"

As if all of the air has left my body, I tell him, "I don't know who I am."

And then he hung up on me.

Usually I'm fearless
But I've become undone
A clown without even a disguise
Now everyone will know that I'm falling
I've fallen in love…

("Falling," Keri Noble)

PARTY'S OVER

NOVEMBER, 1998

"**O**utta my way, I gotta pee so bad! I had to do three laps around the block before I finally found a parking spot!"

As I whiz past her, she yells out, "If you plan on staying here for the long haul, you might want to pay for a parking permit!"

From the comfort of the toilet seat, I yell back, "You're right, I should've just bought one in August, but I never thought in a million years I'd be sleeping on your couch three months later!"

It's nice here. I get to do things like pee with the door open and have girl talk.

"You stay as long as you want, Hunny, I enjoy the company."

Slutty Co-worker opened up her home to me after my surprise party meltdown. Actually, to call it a meltdown is an understatement. The events that occurred that night are still a blur…that's how crazy I was. After Leo hung up on me, I curled up in a ball on the bathroom floor and laid there in a state of panic the likes of which I hadn't felt since my "I FEEL DEAD INSIDE, I FEEL DEAD INSIDE" night ten months earlier. After an indefinite amount of time passed, Kurt got tired of banging on the door, so he broke it down. I lifted my head to find a large amount of people staring at me with shish-ka-bobs and beers in tow. Almost immediately, an argument ensued between my friends and Kurt, something about them wanting to take care of the situation and Kurt thinking he should. I got up, put on a shoe that had fallen off, and headed for the front door. On my way there, things became very quiet, or maybe it was just quiet in my head, but I do remember Kurt grabbing my hand and asking me where the hell I was going. I *think* I said, "to meet my co-workers like I originally planned," and then I left. I vaguely remember my friends telling Kurt to let me go but I'm not really sure, because I haven't spoken to any of them since that night to substantiate anything. I got in my car and drove straight to the restaurant where I was supposed to meet Leo. I thought there might be a chance I'd find him drinking his troubles away at the bar, but not so. The hostess told me Leo punched a waiter for grabbing his jacket in an attempt to force him to leave the restaurant, and after that she wasn't sure where he went. She was just glad he was gone. I almost punched her. I got back in my car and went to the next logical place I might find him: his apartment in Moraga. But if he was there, he didn't answer his door. After knocking for what seemed like forever, I left a note and a message on his answering machine. They both said the same thing.

I have something really important to tell you, and it will explain everything. I'm parked on the street, and I'll wait for you till morning. I'm sorry.

He never showed up, and he never called. The next morning, cold and tired, I drove home to face the inevitable. The TV was on ESPN, but on mute. Dishes were still scattered everywhere, and Kurt was asleep on the couch. I tiptoed to the bedroom and got to work. Just as I was finishing packing up my second suitcase, he came in with two cups of coffee and handed one to me. I felt so horrible about everything I had done to him that I probably would've eaten eggs if he offered them to me.

"You wanna tell me what's going on?"

I shake my head.

"That's okay, I think I already figured it out."

Plop goes my journal right onto the middle of our bed. My legs collapse beneath me and I land Indian style on the ground. Busted.

"What, you didn't think I'd go searching for answers?"

I say nothing.

"Who's Leo?"

Leo's name coming out of Kurt's mouth made my skin crawl.

"He's a…he's a guy who works for one of our corporate vendors."

My God, I marvel at my ability to pull a lie outta my ass.

"What's going on with him?"

"I don't know."

"What do you mean you don't know? You wrote a fucking novel about him!"

"All right, I can explain. I met him at a work function. He's having some trouble in his marriage, and we're having trouble in ours, and we just started talking. He makes me feel… sane."

And I'm sorry, Kurt, but I'm in love with him, and I can't be married to you anymore.

"What I read in that book of yours makes me think you're in love with him or something."

"I enjoy talking to him, Kurt, he makes me think about things."

You know…things like finding true love.

"I don't even know who you are anymore."

You never did.

"Seriously Chrissy, how would you feel if I did this to you?"

Relieved that I didn't have to be the bad guy.

"Aren't you gonna say something?"

There's too much to say. You wouldn't understand. You won't let me go.

"Don't talk to him anymore. I mean it. If I find out you're still talking to him, we're gonna have some trouble."

My gaze shifts from my journal to his face. On what planet does he think those kinds of demands are acceptable and furthermore… doesn't he realize we're already in deep trouble? I hired a therapist, filled up a journal with thoughts of another man, bailed on my surprise party. We're in all kinds of trouble!

"What are you packing for?"

"I'm moving into my friend's place in the city."

"I TOLD YOU THAT'S NOT HOW WE'RE GONNA SOLVE OUR PROBLEMS!"

"They're not getting solved with me here Kurt!"

"Well judging by the crap in that journal, you're not even trying!"

"You're right, I'm not and that's why I have to go."

On the way to Slutty Co-worker's apartment that day, I wondered how the hell Kurt could even *want* me to stay after reading the filth in my journal. It struck me as really odd, almost inconceivable, so I pulled over and whipped it out. To my surprise, I found that most of the inflammatory pages had been torn out. The only explanation I can think of is that after I left the surprise party, my friends must've rummaged around my room looking for evidence of my sins to protect me from further pain and embarrassment. They found the journal and hid my secrets. But even though three months have passed, I'm still too horrified to talk to any of them to confirm my assumption.

Kurt and I talk every couple of days, and essentially nothing between us has changed other than I live somewhere else. And Dr. Maria was right; he continues to be just fine. I begged him to tell his family what's going on, but he says everything's my fault, so it's my responsibility to tell them. Dr. Maria encouraged me to do just that as a first step to freedom, but I can't. Even after everything that's happened, I'm still not ready to be the bad guy.

Leo's back in Moraga, and it sounds like school's going well for him. He's not working at the rock yard anymore. He got a paid internship with some small financial institution, and he's making pretty good money. Probably enough to finally buy a pretty girl a drink at a bar. The Ho-Bag moved out and he's living alone, and as far as I can tell, he's not seeing anyone. I know all this because I'm still a masochistic freak and listen to his voicemail. Since the surprise party, there's only been one message that mentioned my name and it was from Taddeo. It said, "Told you so, buddy. Fuck her."

I really was going to tell Leo I was married that night when I waited for him in my car at his apartment. I had no choice. During that phone call in my bathroom, I could hear the damage my surreptitious lifestyle was doing to him, and protecting my identity no longer seemed as important as his knowledge of it. It no longer seemed as important as his sanity. The rage that exploded from his body when I told him I was in Kurt's presence was frightening. There was a huge disconnect between what I was saying and what I was doing, and I could hear in his voice that he was trying to piece together the reality of the situation. Things weren't adding up. But the love he wanted to believe existed between us made it impossible to do that, so he went nuts. It made me sad and scared and so desperately wanting to end the charade. So yes, I really, really was going to tell Leo I was married that night.

I remember a long time ago when Dr. Maria suggested my secret affair was probably making Kurt insane. But she was wrong. My secret marriage was making Leo insane. I'd like to think I'd still tell Leo the truth, clear things up for him, if he'd give me the chance, but the surprise party was the line in the sand, and I never heard from him again. And so for the last three months, Slutty Co-worker's done everything she can to mend my broken heart. Night after night, she tries to convince me to hit the town with her, but I insist on staying in with my Thai take-out and sad Sarah McLachlan music. Sometimes I venture down to Union Street to take my mind off things, but usually I'm reminded of why it's a bad idea. Seeing all the cute couples walking hand in hand with their groceries and fresh flowers and watching the singles whoop it up at the hip restaurants makes me want to jump in front of a cable car. Everything I see and do makes me crave therapy! But Dr. Maria thought our sessions had become redundant, and she suggested I take a little time off to think on my own. Either she's the most honorable therapist on the face of the earth to pass on my money or she got just as tired of talking about my problems as me. Four weeks ago, at my last session before my hiatus, I asked if Kurt had ever shown up for an appointment and, of course, he hadn't. She asked me if I had spoken to Leo and, of course, I hadn't. I walked out of her office feeling just as dejected as the first day I walked into it.

Immediately after Dr. Maria kicked me to the curb, I scrambled to find help elsewhere. No, not another therapist! Puleez, I may cheat on my husband but I would *never* cheat on Dr. Maria! I bought all the best-selling self-help books I could find. Did they help me? Of course not, but what happened when I was looking for the books did.

Before I tell you what happened, let me explain something to all of you needy mother-fuckers out there. The self-help section at your local book store is the place people go who either don't have enough money for a therapist or simply don't want the frank assessment a good one can provide. Self-help books are jam packed with lively case studies of the moronic and doomed and filled with lists of easier said than done positive steps for improvement, all of which make for a convenient diversion from what self-help book readers really need: therapy. You see, self-help book readers are needy bastards who *looooooove* identifying with the folks in the case studies; it makes them feel like they're not alone and psycho. Take me for instance. I found bits and pieces of myself in every emotionally abused adulteress I read about. Each one of those sluts made me feel like I wasn't alone! But whenever it came to the part of the book that told me how to heal myself, I'd skip pages or throw the damn thing on the coffee table. Let's be honest, most people want validation for their fucked-upness, not a cure for it. Cures are boring and take work. And so we go back to the bookstore the next day to look for more validation and case studies, only to remain forever fucked-up. I know, because I slipped into this dangerous territory for a while. Now onto how my search for the stupid self-help books helped me...

If you're a self-help book virgin, no need to ask the bookstore clerk for assistance locating them, just follow the weeping and moaning sounds. It doesn't matter what bookstore you're in, you round the corner to the self-help section and the entire area is littered with Sad Frumpy Ladies. They're either crying, deliriously laughing or visibly traumatized to the point that their entire bodies are shaking, and every single one of them will look up at you and give you a needy smile and a nod of the head that says, "Hi fellow fucked-up person, come on in, you're safe here." The first time I encountered the emotional carnage sitting on the floor of the self-help book section, my first instinct was to turn and run, but I couldn't. I didn't have the heart to cause those haggard faces and tattered hearts additional damage by rejecting them, so I entered into their bizarre world. And once you're inside those walls, it's very hard to leave, *especially* for a narcissistic person like myself who likes to read about people who have committed similar acts of cruelty and who are now bestselling authors of books called, *How I Committed Adultery, Survived, Wrote A Book, And Got Rich.*

But fortunately for me, the experience ended almost as quickly as it started. On my third visit back to the self-help book section,

I was thumbing through a book that could've easily been titled, *If You Think You're Lost Now, Just Wait A Year And Buy The Follow Up To This Book*, when a clearly emotionally challenged woman said, "Oh you'll like that one, it *really* helped me."

To which I replied, "Oh yeah, then why are you still sitting in the self-help book section?" I got the hell outta there and hid amongst the magazines until I was sure all those crazies had cried themselves to sleep.

I settled into a chair and found refuge with the very best periodical of all time, *US* magazine. Nothing like a celebrity scandal to make your own indignities feel completely manageable. But no, it was not the *US* magazine that helped me to learn how to brush off Kurt's insensibilities and it wasn't *US* that helped me to cope with the loss of Leo. It was what I read on the cover of *Fitness* magazine as I was putting *US* away that helped me heal. Right there on the cover of *Fitness* it said: "Therapy's great, but it's nothing compared to what long walks and yoga can do for your mind...*and your body*."

Well that just cracked me up! Lazy people walk, and granolas do yoga! People with energy and money join gyms and get a therapist, that's just the way things are done! I didn't want to read the article, but the chick on the cover had a great ass, so I decided to flip through to see how she got it.

Without warning I got sucked in like...kind of like I was reading a case study in a self-help book! The article mentioned wonderful things like creating peace of mind and balance, revitalizing the body and soul, and tension relief. I thought...*shit, my gym hasn't done any of that stuff for me!* The article said a spastic personality can only become lucid via quiet physical activity. I thought...*shit, I can use some lucidity!* It also said yoga and walking helps one to gather their thoughts for the next stage in life and aids in the recovery of "life's accidents." I thought...*shit, I definitely have some accidents I need to recover from!* I bought the damn magazine, and on my way back to Slutty Co-worker's, I stopped off at Nordstrom's to buy a solid pair of walking shoes and the exact same yoga outfit the girl on the cover was wearing.

The next day I joined Slutty Co-worker's gym where she told me she secretly teaches a weekend yoga class. The woman shaves her armpits and votes republican! *Who'd a thought*? She jumped for joy when I told her I was interested in giving yoga a try, and she's been an enthusiastic and motivating instructor to me. Seriously, you should see her inner thighs!

For my walking, I picked the reservoir that Leo used to hang out at because I hoped to run into him. I got all glammed up in my trendy work out gear and walked around the damn thing for hours searching for him. I never found him and that's okay, because what happened was even better. I found myself, and I did it by studying other women. I watched all of them. The ones who walk in well groomed packs with all of their gossip and bitching about their ungrateful husbands. Those ones band together real tight. Misery loves company, I guess. Then there are the disheveled ones who walk while pushing their loud and dirty baby strollers. They usually talk about the life they *used* to have and not very many of them seem thrilled about giving it up. Then there are the really old ones. They seem pretty content with life, or maybe it's that they're glad it's almost over. Never could figure it out really. But what I did figure out is that the common topic of conversation amongst all of the women I studied is that they enjoy talking about how much they suffer. And they're not talking about ending their suffering either; they just enjoy bitching about it. I never hear them take responsibility for their unhappiness and not one woman has a plan to correct it. They walk and bitch, and they made me realize there's a very fine line between who I am at this moment and who they are. One wrong move and I'm in a pack of sad angry women...a pack of modern day Francescas! They're alive, and they exist everywhere, and they scare the crap out of me.

Once I became focused on the women around me and my almost certain unhappy place amongst them, it seemed like all of the Kurt and Leo crap that used to clutter my head just disappeared. Don't get me wrong, I still mourn the loss of what I wanted with the both of them, but until I make my life about me, no man will fit into it, and the crazy women circling the reservoir every single day are proof of that. It's clear to me now that a therapist can ask you questions but until you ask them of yourself and give yourself time and space to think about the answers, you're not really making any progress. I remember painfully trying to find answers in Leo's quiet apartment when he lived in Monterey, but failed. Too many of my thoughts were about other people, none of them were about me.

Eventually I blocked the crazy reservoir women out of my mind because, frankly, they made me sick. I started thinking about things like my career and the creative projects I've put on hold because of it. I'd love to learn how to play the guitar, plant a garden, take cooking classes. Shoot, I've always wanted to own my own business. I thought about trivial things like how I would decorate my own place if I had it and what kind of car I would buy if the choice were mine and mine alone. Inspiring and *completely* attainable lists started to fill my head, and soon my trendy work out gear turned into ripped sweat pants and dirty sweatshirts because I couldn't wait to get on that walking path, breathe in the clean air, and think about all the great things that are within my grasp. All of those huge thoughts I used to have about having babies, getting a divorce, and telling secret lovers about secret husbands kept me paralyzed, unable to see the things in life that could make me happy. But I see them now, and I think I'm officially ready to go after some happiness.

NOW OR NEVER

NOVEMBER, 1998

It's finally Friday. Normally I'd look forward to the weekend. I'd sleep in. Slutty Co-worker would bring me a Starbucks, we'd hit up her yoga class, and then I'd drive over the Bay Bridge and walk for hours around the reservoir, dreaming up a bunch of things I want to do with my life. But not this weekend. In fact, I'm actually dreading it.

Six days ago, after a long walk, I was driving through Lafayette in the stormy fall weather looking for a place to grab some coffee, when I came across a man posting a "for rent" sign. I'm not sure if it was my overwhelming fear of becoming a future member of a pack of angry women or my newfound enthusiasm for all the possibilities in life that are within my grasp, but twenty minutes later, I signed a lease for the place. Perhaps the beginnings of the correction phase of my life!

I rented a tiny one bedroom, one bath cottage with lovely old French doors that lead to a massive deck overlooking a roaring creek. It's secluded, peaceful, and perfect, and it's also conveniently located five minutes from a bar and not just any bar: The Round Up.

According to Leo's messages from The Ho-Bag, The Round Up is his home away from home these days. I've been tempted to drop in for a beer when I know he's going to be there, but for the life of me, I can't come up with a lie that would explain why I would frequent a place like The Round Up. The patrons are a unique blend of couch-burning Oakland Raiders fans, construction workers, and uber-rich college kids, and for some inexplicable reason, the crowd clicks. But me…I would NOT click. Maybe one day if the Raiders make it to the playoffs or if I date another college boy (like those two things will *EVER* happen), I'll stop in for a beer. But for now, concocting a plan to bombard Leo at his hang-out goes against any and all of the correcting I need to be doing in my life. But mostly, I'm too scared to play with drugs again. Quitting was way too hard. Nope, part one of my correction phase begins by moving into my heavenly cottage. But before I do that I have to tell Kurt I leased it, and that's supposed to happen tomorrow morning. Hence…the weekend dread.

It's been easy to put the Kurt conversation out of my mind for the last five days because my schedule's been full with interviews for a few positions my company is looking to fill. Every single minute of my week was packed with Donna Karan wanna-be's. Only one more to go, and then I can start to mentally prepare myself for the morning.

Just as the Jewish American Princess Designer and I are picking ourselves up off the floor from laughing so hard at the entitled piece of Euro-trash who just left my office, my assistant knocks on my door to tell me our next interview is waiting, a Ms. Megan Cox.

"Omigod! Let me see this girl's resume, hurry!"

JAP digs in her pile and frantically hands it to me.

"What the hell's the matta?"

I scan down the page to the education part and see that *this* Megan Cox is, in fact, my nemesis. I exhale, "Holy shit, she's got balls."

"Is it good? Lemme see it. Wow, she's studyin' Bitness at St. Mewee's in Mowaga, and she's due to gwaduwate early…next month, acthwally. Wow, and she's been takin' night kwasses in fashion design in San Fwan for the last yeeeea. She's a work-horse, just like we want! Can't wait to meeta!"

"Me neither."

In walks a confident Ms. Megan. Based on her education and her outfit, I think I'd actually like her…if I didn't hate her so much. I rise from my chair, stick out my hand and say, "Hi Megan, nice to see you again," and it rattles her. Totally not what she expected.

"You two know eachotha?"

After I introduce the two of them, I explain that Megan and I have a mutual friend named Leo and then I casually proceed with the interview. I know Megan wants this internship and she won't do anything to ruin her chances of getting it. And I'm right, the interview concludes without any uncomfortable moments, we shake hands again, and I tell her we'll be in touch. That's right, I have your address and phone number now, bitch!

"She'd be good for the job, Kwissy."

"Yeah, she would. Let's put her in our maybe pile."

She might be good for the job, but she won't be good for me if she works here. It would only be a matter of time before she spilled the beans about my relationship with Leo to someone in the gossip, *I mean design*, department. That girl's gone and done it again! Just like she forced me to tell Nicole about Leo, she's going to force me to tell my co-workers that I cheated on who *she thinks* is my fiancé but who *they know* as my husband. Then she'll find out I'm married and…gulp, tell Leo. But she is the best candidate for the internship, and my credibility will be on the line if I argue against her. I have no choice, I'm going to have to beat her to the punch and tell my co-workers I'm separated. Since I'm going to do that, I might as well tell Kurt I want a divorce. And since I'm going to do that, I might as well correct *everything* and just tell Leo I'm married. And if I do that, I'll be sure to tell him it's Megan's fault I'm back in his life. Like I said, I'd like that girl if I didn't hate her so much.

After a restless night pondering my conversation with Kurt about the cottage *and* my new Megan dilemma, I wake up early on Saturday morning and timorously tackle dilemma number one.

"So what do you think?"

"Of what?"

For a split second I consider making up the reason I dragged him here, because I just got the feeling the venti latte I brought him as a peace offering ain't gonna do a damn thing to cushion the blow of what I'm about to say. Not only am I going to piss Kurt off and mark the beginning of the end of twelve years together, I'm about to set him free to have the kind of fun I've been having for the past eleven months. Except his fun will be permissible and encouraged by everyone who's going to hate me for doing this to him. Ugh. Maybe I should've thought this through a bit more. I mean, eventually word will get out about this place and then our status will become public knowledge. It'll only be a matter of time before girls flock to him. Someone's cuteness will grab his attention and he'll feel compelled to act on his curiosity. He'll buy the cute girl dinner, and no doubt she'll be more than happy to thank him with more than a kiss. Omigod, he'll touch her, and it might feel better than it did when he touched me. Because of what I'm about to tell him, because of the legitimate space I'm about to put between us...*he's probably going to realize he's better off without me.* I imagined payback would be a bitch for what I've done to him, but if thoughts like this come to fruition, I might actually die.

"Hello? Earth to Chrissy! I'm running late for a kayaking lesson, can you tell me why we're here?"

But hold on, would I die? Would the pain of finding out that Kurt screwed around with another woman hurt *any more* than knowing I screwed around on him? And if he realizes he's better off without me...could it possibly hurt *any more* than my own realization that I'm better off without him? Hardly. Get real, Chrissy! You killed the relationship when you met Leo, and you were dead in it long before that. So what's it going to be?

"I rented this cottage, Kurt."

"*For what?*"

"To live in. I can't squat on people's couches forever."

"Are you kidding me with this? You're married, with a home in DANVILLE! We can barely afford that mortgage and now you want to layer this on top of it?"

"I got a huge raise, I'm paying for it on my own."

"You got a raise without telling me?"

Oopsy. I didn't mean for that to slip out.

"Well, it's not *that* huge, but it's enough for me to cover this place. I'm doing this, Kurt."

He takes two condescending steps toward me, puts his hands on my shoulders and stares down at me like I'm a lost kid at a carnival.

If I show an ounce of weakness, he'll make me feel confused, clobber me over the head, and drag me back to the cave. He thinks he's talking to the old Chrissy, but I've come too far to give her to him.

"C'mon, Chrissy, what are you doing?"

"I'm moving in here so I can be alone and think." Good girl. Stay strong.

"Think at home."

"No."

"Don't you think it's gonna be a little weird during the holidays?"

"Don't you think it's weird that you committed to hosting Christmas Eve at our house when I don't even live there?"

Man, I hate doing this. I hate acting like him.

"IT'S STILL YOUR HOUSE AND YOU'RE STILL MY WIFE! Look, I've been patient with all the hiding at your parents' house and the running off to your friend's place in the city, but getting your own apartment is plain nuts."

"*It's a cottage.*"

"I don't care if it's Trump Tower! You made a vow to love me for better or for worse, and if you lease this place, it means you stopped doing what you promised to do."

"I DO LOVE YOU!"

"*How is this love?*"

"I'm doing this because you can't see what I see."

"Oh yeah, tell me, Chrissy…what are you so aware of that I'm not?"

"Dammit, Kurt, you're so consumed with finishing what we started that you can't see how wrong we were for each other at the beginning! This is so much bigger than a bike race or climbing to the top of a mountain! Quitting us isn't a sign of weakness, it's admitting we deserve a better, more fulfilling adventure."

"We're not wrong!"

His resistance is killing me, but I can't back down now.

"If I go back to Danville and pretend I'm happy for you and everyone else, what we have together won't get better. It'll get a hell of a lot worse, and I love you too much to end up in a hateful place. Can't you give me credit for being strong enough to prevent that from happening?"

"If you move out of our house, the only thing I'll give you credit for being is a quitter."

If I really were a quitter I'd tear up my new lease and go back home. Hard as this is, I'm NOT going to quit myself, and I'm going to fight this battle for the both of us. In the end, he'll give me the credit I deserve. I think.

"Can't you just choose to be happy?"

"What?"

"Stop *pretending* to be happy and *choose* to be happy."

Like a genie, I bend my arms out in front of me, place my hands on opposite elbows and snap my head downward.

"Zoinks! Nope, still not happy. God, Kurt, my emotional state can't be switched on or off like a lamp, and what brought me to this point wasn't the result of a minor occurrence that I can choose to ignore."

"I'm so sick of talking about bad stuff all the time. I just want to be happy and enjoy life *with a wife* who TOLD ME she wanted the same things as me."

"I tried to want the same things as you, but it's not who I am. This, the woman standing in front of you, this is who I am and you don't like her. You want her to go away, and you want me to keep on pretending. I'm sorry, I'm just not gonna do that anymore."

"I knew I should've made you stop seeing that therapist."

"*You think Dr. Maria's to blame for this*? Give me some credit, Kurt! This separation isn't a result of what a therapist told me to do! Maybe if *you* had continued to see Dr. Maria..."

"I don't need a total stranger to explain my life to me."

"Oh my God, you are so damaged! I can't do this anymore! I can't spend another year, another month, ANOTHER DAY, hoping you'll get it."

"What's 'it?'"

"It...it's...everything!"

"You're losing your mind."

"No I'm not! And please wipe that patronizing smirk off your face.

My God, Kurt, look where I brought you! Listen to what I'm telling you!"

"I am listening, and it's never gonna happen, you're not moving here."

"Yes I am." And then it's my turn to take steps toward him.

"Kurt, you're not afraid of losing me, you're just afraid of losing. I wish so badly it was the other way around. I've *prayed* for it to be the other way around, but it's not. I can't hope for something that's never gonna happen, and you can't tell me what to do anymore. I'm moving out. It's over."

Admitting that to him...to myself...hurt more than I ever could've anticipated. His smirk is gone, and he's silent.

"It's my fault we're standing here now, and I'm more sorry for that than you'll ever know. But I have to get my life back, and I need this cottage to help me do that."

"But we can..."

"No we can't, Kurt. How we were worked for us for a really long time, but so many unfortunate things happened, or maybe it was that so many essential things didn't happen...I don't know, but either way, I don't get us anymore. We don't make sense to me and I'm tired of trying to figure it all out. I just want to move into this cottage and rest. Please, can I rest? *Can we rest*? Please?"

"Stop crying, Chrissy. I don't like seeing you like this."

"But you have to know this is the hardest thing I've ever done."

"It doesn't have to be this way."

"I don't see how it can't."

I want him to be proud of my persistence. I want him to be grateful for my strength. I want him to be apologetic for not worshipping the woman I am. But he's not, he's pissed.

"I'm not a quitter, Chrissy. If you move in here, it's all on you."

I can argue the ownership of "it" until I'm blue in the face, but I choose not to anymore. I'm willing to take one for the team.

"I'm moving in here this weekend. It's time you told your family."

I try to be strong and stand up for myself
I try to speak up with the words that don't come out
Does anyone know this heart of mine?
This heart of mine...

("This Heart of Mine," *Ashley Chambliss*)

SUPERSTAR

NOVEMBER, 1998

When I backed the U-Haul into our driveway on Saturday morning, Kurt still hadn't told his family about our situation. I struggled with being deeply concerned about his denial, but fought the urge to question him by channeling Dr. Maria's words of wisdom that I only have the power to control myself, and I forged on with the move. Together, Kurt and I loaded up all of the guest room furniture and everything from my closet and, like the superstar he is, Kurt did it all with a smile and a whistle. Every time we passed each other in the hallway, I wanted to slap the smile off of his face and scream at him to feel something. When we clumsily carried the mattress out to the truck, I wanted to beg him to stop joking about it and comprehend the seriousness of it. When we shared a beer after the work was done, I wanted to feel like he cared about what he was losing, but all it felt like was that he was thirsty.

Every therapist *and* self-help book says that once a spouse moves out of the house, the marriage is over, the mover-outer has officially given up. If Kurt knew this, I wonder if he would've been whistling. I doubt it, and so it makes me think he thinks I'm coming back. I used to want to protect that side of him, the side that's oblivious to pain, bad and negative, but not anymore. I only have the capacity to protect myself now, and I need all the protection I can get because my heart actually breaks. And so, after two hours of oddly impressive teamwork, I said "goodbye." Like a kid going off to college, Kurt gave me a kiss on the forehead, told me to be safe, and to call him when I got home. As I sat idling in the driveway, we locked eyes and for a second I thought something deep might come out of it. But I was wrong. He glanced at his watch as if I had already taken up too much of his time, shook his head, and let out a condescending chuckle accompanied by his infamous half smile and then proceeded to close the front door on me. After I wiped away what I swore to myself would really, really, really be the last tears shed over Kurt's indifference, I put my rig in gear and headed to Lafayette.

On the drive down Highway 680, all I could hear was Kurt's voice, and it was calling me a quitter, so I turned the music as high as it would go, and I screamed at the top of my lungs to block it out. It certainly wasn't the liberating drive I thought it would be. And all the relief I thought I was going to feel on my big moving day was nowhere to be found when I pulled into my parking space at the cottage. On impact, the place made me feel lonely. When I stepped inside, the freezing cold air was quick to remind me that I forgot to notify the gas company I was moving in. Then when I hit the light switch to find my way to the bathroom, it occurred to me that I also forgot to let the electric company know. For a second, I was grateful for the light coming through the French doors, but then I became horrified at how exposed I was. I thought, "Someone could easily break into this place and murder me!" I rushed back outside to get as much work done as I could before the daylight ran out, but when I opened the back of the U-Haul, the biggest shock of the day slapped me across the face. "How the hell am I supposed to unload this stuff all by myself?"

I started cursing and accusing Dr. Maria of being full of shit when she said this was going to be easier than being a sneaky adulterer. Part of me wanted to call Kurt for help, but I knew he'd only make me feel incapable of surviving without him, so I fought off the urge. I called Slutty Co-worker and asked her for help, but she was quick to remind me that she doesn't perform manual labor. There was no one else to call; I had cut everyone else out of my life. I didn't feel alone, I was alone.

But I was only alone for a few hours. Once I found my CD player, I had Alanis Morissette, Jewel, and Natalie Merchant to keep me company. Nothing like having a bunch of kick ass dejected chicks to motivate you! Seriously, if it wasn't for those girls and their angry words to keep me going, I never would've been able to move all of my crap into my cottage. And for the last two days, I worked like a maniac to make everything just perfect. Pictures got hung, dishes got put away, new pretty linens now decorate my bedroom, and shielding curtains are now hanging over the French doors that just two days ago scared the crap out of me. Aside from needing a few thousand more square feet attached to it, my cottage looks and feels like home.

The nights though...they're a lot harder than I thought they'd be. And it wasn't the exaggerated shadows of *The Blair Witch Project*-like branches that swayed back and forth outside of my bedroom window that made the last two nights unbearable. It was that I couldn't celebrate my accomplishments with Leo. I live closer to him now than I did in Danville, but he might as well be a world away. It took some heavy duty self-medicating to get me through the last two nights, and this morning I wake feeling scared of the task that lies ahead of me at work. In fact, I feel tied to my bed.

You can do this, Chrissy.

No I can't. It's too hard.

C'mon, you've come this far. You should be proud of yourself.

Proud? I'm disgusted. I'm a horrible bitch who ruins people's lives.

Stop that! You're trying to make people's lives better, remember?

Why couldn't I be one of those wives to gracefully accept her fate? You know...a wife who says her wedding vows and sticks to them no matter how crappy her marriage makes her feel?

Because you're better than that.

I doubt that's what everyone at work is going to think when I tell them I'm *separated.*

C'mon...up we go, one foot at a time.

They say the hardest part about exercising is putting on your tennis shoes. Well I say the hardest part about snapping out of a love funk is making it to the shower. *You'll be okay if you can just make it to the shower*! If you can't do that, then you need to immediately call your best girlfriends or your therapist. Since I have none of those at the moment, I have no choice. It's shower or die.

Luckily, I made it to the shower and managed to wash away most of my self-deprecation, and now that I'm settled at the kitchen counter with my cup of coffee, I feel ready to take on the day. Everything in my cottage is pretty and tidy, and I feel calm knowing this is exactly how it will look when I get home. In all of my grown up years, I've never been able to enjoy a quiet cup of coffee before I set off for a busy day at work. I've usually had to stuff down a breakfast I didn't want or race out the door to avoid it. But right now, my bed is made, "Page Six" has been read, and my coffee cup is about to be washed and put away. Everything's heavenly abnormal.

I wonder what Kurt's doing. I pick up my wedding band from the bowl of stuff I have no idea where to put and slide it back and forth across the counter top.

How is this happening to me?

Chill, Chrissy. You're regressing again.

Maybe I'll give him a call. I should probably remind him to give the dog his medicine.

No, dumbass, the dog's an excuse! Put the phone down! You can't make the call! You've been the one to do that too many times in the relationship…and look where it's gotten you!

As I get in my car, I congratulate myself for staying strong. Besides, I can't be pre-occupied with Kurt right now, I have a busy day. On the agenda is to tell the biggest loud mouth at work that I'm separated and then sit back and watch the wildfire spread.

And that it did. By 9:15 the owner of my company was in my office offering his deepest condolences and, *I think,* hitting on me. By 10:15, I had emailed Courtney and Nicole and apologized for being out of touch for so many months. I gave them a status report on my marriage and my new address. Oh, and I asked them to pass the information on to Kelly. I wasn't trying to avoid Kelly, she just didn't have email. She thought it was like Atari and it would be obsolete as quickly as it became a sensation. Too bad she didn't have that same point of view about the Rachael hairstyle. Anyway, I suppose

I could've called her, but I really don't think she cares one way or the other about what happens with my marriage.

What happened when the people at work found out about my marital status totally blew me away! Half of the people never even knew I was married and the other half had a friend they wanted to immediately introduce me to. No joke, for the past few hours there's been a line of kiss-asses at my door who have a "really great guy" they want to set me up with. One by one I tell them, "It's just too soon for me." What? It's not like I can tell them I already have an ex-boyfriend I dream about getting back together with! They'll figure that out for themselves when Megan starts her internship next week.

Normally the thought of my co-workers knowing I'm an adulterer would bother me but right now it takes backseat to the fact that once Megan finds out about my marriage, she'll tell Leo about it. It's definitely not the way I wanted all this to go down and trust me, since the Megan interview, I've toyed with the idea of telling Leo I'm married myself just to beat the bitch to it. But I can't find the right words. I mean, the night of my surprise party, the only truth Leo knew was that Kurt threw it for me and that was cause enough for him to reject me. If he knew I was married to the man, how could I hope for a better reaction than the one he had that night? I can't, and so it looks like Megan will have the last laugh after all. Maybe I'll get lucky and Leo will punch her in the face for being the bearer of bad news! Fortunately for me, I have another week to contemplate the fall out of Megan's arrival, and right now all I want to do is enjoy how temporarily uncomplicated my life is. And what a nice uncomplicated four hours it was.

As I'm leaving the office to pick up some lunch, a sharply dressed man catches my eye and not because I'm looking for some action. He just seems out of place. He's in the parking lot with another interesting looking dude, and they're talking to a girl who works in the production department. They clearly aren't associated with the garment industry, as they're not Jewish or Chinese. These guys have on expensive suits, dark sunglasses, and drive a black Range Rover with the most tinted windows I've ever seen. Once in the car, the guy in the passenger seat rolls down his window and gives something to the production chick. Then he turns to look at me and stares at me until the car makes a left turn and drives out of sight. I follow his gaze until I nearly fall over.

"Hey Chrissy, do you have a minute?"

"Only a minute, what's up?"

I love acting busy when I'm not.

"That guy I was talking to wants you to call him."

"*The black guy*? Sorry, but I'm not down with the brown. I mean, I like plenty of black people. You know Oprah, Denzel, Chris Rock… they're all cool, but I wouldn't date any of them. Well, maybe Oprah because she's loaded…but no, no not even her. Sorry."

"No, not the black guy. The other one. He asked me to give this to you."

She hands me a business card and it reads:

Mark Wisely, Attorney at Law Beverly Hills, California.

On the back he wrote:

I'd love to have a drink with you. I'm in town 'til Tuesday.

"Uhhhh…first things first, what do you need an attorney for?"

"I'm trying to keep it hush-hush, but I got my third D.U.I. last month. The black dude's my lawyer, and he works for Mark's firm. Mark's in town for a bigger case. I think he's the defense lawyer for that pre-school teacher who was drunk at work and killed a three year old."

"Jesus, who'd wanna defend someone like that?"

"I don't know, but he's hella fine. Hey, I'm not gonna get fired because of my D.U.I.'s, am I?"

"Only if you go to jail and you can't do your job." And then I drove off.

By no means is Leo a thing of the past to me and trust me, I've been resisting every urge to enroll in an economics class at St. Mary's, join his gym, or pop into The Round Up for a beer just to catch a glimpse of him. Even though I know he's mad at me and he has some kind of super ability to cut people out of his life, I don't think he can cut me out. I'm special to him. He told me so.

He showed me so. And I think if I found him, he'd give me another chance. But I also think Taddeo's right; I have too much baggage and way more baggage than he's even aware of…for another week anyway. Yes, yes, yes, staying away is what's best for Leo. But it's also really hard to convince myself of all that when I live so close to him now. And to compound the torture of being so close, yet so far away from him, I remind myself that he's probably seeing other people. That's usually about the time I open my second bottle of wine and break out my vibrator (yeah, picked up one of those bad boys a while back). But not tonight. Tonight I break out Mark Wisely's card and give him a call.

Mark's an interesting guy. He's a big time criminal defense attorney and has defended some super bad people and right now he really is defending a woman who killed a kid because she was drunk. It's all reprehensible stuff, but I can't help but be curious about all of it and that's why I take him up on his offer to meet for a drink… tonight…at eleven. I pull up to the Lafayette Park Hotel and valet my car at the same time his chauffer-driven Town Car pulls up. I immediately second guess my nonchalant decision to wear a baseball hat, jeans, and old college sweatshirt because everything about Mark is put together like he's James Bond or something. I'm instantly intimidated *and* intrigued.

"Just so you know, I don't usually get out of bed to meet some-one for drinks at eleven on a Tuesday."

"Just so you know, I don't usually ask women to do that, and I appreciate you working around my schedule. I'm tied up in court for the next two days, and then I have to head back to L.A. I really wanted to meet you before I left."

"*Okay…*Why?"

"You're beautiful, but not L.A. beautiful."

"Whoa!" His comment makes me look at my boobs.

"No, no I mean that in a good way. There are plenty of beautiful women in Los Angeles but not many *smart* beautiful women. The girl who works for you…she said some impressive things about you."

Nice save. I think.

Turns out Mark's thirty-five and doesn't date a lot and not because he's too busy. He's kind of shy. He has a house in Beverly

Hills, one in Palm Springs, and one in Maui. He also has a Harley, a Porsche, an Escalade and some other new fan-dangled hybrid car (whatever the hell that is). The dude's loaded. This is about the time most girls would get all wet and giddy about the gold mine of a guy sitting across from them. They'd be adding up the assets and already excusing his inevitable adultery. But Mark's money isn't what I find intriguing; it's what he does *to get all the money* that I'm curious about. He defends the worst of the worst, people *he has to know* are guilty, just for the thrill of the win and the money. He has no problem with any of the negative connotations about his profession, and he's quick to say, "If I didn't do it, someone else would." He's brutally honest and he kind of reminds me of an older Leo, which makes me sad. I don't want to be sad, so I drink…heavily. Soon I'm feeling pretty comfortable around Mark and I spill the beans (and a few drops of my drink) about being recently separated from my husband who I was cheating on. It's the first time I blurted out the truth to anyone other than my friends and THE DUDE DIDN'T EVEN BAT AN EYE. Gosh, maybe I *could* date him. Maybe Mark and I could be the happy piece of crap couple who shamelessly does shitty things to innocent undeserving people because we're selfish and greedy. Of course, I'd rather be a happy piece of crap couple with Leo but that toilet has long since flushed. And with that thought, I'm sad again. So I tell Mark it's time for me to leave.

"Would you like to have dinner with me this weekend?"

Can I really do that?

"I think I can do that."

"Would you be interested in having it in Maui?"

"*Excuse me?*"

"I was planning on taking a long weekend. I could just fly you up."

I'm fairly certain it looks like a broom just got shoved up my ass because he's quick with a comfort comeback.

"Don't worry, you'd have your own room and everything! You can even bring a friend if it makes you more comfortable."

"Mark, I just met you like five minutes ago. I can't accept a plane ticket to Maui!"

"I'd fly back here if I could, but I already have some meetings lined up there. You don't have to let me know right now. Think about it."

As he walks me to the valet, he loosens his tie, and like a meteor crashing into the hotel, a blast of red, yellow, and orange stops me in my tracks.

"Holy crap, what's that?"

"Oh these--tattoos."

"On your neck?"

"And on my torso and back too. Does it weird you out?"

Fuck yeah it does.

"No, not at all."

He explains that the monstrosity all started with one small tattoo when he got his Harley and soon they became an addiction. He's not really sure when or if he can stop getting them. I can relate; I'm an addict too. When the valet pulls my car up, he gives me a weird kiss, and I hope to all that's Holy, he can't tell how shocked I am. I'd like to be sorta cool about this. Dude's got cash and wants to fly me places! I watch him get into his car and shake my head. I can't go to Maui with a rich guy this weekend, *can I*? This is madness, I'm still married *and* in love with someone else. Dr. Maria would have a field day with this! I tuck myself into bed, and all I can think about is the funny conversation about tattoos I had with Leo the night we met. It makes me laugh and cry all at the same time.

ALOHA

DECEMBER, 1998

"**H**ell yeah, you're going!"

"I can't."

"Tell me one good reason why you can't go."

"I'm in love with Leo."

I regretted saying the words the minute they left my mouth.

"Hunny…Sweetie…he moved on. Has he called you in the last three months?"

"No. But maybe--"

"For fuck's sake, would you listen to yourself? You're holding out for something *that's never gonna happen*. Maui though, that can happen!"

"Gimme a break, what kind of guy takes a girl he barely knows to Maui?"

"Duh, a rich guy who thinks you're hot! Didn't he email you and ask you for the correct spelling of your name?"

"Yeah…so?"

"So he probably needed it to buy an airline ticket!"

"The whole thing is nuts."

"*Ummmm*, did he also ask for the name of a friend you might want to bring?"

"Uh-huh."

I want to slap her six ways from silly to get her to stop bouncing up and down on the chair.

"Did you give him my name?"

"What do you think?"

"Omigod, this is gonna be so awesome!"

"Keep your yoga pants on, that was like two days ago, and I bet L.A. boy forgot all about it by now."

Just then, my assistant knocks on my door and attempts to hand me a FedEx envelope, but Slutty Co-worker snaps it from her before I can even get my hand in the air. She's waving it around like a possessed woman fanning herself at a hot Baptist Church in the deep South.

"Looky here, it's from a Mr. Mark Wisley! Open it! Open it!"

"Oh for the love of God, give it to me." I rip open the envelope and out float two first class tickets to Maui and a note.

Chrissy, I want to get to know you better. Meet me in Maui.
Aloha, Mark

"Holy shit, this is insane! Does he think I'm some kind of Los-Angeles-Playboy-hoochy-koochy-who-will-put-out-for-a-free-trip-to-Maui-kinda-girl? Seriously, what would it say about me if I went?"

"*Ummmmm*, it would say you're fun and spontaneous! Jesus, you don't have to marry the guy. Oh wait, can't do that anyway, you're already married. Okay, you don't have to sleep with him, although I would. I mean, look at all the expense he's going through just to have dinner with you. Yep, you should definitely sleep with him."

"I'M NOT SLEEPING WITH HIM! He's covered in tattoos from his dimples to his dick!"

"Fine, I'll sleep with him if you take me with you."

"I have no doubt. Look, give me some time to think about this, and I'll call you tonight to let you know if you should pack."

"Yay!"

"Now get outta my office!"

Holding the tickets in one hand and tapping the fingers of the other on my desk, my gaze turns to the phone. It's been about a week since I listened to Leo's messages, and no doubt I've been better off without the torment it so often causes me, but like always, my curiosity gets the best of me. I dial his number and enter the secret code.

"You have one new message, sent today at two twelve p.m... Hey, it's Ho-Bag. I'll be at The Round Up around nine. Later."

Fingers still tapping, I have a thought. I press Slutty Co-worker's extension.

"What are you doing tonight?"

"Duh. Packing, remember?"

"I'll tell you what. You come with me to The Round Up and if we don't see Leo, we'll go to Maui."

"Oh, cripes, what if we *do* see him?"

"I'm not sure, but I'll tell you one thing, I won't be in any mood to go to Maui."

"What is it with you and that boy?"

"I don't know, ask my grandpa." And then I hang up on her.

I get home from work and have two messages from Kurt. I have to stay at the house next weekend to watch the dog and I have to cut him a check for half the bills. I feel terrible that I left him with an entire household to take care of, but even so, I hate getting pulled back into the responsibility. I'M SO SICK OF RESPONSIBILITY. That being said, maybe I should be spontaneous and go to Maui. I'll let Leo be the answer to that. A shower and a glass of wine later, a very annoyed Slutty Co-worker arrives to pick me up. Ten minutes later, we park at The Round Up right next to Leo's jeep. Slutty Co-worker is not a happy girl.

"Great. So I guess this means no Maui."

"Would you like to go to Korea instead?"

"What the hell are you talking about?"

"The Ho-Bag's in there with him."

"Very funny. So what's your big plan?"

"I don't have one. You wanted me to be spontaneous, right? Come on, let's go."

Okay, The Round Up is quite possibly the grossest bar I've ever been in. Once inside the saloon doors, we're stared down by a couple of fat girls with pierced belly-divulging tee shirts. They're trying to sing "Baby Got Back" on karaoke and the vision is quite scary. I'm going to take a moment away from my quest to find Leo to ponder the horrific style choices of today's youth. Who the hell is giving these kids the idea that it's okay to be fat and expose their flesh? In the fashion industry, we don't glamorize chicks like these by calling them "curvy" or "real women." We call 'em what they are. FAT! Anyway…

So right next to the FAT girls is a shuffle board and pool table and they're beat up as all hell. And in the back of the room, is an antiquated juke-box that's fiercely trying to compete with the FAT girls by blaring "Sweet Child O-Mine." I grab Slutty Co-workers hand to pull her to the bar, and when we turn toward it we're instantly eye-fucked by a dozen or so manual laborers. Every single one of 'em is filthy dirty and looking at Slutty Co-worker and me like they want to jackhammer us. We're clearly fish out of water at this dive and as bad as I want to be here, I want to leave even more.

"You know what? This is stupid. Let's get outta here."

"Thank God. Something tells me they don't have chardonnay here. Good-bye Round Up, *hellooooo* Maui!"

I turn to make a run for it but as fate, or my grandpa, would have it, I notice Leo sitting at a table drinking beers with his buddies. He can't see me, so I know I can leave without him noticing but…OH MY GOD there are girls at the table! There's NO WAY I'm going home with that vision.

"Shit! Grab a seat at the end of the bar and pretend like we don't know he's here."

"Fine."

"I want my back to him so you take the seat facing his direction."

"Fine."

"And can you please act like you're having fun?"

"No."

"Hi, ladies, what can I get you to drink?"

Before I have a chance to answer the bartender, Slutty Co-worker sits up and barks, "We'll have a couple of Jack and Cokes and it's on the guys sitting at the table over there."

"*What*? Noooooooooooooooooo!"

But it was too late. Before I could articulate my mortification and recall the order, bartender's half-way to Leo's table to confirm everything.

"WHY THE HELL DID YOU DO THAT?"

"Cause I'm pissed about Maui. Plus, I showed that little Korean guy a good time last January. Least he could do is buy me a drink."

"Holy shit, are they looking?"

"Uh-huh."

"What's Leo doing? For fuck's sake stop waving!"

"He's staring at your back…Okay, now it looks like he's trying to make sense of this…ahhh, yep…he gets it. He's walking over here. Damn girl, he looks *goooooooooood*."

"I'm so gonna kill you."

"Hiya, Leo, long time no see. Is that my little Ho-Bag over there? I think I'll go say hi. I miss that little fucker."

Without taking his eyes off of mine, Leo slides onto Slutty's vacant barstool. He's wearing a black baseball hat backwards, and it's just about the sexist damn thing I've ever seen. Really, when worn correctly, a backwards baseball hat can win over just about any girl. It can't be one of those white trash sideways crooked looks, and it can't be combined with a do-rag like the ghetto boys kid themselves into thinking looks good. It's gotta look just like he has it.

"What are you doing here?"

"I live here now."

"You live *here*?"

"Well no, not here at The Round Up. I moved into a cottage up the street."

"*By yourself*?"

"By myself."

I can see his mind racing.

"I'm so sorry about what happened in August. I came by your apartment to ex…"

"I know, I saw the note."

"You didn't call me."

"I was done getting hurt."

It was almost a year ago that I met this guy and realized that nothing in the world feels better than the tell-it-like-it-is vulnerable love he showed me. Maybe I've been using the whole 'he deserves better than a chick who lied to him' thing as an excuse. Maybe I'm the one who's too scared to take a chance on a guy who's so much younger than I am. Maybe Dr. Maria's right and I care too much about what other people think. Maybe I'm afraid I'll be laughed at. I mean seriously, divorce *and* a twenty-three year old...*at the same time?* I'd be taking bullets left and right! But maybe it's not any of that. Maybe I'm afraid *he'll* hurt me like I've hurt him. Good Lord, for someone who says she wants vulnerable love, I sure do a good job of talking myself out of it. But you heard him, he said he's done! I'd be stupid to be vulnerable now. Must keep this casual.

"You look good, Leo. You doing good?"

"Yeah."

That's it?

"Yep, good here, too. Just letting off a little steam after a crazy day at work." Was that too blasé? I certainly don't want to scare him away.

"I'll let you get back to your drink, then. Hope you like it. I think it's on me."

Crap, I scared him away! With each inhale and exhale I go from a bulging B cup to what's gotta look like a double D cup. That's how fast my heart is beating. That's how badly I want him.

"Good seeing you, Leo."

I'm changing my life to make room for you, Leo. I want to have a million babies with you, Leo. I'll love you forever, Leo. Sigh. Good-bye, Leo.

He's about five steps away and then he turns and says, "Hey, remember at The Red Devil Lounge when I told you I didn't like the thought of you in a place like that?"

"Yeah?"

"Well I don't like the thought of you in a place like this, either."

If he only knew it was him that I was following into places like this...

"Look at these people, you don't belong here. Jesus, hold on. Hey Bruno! Quit fucking staring at her like that!"

Not quite the romantic exchange I was hoping for, but it'll do. Sure sounded kind of vulnerable. Maybe I should reciprocate. Just be careful, Chrissy, take it slow.

"Let's go back to my place then."

Who am I, the Mario Andretti of hooking up?

He stares at me for like ten seconds, and I can tell that he too is contemplating the vulnerability factor. I finally get the sensation of time standing still and it's horrible. So horrible that I wish I could rescind the offer. If he says "No thank you," it's over…done. He will, without a doubt, have put me behind. And it looks like that's the response I'm going to get when he takes a few serious steps toward me. But he says nothing. He just grabs my hand and leads me to the door.

I glance over my right shoulder and hear The Ho-Bag say to Slutty Co-worker, "Looks like it's just you and me again, Baby."

Leo's quiet on the short drive to my apartment, and I'm scared he's going to have second thoughts about coming with me, or worse, he's waiting to be alone to tell me what a shitty person I am. I've been doing so well with my quest for true happiness with the yoga and the walking and with the renting of the cottage and the going on dates with rich tattooed guys. I'm making smart choices for once. Is bringing Leo to my cottage like throwing my life in reverse? Will more shittyness come as a result of bringing him here?

Ten minutes later, as I unlock the door to my cottage, he's still by my side…and quiet. I can smell his skin and I can feel the drug enter my body. Nothing shitty about that.

"I'll get the lights."

"Leave them off."

Whenever we were together before, I felt like I was the one in control. But not right now, right now I'm totally at his mercy.

"Wine?"

"Sure."

Assisted by only the street-lights shining outside, I'm making my way to the drawer that contains the bottle opener when he walks up behind me and starts to kiss my neck. Too weak to hold up my head, it falls back in little semi-circles. After a minute, or maybe an hour, he turns me around to face him. We're inches apart, searching for answers in each other's eyes.

"Don't you want to talk about what happened in August?"

"I thought I did. Actually I wanted to yell at you for what happened in August. But in five minutes you could be gone again. I'm not sure that would be spending my time wisely."

"I don't wanna be gone, Leo."

"Could'a fooled me."

Like a shamed child, I tilt my chin to the floor, and in barely a whisper, I say "I have something to tell you."

It's time.

"No. Let me decide how to spend the five minutes."

Maybe it's not the time.

"Unbutton your shirt."

Definitely not the time.

"Now take off your jeans."

Without leaving his eyes, I do what I'm told.

"Now put your shoes back on."

The guy could ask me to kill someone and I would. As I slip my heels back on, he steps closer to me and whispers, "I miss you so much," and then slides my blouse off of my shoulders. He leans into me like he's going to kiss me, but instead he tells me to turn back around. I do. He gently moves my legs apart with his feet and places both of my hands on the wall. I can barely hold my legs up as he caresses my body from underneath my breasts down to my inner thighs and then back up again. Thank God for all of that yoga. He kisses my neck as his index fingers toy with the waistband on my panties. He glides his hands over to my stomach, back down to my inner thighs and then back up my belly to my breasts, where they settle as he leans his body against mine and holds me. His breath is powerful, mine is nowhere to be found. He finally unhooks my bra, and I drop my hands down to let it fall to the floor. He places them back where he wants them. I want to kiss him so badly but when I try to turn around he says, "No, not yet." He backs away and I can hear the sound of his clothes coming off. A moment later, I feel his body warm against mine. With my head resting against the wall I bend slightly over and he takes my move for what it is, an invitation. After a few minutes of euphoria, he spins me around, picks me up and places me on the kitchen countertop. I grab his hair with my hands, wrap my legs around him and admit to myself that the balance of power between us has shifted. And then there's a knock at the door.

HOLY F***ING SHIT!

DECEMBER, 1998

"Chrissy, you in there?"

The pounding on my front door jolts me off of the counter-top.

"Oh my God!" Wide-eyed and in total shock, I grab Leo's shoulders in a failed attempt to keep him from freaking out.

"Who the fuck is that?"

"Okay, Leo…you need to stay calm."

"No I don't."

"No, you do. Promise me you'll stay calm." It's useless. He's a deranged lunatic.

"Tell me who it is, Chrissy."

The knocking is so hard, the walls are vibrating.

"Chrissy, I see your car, and I can hear you in there. Open the door!"

Holy fucking shit, holy fucking shit, holy fucking shit! I frantically scoop up my clothes and scramble to come up with an explanation for who's at the door, but it's pointless, there's no way outta this. I grab Leo's arms as if I can actually prevent him from doing anything, and then I drop the bomb on him.

"It's Kurt. But wait! I can explain everything. Please, I'm begging you to stay calm."

"I'm gonna kill this guy! You're back in my life for like thirty seconds and SURPRISE, so is he! What the hell?"

As I reach down to pick up one last article of clothing, Leo bolts for the door. I grab his leg, because frankly there isn't much more to grab onto. The dude's naked.

"No, you're not gonna kill anyone! Please Leo, he's not who you think he is! Please, please, please just go in my room, and I'll be there in a minute to explain."

Reluctantly he picks his pants up off the floor. "If you're not in to get me in five minutes, I'm gonna fucking freak out."

Once I'm sure he's tucked away in my room, I grab my robe, take a deep breath and open the door.

"What's going on, Kurt, it's ten-thirty?"

I sound like I'm tired and mad, but the truth is, I'm not really sure what to feel about him being here. It's the first time since I moved out that he's made the effort to show up.

"Look, you made your point, and I get it. I'll go to therapy…just come home."

Kurt's not a drinker, but I can tell he's had a few tonight.

"It's not a good time right now, I'll call you tomorrow."

"Let me come in and talk to you."

He's not budging. I'm going to have to tell him something so atrocious that he'll want to get as far away from me as possible. And I have to do it quickly because the clock's ticking on Leo's patience. This isn't what I had planned…but I have to do it, AND NOW!

"I'm seeing someone else, Kurt."

Holy fucking shit, holy fucking shit, holy fucking shit! It's out! The line has officially been crossed. I never thought about what this moment would feel like because, ever since I met Leo I planned for him to stay on the side of the line that remained a secret. I thought that somehow I could lock him up in my heart long enough to avoid the horror of this moment. I wanted to divorce Kurt for all of the reasons I told him I wasn't happy, because, after all, *those are the real reasons.* I never wanted him to have my unfaithfulness to blame things on. But now, there's no erasing the impurity I just admittedly scribbled onto what was once an enviable relationship, and surely it will go down as the reason Kurt and Chrissy didn't work out.

"What are you talking about?"

He's running his fingers through his hair and pacing back and forth on my small porch. Couple it with Leo's pacing in the room behind me and it feels like I'm surrounded by a pack of angry wolves.

"And, I think you should see other people, too."

Of course, I don't want him to. I want him to sulk about me the rest of his life, but I have to be realistic.

"I can't believe you're doing this to us!"

And that's how this marriage will go down. We're irrevocably shattered, and it will always be because of what *I did to us*. Everyone will say we could've solved our problems if *I didn't* decide to see other people. No matter how much I try to justify my actions, there's no fixing adultery, and that's what will always make me the bad guy. It's time I accept my fate.

"I'm sorry for my part of our situation."

"*Your part*? You're part *is* the situation! I didn't tell you to go to therapy. I didn't tell you to move out. I didn't tell you to date other people. You did all of that stuff on your own. You made this marriage what it is. Fuck, what is it, anyway?"

"Kurt...please just go."

"*IS THE GUY HERE?*"

"No! God, no!"

Then, there they were, the tears I doubted existed.

"What happened to you, Chrissy?"

With more hate in his eyes than I've ever seen, he accuses me of being the thing he knows will hurt me the most.

"You're a quitter."

With more strength that I ever thought I was capable of, I place my hand on his chest and softly nudge him back.

"Actually, I'm just trying to survive."

And with that, I close the door on him and all hope of our happily-ever-after life together. I watch through the window as he circles his car a few times, mumbles something, and then finally gets in and drives away. My heart is breaking for the both of us, and I hate that he's alone, and dare I think...confused. For a split second I want to chase him down. I open the door but quickly close it again. "I won't live my life like Francesca!" And then just like her, but with a completely different outcome, I take my hand off of the door handle.

Doing that to Kurt was the hardest thing I've ever done in my life. Now I'm about to do the second hardest thing. Leo's dressed and ready for battle when I open the door to my bedroom.

"This is bullshit! Every single time you walk into my life, he does too. When's it gonna end?"

"Leo, I have something to tell you, and if you thought you hated me after the surprise party, you're really going to hate me now."

He follows me to the couch and sits beside me. I start shaking, I mean *really* shaking.

"I don't know if I can tell you this. It's really, really bad."

My jibber jabber of how horrible a person I am goes on for like ten minutes, and it would've gone on much longer if he didn't pull me onto his lap.

"Just tell me."

"I can't. I'm so afraid of how you'll react."

"Are you gonna leave again?"

"I don't want to."

"Then I can handle it."

"I lied to you. I'm not who you think I am."

He pulls back about an inch and looks instantly nervous.

"Leo, what's the most horrible thing you could possibly imagine about me?"

"Jesus, are you dying?"

Wow, it's so sweet that he really did go to the most horrible thing imaginable.

"No, I'm not dying."

"Chrissy, this is killing me. Just tell me."

"I can't, because when I do, you'll never look at me like you are right now. Worse, you'll walk out the door."

"You're the one who keeps leaving, not me."

"I lied to you real bad, and I know how much you hate liars."

"Is it something you think I can get over?"

"No. What I did is unforgivable."

"Let me be the judge."

"Leo…I didn't think this…you and me…would turn into anything real when I sat next to you at Buckley's that night. I didn't think I was gonna fall in love with you so hard and so fast. I didn't think you were gonna be the best thing to ever happen to me...I wanted to believe I already had it."

He looks confused. Here it goes.

"I was never engaged. Well, I mean, I was at one time."

He still can't see it coming. Time to end the insanity.

"Please don't hate me." Deep breathe in. "Kurt's my husband."

Everything's finally out. Kurt knows where my heart is, and Leo knows where it's been. Let the chips fall where they may. One thing's for sure, I'm never going to tell another lie.

"Please say something."

"It's over, right?"

Okay, that was NOT what I was expecting him to say.

"Yes."

"And you're getting a divorce?"

"Yes."

"It's gotta be final soon then, right?"

Uh-oh.

"What do you mean?"

"We met almost a year ago. How long can it possibly take?"

Son of a bitch.

"Should be final in a few months."

Honest livin' sure was fun for the ten seconds I experienced it.

SURVEY SAYS!

JANUARY, 1999

Don't get me wrong, my search for true happiness has been great. The yoga, the walks, even the new cooking classes I signed up for...all of it has been fantastically liberating. But the problem is, I do all that stuff in the daytime. My nights continue to be hell. From the moment I moved into my cottage, the Kurt guilt and Leo loss weighed heavy on me, and I ended up spending most evenings crying on the couch with a bottle of whatever, while old episodes of *The Family Feud* aired on The Game Show network.

Why tune into the Game Show Network, you ask? Easy, those old game shows offer me a respite from the hellish nightmare my life has turned into. They take me back to when I was a little girl, back to when I believed in fairy tale weddings and happily-ever-afters. Occasionally, I tried to take a break from Richard Dawson and flipped through the channels, but once I saw how close my real life shenanigans resembled the ones of ditzy sluts like Ally McBeal and Amanda Woodward, I only became more disparaged. Sometimes I gave shows like *Dateline* and *20/20* a chance, but the reality of how royally fucked-up our world is scared me even more than my current state of affairs. And so usually, just minutes after abandoning Richard, I found myself back to him and the comfy coziness of the 1970's. I suppose I could've forced myself to go out with friends, do all the things I dreamed of doing once I had my own place. And I guess I could've enrolled in a night class or started knitting to take my mind off of Kurt and Leo, but I didn't. My evenings became the time when I decided to pay the price for all my bad choices.

And night after night, without fail, *I paid that price.* As Richard Dawson welcomed his horny little contestants, I'd sit in the middle of all the love letters I ever wrote to Kurt and sob over my tainted fairytale. To calm myself down, I'd blast the *Braveheart* soundtrack and soak in the tub. Obviously, that move only resulted in more self-degradation and tears. I was a fucking mess! Night after night, I found myself in a perpetual ping-pong game of anger and heart-ache, and the only way it ended was when my Tylenol PM kicked in. But the next day, the heartache, accompanied by a massive head-ache, ensued. You know...I'm sure the makers of Tylenol PM are accurate in their claim that you wake up feeling rested and refreshed after taking the recommended dosage. But when the recommended dosage is doubled *and* accompanied by a bottle and a half of wine... not so much.

Then miraculously (via phone hacking), Leo reappeared. And I thought once he was back in my life, my cottage would cease to be a personal torture chamber and The Game Show Network would be a thing of the past, but unfortunately, it wasn't.

Surprisingly, Leo took the news of my marriage a million times better than I thought he would. In fact, he was glad I waited as long as I did to tell him. He said, any earlier and he wouldn't have been in love with me enough to tolerate it. Never in a million years would I have thought delaying telling him I was married would be a good thing. After I explained the specially selected details of my past to him, we shared a bottle of wine, as he tried his best to make me feel better about all of my stupid mistakes and choices. We made love in my bed and, for the first time since moving into my cottage, I slept soundly in it. Morning came; we made plans to see each other that night and kissed good-bye. Then...once I closed the door...I was back in my torture chamber! My newest doozy of a lie imme-diately started chasing me around my cottage and it hasn't stopped. How in the hell am I going to finalize a divorce in two months... in a state where it takes at least a year...to a husband who hasn't been formally notified of one? Exactly. I'm not. And because I'm scared of Leo finding out the truth, I'm pushing him away...again. I cancelled on him that night and it's been weeks since I've seen him. And so, even though we're technically back together, night after night I sit alone with my bottle of wine, my Tylenol PM, and my *Family Feud*. I don't know what to say...to anybody. Time to call Dr. Maria.

Sad Frumpy Lady's wearing the usual outfit and her usual scowl. Even so, I'm happy to see her. Oh, finally...

"Hi, Hunny, come on back."

I rattle on to Dr. Maria about my two huge triumphs, moving out and telling Leo I'm married, and she's obviously proud of the steps I've made.

"I don't understand something, though."

"What's that?"

"Well, I finally got my own place. I told Kurt I'm seeing someone, and I told Leo I'm married. But I don't feel how I thought I'd feel."

"How do you feel?"

"I'm really sad."

"What makes you sad?"

"Oh, let me see...that I hurt Kurt and I have to hide from Leo how horribly bad that makes me feel because he'll go ballistic. That I lied to Leo about being closer to divorce than I really am. That *I haven't even told Kurt I want a divorce*! That I live in a tiny little cottage and spend my nights alone in it to hide from all of the things I should be doing to fix everything I just told you. Tell me, *how is this my life?*"

"You made it this way."

All right already, *Maria*! I'm all about accountability, but FOR ONCE give me some real fucking answers!

"Right, and on therapy paper, it looks like I made some really good changes for myself, but in all honesty, it doesn't feel any different than it did before I let all the cats out of the bag. I still feel like I'm in prison."

"That's probably because you're still letting Kurt control your feelings."

"How long will I be stuck in limbo?"

"Until you file for divorce. If that's what you still want, anyway."

"For God's sake, I just told him like a week ago that I want to see other people. I can't drop a divorce bomb on him; that would be like fast-tracking the whole thing."

"It would only be like fast-tracking it *for him*."

She's right. It's always been for him, for him, for him. How long until I stop putting his feelings before my own?"

"Are you considering staying married to Kurt?"

What was it that Courtney said? Oh yeah…it'll take six months for every year we were together before I stop considering it…him… us. Good grief, that'll be like the year…2005! There will probably be fucking hover-craft cars by then.

"You know, for so many years I loved Kurt with all my heart. And I used to think he loved me with only half of his; that's where so much of my sadness and resentment came from. But after all my therapy and alone time, I realize he gave me as much of his heart as he possibly could, and in a lot of ways, it makes me love him more now than I ever did."

"So you *are* considering it."

"I know now that I'm the most important thing in the world to him. And you know what, if I had started therapy and learned to be authentic with Kurt before I met Leo, I think I would've been able to see the bright side of things with him, and I'd really consider staying married to him. But it didn't happen like that, and that's what makes all of this so tragic."

"Explain the tragedy to me."

"It took meeting the love of *my* life to figure out…I've been Kurt's all along."

"So, you've always had the thing you thought was missing with Kurt."

"Yeah…I've always had his whole heart."

"I can see the tragedy there. Tell me, is it enough?"

"Is what enough?"

"Kurt's heart, is it enough?"

"No."

"How do you know?"

"Because half or whole, it's still the same ol' heart, and it won't be enough to make me fall out of love with Leo. And that's why, to answer your question, I'm not considering staying married to Kurt."

I leave without asking Dr. Maria where to go from here, and then I race to the city to meet Slutty Co-worker for the last yoga class of the night. I settle into child's pose and wish I could stay there forever.

TORN

MAY, 1999

For the last four months, every week has been the same. I go to work every single day, even on the weekends and not because I'm gaga crazy about my job, either. It's because I'm like every other single gal out there, and I gotta make my own jack to support myself. My boss is preying on my vulnerability, too, and it's really starting to piss me off. It's like he assumes I've got nothing better to do and he's taking advantage of my dependence on a paycheck by piling on the work and the guilt for not getting it done fast enough. Of course, he'd back off if I slept with him, but that's the biggest thing that sets me apart from every other chick at this fucking company.

Megan started working at my office right after holy fucking shit night, so by the time she found out I was married and called Leo to blab the news to him, he said, "I already know, and I thought I told you never to call me again." The poor girl thinks I'm the chupacabra, so she does her best to avoid me in the office. As far as I know, she's doing a fine job with her internship, and as long as she stays out of my business, she can keep it. My co-workers are still trying to set me up with old rich guys, but I happily tell them no, I'm already pursuing a young poor one. All that judgment in the workplace that I was so afraid of never came to fruition, at least not that I'm aware of or care about. Dr. Maria was right; once I got far enough away from Kurt, I've starting caring a whole lot less about what people think of me.

It's been six months since I moved into my cottage and the bad news is it's still a torture chamber. I literally run a million miles an hour to avoid the inevitable. The inevitable being that I have to divorce Kurt, and Leo's going to find out that it's happening later rather than sooner. According to the timeline I gave Leo on holy fucking shit night, I should've been divorced two months ago. Obviously that hasn't happened. And not because the folks in the Contra Costa County recorder's office aren't doing their due diligence either, it's because they don't even know about Gibbons vs. Gibbons yet! Leo, on the other hand, *thinks* things are moving along…at a slugs pace. I told him there was a log jam of other stupid ass idiots that got married for all the wrong reasons, and things are going to to take a little longer than expected to get finalized. Then I asked him not to ask me about it again because it really stresses me out. I guess he was afraid I'd bolt again if he pestered me about it, because, miraculously, he hasn't brought it up once. My old fear of him finding out about my marriage is now replaced by my new fear of him finding out I haven't even filed for divorce yet, except this time, I'm more fearful of the outcome if I'm exposed. Until I get the courage to drop the hammer on Kurt, I only have one option and that's to make Leo fall even more in love with me to cushion the blow of the truth when it's finally exposed. Maybe then he'll only slightly murder me.

And fall deeper in love we have. Earlier this year we spent a snowy weekend that was absolutely fabulous at my timeshare in Tahoe. Every night we snuggled by the fire as we watched the sunset over the Sierra Nevada Mountains, and we talked until it reappeared. He let me cry over the mistakes of my past and offered me the reassurance I needed for my sanity that everything happens for a reason. Hard as it was for him to be glad I was married before, he admitted, if I wasn't, I most likely wouldn't have been at Buckley's that night.

A few weeks ago, we spent an incredibly romantic weekend at The Cliffs at Shell beach near San Luis Obispo. We picnicked on the beach, got shit-faced at the hotel bar, and broke into the pool after hours and went skinny dipping. We even went wine tasting and made our first couples purchase together, a wine of the month club.

The bulk of the trip was paid for by me because Leo's still struggling to get through college, but he insisted on paying for half of the wine. Now each bottle we drink together reminds me of how much he loves me and that he'll do anything to make me happy, even eat canned chili for ten days straight because the wine club purchase busted his budget.

Now it's May and in one month, Leo will FINALLY graduate from college. He even has job offers from two investment banks. One is from Robertson Stephens in San Francisco and the other is with Lehman Brothers in New York. Even though I'd be devastated if he went to New York, I've said nothing to persuade his decision one way or the other. If anything, I'm acting more supportive of the New York job just so Taddeo doesn't think I'm trying to hold him back. He told me he'll have his choice made by the time we go to Mexico, a trip we have planned the day after he graduates.

The last time I saw Courtney, Kelly, and Nicole was at my cottage in January to celebrate the New Year, and to tell you the truth, it was just plain awkward.

"Wow, so this is the new place, huh? It's cute but it's just so... small. I could *never* live here after living in your house."

A compliment accompanied by a slam. That's Kelly for you. Seriously, sometimes I think she's going to rip a mask off of her face and it's really Kurt under there.

"How long do you plan on staying here?"

"Why? You don't like it?"

"You could be back home if you wanted to."

"Damn it Kel..."

"Just hear me out. Kurt went out with the guys a few weeks ago, and he told them he wants you back big time. Says he'll do anything."

One by one, I look at their dopey grins. They still don't get it.

"I'd want me back big time too. But it's not possible because the only time in my life I ever felt like I was good enough to want back was *after* I met Leo, and it was him that made me feel it. I can't go back to Kurt knowing that."

The rest of the evening was a struggle for all of us. Nicole tried to express interest in what was going on with Leo, well mostly what was going on *sexually* with Leo. But Courtney and Kelly said they felt weird talking about my "lover" when I still had a husband. I sort of get it but if you can't talk to your best friends about your "lover" who can you talk to? After that night, it seems like we've given up on each other. Aside from a few frivolous emails, I haven't had meaningful communication with any of them for months.

So to sum up the last four months, everything's changed and nothing's changed, and in so many ways, I'm right back where I started. Right now I'm on my way to the house in Danville to pick up some of my mail and let the dog out to pee. Kurt has to work late or play softball, I can't remember which, but he asked me to help him out, and I want to. After saying "hi" to a few curious neighbors that I make more curious by not telling them what the hell is going on, I walk around the house that doesn't feel like mine anymore. The bed's not made, dishes are piled high in the sink, and the toilet seat is up...in all three bathrooms. I search for clues that another woman's been here. In March, I cracked into Kurt's email account, (like a guy moron he didn't change the password after I moved out), and I read one very flirtatious email from a chick named Kayla. What a stupid name, *Kaaaaaayla*. I checked the date of the email to make sure it was sent after holy fucking shit night when I told Kurt he should see other people, too. It was. After I swallowed the bile that crept up my throat, I reminded myself that I didn't have justification to rip his balls off. He's just doing what I told him to do. Satisfied that *Kaaaaaayla* hasn't been in my house, I make my way to the office to pick up some of my mail.

"What's this?"

Our wedding album is sitting on the floor and right next to it is a list of songs and a cassette tape.

"Kurt and mixed tapes?"

This is a sight I never thought I'd see. I pop the tape in the stereo and the only song on it is 'Torn' by Natalie Imbruglia.

"You couldn't be that man I adored... you don't seem to care what your hearts for... I'm all out of faith... illusion never changed into something real."

He's searching for answers, he's contemplating failure, he's growing, and I'm moved to tears. I hold the cassette tape to my heart for a minute before I put it in my purse and kiss the dog on the nose, "See you soon, Buddy." I miss my pretty house, and I miss the dream, but I don't think ten thousand mixed tapes could get me to move back here.

Here's to the nights we felt alive
Here's to the tears you knew you'd cry
Here's to goodbye
Tomorrow's gonna come too soon

("Here's to the Night," *eve 6*)

LO SIENTO

JUNE, 1999

The day has finally arrived: Leo's college graduation! And in addition to celebrating that gigantic accomplishment, it's also his twenty-*fourth* birthday. We're going to do a lot of celebrating today, and then later tonight when we're back at my cottage, he's going to tell me which job he decided to take. I'm excited and nervous all at the same time! I'm excited that I'm no longer dating a poor rock yard working college guy, but I'm nervous that my new investment banker boyfriend might be going to New York and taking his new money with him. Friggin' Taddeo's been putting the pressure on him to take the Lehman Bother's job and his messages have been ruthless.

"Dude, you gotta come to New York! You can't pass up an opportunity to work at the top of the World Trade Center. Are you kidding me?"

"Dude, she left you like a million times. It's your turn now, just see what happens!"

"Dude, I just signed a lease on a killer place. You're gonna live with me and we're gonna go crazy in this city. Blehhhhh!"

I also keep telling myself that if he goes, I'll be okay, I'll be okay, I'll be okay.

It's an exceptionally hot June day, around a hundred and five degrees, and I'm sweating my ass off in the bleachers of the St. Mary's stadium with Leo's family. I marvel at how perfectly I fit in with them. They're dysfunctional as all hell, but they acknowledge it and make fun of themselves. Refreshing! Leo told all of them about my divorce (gulp) and the only thing his mom said to me was, "Hunny, I waited until I was fifty to get a divorce and trust me, sooner rather than later is best." She's a real fire cracker. I notice a tattoo on the ankle of one of Leo's brothers and think back to the night at Buckley's when he told me how stupid he thought it was. My God, that was a year and a half ago. I'm thrilled that Leo's family came together on this really hot day to watch him get what he's worked so hard for and, despite how much he complains about them, I think he is, too. For a second, it makes me sad all over again for Kurt that his family missed his college graduation. I remember him sitting amongst the other graduates with his cap and gown and his huge smile, feeling so proud that he was the first ever Gibbons to receive a college diploma. I stood up to wave, and when I got his attention his smile slowly vanished when he realized his family was nowhere around me. I push the sadness out of my mind as quickly as it enters it. He chose not to let it bother him, so I have to stop letting it bother me.

Finally the graduates make their way onto the grassy field, and I immediately notice Leo. He's a good two inches taller than everyone else. He gazes up into the jam-packed bleachers, and I watch him as he scans each and every row...he's looking for me. Instead of standing up and yelling his name, I sit and soak up the intensity of his search. After a few minutes of treasuring his determination, I will him to find me and just like the night at Buckley's, he does. When our eyes meet, we smile at each other and through my tear-stained eyes, I mouth the words, "You did it." Through his own, he says, "We did it."

When Leo left Cal Poly, he took so many huge, scary, and expensive steps backwards to fulfill his dream of becoming an investment banker and the move set him back a good two years.

When his friends graduated on time and started making real cash, he was shoveling rocks and dirt into the backs of other people's trucks, making just enough money to cover the part of his rent and tuition that his grandparents couldn't. While Taddeo was feasting on lobster at Tavern on the Green, Leo was surviving on Top Raman. What I think is the most distressing of all of his sacrifices is that he hasn't bought a single article of clothing in over TWO YEARS! It's all amazing stuff, but the most amazing thing about the last two years of Leo's life was that he didn't complain about it. He once said to me, "If this is the hardest thing I ever have to do, I'm lucky to get it over with when I'm so young."

Looking at him now, sitting in his seat with his head resting on his hands and his gaze toward the ground, I can only imagine what's going through his mind. As proud as we all are of him, it can't come close to how proud he must be of himself for fulfilling a dream. It inspires me to fulfill mine too. I want a fresh start, I want it with Leo, and I want it now! I want it to really mean something when he says the words, "We did it." Just as Leo's crossing the stage to receive his diploma, I walk to the back of the stadium, pick up my cell phone and call Kurt. I get his voicemail.

"Kurt, it's me. I can't do this anymore. I'm going on vacation and when I get back, I'm filing for divorce. I'm sorry to tell you like this, I just didn't…I just didn't…know how else to do it."

Gazing over at Leo's sixty-something year old mom, I think, if getting a divorce is the hardest thing *I* ever have to do, I'm lucky to get it over with when I'm so young…*and* without kids. I'm ready.

I felt a huge sense of relief after leaving the message, and the rest of the day Leo and I celebrate at the Mexican fiesta his mom throws for him. For once, I feel twenty-nine instead of forty-nine and as we swim, kiss, and drink margarita after margarita, Leo and I talk non-stop about the trip we're scheduled to depart on the day after tomorrow. It seems like both of our dreams are about to come true, and like a couple of fools in love, we say goodbye to everyone at midnight and giggle our way back to my cottage.

"Baby, I can't believe I'm finally done with college, I'm with you, *and* I have my dream job ahead of me. This is unbelievable, it's like I have to pinch myself to make sure it's all real."

"You deserve all of it. But here, let me pinch you just so you know for sure!"

I jump on top of him and start kissing him with every ounce of love I have inside of me. It's ironic that I'm finally on my way to being single and he might leave to take a job in New York. Well, it's more bullshit than it is ironic really, but I only have myself to blame for New York even being a consideration. It was on our last "break" that Taddeo talked him into applying for a position at Lehman Brothers.

"I'm gonna accept one of the offers before we leave for Mexico on Monday."

Oh God, here we go.

"Oh, and I have a surprise for you after I tell you which job I picked."

"*A surprise for me?*"

"Yeah and I'm even more excited about that than my job."

"So…tell me!"

It wasn't the phone ringing that alarmed us so much; it was that it was ringing at one in the morning. Being the drunk fool that I am, I answer it. Damn those margaritas! I totally forgot about the message I left for Kurt hours earlier but the minute I heard his voice, I sure remembered.

"Chrissy, we have to talk. NOW!"

Uh-oh…maybe dropping that bomb on Leo's big day was a mistake.

"Why would you say all of that, *in a message?*"

Man he sounds bad. But I have to keep this low key or else Leo's going to freak.

"Can I call you in the morning?"

"ARE YOU FUCKING KIDDING ME?"

Oh crap.

"I'm gonna have to call you back in a minute…uh-huh…I promise, one minute."

Even though I can tell he already knows the answer, Leo asks anyway.

"Who was that?"

My look confirms his suspicion.

"For some reason that guy doesn't get it that the two of you are over."

I want to tell him there's a reason Kurt thinks that, but now's not the time. It's an important day for him.

"What the hell did he want?"

"I don't know, but I have to call him back."

"You're kidding, right?"

"No. I'm sorry, Leo. He's really upset about something and I can't just blow him off."

"But you can blow me off?"

"I'm not blowing you off! I'm *here* with you, we're *going* to Mexico the day after tomorrow, I want *to be* with you…forever."

"If you want to be with me forever, you better not call him back."

I'm flattered by his jealousy and shocked by his threat all at the same time. If I hadn't just told Kurt I want a divorce, I'd be leaning more toward the flattery side, pounce on him, and have massive sex, but Kurt may just get in his car and drive over here if I don't call him back. I'm going to have to react according to what's going to get me on the phone as quickly as possible in order to avoid a face-to-face meeting between these two guys. Queue shocked.

"*I have to call him back*! We're in the middle of a divorce!"

"Right, so what the hell is there to talk about?"

Good point. Fuck!

"You wouldn't understand. You've never been married!"

"No, but I've been in love, and I wouldn't blow off the person I'm in love with."

"I'M NOT BLOWING YOU OFF!"

"Who's it gonna be, Chrissy, me or him?"

"I can't believe you're doing this to me."

"I'm doing this to *you*? You sure you wanna go there?"

"Leo, I've done horrible things to that man!"

"YOU'VE DONE HORRIBLE THINGS TO *THIS* MAN!"

Again, good point. Jesus, he should've been a lawyer instead of an investment banker.

"Look, you might despise him because he didn't take care of me the way you would've, but he did the best he could. And for most of the time I was with him, I made him think his best was good enough.

None of this is his fault, and I'm not gonna be mean to him just because I fell ass-backwards into your lap at some bar!"

Oopsy. I think I just ruined graduation night.

"Hey, I didn't ask you to talk to me at Buckley's! I was willing to let you walk away, remember?"

"Here's a good idea, let me walk away now!"

I slam the door to my bedroom and pick up the phone to call Kurt back. But before I start dialing, I press my ear up to the wall to see if I can figure out what Leo's doing. Silence. The line rings only once before Kurt picks up.

"Chrissy, *divorce*?"

"Yeah."

"That's all you have to say?"

"I'm sorry, Kurt. I don't know what else to tell you. I guess that's why I left it on your machine."

"My family doesn't even know we're…what am I gonna tell them?"

"It's your choice how you want to handle it."

"*Why are you doing this*?"

"One day, when you're far away from all of this, it'll all make sense."

"Are those Dr. Maria's words or yours?"

"Kurt, I gotta go. We can talk more when I get back from Mexico."

"Who the hell are you going to Mexico with?"

Remember Chrissy…no more lies!

"I'm going with that guy, the one I'm sort of dating." That sounded plain old icky.

"But Kurt, don't freak out, it's no big deal."

"NO BIG DEAL? *Are you serious about this guy*?"

Here's the thing. Since I met Leo, I've been trying to convince myself that I'm not leaving Kurt for him, I'm leaving Kurt for myself. And even though all of my failed attempts to break it off with Leo prove otherwise, it's the truth; I'm leaving Kurt so that I can be free to fulfill my dreams, if Leo's a part of those dreams…great. If he's not, I'll be better off alone than I'll ever be if I stay married to Kurt. I'd *like* to tell Kurt I'm serious about Leo because I'm tired of hiding and pretending, but if I do, he'll ignore all the *real* reasons I told him this happened to us. Kurt can call me a quitter all he wants, I just want him to be as knowledgeable as possible about why I quit. I CANNOT have Leo be a distraction from the truth.

"No, I'm not serious about him! It's just a trip to Mexico with a group of people and he'll be there too."

"He's gonna try to sleep with you! What are you gonna do when that happens?"

"I'm a big girl and I can take care of myself."

"But I don't want you to be in the position to have to say 'no' to him. I'm not gonna get off the phone until you promise me you're not gonna go to Mexico!"

"Kurt, I paid for the trip and I'm going."

"Chrissy, it's not too late for us to fix whatever mistakes we made, but if you go on this trip, it will be!"

The *only way* he'll recognize it's too late to fix us is if I *do* go to Mexico.

"Babe, c'mon, don't be stupid about this."

"Kurt, I... I..."

"You what?"

Hold on, that wasn't Kurt's voice. Oh my God, *is Leo on the phone?*

"Who the hell was that, Chrissy? CHRISSY!"

Ignoring Kurt, very slowly, with the receiver glued to my head, I open my bedroom door and peak around the corner to find Leo in the kitchen holding the other receiver. His eyes are cold and violent and they're glaring right at me.

"Go ahead and tell him who it is, *Babe*. Wait, before you do that, why don't you tell your husband if you guys can be fixed."

"Hey Asshole, don't talk to my wife like that."

"Hey Asshole, you've been talking to her like that for years."

FIGHT! FIGHT! FIGHT!

"Are you the fucker who thinks he's going to Mexico with my wife?"

"Listen to you...*my wife, my wife*. Last I heard she wasn't *your* wife anymore."

Oh shit, I gotta put a stop to this.

"Hold on a sec, guys! Can we just hang up and--"

"Fuck you! You don't know what the hell you're talking about. Up until today I thought we were trying to work things out! Chrissy, I'm on my way over there, and when I get there, that punk better be gone!"

Leo slowly places the receiver on the counter, tilts his head to the side and glares at me. He looks like Charles Manson…no wait… Mike Tyson. This is NOT going to end well.

"You were working things out?"

I am so busted.

"Leo, calm down. I told you I needed to take this slow."

"How can *he* think you're working things out when you told me you already filed for divorce?"

I finally did the hard part by telling Kurt about a divorce this afternoon. Everything after that was supposed to be easy…except I hadn't figured out how I was going to explain the year long delay to Leo yet. I *thought* I had at least a week to work out the logistics of that.

Leo walks up to me and stands about an inch away from my face. It actually makes me flinch a little. Dear Lord Jesus that I don't believe in, please don't let me end up like Nicole Brown Simpson tonight.

"He has no idea who I am, does he?"

Shaking my head.

"He has no clue you're anywhere near divorce, does he?"

Still shaking my head. He's literally scaring me straight.

"WHAT THE HELL HAVE YOU BEEN DOING TO ME?"

"Leo, wait! I've been trying to be sensitive to the situation, but I realize I've made a much bigger mess of things than…"

"Sensitive? Fuck you! You've been manipulative and you've been jerking me around for almost two years. You knew exactly what you were doing, and now I do, too. There's no Mexico, there's no more us. Do you understand?"

"Wait, please don't go. I can fix this!"

I grab his arm as he attempts to leave. His muscle is flexed crazy huge and it scares me just as much as his eyes.

"Leo, please…I'm almost free to be with you."

He jerks his arm away from me and sneers, "You'll never be with me."

I'm hysterically crying but that doesn't stop him from continuing to beat me down.

"You know what, Chrissy, I was gonna take the Robertson Stephens job. I even found an apartment in San Francisco that I wanted us to move into, and I was gonna take you to see it tomorrow. I wanted to start a life with you and give you everything you ever wanted because that's what I *thought* you've already given me. But you've done nothing but suck away two years of my life. I changed my mind, I'm taking the Lehman job. I'm going to New York so I can be as far away from you as possible. Stay married to that guy, for all I care."

After he slams the door, and I hear his car peel away, I fall to the floor in absolute horror. It's over, I've been exposed. If it wasn't for the hard knock at the door fifteen minutes later, I'd probably still be sitting there in shock. "Oh thank God!" I scramble to the door in a sort of half crawl jog motion and fling it open, hoping to be scooped up by Leo and carried to my bed.

"This little marriage hiatus you've been on is over. We're packing this place up tomorrow, and you're coming home so we can actually try to put this relationship back together."

Deflated, exhausted, and crushed, I close my eyes and exhale when I address him.

"I am home, Kurt. I have an attorney, and if you want to end this amicably, she's willing to represent both of us. I'll have her draw up the papers and you can decide what you want to do after you read them. Good night."

I slump down the back of the closed door and similar to what some say happens in death, the happiest moments that I shared with Kurt and Leo start to flash through my mind. The visions are a jumbled mess, but each one is as crystal clear as the pain I feel in my heart right now: my first official date to the ice cream parlor with Kurt when I was sixteen, sitting on the barstool next to Leo the night I met him, getting the keys to my first dilapidated home with Kurt, standing in the rain searching for Leo the day after I met him, my first camping trip with Kurt, making out with Leo at The Sweetwater Saloon, the day at the beach when Kurt asked me to marry him, the trip to Banana Republic when Leo bought me my ring, the day Kurt and I got our dog, the night I completely gave myself to Leo, my beautiful wedding day, slamming into Leo at The Red Devil Lounge, the first time I held Kurt's hand, when Leo's hand reached out to grab his college diploma.

"I'll be okay, I'll be okay, I'll be okay."

I crawl over to the two glasses of champagne I poured an hour ago.

"Here's to goodbye."

Tomorrow's going to hurt real bad.

OUCHY

AUGUST, 1999

Not only did the day after the double break-up hurt real bad, but so has every day after that, especially the week after Leo's graduation when we were supposed to be in Mexico. I showed up at the airport hoping he had decided to forgive me, but he hadn't. I boarded the plane and spent the next five days at the Palmilla Resort crying myself to death in front of the bartender named Cornelio, or was it Cordero? Who cares, I don't even think he understood a word I was saying and it wasn't the language barrier that got in the way either; it was the babbling baby talk made even more unclear by the never-ending cascade of tears streaming down my face.

I've been back on Dr. Maria's couch more times than I've had the cash in my pocket to pay for, and sometimes we don't even talk, I just don't want to cry alone anymore. My job satisfaction is at an all-time low, I hate everyone there, and I hate getting up in the morning to face them. They're all selfish savages that suck what little amount of life I have left in me. Most days it seems like the only thing I have the energy to do is lift a wine glass. The only good news I have to share is that I finally met with my attorney to get the ball rolling on the divorce.

Confirmation of Leo's move to New York came when I hacked into his voicemail and heard a lovely message from Taddeo. In it he said he'd pick Leo up at the airport on July nineteenth at five in the evening, show him "their" place, and then hit the town for a night of "debauchery."

The message was topped off with a nice big *BLEHHHHH*. I can only imagine the debauchery; it makes those two bar hopping gutter sluts he was with at the Red Devil Lounge seem like a couple of nuns. I do my best to shake off the sick thoughts of Leo sleeping with other women in New York City by almost doing it myself. Yes, to numb my pain, I've turned into quite the Courtney Love party girl these days, even traveling to Los Angeles to hang out with Mark, the tatted-up defense attorney.

For security reasons, I brought Slutty Co-worker with me to L.A. During the day, we lunched at The Ivy where she made a fool out of herself gawking at celebrities, and I drank myself into oblivion. Then at night, we partied our asses off in the V.I.P. section of The Viper Room. No waiting in line for anything. Mark is super dialed-in and hangs with people that I'm fairly certain I see every night on Entertainment Tonight. Normally his posse would scare the crap out of me, but the massive amounts of alcohol I now consume makes me comfy cozy around pretty much anyone. It's like I'm one with the Playboy bunnies and drug dealers we sit amongst. I'm not the fun kind of party girl, though. I'm the sarcastic one who drinks as much as she can to forget about what a mess her life has turned into. But drunk or not, my intentions for going to Los Angeles were clear. Do the things with boys that Leo's doing with girls.

"Can I get you another vodka tonic?"

I can't tell if Mark has one head or two or if it's even him I'm staring at for that matter.

"I'll take four."

"You're cute, you know that?"

"Yep."

"Dance with me."

The last time I danced was with Leo at The Red Devil Lounge. He held me so close. He smelled so good. I NEED MY DRUGS!!!!!!

Shake it off, girl!

"Nah, I don't think so."

"Come on, I won't hurt you."

You can't.

Mark pulls me to my feet and out to the dance floor where he wraps his neon dragon painted arms around my waist. This doesn't feel right. Who cares though, Chrissy, just be a guy! Think of how many times Leo's probably done this since he went away. Oh my God, I want to kill someone right now! Shake it off!

"Are you okay?"

"Just a little tipsy, I guess."

"Are you too tipsy to feel this?"

And then there it was, my first skanky unfamiliar kiss. Granted I didn't know Leo very long before I kissed him, only a few hours. But it was as if I knew him my entire life. This feels dreadful. I pull away.

"I'm sorry, Mark. My mind is elsewhere these days, and I can't do this."

"It's cool. Maybe I'll do something throughout the night to make you change your mind."

And by that he meant buying me drink after drink and repeatedly trying to kiss me. Once I had enough of his machine gun style kissing tactics, Slutty Co-worker and I excused ourselves to go to the bathroom and never returned. That was the last time I ever saw Mark. But sadly, it wasn't the last time I attempted a skanky unfamiliar kiss.

About a month after the Viper Room incident, Slutty Co-worker and I were back at Buckley's searching for a way for me to get back at Leo. And boy, did we find one. Well actually, we found five. Five guys from the Cal football team. Amazingly, I managed to hook up with a guy *even* younger than Leo. This, if my memory serves me, means the next most unlikely event to occur is that the Oakland Raiders will go to the playoffs.

My guy, who was the quarterback, invited Slutty Co-worker and me back to his parent's house (yeah, you read that correctly) for a late night BBQ and make-out extravaganza. Apparently he was "house sitting," but truth be told, I wouldn't have cared if his mom were standing in the kitchen with milk and cookies. I wanted pay back for what my mind had convinced me Leo was doing. I no longer cared about the all-important emotional connection, and I was willing to suffer the day-after repercussions of my actions and get dirty with the guy.

"Hey, let's go in your old bedroom."

"Uhhhhh, my mom turned it into a scrapbooking room."

"God, that's gay. All right then, let's go to her room."

About half way down the hall, I grab QB's belt loop, yank him toward me, and mack on him hard. I *think* he's cute. Pull away, get another look of the face, good enough, dive back in. Damn it, if Leo's doing it, why shouldn't I? This isn't about pleasure, it's about retribution!

I grab at his pants and pull him to the floor, and the kisses are flying everywhere as the dry humping commences. Wowie, his stomach is as rock hard as a twenty-one year old football player's…oh wait!

"Are you sure we should do this? How about if we go out tomorrow night and get to know each other better?"

"Dude, isn't that what a girl would say?"

"I know, but I don't want to blow it. You're just so pretty and stuff.

I'd like to get to know you and…"

"How about we do this first and get to know each other later?"

"Are you serious, you wanna have sex?"

"No, you're right, let's just cuddle."

"Wait, are you being serious about that?"

"No, dumbass, I'm not being serious about cuddling! Come on, let's just have some fun, can you do that?"

"Hell yeah, but…you just seem so nice. Why don't we hang out and talk for a while."

"Man, you're about as gay as your mom's scrapbooking room."

All I want to do is have sex to get back at Leo, and this guy wants to snuggle! I can't catch a break. I grab my clothes that are strewn down the hallway and yank Slutty Co-worker off of the wide receiver's lap. As we make our way to the car, the quarterback comes running out with his pants unzipped.

"Hey, I was serious! Will you go out with me?"

"Sure. I'll call ya."

As we drive off, I hear him yell out, "But you don't have my *numberrrrrrrrrrr.*"

Yesterday, after I got done telling Dr. Maria about the sexual shenanigans of Chrissy Anderson, she surprisingly had a smile on her face.

"Dr. Maria, I swear when I look in the mirror I don't even recognize myself. I'm spinning in a million different directions at a million miles an hour, trying to escape my thoughts. But seriously…*a college quarterback?* I'm making everything worse."

"You know what the best thing about you is, Chrissy?"

"My ability to repeatedly make an ass out of myself?"

"That you *know* when you're making an ass out of yourself and you *know* when to get help with your destructive behavior. Look, what you're doing is perfectly normal. You just have some kinks you need to work out of your system. But you might want to cut back on the drinking and go back to the yoga. You found a lot of answers with the meditation. It's hard to meditate when you're drunk."

She was right. Last night I went to yoga class, and instead of drinking a bottle of wine, I drank a bottle of water, and I slept better than I had in a long time. In the morning, I'm jolted out of my deep slumber by the pounding on my door. *Leo?* Just in case, I quickly check myself in the mirror before I open the door. Deep breathe in and…

"Hi there, sign here please."

Damn. But maybe the flowers are from him. My hands are shaking as I open the card.

Happy Birthday, Chrissy. We hope you find what you're looking for this year.
Love, Court, Nic & Kel

Holy crap, today's my 30th birthday. Where's that bottle of wine I didn't drink last night?

I know your life is empty
And you hate to face this world alone
So you're searching for an angel
Someone who can make you whole
I cannot save you
I can't even save myself...I am just as fucked as you
So just save yourself

("Safe Yourself," Stabbing Westward)

REUNITED

OCTOBER, 1999

Slutty Co-worker's been seeing the wide receiver she met on the night of my quarterback catastrophe. I don't think the relationship will go anywhere, but she sure is having a great time playing in his end zone. Suffice it to say, she hasn't been as available to help me deal with my emotional mini-breakdowns as she has been in the past. And lately I've grown tired and *broke* from spending my evenings on Dr. Maria's couch. So, per my therapist's suggestion, I do what I should've done a long time ago- call my best friends. I decided to make up for being absent for so long by taking them to lunch. We hit up a restaurant in Danville because for some reason I can't help being a masochistic freak who tortures herself by going back to her old neighborhood that reminds her of just how little progress she's made in her pathetic life.

"Wow, how long has it been, guys?"

"Long enough for most of us to turn thirty, you...you...you friend abandoner!"

"I know, Nic, I suck. Honestly though, it was for the better. I needed to sort through everything alone."

"*Well*...did you?"

"I think so."

"And how do you feel? I mean, you look good…does that mean you feel good?"

"I feel okay. All the work with the attorney is done. Now all we have to do is just sign the papers, sell the house and split up the stuff. Of course, he still thinks I'm throwing him away and I'm a big fat quitter and all that. I swear, it's like he'll never really…God, I'm so sick of *everything* being about me! Tell me, how are *you* guys doing?"

Nicole and Courtney give me a quick re-cap of what I missed out on over the last nine months. Their stories are interchangeable and boring and they make me think I don't fit in anywhere anymore. Then I realize Kelly's paying about as much attention to the two doctors as I am. Actually, considerably less. I think she's falling asleep.

"Kell…everything okay?"

"Oh, I'm alright, just a little tired these days. I'm starting to think I have a thyroid problem. I have an appointment with my doctor in a few weeks. Hopefully he'll give me some pills and it'll just go away."

"Why haven't you talked to me or Nic about any of this?"

"It's no big deal, Courtney, that's why I didn't bother you with it."

"What are your symptoms?"

"For crying out loud, I'm telling you, it's no big deal."

"Then you should be able to tell me."

"Fine. Some abdominal pain that never really goes away, and I guess I don't have much of an appetite. Really, I'm sure it's nothing a pill or a really long nap won't take care of."

"So the abdominal pain is chronic?"

Perturbed, Kelly scoffs, "I guess you could say that."

Just as she bends over to grab her purse, I catch Nicole give Courtney what looks like a worried look.

"Why'd you just look at each other like that? Is she okay?"

Kelly glances up and rolls her eyes while Nicole chastises me.

"Calm down, Sensitive Susie! There was no look. I'm sure it is just a thyroid problem or maybe it's hormonal. I'm not concerned, are you, Court?"

"Nope, no concern here. Don't let Chrissy's paranoia worry you, Kelly, you're fine."

Without lifting her head from her purse Kelly says, "You guys are freaks."

During lunch, the four of us make long overdue plans to celebrate our thirtieth birthdays. We're going to Arizona in December, the weekend Courtney officially becomes as old as us. Other than talk of our trip, the meal is tedious and uneventful. The two doctors talk about their typical confusing doctor stuff, which is usually fine, because Kelly and I spend the time gossiping about every single person we know. But this time Kelly was in no mood to talk, and it made the lunch completely blah. Finally, we hug goodbye.

Before I head back to my cottage, I make an impulsive detour and head to my old house to say a quick hello to the dog. As I drive, I wonder if Courtney and Nicole noticed what I did, that underneath Kelly's baggy sweater was nothing but skin and bones. It looked to me like she lost about ten or fifteen pounds since the last time I saw her. She did mention that she took up jogging...I'm sure that's what did it, the jogging! Jesus, I've got to stop finding things to worry about and start enjoying my life a little bit more. Lord knows Leo's having fun. And only the Lord would know, because soon after he left for New York, the voicemail account was shut off. The minute I realized the phone had been disconnected, I drove to his apartment and parked out front like a total stalker. I wanted to rehash the past, to pretend I was showing up unexpectedly just like I used to, to hope some miracle would happen and Leo would come bouncing out of his front door when he noticed my car. But all of my assumptions about Leo leaving me behind to start a new life were confirmed when I saw a couple of overly pierced white trash losers stumble out of what was once my love palace.

Speaking of contaminated former love palaces...ten minutes after leaving the restaurant, I pull up to my house. Hmmmm...there's Kurt's truck, but whose piece of crap Audi is that?

I take a mental note of the Stanford University parking permit, the tennis racket and the bathing suit on the passenger side seat, and after almost permanently flattening my nose onto the car window, I can make out the name Kay something or other on a term paper. *Kayla*? The chick who emailed him? But this couldn't possibly be…he wouldn't bring a girl into our house would he? Do I go in? Hell yeah, I go in!

"Hellooooo? Kurt…you home?"

No answer. Hold on! God, I'm so stupid! It's not like we're the only people who live on the street. That car must be one of our neighbor's friends or something. Sure the marriage is as good as done, but he would *never* disrespect what we once shared by bringing another woman into our home. For God sakes, some of my clothes are still hanging in the closet. Our wedding picture is on the mantle, and my doggie lives here. Bringing a woman here would go against everything… *HOLY HELL, IS THAT A BRA?*

All of a sudden my eyes adjust to what I really see in my house and not what I wanted to see. My once beautifully decorated family room looks like the Sigma Chi frat house. There's beer bottles strewn everywhere, take-out food containers spilling onto my carpet, an ashtray filled with pot, and right next to that are some blankets and pillows that should be on *MY* bed. Then I really focus in on the carnage! Hanging off of the corner of my wedding picture that's perched atop the fireplace mantle, is the bra. I can't resist. I walk over to it…34D. Bitch!

To stabilize myself from the nausea that just set in, I rest my hand on the kitchen table, but it slips on the small stack of papers sitting on the edge of it, and I fall flat on my ass. I watch for an eternity as the tiny strips of paper that caused the commotion fly into the air, then float down and rest around me.

"God, could this day get any worse?" I reach out and grab the closest strip of paper. "What the hell is this?" I grab another and another and another until it starts to make sense to me. Airline tickets to Mexico! "Oh you've got to be kidding me!" Kurt's going to Mexico with some girl named Kayla, and they leave tomorrow. Is this some kind of sick payback?

I've got to get out of here! Just as I'm about to get in my car, I see the two of them with *my* dog riding their *stupid* bikes back to *my* house. As they get closer, Kurt and I lock eyes. There are no words to describe the look on his face. It's like grief and terror all crammed together. It's grerror.

"Chrissy, what are you doing here?"

Without taking my eyes off of the girl, who by the way isn't as impressive looking as her bra, I answer him.

"It's my house too, Kurt."

"You have your apartment, and you asked me to stay away from it. This is my space now, and you can't just pop into it whenever you feel like it."

"It's a cottage, dammit!"

"Whatever."

"God Kurt, why don't you have the guts to say what you want to say?"

"What's that?"

"That you're mortified you got caught because now you don't look like the victim you wanted everyone to think you were. That you'd give anything in the world for me to be the one on the bike next to you instead of *that* girl. That you wish you could go back in time and do and say everything you know you should've to have prevented me from leaving you. That you know I'm strong, you know I'm beautiful, and DESPITE what you wanted me to believe for all of these years, you need me more than I need you. But *nooooooooo*, you can't say any of that because your pride or your fear or your WHATEVER is *soooooooo* fucked-up that it's easier for you to lose everything than expose your heart."

Rather calmly he says, "You should leave."

"Nice that we're on the same page for once."

Normally I hate being a hostile bitch, but not right now. Not when her boobs are front and center and petting MY DOG!

"You know what though? Before I go, answer this for me. Don't you think it's hypocritical of you to take a girl to Mexico when you told me...*Hoooooooold* on a minute! Just how far back does this little fling date back to?"

"It's none of..."

"I'M NOT TALKING TO YOU, I'M TALKING TO HER!"

The poor child is scared out of her mind.

"What...you can hang your bra on my wedding picture and spill food on my carpet, but you can't answer my question? Wow, she's perfect for you, Kurt. A young dumb girl who likes to ride bikes and won't speak up during a confrontation."

"Shut up, Chrissy."

"Are you *actually* coming to her defense? Wow, it must be love, Hunny because that's something you never did for me."

"THAT'S BULLSHIT AND YOU KNOW IT!"

"Do you really think this is where we'd be if I thought otherwise?"

"Just go, you're making a fool of yourself."

"Fine. But know this. I'll forever be sad that we failed, but the guilt of why our marriage imploded is something I certainly won't carry with me the rest of my life because for most of the time we were together, I know how hard I tried to make you happy. You'd be a liar if you said the same. You carry the guilt!"

He's shaking his head in pity.

"Mock me all you want! Eventually everything you *didn't* do will come back to bite you on the ass, and when it happens, you'll either be alone or worse...with someone like her."

He's signaling the end of the conversation by walking away, but it only makes me yell louder. "The difference between me and you is that I admitted my mistakes to myself, to you, my therapist, and my friends! I'm free. But you, you'll be locked up in your own personal Hell forever and you don't even know it!"

Screeching away, I look in my rear view mirror and I'm horrified at just how many of my old neighbors witnessed the spectacle that just took place. It makes me wonder, which love palace is more white trash now, the one in Moraga where Leo used to live or this one?

ANEMIC

DECEMBER, 1999

"I can't believe it Chrissy! You knew Kurt was seeing someone for the last two months and waited until now to tell us?"

"Sorry, Nic. I guess after everything I did to him, it didn't seem fair to trash him."

"But you've been so concerned about being the bad guy and all. I'm surprised you didn't shout from the roof top that he had someone on the side."

"I guess I settled into the role, and I stopped caring who points their finger at me for causing the BIG break up. In therapy we call that growth."

That was supposed to be funny, but clearly their alcohol hasn't kicked in yet.

"Well, the thing that pisses me off is that he was seeing someone else while he was telling *our* husbands he was devastated about the divorce. I love Kurt, but I mean, really, what the hell?"

"Listen to you guys! What did you expect him to do? Sit around for another year and wait for Chrissy to call the next shot?"

Nicole, Courtney, and I simultaneously snap our heads up from our lounge chairs to look at Kelly. We arrived in Phoenix for our girls' birthday weekend a couple of days ago and things have been nice and relaxing, mostly because I haven't brought up my man troubles.

Those usually cause tension between us (á lá this very moment), and I promised myself I wouldn't say a word about Kurt or Leo, but damn the margaritas at this resort!

"It's okay you guys, Kelly's right. He needed to get on with his life."

"You drove him to her, you know."

Wowza! I tried to take responsibility, you know, be the bigger person. But she's really going for the jugular. Time to defend myself.

"I'm aware of that, Kelly."

"He wanted to stay married to you, but you didn't give him any other choice."

"All right already, I get it!"

"Do you, though?"

"What are you talking about?"

"If you "get it," then why haven't you signed the papers? How fucking long are you gonna drag this out?"

In all the years I've known Kelly, I've never heard her use the F-word.

"Geez, Kel, I'm *sooooooooooorry* I'm dragging my feet on the thing that's gonna rip my life apart."

"Oh my God, you have to stop being so dramatic, Chrissy."

"Okay, obviously you think what I'm going through should be a lot easier than it is. But let me ask you this, what do you think happens to my house when I sign the papers?"

Silence.

"That's what I thought you'd say. I worked my ass off to buy that thing, Kelly, and when those papers get signed, I have to sell it! Oh, and that dog I've had with Kurt for nine years…bye-bye. Kurt gets him! He says it's the least I can do for ruining his life. But you know what the worst thing about all of this is, Kell? Once we're divorced, where does the last decade of my life go? And all of those experiences I had with him…who the fuck wants to hear about those?"

More silence.

"Exactly. Nobody. If I talk about them, it means one of two things: either I can't get over the past or I'm bitter. You're talking thirteen years of my life that are now taboo! Thirteen years of my life that all of a sudden make everyone feel uncomfortable. But *you*...you still get to be a part of his life. You can talk about our college days, the parties we went to, the camping trips we had, the weddings we all participated in together, all the good times! Christ, Kelly, I've been with Kurt since I was *sixteen years old,* and excuse me if it's taken me a little longer than the average adulterous bitch to deal with losing him!"

"Jesus, you guys are more annoying than bagpipes! This is a nice place, can you bring it down a notch, please?"

"You're right, Court, this adulterous bitch should leave."

I start gathering my things but then Kelly stops me.

"You stay. I'll go."

"Oh for cryin' out loud, why do either of you have to go?"

Slightly embarrassed, I plop back down on my lounge chair. "Kelly, you gotta give me a break. I'm doing the best I can."

"I'm sorry, Chrissy, call it tough love but you can't stay in limbo forever. It's exhausting, and if it's this exhausting to us, I can't imagine what it's like for you."

"I know, and I love you for caring... even though you show it in the most scary and militant way possible."

"Here you go again with the 'I love you's.'"

"Ahhhh come on, tell me you love me, Kel."

"No."

"Tell me!"

"No!"

"Stop throwing ice at each other! The bartender's eye balling us, and he's gonna cut us off!"

"Okay, okay, Nicole! Hey, why are you still packing up your things, Kelly?"

"I'm gonna go back to the room, after all. I'm a little tired and I want to take a nap before dinner."

"It's noon!"

"You want me to stay and yell at you about your divorce some more?"

"You're right, you should go!"

Once Kelly's gone, we order another round of margaritas, and before I'm half way through with mine, I doze off into a nice tequila-induced nap. An hour, or maybe it's just twenty minutes later, I wake to the chatter of Courtney and Nicole, but I don't let them know I'm listening.

"Did she ever tell you what her doctor said?"

"All she told me was that it wasn't her thyroid and that she was undergoing some blood work to rule out anemia. She doesn't look good, though."

"I know. She won't take her bathing suit cover-up off, but the weight loss is obvious to me."

"Me, too."

"And I haven't seen her eat a damn thing. I don't know, Nicole… doesn't seem like anemia. Do you think she might be diabetic?"

"Can't tell. You think she's being honest with her doctor about everything?"

"What do you mean?"

"You know Kelly… everything has to be perfect all the time. She's got her stupid lists and timelines just like that one over there." I can feel their eyes look my way. "What if she's not being honest with her doctor about her symptoms because she's afraid that whatever's wrong will mess up all her plans?"

"Nahhh, I can tell she's worried. I don't think she'd hold back any information from her doctor. Besides, Craig wouldn't let her."

"Should we talk to her?"

"Let's give it a month or so. I just asked her about the thyroid thing. You know how she doesn't like everyone fussing over her. Press her too much and she'll attack us like she attacked Chrissy!"

Anemia? Diabetes? Gosh, now I feel terrible about yelling at her.

"Excuse me, ladies, is one of you Chrissy Gibbons?"

I lift my head like the bartender just woke me up.

"Sort of." He looks confused. "Yeah, yeah, yeah, I'm still her for another few months. What's up, credit card maxed out?"

"Phone call for you, ma'am."

"Ma'am? I'm thirty, not fifty!"

Must be someone from my office. I turned my cell phone off, but those bastards always seem to find a way to reach me.

"Nicole, I'm too drunk to talk. Go tell whoever it is that I'm in the middle of a massage."

Courtney and I are in the throes of debating the hotness of George Clooney versus Harrison Ford when Nicole jogs up.

"Guys, we gotta go!"

In unison Courtney and I say, "Where?"

"That was Kurt's mom."

"Gimme a break, Nicole, I know you love your jokes, but you couldn't come up with anything more clever?"

Stuffing all her crap in her bag, "I'm serious, Chrissy, Kurt got in a motorcycle accident, and he's been airlifted to a hospital in Sacramento."

I slowly arch my back up as I watch her go to work, and, at once, a million thoughts are racing through my mind. Is this for real? Holy crap, is Kurt *really* hurt? She's gotta be joking. Oh my God, what if Kurt's dead! I'm going to kill her if she's joking. If it's true, what's my role in this nightmare? What does everyone expect me to do? I'm at a crossroads! *Grandpa?*

Strangely composed, I say, "Is he okay?"

She stops stuffing and snaps her head at me.

"You're calm? *Why are you so calm?*"

"Nicole...IS HE OKAY?"

"Okay, that's better. She didn't know."

"When will she get to the hospital?"

"She's on her way from Fremont now, should be a couple of hours. But Chrissy, I think you need to know--"

"Okay then, I'll call her back and give her my cell phone number. She'll give us an update once she arrives. If it's bad, we'll go. But there's no sense rushing off if it's minor. Given everything I've put Kurt through, I'm not even sure he'd want me by his bedside. Maybe he'd rather have *Kaaaaaayla* there instead."

Satisfied with my plan, I plop back down on my lounge chair.

"Ummm Sweetie, we have to tell you something."

Instantly unsatisfied, I pop back up.

"I mean, Jesus! What the hell was he doing in Sacramento anyway?"

"His mom said something about some dirt bike race thing. You have to--"

"Oh, that's it! I'm NOT ruining my vacation because of his dumb decisions! Seriously, what kind of retarded thirty-one year old man goes on a dirt bike race? "

"CHRISSY, WOULD YOU SHUT UP FOR A MINUTE! We have to tell you something."

"What?"

"Kurt hasn't told his family a single thing about what happened--you know, between the two of you."

"Yep, as far as they're concerned, you two are as happy as the day you got married."

"Son of a bitch."

Welp, that answers that question. My role in this nightmare is that of wife, and no matter how superficial his wounds may be, everyone will expect me to ditch my vacation to be by his side. *Not* what I was looking for, Grandpa!

"It doesn't mean you have to go, Chrissy."

"What are you talking about, Nicole? Of course she has to go! He's still her husband."

"It's not her fault he hasn't told them anything."

"But it *is* her fault she hasn't gone through with the divorce, so as far as I'm concerned she's obligated to go!"

Of course, I'd hop on the first flight out if Kurt was severely injured, no matter if it's today or ten years from today. But I've created another situation for myself where I'm *obligated* to put his well-being, even if he only has a slight wound, ahead of mine. Son of a bitch! I was so close to being able to disassociate myself from the word obligation! Unbeknownst to everyone, I even signed the divorce papers immediately after the run-in with Kayla at my house. It no longer seemed important to remain attached to a man who's toting around a 34-D cup girlfriend. *But did I send them?* Of course not! And all because I wasn't ready to stop talking about my past with him, because I wasn't ready to split my assets, because I wasn't quite ready to let him be happy without me. But now I might have to rip up those papers. *Never* in a million years will I have the courage to divorce Kurt if he turns me into Mrs. Christopher Reeves! I was already *barely* going to make it into Heaven with all that adultery business, but there's no way I'll make the cut if I abandon a paralyzed spouse. Looking like I'm the anemic one, I slowly start to gather up my belongings.

"Call the airline, Courtney."

Hours later, I enter Sutter Memorial Hospital with my three, still somewhat inebriated, friends in tow. We took every single bottle of liquor from the hotel mini bar and pounded the entire flight over. I park them right next to Kurt's mom, who looks a little inebriated herself, and tiptoe my way down the hall.

"Excuse me. I'm looking for Kurt Gibbons."

"Are you his wife?"

"Uh-huh."

"Oh good, he's been asking for you."

"Is he okay?"

"He's pretty banged up, got a nice road rash across his chest. He just got out of x-ray, I'll know more about the damage to the spinal cord once I'm able to review them."

"Ho…ho…*hooooooold* on there, Doc…*Spinal cord*?"

"Ma'am, your husband took a serious blow to the head and neck when he was thrown from the bike. My best guess is that he's suffered a severe contusion to the spinal cord, possibly also with multiple herniated disks."

What the fuck is it with the "ma'am" stuff today?

"I can let you in to see him, but it's important that he lies as still as possible, we're worried about some possible paralysis."

Paralysis?

"Look, I've gotta run. Go be by his side, try not to worry, and I'll be in to see you as soon as the x-ray results are ready."

No, No, No, No, No! This cannot be happening to me. I stabilize myself by holding onto the wall outside of Kurt's room. *Paralysis*? I need Dr. Maria, a pill, another margarita, something! I'm like a car teetering on the edge of a cliff, and if so much as a bird lands on the hood, the whole thing's going to topple over into a ravine and burst into a ball of flames. Shooo birdie! Shooo!

"Chrissy, you okay?"

It was Kelly, the least intoxicated of my three friends.

"I don't think so."

"What can I do?"

"Tell me what to do."

"I wish I could, but I can't."

"No, I really need you to tell me what to do! I feel like I'm the paralyzed one right now! I can't breathe. Tell me what to do! Someone has to tell me what to do! Omigod, I feel like I'm gonna pass out."

"Here, sit down."

"Kelly, I can't do this. I'm not the cold-hearted bitch you think I am. If I go in there and see him strapped to a board, bleeding...*paralyzed*! I'll have to go back. I, I, I...I can't turn my back on someone I love like that. He'll need Francesca! I'll have to be Francesca!"

"Francesca?"

"You don't understand, the last year and a half has been so hard. To get my freedom, I had to cut everybody off...him...you guys. I didn't want to, but I knew if I didn't, you'd all convince me to go back to a life that wasn't right for me."

"I know that now."

"But I can't cut this off! I'm gonna have to take care of this!"

"Chrissy, you didn't do this to him. Not wanting to be married to him has nothing to do with this accident."

"But I'm *still* married to him! You heard the doctor, he's been asking for me, ME! His mother is out in that hallway waiting for a report from ME! How the hell do I distance myself from that now without being a monster?"

"You're not a monster."

"Kel, I want to go to him because I care about him, but what about after that? I mean, what if he's really, really hurt?"

She shrugs her shoulders and shakes her head and says, "I dunno."

I dunno? Kelly's a good friend to be by my side but she's like Kurt in so many ways. She states the obvious but when hearts need to be laid on the line, she's dismissive. After a not tight enough hug, she walks away. I brush the tears off of my face and take a deep breath before I enter the hospital room.

"Kurt? Can you hear me?"

His face and hair are covered with dirt. His motorcycle gear is ripped to shreds, some of it caused by the fall and some of it caused by the scissors used by the EMT's to get to his wounds. He has a brace around his neck and his forehead is taped to the board his limp body is laying on. He slowly opens his eyes and smiles up at me. His teeth are covered with dirt too.

"Sorry to ruin your trip."

"Don't worry about it; I wasn't having very much fun anyway. Oh gosh, don't laugh. The doctor said you aren't supposed to move."

He wiggles his right fingers to motion me to touch them.

"Hey, good to see those things are working."

Squeezing my hand tightly, he whispers, "It's my legs." And then I see a solitary tear travel down his cheek.

"It's okay. It's gonna be okay. Let's just see what the x-rays say before we get all crazy, all right?"

"All I could think about was you, Chrissy. As I was falling, when I was in the helicopter...all I could see was your beautiful smile. I don't want to lose you. I need another chance to make things right."

"Shhhhh, just rest. We'll get it all figured out."

"I love you so much."

"I know. Love you, too."

I wonder if he realizes the painful difference that was unmistakable to me all those years.

Two hours later, I wander out into the hallway. The nurse informs me that my friends booked a room at the hotel next door and would be waiting for me there. I make my way over to Kurt's mom and give her the news. Kurt indeed has a severe contusion with marked swelling to the spinal cord, and he has multiple herniated disks. Right now he has limited use of his legs but with surgery, steroids, and physical therapy, he *should* be able to regain full use of them. It'll take a few months, but with hard work and dedication, which Kurt's committed to doing, he's going to be fine...maybe. I give her a hug, promise to return in the morning and resignedly leave to meet up with my friends.

"Okay...it's not as good as we wanted, but it's not as bad either, Chrissy."

Nicole rolls her eyes at Courtney's glass is always half of some bullshit comment and says, "*We* don't matter. What do *you* think of everything, Chrissy?"

"There's a really good chance he could get back full use of his legs. Of course it's good."

They could give two shits whether I think Kurt's recovery is good or bad, they only want to know what part I plan on playing in it and they're too afraid to ask. They're just staring at me.

"Guys…relax. Once he gets released, I'll take him back home and stay with him until he gets better. It's okay, I'm fine with the decision."

"What if he doesn't get better?"

"I dunno, Nicole, I haven't thought it through. Helping to rehabilitate a partially paralyzed soon-to-be-ex-husband was never on that list I made when I was sixteen. I just gotta take this day by day."

"That's a good attitude, Chrissy."

"Yeah, and it only cost me about five thousand bucks in therapy and yoga to get it."

"I have a question."

I roll my head up at Nicole in a way that tells her it's her last.

"What would you do if Leo was still in the picture?"

They're on the edge of their seats waiting for my answer, and I think long and hard before I give them the best one I can think of.

"I'm starting to get the feeling that obligation will always kick love's ass. It's good he left when he did." Without changing my clothes, I pull the blanket over my head and quietly start to cry. I'm not sure which one of my friends it was who rubbed my back until I fell asleep.

BUCKAROO

FEBRUARY, 2000

The drive home from the hospital two months ago reminded me of the drive on the night Kurt convinced me to leave my parents' house and go back home with him...Well, except this time his legs didn't move. Even so, he was all smiles. He didn't even care when he had to boost himself up from the wheelchair, balance the entire weight of his body on his crutches, and wriggle his way into the passenger side of the car. He was just happy to be with me and on our way home. On the long drive, he gabbed about all the things going on with our neighbors that I didn't know about since I'd been gone for so long. He got me up to speed with his job, and told me about his promotion to Vice President of International Sales, *and* he apologized for the Kayla fiasco...sort of. There was no admission of grossness for bringing her back to our house and no confession of a double standard about going to Mexico with her. And also not surprising was that there was zero mention of Leo. Everything was one hundred percent positive and great. He was one hundred percent Kurt...but again, without the legs.

Moving back home allowed me to make up for a lot of the horrible things I did to Kurt over the last two years. Obviously nothing I do will ever erase all of the indecencies, but helping him to get dressed, driving him to work, to physical therapy, even taking him to the shitter…all of it was penance for the crimes I had committed against him. And I didn't resent a second of my time with Kurt, either, because I knew that seconds were all we really had left together. No, no, no, he didn't die! In fact, after two months of intense physical therapy, spinal fusion surgery and gallons of steroids, he's almost totally rehabilitated. I'm sure he wishes the same could be said about our marriage, but it can't, and he realized it the moment we walked into the house after that long drive home from the hospital that December morning.

"Where's all your stuff?"

"Right there."

"That's just a suitcase. I mean where's the furniture, the dishes, all the stuff you moved out with?"

"At my cottage."

"Why?"

"I'm not moving back here, Kurt. I'm staying with you for as long as it takes to get you better, but my cottage is my home, and I'm keeping it."

"Babe, I meant everything I said to you at the hospital, and I'm gonna make it all up to you."

"Make all of what up to me?"

"You know, making you feel more appreciated…cherished. All the stuff you and Dr. Maria talked to me about that one time."

"How are you gonna do that?"

"Why are you being so antagonistic about this? I'm saying good stuff!"

"Kurt…please…"

Seeing him struggle to turn around in his wheelchair to face me almost makes me hold back what I have to say. *Almost.*

"Let me finish and then you can get as mad at me as you want."

"Fine."

"However you plan on making me feel cherished…it won't be enough. However much you try to open up your heart to me…it won't be enough. Whatever wonderful things you try to do and say to make me forget about everything I've learned about myself, none of it will be enough to erase it."

"You don't know that!"

"Please…for so long, I thought you were holding out love for me in order to control our relationship and it drove me CRAZY insane. And I thought if you could just learn how to stop being so damn controlling, we could magically be that perfect couple I always wanted us to be."

"I NEVER held out my love for you!"

"I know that now! From the start you gave me 100% of your heart. You cooked good food for me because you wanted me to be healthy. You took me on adventurous trips and encouraged me to try things I'm afraid of because you thought I'd feel the same rush as you and you wanted me to experience that joy. You bought me camping gear and roller blades and bicycles because you wanted to do all of the things that you love…together, *as a couple*. You didn't want to talk about really painful stuff with me because I think you wanted to protect me from the kind of pain it caused you. Those are all the ways you tried to make me feel appreciated and cherished and I see that now. That's why I'm here."

"Then why would you leave?"

Telling him all of this with two good legs would be hard enough, but doing it now when he's so helpless looking is horrendous.

"Kurt, for some lucky lady your 100% is gonna be more than she ever dreamed of, but for me, it'll never be enough."

"I don't want another lady. I want you."

"I know and for a really long time, I fought those same feelings. It's hard, *but you have to believe me*, when you find the woman you're supposed to be with, it'll be like peace and sanity and relief and safety wraps around you like a cocoon and all the things you ever *thought* you wanted no longer exist because she'll be all you ever need. Everything will feel calm…comfortable. Like a dream come true. You have to believe me. Please tell me you believe me because your trust in what I'm telling you is the only thing that'll set me free."

Right there in the entry hall, I settled onto his wheelchair-burdened lap, wrapped my hands around his neck, and held him as tightly as I could and I begged him to believe me. Once he told me he did, and our positioning became incredibly uncomfortable, he used all of his strength to lay me on the floor where we spent the rest of the afternoon talking, laughing, kissing, and crying. Everything we said and did that day was centered around how little time we knew we had together, and so instead of fighting about all the things we did wrong, we focused on everything we did right. We talked about how sorry and scared we both were and promised each other to always speak highly of our marriage because as we agreed, it was the most precious learning experience of our lives. The next day, with new attitudes and a rediscovered respect for each other, we aggressively tackled Kurt's leg situation. For two months we worked on getting him better and the teamwork paid off, because today he's getting himself dressed, driving himself to work and wiping his own ass.

INVISIBLE

FEBRUARY, 2000

With Kurt safely on the road to recovery, I'm back at my cottage and trying to catch up with everything going on at work. It seems like everyone...except Megan, is glad I'm back. I think the time apart did her and me some good though. Now that Leo's long gone, and the stress of juggling two men at once is over, I no longer feel the need to scare the crap outta her on a daily basis. In fact, I even made nice talk with her in the break room yesterday. I try to stay outta there at noon because that's when the Chinese sewing ladies are squealing away at the break table while they eat their monkey brains and rat embryos, but I had to refill my water bottle. It was at the exact same time Megan was refilling hers.

"How's it going with the internship?"

"Are you talking to me?"

"Well, no one else in here speaks English so...yeah I'm talking to you."

"Oh, um...it's good. Different than I thought, but good."

"It's certainly not the glamorous industry everyone thinks it is, huh?"

"Totally not. It's like my friends think I sit around and read Vogue and then share my fashion inspiration in chic trend-forecasting meetings. But all I really do all day is unroll fabric and count buttons."

"Stick with it and you'll get more responsibility soon. In fact, I suggested they take you to Dallas with them for March market. I think they could use your help."

"*You did?*"

"Megan, work is work. Whatever happened outside of here has zero impact on what I think of your performance here. Got that?"

"Got it."

"Welp, I'm off to New York this evening, so I'll see you next week."

"Do you see Leo?"

I come to a screeching halt just outside of the break room, turn and peek my head back in.

"What'd you say?"

"When you go to New York, do you see him?"

"Noooooo. Have *you* talked to him since he moved there?"

"I'm not allowed to, remember?"

"Megan, I…"

"No, it's okay, it's my fault all that happened."

"No, I acted childish."

"You were right though, Chrissy."

"About what?"

"I was totally in love with him."

Hearing her say that should make me mad, but it just makes me sad. Because of me, both of us can't know him anymore. Such a shame. With a heartfelt sigh, I say, "I know you were."

"It's cool though. I mean, it wasn't at first, but then I met Mick in Shipping & Receiving, and we're like totally seeing each other and I dunno, I think I'm supposed to be with him. Sounds silly, I know…"

"No, not silly at all. Everything happens for a reason. Maybe Mick's the bright side of all that stupid stuff that happened between you and me. Just a heads up though…Erika in Production has the hots for him, and she's a huge slut. I'd keep my eye on her."

We actually share a little laugh before I set off down the hallway again.

"He asked about you, ya know?"

Now it's her head that's peeking into the hallway. I whirl around so quickly that half of my water tumbles out over the rim of my bottle.

"*When?*"

"My roommate's boyfriend is old high school buddies with Leo and Taddeo. He went to New York to visit them, and Leo asked him to ask his girlfriend to ask me if you ever got divorced. Of course, I wasn't supposed to know that it was Leo who wanted to know because he still hates my guts and…"

"What did you say?"

"I said 'I don't know' because I don't know."

"Did you say *anything* else?"

"Are you gonna be mad?"

I raise my hands in the air and bug my eyes out at her.

"Okay, okay okay…all I said was that you look sad all the time and that I thought ever since he went away you've been…you've been…"

"I've been what?"

"Lost."

Oh great. I bet he's enjoying his fabulous New York Investment Banker single life so much more knowing I'm a total wreck.

"Chrissy, I'm sorry! I had to! You know how Leo hates liars!"

She was trying to be funny to shake me out of my funk, but she failed.

"Better than anyone."

Usually on my red eye flights to New York I spend the first two hours reviewing reports for my meetings, then I order a vodka tonic, pop a melatonin, throw the shitty airline blanket over my head, and snooze until we hit the ground. But last night, I put the *Braveheart* soundtrack on my Discman and stared out of the window into complete blackness for five whole hours as it played on repeat. Slutty Co-worker, who had arrived a few days before me for some sample shopping, was waiting for me in the lobby of the W Hotel with a cup of coffee and a bagel. She always takes such good care of me.

"I don't even know why I'm here."

"The Macy's appointment. Jesus, Hunny, how many fuckin' melatonins did you take?"

"No freak, I know why I'm *supposed* to be here. I'm just not into it anymore. Work used to be so important to me because it was the one place I could be myself. But after meeting Leo…after having the kind of happiness with him that all of this used to give me…I dunno, now that he's gone, it just doesn't fill the void it once did."

"What are you saying?"

"I don't wanna do this anymore."

"What do you want to do then?"

"I have absolutely no idea."

"Hunny, just go find him so we can all get the fuck on with our lives."

"Oh yeah…and tell him what?"

"That you love him!"

"Tell him I love him so much that I'm not even divorced yet? Yeah, that'll win him over."

"I bet my last buck, he's just as unhappy as you."

"I'd take that bet if there was a way to find out."

"There is. Go take a nap and a shower, and I'll meet ya back down here at four o'clock."

"What about the Macy's appointment?"

"You don't want to do it anymore…then don't do it anymore. I'll take care of it."

"Are you serious?"

"As serious as your love is for that boy."

Not knowing what to expect, at four o'clock on the dot, I show up in the lobby. Slutty Co-worker yells to me from a town car outside.

"Chrissy! Over here!"

"Fancy. Where we headed?"

"Driver, World Financial Center please." Then turning to me like a five year old on Christmas morning, "I did some detective work, and it looks like Leo leaves work at around four-thirty and occasionally stops off at a bar across the street from his office. Let's see if he's thirsty today."

"*You did some detective work?*"

"Hey, you're not the only crafty bitch in town who knows how to hack into voicemail. I have my ways."

I'm quiet on the drive. It's been eight months since I've seen Leo, and I don't really know what good can come out of watching him drink beer at a bar. But my reservations do nothing to turn the car around. I have to see what a successful Leo looks like.

Sixty minutes and three overpriced New York drinks later…

"Are you *sure* that's the place?"

We're sitting at a restaurant across the street from Leo's supposed hang out, and it's beginning to look like either Slutty Co-worker took us to the wrong place or Leo has better things to do today.

"Yes, calm down. You're getting on my nerves. Have another drink, for God's sake."

"Jesus, let's just go, this is stupid and--"

"Omigod, there he is!" Clapping her hands she sings, "Told you so! Told you so!" over and over again.

Walking across the windy street with his black hair smartly slicked back, wearing a crisp white collared shirt, black slacks, shiny black shoes, and a black trench coat, is my Leo. He looks everything and nothing like the rock yard worker I met just over two years ago. Wow, he really did it.

"I gotta get outta here."

"What? W*hy?*"

"This is pathetic. I went from being a twenty-eight year old adulterer who stalks twenty-two year old college kids to a thirty year old divorcee who stalks out of state twenty-four year old investment bankers. Call the driver."

"Well, technically, you're not divorced yet."

"Exactly. Another reason why this is so pathetic! Call the driver now!"

"Just go talk to him."

"*And say what?* Hi, Leo, I'm still the pathetic loser who can't seem to shit or get off the pot or should I lie to him *AGAIN* and pretend I've made all these wonderful changes in my life, only to woo him back *AGAIN*, fall madly in love with him *AGAIN,* and get dumped when he finds out the truth about me…*AGAIN?*"

"You're killing me, girl. I've never met anyone better at screwing up a good thing."

"Me neither. Now give me my money and call the driver."

"What money?"

"You bet me your last buck that he's just as unhappy as me. Look at him."

Slutty Co-worker confirms my worst fear by handing me all of the money in her wallet as I broodingly watch Leo laugh with the banker boy sitting next to him while he cheers on some stupid sport. I clumsily move to the other side of the table to collect my winnings so I won't have to see Leo's beautiful happy face anymore, and that's when he notices me. Not only did my version of musical chairs disrupt the five angry New Yorkers sitting around me, it also got the attention of Leo who was fifty feet away across the street.

"Uh-oh. Looks like he's leaving, Hunny."

"I can't care anymore."

"But you *dooooooo*, that's what makes everything you say and do so weird!"

"Where's the damn driver, already?"

Admitting her defeat, Slutty Co-worker takes a deep breath and shakes her head at me.

"Just pulled up."

"Good. I wanna go back to the hotel, take a bath, and forget this ever happened."

What that really means is I'm going to go back to the hotel, raid the mini-bar, and pass out. I slap twenty of my new bucks on the table, quickly gather my belongings, and yet again, annoy everyone around me as I bash their tables with my big fat handbag on the way to the door.

"Chrissy, wait!"

I'm one foot inside of the car when I hear it. I cup my hands over my mouth and snap my wide eyes toward Slutty Co-worker in a way that suggests that if I don't move an inch or say a word I can be invisible. It didn't work.

"Chrissy, over here!"

I slowly peak my head up over the roof of the car, pause for a moment, and then slide back down. "How in *theeeeeee* hell did he notice us?"

"Uh gee…the restaurant's a wall of windows, Hunny! Maybe you shoulda thought of that before you decided to knock down four tables on the way out the door and cause a big fucking scene!"

I take another peak over the roof, and Leo puts his hands in the air like he's asking "What the hell are you doing here?" He's trying to make his way over to me, but he's at the mercy of the crosswalk, the outrageous New York traffic, and the hordes of people who evidently have more important places to go than him.

"What are you gonna do, Sweetie?"

I raise my hand up to wave at Leo, but it looks more like I'm taking an oath on the bible. His crosswalk turns green and, for a moment, I watch his trench coat flap in the wind as he maneuvers through the crowds of people to make his way toward me. By the time he gets there, I'm gone.

DUCK, DUCK, DUCK... GOOSE.

MARCH, 2000

"That's it?"

"Yep."

"When was it?"

"Couple of weeks ago."

"And you haven't heard from him?"

"Oh no, I heard from him."

"Omigod! What did he say?"

"He emailed me and asked me why I ran away. Oh, and he also wanted to know what my situation was."

"Situation?"

"Yeah, like if I was alone or still married."

"Oh boy, what'd you do?"

"Nothing."

"*You did nothing*?"

"What the hell was I gonna do, email him back and tell him I was stalking him and yes, I'm still married?"

"She's got a good point."

"Yeah, she does."

Since our trip to Arizona, Nicole, Courtney, Kelly, and I made a promise to resume our monthly lunches and we've been diligent about keeping that promise…at least three of us have, anyway.

"You know what, you guys, let's change the subject."

"All righty, have you signed the divorce papers yet?"

"Not the subject I was hoping for, Nicole, but yeah, I signed them."

"Good girl. Did you send them back?"

"Not yet but…"

In unison Courtney and Nicole blurt out, "*Oh…my…God!*"

"I know, already! But here's the thing. I actually signed them in December, before we even went to Arizona but then all that stuff happened with Kurt, my mail piled up at home, and I'm still trying to get caught up with it. I promise, the minute I find them, I'll put 'em in the mail."

"You're a train wreck you know that, Chrissy?"

"Tell me something I don't know, like…where the hell is Kelly?"

"You haven't heard from her either?"

"No, I was hoping you guys have."

"I talked to her about two weeks ago, she said she was going back and forth between doctors to try and get to the bottom of her abdominal pain."

"Should we be worried?"

"You can be worried, Chrissy, God knows it's what you do best. Nicole and I will keep pressing her for more information, and we'll let you know when you can relax."

This lunch, like the three others before it, was quite boring. Without Kelly to talk to about Hollywood gossip and the losers from our old high school days in Freakmont, I'm stuck listening to stories about triage, code reds, and hypoglycemia. *Bleckh*!

After lunch that day, I went straight back to my cottage to look for the divorce papers. Not just because it was time to shit or get off the pot, but because I was tired of asking myself what I would've done on that New York curb if I had sent the damn things in already. Like if I could've told Leo I was divorced, would I be in his arms right now? I want to free myself up so that if I'm ever lucky enough to stalk/run into him again, I can say I'm officially single. After turning my cottage upside down, I finally locate the papers underneath ten unread copies of *Cosmopolitan* magazine, all with headlines like:

"What to do if you're thirty and single"
"No man? No sweat. Here's ten ways to pleasure yourself"
"Maybe you're the reason you're not in a good relationship"

Huge note to self...cancel your subscription to *Cosmopolitan* magazine. With a martini in hand, I settle onto my bed and carefully re-read the divorce papers, my fingers gliding over every one of my perfectly crafted signatures. At the time I signed them, I took extra care in writing my name, thinking it would be the last time I'd be Chrissy Gibbons. Little did I know it'd take another five months before I sent them off. I gently placed the papers back in the large envelope they arrived in and ceremoniously deposited them in the mailbox by taking a giant sip of my martini, as they slid down the shoot. The divorce should be final sometime in the fall, my favorite time of the year. The leaves on the trees will be falling as quickly as the likelihood of a thirty-one year old divorcee finding a man as perfect for her as the one she left on the dirty streets of New York. Now that would make a great article in *Cosmo*.

The month of March trickles away like the Northern California rain that always belongs to it. My weekdays are filled with work and exercise and my weekends are filled with...just exercise. I took a lot of time off from yoga while I was helping to rehabilitate Kurt, but I'm more than making up for it now. I found a hole-in-the-wall place near my cottage in Lafayette to start practicing because the drive to the city to do it with Slutty Co-worker was stressing me out to the point that it made yoga completely unenjoyable. Those assholes coming out of the Bay Bridge toll booth DO NOT know how merge! I don't have to worry about it anymore though because just fifteen minutes from my cottage is an old, dilapidated yoga studio where almost seven days a week, I contort my body into positions that I dream of showing to Leo. It's the only hour of my day that I feel focused and, sometimes, my mind even drifts off to a place where I'm happy and I feel at peace.

Work has become even more hum-drum than ever. I drift from meeting to meeting without a care for whatever it is I'm supposed to care about, and whenever I'm not pretending to be a corporate cheerleader, I lock myself in my office and search the internet for ways to make money doing the things I like to do. But those soul-searching intervals only end up pissing me off because...*I don't know what the hell I like to do!* And it seems like no matter what I do to fill up my nights, they always end up with me in front of my computer where I read Leo's email over and over again.

Chrissy, I'm not sure why I'm writing to you. I guess my mind is getting the best of me. Why did you bail on me after I saw you in New York? If I don't hear back from you, I'll assume it's because your situation prevents you from doing so. By the way...what is your situation? Leo

For weeks I've tinkered with all kinds of responses. They range from the sexpot kind where I ignore the entire content of his email and talk dirty to him to the idiot kind of response where I play dumb and pretend I don't know what the hell he's talking about. *New York? Bail on you? I have no idea what you're talking about.* After spending an hour on tonight's response, I decide that this is the email I'm going to send. I carefully type his email address, close my eyes, and hit send as I enjoy the rush of my Leo drug as it sails through my body. Moments later, as I'm pouring myself a third glass of wine, I wonder if my chutzpah to send the email came from the first two glasses. Crap, I should know by now that email and alcohol don't mix! I race to my computer, re-open the email and read it again.

Leo, Whatever situation I'm in, it could never prevent me from responding to your email. I'm only sorry it took me this long. I bailed on you in New York because I'm scared. Scared of what, I still don't know. Chrissy

Shake it off, Chrissy, it's a good email, and it's vague. I'm sure nothing will come of it anyway, so calm down. And then the phone rings.

I look up toward the Heavens and silently thank my Grandpa. Then I give myself a little pep-talk. Okay Chrissy...whatever you do, tell him the truth about where the divorce stands. It's his choice how he deals with it. Only the truth will set you free, Baby!

"Hello?"

"Chrissy, it's me."

My heart sinks. Totally not who I expected to hear.

"Oh...hey Nicole. Let me guess, Kelly's not coming to lunch again tomorrow."

"She's not."

"What's her excuse this time? Bad haircut...baby sick again?"

"I just got off the phone with Craig."

Nic's voice...it's scared or something. My voice is scared right back.

"Why were you talking to Craig?"

"I don't know how to tell you this."

"Nicole?"

"She's got cancer...Kelly's got cancer."

For the first time in my entire life, I'm speechless.

"Are you okay, Chrissy?"

"Tell me this isn't real."

Silence.

"She'll be okay though, right? We can beat it, can't we?"

"Not likely. It's pancreatic."

"How much worse is it than all the other cancers?"

"Way worse."

"Nic, you gotta tell me something good. This is...this can't..."

"Do you know *anything* about pancreatic cancer?"

"Well no, but she's so young. She's strong and otherwise really healthy."

There's a long pause. Too long.

"She'll be okay, won't she?"

"No, I'm telling you, she won't."

"Stop it! How do you even know that?"

"Chrissy, no one survives this kind of cancer."

"So what the hell are you saying?"

"I'm saying Kelly's gonna die."

I slide down the wall in my kitchen and not in the normal dramatic Chrissy sort of way either. My body took me there all on its own.

"Are you still there?"

"I don't understand how you can just say that. You're talking about Kelly!"

"Maybe it's the doctor in me. Maybe it's that I want you to start processing the reality of the situation as soon as possible. Maybe I'm in shock, too. Courtney and I are on our way over to your place now. We thought we should be together right now."

"How long will…OH MY GOD NICOLE, THE BABY! WHAT ABOUT HER BABY?"

I sit on the floor and try to process what Nicole just told me, my head wobbling from side to side like I'm a hundred year old with a completely degenerated nervous system. But we're only thirty. Not Kelly. Not us. What will Craig do? No, no, no, no…this isn't happening. I have to talk to her! She'll tell me it's not as bad as Nicole said it was. She'll make me feel better. I grab for the phone and punch in Kelly's number, but the machine picks up. I call again and again and again…every single time the machine picks up. I hear Nicole's car pull up, so on my last attempt, I leave a message.

Kel, it's me. I need to… I don't understand…I don't know how to do this. I have to talk to you. Please call me. Don't be mad at me for saying this… I love you.

I open the door, and the three of us hug without saying a word. I can't remember the last time any of us were this quiet this long. After we help each other wipe away the tears, we stagger over to the couch.

"Do you guys want tea? I might have some."

"I don't drink tea."

"Me either."

"I don't either. What the fuck was I thinking?"

"You're not. None of us are."

"Please, someone tell me how this happened."

"How do we really know how anyone gets cancer?"

"I need some answers, guys. She's only thirty! She hardly drinks alcohol, exercises regularly, doesn't smoke. *Why her*? Courtney?"

"It's random, Chrissy. Could've just as easily happened to one of us."

I remember that stupid toast I made at dinner last year, the one where I joked about the chances of one of them getting a horrible disease, because I had already suffered enough as the divorced one. I'm such an asshole.

"Yeah, it's like sometimes I think God's up there playing duck, duck, goose with us."

"*God*? There's no God, Nicole! What kind of a God would take a young mother away from her baby? I have to talk to her!"

"Not a good idea, Chrissy. Right now, we have to respect her wishes."

"She has wishes?"

"Craig said she wants to be left alone. She doesn't want any of us making a fuss about this. You know how Kelly is, so don't even think about picking up the phone and leaving her some gushy message. Got it?"

I'm so much more than an asshole.

"Craig says they're working on an aggressive treatment plan. She starts radiation and chemo next week."

"That's positive news, right? I mean, her doctors wouldn't do all that stuff if there wasn't hope…right?"

"In her case, I think it's just a plan."

Nicole's no use. I turn to Courtney.

"Can't they just cut the cancer out of her?"

"They could do something called the Whipple procedure. But according to Craig, the tumor's pretty large so they'd have to shrink it before they consider surgery. That's why they're getting started so fast with the chemo and stuff."

"Well, how did it get so fucking big? I mean, she's been complaining about pain for months! All those trips to the doctor…why didn't they see it?"

"The pancreas is located smack dab between the spine and the stomach. It's in a truly God-awful place that makes this kind of cancer nearly impossible to detect until it's too late."

"And the really horrible thing about the disease is that it usually causes no symptoms. People don't know they have it until the tumor is large enough to detect, and by then it's inoperable. I'm afraid Kelly might fall into that category."

"Does *anyone* survive this?"

The long stare they give each other offers me no comfort. I start pacing the room like I'm the one who's going to come up with the cure.

"Chrissy, come and sit down. Her doctors are gonna do everything they can to shrink the tumor."

"But Nicole, you just said yourself that you don't think she can survive! That you think the tumor is already too big to do that Whipple thing! So what happens to her today? What will her doctors do for her right now?"

Again with the long stare. Sometimes I feel like a child when I'm with these two. That feeling is multiplied when they talk to me in a whisper, like Courtney's doing now.

"Eventually, *probably soon*, her treatment will be designed to improve her quality of life for the duration of it."

Why are they throwing in the towel on her? I'm back on my feet, pacing around the room, searching for answers. Shouldn't they be too?

"Why can't they just take out her pancreas?"

"It's more complicated than that."

"Well, I'm sorry I'm not a doctor and smart like you guys! I solve problems at my job! I don't KILL projects when they don't work the way everyone wants them to! I keep at stuff until I'm satisfied with the outcome. Oh, I see that look on your face! Don't even bring up Leo or my divorce! Now's not the time!"

"Okay, okay everyone, calm down! I'm sorry we're being so blunt, Chrissy. I think we just came here prepared to take care of you, that's the doctor in us, but believe me, we're just as horrified about this as you. Nicole, say you're sorry, too."

"Sorry."

"Guys, please tell me what I'm supposed to do."

"Just do nothing, Chrissy. That's what Craig said she wanted... nothing."

"*But we're her best friends*! How can she expect us to stay away?"

"Craig said he'd call with updates and when Kelly's ready for visitors, he'll let us know."

"Visitors? We're not fucking door-to-door Jehovah's Witness freaks. We're us! Look, if everything you guys said is true, then we're gonna have to live with her death. She'll be dead, she won't have to feel the pain that we feel. I don't know about you, but I have to tell her everything that's in my heart. If I don't…this is gonna kill me, too."

"But Chrissy, this isn't about you."

I'm speechless. I don't know how to function when it's not all about me.

LIGHT'S OUT

APRIL, 2000

I'm far, far away from my care free days, the days when my three best friends and I would ditch class and go to Santa Cruz. We'd stare out at the ocean as we drank the alcohol we stole from our parent's liquor cabinets and talk about boys as we listened to "Forever Young" on our tape recorder over and over again. I'm far away from the days when I married the boy I dreamt about since the moment I laid eyes on him. Far away from the day I turned my back on that boy and met the man of my dreams and he showed me I didn't have to dream anymore. Everything's a blur now, now that death and its dream-killing qualities have taken over my life.

Kelly won't take my calls. It's been three weeks since I found out about her cancer, and I still don't know any more today than I did on the day I found out about it. I take that back. I know a shit load about her disease, just nothing about how she's coping with it. My office has literally turned into a research center. Books and pamphlets about pancreatic cancer litter my desk and my voicemail is maxed out with messages from John's Hopkins, Virginia Mason Medical Center, University of Chicago, and a dude named Charlie Spencer. Poor Charlie…he's a guy I found in an Internet chat room and is near death from the damn disease. Just like I've attacked everything in the past, from trying to be popular in high school, to making Kurt fall in love with me, to Leo in the front seat of my car on the night I met him, I've attacked Kelly's pancreatic cancer with the hope of curing it. But I'm failing miserably. Like Charlie told me, there's nothing I can really do for her except love her and support her. Charlie doesn't know Kelly.

The only thing I know how to do well these days is go to my church and pray; which in my world means going to the old dilapidated yoga studio and striking a pose. Every day, to my boss's condemnation, I leave my research center/office early, drive straight to the yoga studio, and try to make some sense out of everything that's happening. It's quiet, it's cleansing, it's nurturing and I just found out that I, too, is dying. The owner has three months left on the lease and then she's moving to the beach to retire.

I was dealing with my divorce from Kurt like a champ. I finally started coping with the loss of Leo with grace, and I've been processing Kelly's disease with courage. I've been able to semi-handle everything on my own because I had my safe yoga studio to hide out in, to process my pain in, to sweat out the tears in. But now that my sanctuary's going to kick the bucket, just like everything else in my life, I'm back in Dr. Maria's office. It's been months since I've been here, but the magazines are still the same and, unfortunately, so is Sad Frumpy Lady. Same outfit, same blank stare, same nothing.

"Everyone's dying."

"No, just Kelly."

"Leo's long gone…might as well be dead. Kurt'll have to be dead to me when the divorce is final. Kelly's got God only knows how much time left, and now my yoga teacher is leaving me. I'm fighting to do all the right things, make all the right choices…but still, nothing good is coming of it!"

"Then you have to fight harder, make even better choices. What's the alternative?"

"Quitting"

"Quitting what?"

"Life."

"You mean kill yourself?"

"Hell no, do you really think I'm capable of that?"

"Well, no but…"

"I mean I should just quit caring, stop loving, stop trying to make something of myself and accept the fact that this is my pathetic life, so stop expecting something more."

"Yeah, that sounds like a great plan."

"Well, let's see…I'll never find love like I had with Leo. I'll always have to work for an asshole because I'm not rich and, essentially, I have zero creative talent and my best friend is about to die for no reason I can make sense out of! I can love and care and try all I want, but nothing's gonna change any of that stuff. There's no silver lining."

"You have to create it."

"OUT OF WHAT?"

"Out of your dreams. They can come true, you know."

"You sound like a Disneyland commercial."

"Think what you want. But know this: no one will want your dreams to come true more than you, so you *alone* have to make them happen, Chrissy. Don't expect much help."

"All the dreams in the world can't change the fact the Kelly's gonna die."

"You might be right about that, but let's think rationally for a minute. You *had* dreams with Kelly that came true, right?"

"What are you talking about?"

"Well, you two dreamt of going to college together and you made that happen. You two dreamt of getting your first apartment together and you made that happen. You two dreamt of being each other's maid of honor and you made that happen. *You* made realistic dreams come true."

"And I still have dreams that include her!"

"It'll take time, but you'll replace the dreams you had with her with new ones…if you let it happen."

"I don't want new dreams."

"Okay then, quit dreaming. My colleague here has a client who did that. It's a very, very sad case. The worst I've ever heard."

I'm relieved that I'm actually not the worst case she's ever heard of but also frustrated that I have to ask, "Well, aren't you gonna tell me about it?"

"Her patient, a woman…she was a brilliant professor at UC Berkley. Had so much to look forward to…so many dreams. She married her first and only love right out of grad school and a few years later, had a baby girl. All of her dreams were coming true, but then God interfered."

"What do you mean interfered?"

"Her husband and daughter were caught under the rubble of the Cypress structure when it collapsed in the Loma Prieta earthquake in 1989."

"Oh, no! What happened to them?"

"They died and, in a sense, she died with them. She won't get rid of her husband's clothes. She won't change a thing about her baby's room, left it exactly how it was the day of the earthquake. Her hair is the same, her clothes are the same. Basically, she stopped looking forward."

"Geez, that earthquake was like…eleven years ago."

"I know. The poor woman stopped dreaming eleven years ago. I'm not saying anyone could or should get over something so terrible, but to stop dreaming all together…well that's just another form of death. I thought you knew that better than anyone, Chrissy."

D'oh! I'm so sick of Dr. Maria and her full circle trickery!

"You're making me feel like a fool."

"I'm not trying to. I'm just trying to make you see that if we open our hearts and minds, I mean *really* open them to the point that it feels uncomfortable to do so, even in the midst of tragedy, there's an opportunity to find some good stuff that we never knew existed."

"What do you mean?"

"I mean good can come out of even the most horrific experiences. Who knows what that woman's life would be like now if she were able to open her heart and mind to love. Maybe she would've met another man…had another child. They wouldn't replace the ones she lost, but she wouldn't be haunted by dead dreams anymore. Those would be put to rest by the new ones she has for herself and the new ones she loves."

I think about how much I've been haunted by dead dreams, the ones I had with Kurt…the ones I had with Leo. I'll friggin' implode when I have to layer the dreams I had with Kelly on top of those. I'll be like dead girl walking.

"My yoga studio's been the only place where I come close to opening my heart and mind. I'm a mess outside of it. I hate my job, and all I do at my cottage is drink wine and pace around. When I'm at the studio, doing my thing, I'm strong and hopeful. I'm confident that everything will work out, that I'll be okay no matter what happens. I'm not sure why. Maybe it's because yoga is something I never considered doing; it's so opposite of who I thought I was. But once I opened my mind to it, I found something I love, something I'm really good at, something I depend on... Wow, that's kinda what you were just talking about."

"Kinda, Hunny."

"I can't let that place die."

"Then you better start dreaming up a mess of something good."

MOMMY DEAREST

JULY, 2000

I'm rich! And Lord knows it's not because I'm rich in love and happiness and all that other crap, either. It's because Kurt and I sold the house in Danville. Sad as I was about losing my dream home, the money couldn't have come at a better time. My boss has been quite unsatisfied with my job performance, and he's given me one month to "get my shit together" or no raise for me at review time. Can't blame him really. For starters, I won't sleep with him, but that was always the case and it didn't prevent me (or him) from getting raises before. It's mostly because half of my office has turned into the west wing of the Mayo Clinic and the other half looks like an Ashtanga yoga clinic. I literally don't do a damn thing at work other than obsess about pancreases. Then, when I need to de-stress from how hard it is to fix the fucking thing when it's tainted with cancer, I drop down on my yoga mat for some much needed relaxation. Then when those two things become exhausting, I ditch work and head to Kelly's house where I do all the things I know she wishes she could do for herself. Well, technically I do everything on the *outside* of her house that she wishes she could do for herself. She won't let me in. She won't let anyone in, and other than sneaking out to her doctor's appointments, she won't come out.

Nicole and Courtney got so mad at me when I told them about my day trips to Kelly's house. They said I was defying Kelly's request that we stay away, but I think they're angry because instead of following directions, I'm following my heart, something neither of them are capable of doing. Here's how their brains work: "Kelly's dying and she told me to stay away. Therefore, I must do what I'm told or else I will get a bad grade, oops, I mean get in trouble."

Here's how my brain works: "Holy fucking shit, my beloved Kelly is dying! Even though she told me to stay away, I have to go to her, be by her side! Whether she likes it or not I have to tell her I love her and that I can't imagine my life without her."

And so, that's exactly what I did. Well, sort of. Since she won't let me inside, I sit on her front porch and write her gooshy letters about our high school days, college days, and wedding days until Craig comes out to give me something to do. I go grocery shopping, take the baby for long walks in her stroller, mow the lawns, and plant flowers so that Kelly always has something beautiful to look at. In a lot of ways, I'm fulfilling my dream of being the perfect stay-at-home mom. Yep, it's my own little fucked-up heaven. This is what I'm writing about to Kelly today when the front door opens.

"Oh, hey Craig, what's on my list to... Kelly!"

There she was. Standing in the doorway, drowning in her denim overalls, her thinning hair pulled into two scrawny pig-tails, pale as a ghost, and mad as the devil. God, it's good to see her.

"Chrissy, what the hell are you doing?"

"Being your best friend."

"No, you're being a pain in the ass. Stop coming here, and for God's sake, stop writing all those damn letters. I don't read those things, you know."

"Yes, you do."

"No I don't! I don't have time to be sad."

Is it because death is on the horizon? Or is it because she and her doctors are working diligently on a cure? I want to know why she doesn't have time to be sad, but I can't ask her, she'll freak. Freaking will cause her to slam the door on me. Freaking will put an abrupt end to this moment that I've waited four months for.

"Come here, Farmer Ted. Sit next to me."

I pull the hem of her overalls, and she reluctantly gives in to my request. She smells like medicine.

"I don't write them to make you sad, Kel. I write them to make you happy and make you laugh. And I like coming here. I regret not doing it more often, before the canc--"

"We don't talk about it, Chrissy. Got it? You want to sit with me and chat? Then it's gonna have to be about something else."

"Okay, okay. I'm sorry."

Craig told me it was like this. Sometimes when it's late at night and Kelly and the baby are asleep, he joins me on the front porch. We drink beers, and I listen to him cry as he spills his guts that are so full of fear and anger. Kelly won't let him do it in front of her. Whenever he starts to well up, she asks him to go to the garage. Can you imagine? The man wants to grieve with his wife, and she sends him to the garage to do it alone. Actually I can imagine it; I lived it with Kurt.

"Your daughter is beautiful, Kel. Such an angel."

Oh fuck, I did NOT just say that. Cancer…death…angels!

"I'm sorry, Kelly, probably gonna keep putting my foot in my mouth if you don't lead the discussion."

"You divorced yet?"

I should've known this is where she'd head.

"Looks like it'll be final in December."

"'Bout time. You back together with that Leo guy?"

"Looks like that'll never happen."

"Sorry to hear that."

Okay, now I'm confused.

"*You are?*"

"Yeah, I never took you for a quitter."

Damn that word.

"What are you talking about? You were totally in Kurt's camp during that whole ordeal."

"Noooooo, I was in my camp."

"What's that supposed to mean?"

"If you haven't noticed, Chrissy, I don't like change. I married my high school sweetheart just like you did…except I got lucky. I never left Fremont, never even changed jobs since I graduated from college. For cryin' out loud, look at what I'm wearing! You think it's because I'm trying to hide how skinny I am, but the truth of the matter is, I wear these every Friday…*every single Friday for seven years*. Change does *NOT* come easy for me."

"Let me get this straight. You didn't want me to divorce Kurt because of how it would've affected *your* life?"

"I dunno…I guess so. I didn't like the thought of choosing a side, having to hide details of each of your new lives from each other, having to decide between you or him for the annual group camping trip. Stuff like that."

"I'll help you out with that, he can have the camping trip."

I thought that was funny, but when our eyes meet, hers tell me there are no more camping trips for her either.

"Look, this…and let's not put a name to 'this' because I told you I didn't want to talk about it. But what's happening to me and my family should hopefully put a lot in perspective for you."

"It does."

"Not as much as it probably should."

"What are you talking about?"

"I'm pretty pissed that I'm now this person who people can use as some kind of barometer for how great their lives are after all. I hide in my house because everyone's pretty damn relieved not to be me, and they do a bad job of hiding it."

"That's not true."

"Sure it is. Everyone's relieved to have more time with the spouse they used to resent, the kids that used to bug the shit out of them, to have the job they used to hate. They feel relieved and then they feel guilty, and that's why they show up to help Craig and me. I resent everyone's new lease on life."

"Nothing about what you're going through is a relief for me, Kel."

"Let me finish. Even though I hate being the big reminder to everyone to start appreciating their life, if I had to choose one person for my situation to be an example for, it's you, Chrissy."

"*Me?*"

"You're different than everyone else. You're not here because I jump-started your once pathetic life, and you're not rejoicing in second chances. You're here because you're resentful…just like me."

"Well, we always have been attached at the hip."

"But it's not good to be attached to me now. Don't use my 'this' as another reason why you don't get on with your life. You've already wasted so much time and no thanks to how unsupportive I was over the whole Kurt and Leo thing, I'm sure."

"Kelly, stop."

"No. That's why I'm on this porch right now, to tell you to be like all those people I'm hiding from and use my 'this' as a reason for you to take chances and be happy. Go find a man you don't resent, have a kid that doesn't bug the shit out of you, find a job you love. Do something except come here."

"I didn't want our time together to be about me, Kel. I feel like there are so many more important things to be talking about."

"But *are* there more important things to talk about? I mean, aren't you sort of clinging to life, too?"

"Not like you."

"But you will be one day. You need to stop taking each day of your life for granted and spend it with the ones you love the most, *the ones that make you feel the most loved.*"

"But..."

"Yeah, yeah, yeah, I know you love me and all that stuff, but I'm not the person you should be investing your time in right now."

"Stop it! Don't say that."

"I won't stop, and you will listen. For once...just listen. None of the people you've surrounded yourself with have ever given you what you need to feel whole. Not me, Nicole, Courtney, or Kurt. It's why you've always needed us as a package. As a group, we possess everything you need to feel good about yourself, but when just one of us disappears, you almost can't function. But your package is broken, Chrissy, and it's not broken because of the divorce and it's not broken because I have 'this.' It's been broken for a really long time, and for years I've watched you try to glue it back together."

"Oh, c'mon...that's not true!"

"Give me a break, it was always you who put an end to the arguments I had with Courtney and Nicole and the arguments they had with each other. You never gave us enough time to solve our own conflicts because you knew if you did, they might not get solved.

And we went along with whatever you asked of us because frankly it was easier than watching you sulk about the impact our conflicts had on your life."

"I'm not that bad!"

"Worse! I bet the only actual birthday any of us have on our calendar is yours! Yeah, we're all scared shitless to forget. Afraid you'll jump off a bridge or something."

"So, I *guilted* you into doing nice things for me?"

"No, Chrissy, I *wanted* to do nice things for you, but I have to admit, what I *wanted* to do took back seat to your hypersensitivity."

Wow. I'm actually pissed at my cancer-stricken friend.

"And you *always* made excuses for Kurt when he was so obviously indifferent to your feelings. There you were solving problems and fixing things that no one asked you to fix, *always* making sure your package was perfect. But none of us ever asked you to do that for us. Want to know why?"

"Not really."

"Because with or without you, we're whole. Court, Nic, and I have stuff in our lives that makes us feel whole. Whether it's our husbands or our jobs or our children, we have really good stuff. And Kurt...well he's just in love with himself."

"Wow, you sure are mad that I keep coming here and writing you letters."

"No, I'm mad that you're taking me away from my family...the people who make me the most happy...the people I want to spend all of my time with right now. I'm mad that every time I hear your car pull up, it distracts me from the things that I want to be doing. You're making me worry about *you*, Chrissy. It was enough when I was healthy, but now it's just really pissing me off."

I'm horrified, and I don't know if it's because Kelly just made me feel like my love for her means nothing or if it's because I'm taking her away from the people she justifiably loves more than me. All I can say is, "I'm sorry, Kelly," and do everything I can to hold back the tears so I don't continue to piss her off. It's quiet long enough for nearby crickets to return to a loud rolling chirp.

"Look, all I know is when you were seeing Leo, you stopped caring about how well your best friends got along or if they called you on your birthday or Christmas. You seemed to stop caring whether people thought you and Kurt were the perfect couple. I can only imagine all that stuff happened because he made you feel whole."

My tell-it-like-it-is friend is always right.

"But now that he's gone, there you are with your glue and tape, trying to mend the package."

"Even if Leo was in my life, I'd still be sitting on your porch writing you letters, buying you groceries, and spending time with your daughter."

"But not every day! Most days you'd be with him because he'd be helping you through this."

"You're breaking my heart, you know."

"No, I'm trying to put it back together. Look Chrissy, the only reason I can do 'this' is because there's nothing I look back on with regret. I have everything I ever wanted."

"If you're so whole, why can't you let Craig cry? Why can't *you* cry?"

And the floodgates are open. Mine, not hers, of course. I'm scared of her reaction and surprised when it's actually sweet.

"If I start, I'll never stop, and that's not how I want to spend my time right now. Chrissy, this…this thing I have…it's gonna hurt real bad. But it doesn't have to hurt as bad as you're making it. Go find him. Go find *something* to make you whole. You're gonna need something other than vodka to get you through your tough times."

My moment with Kelly on her porch wasn't just something I waited months for…it was something I waited almost eighteen years for. She laboriously lifts herself up to go back inside. Just before she reaches the door, I give the hem of her overalls one last tug.

"I love you, Kelly."

"I know, I know…I love you, too. Now get out of here before I call the cops. You look like a Goddamn stalker."

NAMASTE

AUGUST, 2000

"This has to end."

"You think?"

I look up from my downward dog pose just long enough to flash Slutty Co-worker a dirty look before I transition into pigeon pose.

"I can't believe they're paying you over a hundred-fifty grand a year and you sit in your office and do this all day."

Looking up at her like I could give two shits, I ask, "How much longer do you think I can get away with it?"

"Word on the street is you have about a month to clear all of this medical shit outta here, change your attitude, and get back to work."

"So then...I guess I have a month to figure out what I want to do with my life."

"Not many places you can go and make the kinda money you make here, my love."

"It's not about the money anymore. I, we...*we* only get one life. Screw the money."

"That attitude of yours isn't gonna pay the bills. But here's an idea, when you get fired, I'll set you up with some of those old farts I used to date. *Theyyyyyyy* gave me a lot of money! Wow, where did you learn that pose?"

"From my lady at the Yoga Shack."

"How much time do you have left with her before the place closes down?"

My eyes focus on a picture of my three best friends and me on my desk.

"I'm sorry, Hunny, I didn't mean for your mind to go there."

"It always goes there. Anyway, the studio closes next month. She can't find anyone to buy--"

All of a sudden, I hop up from the ground and grab Slutty Co-worker's shoulders.

"Oh my God, I can't believe I didn't think of this sooner!"

"You're freaking me out, Hunny! Tell me what that pretty little head of yours is thinking."

"I'm a good business woman, right?"

"Well, you *used* to be."

"And I love yoga, right?"

"That seems to be all you love these days. Certainly haven't seen any men in your life...What a waste of a good body."

"...And with the sale of my house, I have more money than I know what to do with... Oh my God! This is it! How could I have not seen this before?"

"Seen what?"

"Here are my car keys. Start taking my pictures off the wall and put them in my car!"

"Chrissy Anderson, what are you about to do?"

"And do it fast! I'm probably only gonna have a few minutes to clean up five years of crap after I tell that pervert boss of ours what I'm about to tell him. He's gonna go ballistic."

And that was an understatement. When I quit my job, my boss literally chased me all the way down the hallway back to my office, yelling at me the entire time."

"This is the thanks I get for letting you sit in your office day after day crying over death and divorce? You haven't done one thing in the last six months to contribute to the success of this company! I should've fired you a long time ago!"

I mentally block out the immense amount of profanity flying out of his mouth as I flip through client files that once meant the world to me. I hardly noticed the pounding of his fists on my desk as I delete emails that used to be as vital to me as the bible is to others. And I barely notice the sudden softening of his voice as I strip the keys to my office from the key chain that Slutty Co-worker just handed back to me.

"Okay, okay, okay! Hold on a minute! I overreacted and I apologize for that. It's just that I thought I was doing the right thing by giving you time to figure all your shit out. And now I'm just a little upset that this is how you're repaying me. We can work this out, can't we? Jesus, we're in the middle of a major factory change in Hong Kong! Who's gonna be able to pick up the pieces of that mess? *C'mon, Chrissy...you don't want to be a quitter do you?*"

My homicidal eyes roll up from my key chain and glare at Slutty Co-worker. Like a scared child, her head drops down into her hands anticipating the wrath of me being called the Q word.

"No, pervert, you're upset because I'm the only one here who refuses to sleep with you, and now that I'm leaving, you'll never get the chance! Here's some advice, Boss, instead of cheating on your wife and using sex as a stress reliever, why don't you drop into my new yoga studio sometime. Try working out your frustrations that way! Oh, and as is the case with your adultery, quitting isn't ALWAYS a bad thing!"

As I exit the office that I spent the greater part of my adult life building, I can hear the entire production department simultaneously ask each other, "Did *you* sleep with him too?" He's so busted.

"Chrissy, wait for me!"

I whirl around to find Slutty Co-worker jogging after me with one teeny tiny dead plant in her hand.

"Hey, Doll, you're a great business woman with a lot of cash and all, but don't you think you're forgetting something?"

"What's that?"

"You're gonna need a great yoga instructor if you really want to make that place fly."

"*Are you serious*? You wanna come with me?"

"The only reason I stayed here this long was to take care of you."

Pointing at her hands and laughing, "After all these years, is that really all you have to take from this place?"

"Well...you already left."

Then in the middle of our hug we hear, "Wait for me, guys!"

"Megan, what the hell are you doing?"

"I have a great idea for a yoga clothing line and all they let me do here is count buttons! What do you say, Chrissy, will you give me a shot?"

"Who am I, Jerry Ma-fucking-guire?"

"No, he asked people to go with him. We're asking you to take us with you."

And off we went. The three of us piled into Slutty Co-worker's convertible and left the security of our cushy jobs at the big successful clothing company and high-tailed over to the Yoga Shack to make the owner an offer she was relieved to get. I was so excited about my new adventure that I forgot all about death and lost loves and, for the second year in a row, I forgot it was my birthday.

For the next sixty days our little motley crew painted walls, refinished hardwood floors, installed a new bathroom, and launched an aggressive marketing campaign to rebrand the Yoga Shack and turn it into the ever so hip Forever Young Yoga Studio, which was accompanied by the ever so sassy Forever Young Yogawear collection. We worked non-stop to make our grand opening a huge success and, on October 2nd, we opened our doors, and immediately a waiting list ensued. We have more customers than we have space for and talks are already under way to open a second studio in Moraga. Asked by a local newspaper reporter why I chose Moraga, I answered, "I experienced a lot of love there." The news was read by almost everyone I know, by my pissed-off former boss, by my incredulous soon to be ex-husband, even by Leo's mother.

Normally I would obsess about wanting Leo to know where I am and what I'm doing. There was a time when I would check my email and voicemail fifty times a day hoping to have a message from him. But I never heard back from him after I replied to his email in March. And it makes sense that I didn't. He never got the email. Unbeknownst to me, the vintage cable connection at my cottage timed out before it was successfully sent and instead of checking on it, my attention turned to Nicole and Courtney when they arrived at my apartment to tell me about Kelly's cancer. Leo thinks I ignored his original email because my "situation" prevented me from doing so, and he has since made a determined decision to get on with his life.

And normally, I would want Kurt to catch wind of what a badass yoga studio owner I am. In his own words, he said he didn't think I could survive without him, let alone quit my job, take employees with me, and start not only one, but TWO yoga studios. Normally, I would make damn sure I told every person we shared a relationship with about my successes so he'd find out, see me in a new light, and obsess about me for the rest of his life, ultimately landing him in much needed therapy.

And normally, I would've called my best friends to gloat about my success because I always felt like they had accomplished so much more than I had. In the past, I would seize any opportunity to show them I'm just as good as they are. I would've sent them a copy of the newspaper article and waited for their phone calls full of praise. I'd do anything to make them shower me with attention.

But something happened in the sweet chaos of starting my own business…of dreaming. Other than missing Leo, which is all I allow myself to do with him anymore, I stopped trying to mend my "package," and I started the process of becoming whole. Wondering if people think I'm nuts for letting Kurt go has become a nonexistent thought. I'm simply too busy to care what irrelevant people think about me. And hoping that Kurt seeks therapy is now more laughable than it is necessary. Wondering if Courtney remembered to send Nicole a birthday present only lasted for a second, and I stopped trying to find the cure for pancreatic cancer. I haven't stopped caring about the people that I love, but I have stopped trying to make them love me, and I've stopped trying to fix things I have no business fixing. The choice to call me, to need me, to love me, is theirs and I've never felt better. *Almost.* But I bet Leo and I wouldn't even work out now that I'm just plain old me.

"Well…you'll never know, will you, Hunny?"

"Oh, stop egging me on, Dr. Maria. He didn't even email me back last March. I'm sure as heck not gonna chase someone down who ignores my email. In my opinion, that would make me so much worse than anything I was in the past."

"How are you handling the fact that he didn't email you back?"

"It hurts bad, but I feel like it's only fair considering how many times I rejected him. But I miss him. I miss him a lot."

"Tell me about Kurt."

"Nothing to tell, really. The divorce is under way, and I haven't heard from him since I opened the studio."

"Oh yes! The studio! Congratulations on that, Hunny! Boy, when I told you to dream up a mess of something good, I had no idea you would go to such extremes."

"Just following my heart."

"Keep listening to it. It'll take you where you need to go. And Kelly? How's she doing?"

"I only stop by once a week now. Craig comes out to give me an update. It's usually pretty dismal. I give him a letter for her and I leave. I don't walk the baby anymore; I don't plant flowers…It's not that I don't want to do those things, but I don't think those things made her happy." As my voice trails off, "I think doing them only reminded her of what she couldn't do for herself anymore."

"Are *you* doing okay?"

"I'm doing okay, Dr. Maria. Despite it all, I'm doing okay. Tell me, how's that woman doing? You know, the one whose family died in the Loma Prieta earthquake?"

"As long as she keeps coming here, she has a chance."

"Looks like she's hanging in there, she's always in the lobby whenever I'm here."

"Yep, definitely have to give her credit for sticking with it."

Dr. Maria realized her slip-up the second she made it and rolls her wide eyes up at me over the rim of her glasses.

"Wow, you're one clever woman, Chrissy Anderson. I could get in a lot of trouble for exposing her identity."

Laughing hard, "Considering how many secrets you have on me, it's only fair I should have one on you!"

Throwing pillows from the couch at me, she says, "I take that back…you're not clever, you're manipulative!"

"I know. It's about time I start getting credit for it!"

FREEDOM

DECEMBER, 2000

The last four months have been the fastest of my life. Between the two yoga studios and the clothing line, I barely have time to breathe, and I can't tell you how much I love being out of breath. Making things happen is so much better than waiting for things to happen. Waiting for love to happen, for death to happen, for divorce to happen...it's all so damn exhausting.

"*Ahem*, Chrissy...Kurt's here to see you."

"Very funny."

Not really believing Megan, I continue to sift through thermal fabric swatches for the hoodie sweatshirt she's working on.

"No, really, he just walked through the door. Wow, he's a hottie!"

I look up and see Kurt walking toward me with a dozen red roses.

"Well, hello there, Stranger, a little late to try and win me over don't you think?"

I lean in to give him a kiss on the cheek, and he whispers ,"It's final," in my ear.

"What's final?"

"The divorce. I got the paperwork last week. I know how busy you've been with all of this, assumed you haven't been opening your mail at home. I thought I'd drive over and tell you the news myself."

I had months…*years even*, to prepare myself for this moment. I'm confused that I feel so…confused.

"Oh…I thought we had until December."

"It is December."

"Wow, I guess you're right. So, we're not married anymore?"

"Nope."

"I'm not Chrissy Gibbons anymore?"

"I don't think you ever were."

"Ouch."

"I'm not here to hurt your feelings. Just wanted to give you these, they're called freedom roses."

"I bet there aren't many girls out there who get a dozen red roses from their husband when their divorce is final."

"Not a dozen, fourteen. One for every year we were together."

I hear Slutty Co-worker say to Megan, "What is this…a divorce or a first date?"

I glare at the two of them as I grab Kurt's hand.

"Come on. The evening meditation class just finished, let's go inside the studio for some privacy."

The studio is still lit by candles and the music is softly humming in the background. It kind of does feel like a first date.

"Let's dance."

"You're not gonna make me cry, are you, Kurt?"

"Isn't that what I do best?"

Laughing, we slide together just like we did on the night we met at his high school graduation party in 1986. Who knew it would take me this long to grow up?

"Dr. Maria told me I could find you here." I pull away.

"*You* went to see Dr. Maria?"

"Not to talk about me, believe it or not, I'm okay with who I am. I wanted to ask her if you were okay…if you were finally happy."

"What did she say?"

"She told me to come and ask you myself."

"Sounds like something she'd say. Kurt, I--"

"You don't need to say anything about what happened any more. You were right about us not being a good fit."

I pull away in shock.

"*You really think that?*"

"Yeah. I always thought I was the strong one, the one who knew better for the both of us, but I was wrong. You saw what I didn't have the courage to see. For that, I thank you."

"Please don't thank me. I did a lot of stuff I'm not proud of. Stuff I don't know if I can ever forgive myself for."

"I know, and I didn't deserve a lot of it. But I forgive you, Chrissy. And if I can forgive you, then you should forgive yourself."

"I have a lot of guilt, Kurt. It's not quitter guilt, it's just guilt."

"Is guilt the reason why you're not with that guy?"

"There are a lot of reasons I'm not with that guy, but I'd definitely say guilt is at the top of the list."

"Chrissy, what good is your freedom if you're not gonna use it to go after the things you didn't think you could have with me?"

"So you think I should try to find him?"

"Alright, alright...I'm your ex-husband, not your girlfriend! I'm done talking to you about this."

After a few minutes of silent spinning, "Are *you* happy, Kurt?"

"I'm gonna miss calling you my wife. Just like you, I wanted this to be forever. But I know why it can't be, so yes, I'm allowing myself to be happy. You know me; I don't spend too much time on sadness and stuff like that."

"Are you still with *Kaaaaaayla?*"

"Don't you think it's time to stop saying her name like that?"

"The thought of you kissing another woman makes me sick to my stomach."

"I know the feeling. Yeah, I'm still with her. She likes to camp, you know. She loves basketball and hiking and..."

And there it was, his million-dollar smile, as big and beautiful as ever.

"Okay! Okay! Stop! I'm happy for you...I think."

"But she doesn't like yoga and yoga chicks are hot."

"I know! Look at this butt I have now!"

"Oh boy, I should probably leave before I ask you on a date." He moves to pull away, but I cling tightly to him.

"Just one last dance."

"You got it."

When we're done, he wipes a solitary tear off of my cheek with his finger. As he's doing it I ask, "How come you don't have any of those for me?"

"If I started, I'd never stop."

I pull away in amazement as I'm reminded once again of just how similar the two people I'm losing really are. He asks me how Kelly's doing, and after a brief and not so great update, he puts his arms around me one last time.

"Craig told me that you're one of the few people who's been able to talk to her in person. I'm glad; I know you need that kind of closure."

"Is that why you're here?"

"That's exactly why I'm here."

Grabbing both of his hands and studying every line and scar on his face, "We're not gonna be able to be friends, are we Kurt?"

"Would you be able to move on if we were?"

"No."

"Then why'd you ask the question?"

"Stalling, I guess."

"I should probably go now. Seriously, that new butt of yours is working its magic on me. Walk me out to my car."

On the way out, I make one final scan of his body. I take a mental picture of his crew cut, of the tiny lines that form on the outside of his smile, of his...

"Kurt! *Is that a fucking Porsche?*"

"Yeah, I bought the roses for you and the car for me. Pretty sweet, huh?"

After Kurt left the studio, I drove straight to Freakmont to sit on Kelly's porch and write her a letter about the divorce *and* the Porsche. I thought she'd get a good laugh out of both.

Kurt bought the car a few months ago. He admitted it was partly out of spite, a foreign feeling for him, but he went with it. I guess I can't be too angry that he bought the damn thing because all of his driving around in it afforded him some much needed time to think. And the more he thought, the more he agreed with me that we weren't right for each other. He also realized he'd much rather have a Porsche at this stage of his life than children, and secretly he became pretty damn thankful that things were the way they were. Right now, his new true love is the Porsche, but he admitted to me at the yoga studio that it might not be long before it was Kayla. And then he thanked me for his second chance to find true love. It was the second chance part that I thought Kelly would get a real big laugh at. I wanted to tell her she wasn't the only one in town who could spread them around. But I never got an opportunity to write the letter. When I got to the house, I saw an envelope taped to the front door. It said "Read before you write." I slump down into my usual spot on the porch and hesitantly open the envelope.

Hey Loser, I already know about the divorce and the Porsche. Kurt told Craig about both of them last week. And yes, I laughed my ass off when I heard about the Porsche. Well, as much of my ass that's left. What I don't know is why this is the first place you came after you found out that you're a free woman. Don't you think there's someone in New York who wants to hear about your divorce more than me? Someone you can actually have a life with! Go find him, Chrissy. I know he's waiting for you.

Did you know that since I got sick you're the only person who had the audacity to ask me, "What will I do when you die?" No one else would touch that question with a ten-foot pole! But you... you just had to go there! You always ask the questions that no one else has the guts to ask, and I've always admired that about you. I never answered your question, Chrissy because I really thought I could beat this. But I was wrong, it's kicking my butt. So, I'll answer your question now. After I die, you'll live and you'll love. Now get the hell out of here and get moving on those second chances. K.

p.s. Make sure you give my eulogy. C & N will be way too serious. Craig's gonna need to laugh.

p.p.s. It's Friday and I'm wearing my overalls!

p.p.p.s. Here are your missing journal pages. Damn girl, you're a freak!

I reach back in the envelope and pull out the small stack of familiar papers. One by one, I glance at the incriminating pages that were ripped out of my journal on the night of my surprise party. This whole time I was wondering what happened to them, and Kelly had them all along, never in a million years would I have thought it was her who came to my rescue. I refold the letter and gently place it back in the envelope, careful not to let my tears smudge any of her writing. Just then, Craig comes out to sit with me.

"Are you okay?"

"No, are you?"

"No. She wants you to have this, Chrissy."

My mind is racing as Craig hands me a tiny box. Is it her pearls, the something blue we shared on our wedding days, a special picture of the two of us?

"It's her American Airlines frequent flier card. She enclosed her username and password so you can transfer the miles to your account."

"What the?"

"She really wants you to go to New York...tonight. She wants you to tell that guy everything you came here to tell her."

"You've got to be kidding me! I can't fly somewhere at the drop of a hat. I have to work."

"She knew you'd say something like that so she wanted me to remind you of how many times you barged into her life and tried to make her feel emotions that don't come easy to her. She said it's her turn now."

"But this is different."

"Hey, I'm just telling you what she wants. Besides, don't you want it, too?"

After thinking for a lot longer than the guy has time for, "Craig...I want it so badly that I'm too afraid to go after it and find out it's gone. It's been a year and half since he went to New York. It has to be gone...doesn't it?"

"Only one way to find out."

I take the box, stand up, and dust myself off. Craig and I hug goodbye for a lot longer than usual. We both need it. Before I get in my non-Porsche car, I look up and see a faint outline of Kelly peeking thru the curtains. I step forward, but she puts a hand on the window in a way that tells me to stop. I clutch the box and the envelope to my heart and mouth the words "thank you." It's hard to see what she looks like, and I squint to get a better view, afraid of what I might see. As if she knows I would be, she gives me a shaky thumb up and then lets the curtains fall back together.

Have you seen my love
Is he far away
Have you seen the one for me
Whose face lights up my day...

("Have You Seen My Love?" *Rosie Thomas*)

WISHING

DECEMBER, 2000

What's a girl to do? Should she fulfill the wish of her dying friend or should she protect herself from almost certain heartache and embarrassment? On the one hand, Kelly will never know if I went to New York, so technically I can ignore her request. But on the other hand, what if she's right and I can get Leo back simply by telling him I'm divorced. What if it's that easy? About an hour into the drive to my cottage, my brain is about to explode from all of my psychotic back and forth debating, so I flip on the radio hoping to take my mind off of Leo for two minutes, but guess who's there yelling at me! My grandpa, and he's telling me to go to New York, too. No matter what station I switch the dial to, every song that I shared with Leo and every song that reminds me of him is playing. Dave Matthews, Sarah McLachlan, Jewel...all of their voices sent by my grandpa to haunt me.

"... And I have the sense to recognize
That I don't know how to let you go
every moment marked with apparitions of your soul..."

Shut up! Shut up! Shut up, Sarah McLachlan!

"... I'm ever swiftly moving
trying to escape this desire..."

403

I am, and it's exhausting. Maybe New York isn't such a bad idea. Not because I think Leo's going to swoop me up in his arms the second he sees me, but because the only likely way to rid myself of the desire I have for him is to hear it directly from him that he's done with me. I guess he technically already told me that when he slammed the door in my face, sped away, and moved three thousand miles away. But I was still married then, he didn't have a choice but to react any other way. But to get that kind of rejection from him now that I'm officially divorced and fully ready to commit to him could be officially desire-killing! It's the opposite of what I hope for, but at least it'll result in some kind of closure, and I *think* that's what Kelly wants for me. Apparently my grandpa does, too. Looks like I'm going to New York tonight.

I get back to my cottage in just enough time to pack a small bag and leave Slutty Co-worker a message about my trip and where I'll be staying in case of an emergency and then I dash off to make the red eye. Where do I go when I land? Do I just show up at his office? Shit, what if he doesn't even live in New York anymore? I thought the six-hour flight would afford me enough time to come up with a really good plan of attack, but it didn't. And after creating three pages of the pros and cons of finding Leo, and chugging down six vodka tonics, the plane starts its descent into New York City… without a plan. *Already?* I peek out the window, and when I catch a glimpse of the World Trade Center, I quickly close the shade as if he can see me. The closer the plane gets to the ground, the more I turn into a chickenshit, and by the time we touch down, I decide the least scary course of action is to check into a hotel near the World Financial Center and just wander around. I'll have fulfilled Kelly's wish, while at the same time fulfilling my desire to *not* make an ass of myself. Good plan, except little did I know, Slutty Co-worker was busy making me look like an ass on her very own. At one in the morning, after returning home from an evening of tawdry raunchiness, she listened to my message. Without hesitation, she woke up Megan, who she made wake up her friend, who then woke up her now *ex*-boyfriend to get Leo's phone number. By the time I check into my hotel, Slutty Co-worker had woken up most of Contra Costa County *and* called Leo to tell him where I was. Four hours later, after a quick nap and a cold shower, I reappear outside of the hotel. Unbeknownst to me, Leo's there, too.

Without a plan, I look to my left and to my right, take a deep breath, and walk in the direction of the nearest coffee shop. Leo follows a safe distance behind, careful not to let me see him. For over an hour, I sip on bitter coffee and stare at the nauseatingly happy Christmas shoppers as I absorb the real reason I'm here. On my third cup, I remove the list of pros and cons from my purse and review each line item again, now ranking them in order of importance. From across the street, Leo watches me have a bizarre mental conversation with myself as he contemplates his next move.

After what seems like forever, I come to the conclusion that the #1 pro associated with tracking down Leo is that he *might* profess his undying love for me. All good, but the #1 con associated with tracking him down is that he might tell me he's in another relationship. Well, that answers that! There's no way in hell I'm going to track that guy down and find out he's happily bangin' some other chick! I violently crush the pieces of paper into tight balls and shove them in my purse. I'm definitely sticking with my chickenshit plan, and I'll be spending my day wandering around NOT looking for Leo! I'll do some shopping, have a nice dinner, and take the first flight back tomorrow. I pay the bill and get a smart ass remark from the waitress for taking up her booth for so long and then I venture back into the angry New York fray. Goddamn, the people here are mean.

I walk for hours, down West Broadway, over to Park Place, and finally landing on West Street where I dart into the Winter Atrium. It's a huge reprieve from the cold, and if I had my wits about me, I probably would've heard Leo mutter, "It's about time," from a few feet behind.

The Atrium is truly spectacular, and I've always wanted to visit, but never had enough time to venture to this side of the city. Its architectural beauty definitely provides an upside to this waste-of-time trip and, for a second, I forget why I'm even in New York. As I make my way over to the garden area that overlooks the Hudson River, my heels click click click LOUDLY on the mosaic tile floor of the scarcely populated lobby. I get the weird sense that my shoes are making me the target of some young person's shoe envy or an old person's shoe mockery, so I pause and scan the room to see if anyone's looking at me. As I turn around in a circle, Leo darts behind one of the massive palm trees scattered throughout the Atrium, just missing my glance. I shrug off the weird vibe and press on, cursing my love of impractical footwear for the remainder of my walk of shame to the garden area. I immediately forget about my shoes when I get to the overlook and see the sunset. It's beautiful. Although…it would be *more* beautiful if the two love-struck assholes next to me weren't making out so hard. From behind the palm tree, Leo watches intensely as I glare at the kissers, roll my head back, look up at the Heavens, and shake my head in total frustration. Badly needing a drink, I interrupt the assholes and ask where the nearest bar is. They send me to P.J. Clark's on Vesey Street "cuz it's like totally awesome!" I'm like, you two can go fuck yourselves.

Finding P.J. Whatever's isn't as easy as the love-idiots said it would be, and I'm irritated with myself for choosing a hotel in the financial district as opposed to the garment district. I know where a hundred bars are there! "Oh finally, there's Vesey!" Rounding the corner, I stop dead in my tracks.

"*What the?*"

Confused, I look around in a million different directions and then ever so slowly, images of my close encounter with Leo from last February flash through my mind. My head snaps to the left. There's the intersection! Then to the right. There's the curb! Then straight across the street.

"Holy Shit!"

P.J. Clarke's is the bar Leo goes to after work! I take my gaze across the street from Leo's hang out and recognize the small restaurant where Slutty Co-worker and I spent time stalking him. How am I here right now? Grandpa, talk to me!

From a block behind, Leo folds his arms across his chest and leans against a building. He's realizing it wasn't my intention to find him. Hastily, I grab at my wrist and check the time. Five o'clock.

"Shit! Shit! Shit!"

He might be in there RIGHT now! I squint to get a better look inside, but the bright sunset against the window makes it impossible to see anything. I quickly grab a coin out of my pocket. If it's heads, I'll go in, tails I'll hail a cab.

"Heads! D'oh!"

I check my hair and makeup in the nearest window and turn sideways to get a look at my butt and waistline. I'm so glad I didn't eat lunch. Leo stirs, runs his fingers through his hair, and wonders what to do next.

"Here goes nothing."

Thinking that he might actually be looking at me through the window of P.J. Clarke's, I find it hard to walk across the street correctly. My arms and legs won't function in a way that makes me look calm, cool, and collected, and I literally stumble toward the bar like a zombie from an episode of Scooby Doo. Seriously, I look like a fucking idiot who forgot how to walk. A cab rolls by and for a second I consider calling for it, but then I hear ten thousand voices in my head screaming "QUITTER!" so I don't. Someone or something put me at this intersection for the second time in my life, and I can't ignore its will. I have to see this through. I have to have faith. Once inside the door, I make a beeline for the closest available barstool and immediately pretend to look for something in my purse, so that I don't have to look around. If Leo's here, he's going to have to make the first move. I used up all of my courage getting across the street.

"Mind if I sit here?"

My disappointment rivals Leo's anger as we focus on the guy asking the question. He's a total player from Leo's office. The kind of guy who bangs a different girl every night of the week...like the one's Buckley's was full of the night I met Leo.

"It's a free country."

"Whatcha drinking?"

"Anything."

"Hey, Rocko, couple of manhattans over here!"

"Sort of cliché, don't you think?"

"What, a manhattan in Manhattan or a bartender named Rocko?"

My slight smile makes Leo clinch his fists.

"Both, I guess."

"Got a name?"

"Maude."

Player boy makes a smelly fart face, and I can barely contain myself.

I've come up with some awful fake names before, but Maude takes the cake.

"Yo, dude...I thought you were taking a sick day! Come on over and meet Ma... this great gal!"

Not interested in meeting one of Player's player friends, I stare at the television and drink my drink.

"I already know her."

That voice.

"Oh yeah, and just how well do you know this pretty lady?"

"Better than you ever will, now get the hell away from her."

As soon as Player meanders away with his tail between his legs, Leo takes his seat. Everything wonderful that I remember about him washes over me like a tidal wave. I take a deep breath and muster up every ounce of courage to speak.

"Hi."

Just silence and an ice cold stare.

"You and Player...friends are you?"

"We work together, that's it."

"Are you really sick?"

I've dreamt about this moment for a year and a half, and these aren't the questions I dreamt about asking! First I can't walk and now I can't talk!

"No, but when I heard you were gonna be in town, I needed some time to think."

"You heard I was gonna be in town? Who the? *Ahhhhh.*"

Damn that woman.

"She called me in the middle of the night, told me where you were staying and stuff. I don't know why, really."

He's acting just like he did that night at Buckley's. I should too. Focus, Chrissy! Be cool, stay interesting, channel beautiful. It worked for you then.

"I'm sorry, she shouldn't have done that."

"So...why?"

"Why am I sorry she did that?"

"Why are you here?"

Shit, what's my story again?

"I…umm…just doing some Christmas shopping and…felt like having a drink and…ended up here."

Good job, idiot. It doesn't get anymore uncool and uninteresting than that. I wonder if it's too late to count on my looks.

"I knew you'd say something like that. I'm outta here. Merry Christmas, Chrissy."

So much for my looks.

"Okay! Okay! Okay, that's not true!"

I grab his hands to pull him back. They're still as strong as ever, but there's no trace of rock yard on them anymore.

"I'm sorry…I'm nervous, and well, you didn't email me after I emailed you back. I thought you got scared or maybe met someone new. I guess since I don't know which one, it's hard for me to tell you why I'm here. I kinda have an answer for each reason."

"You have an answer for everything, don't you?"

Not wanting to prove him right by answering, I stay quiet.

"I never got the email."

"*What?*"

"Never got it. I assumed your situation prevented you from responding. Your situation was *always* the reason for not getting back to me quickly."

"Not this time, Leo. I don't know what happened to the email, but this time there's no situation. I promise."

Man, those eyes.

"I know. She told me about your divorce when she woke me up at three this morning."

There's no trace of delight on his face. I was stupid to think he'd be happy to hear about it after all this time. Time to lower my desire-killing force shield and let him get it over with.

"Did she also tell you about the yoga studios?"

That was my attempt to recapture cool and interesting, but he shot back, "Yeah, but I already knew about those. My mom mailed me the newspaper articles."

Wow, she's on my team? Maybe I stand a chance here. Force shield re-activated.

"Chrissy, why are you here?"

"I don't know how to explain it."

"Try."

"My friend Kelly, you never met her…she's really sick."

My voice unintentionally cracks and my eyes become teary as I say the words, "She's dying."

He looks uncomfortably apologetic for being so mean.

"I've been spending a lot of time with her, well not really with her, as much as with her front porch, but the time on her porch … well, it made me realize some stuff."

"I know about Kelly, too."

"Wow, is there *anything* that woman didn't tell you on the phone?"

"She didn't tell me why you're here."

Hard as it will be to receive the total rejection that's going to ensue after I put my heart on the line, I have to do it. He did it for me.

"Fine, Leo. Here it is. I dream about you…about us. I dream about all of the things we talked about. The conversations play over and over again in my head, they won't go away! I dream about the way you touched me, about how you wanted to protect me…wanted to give me everything I ever wanted. I never stopped loving you and…"

"And what?"

"I'm in New York to see if we still have a chance."

"*A chance at what?*"

He's really making me pay.

"Please don't do this. If you don't feel the same as me, then fine, but don't treat me like you hate me, Leo. That's the one thing I never wanted to happen."

Nothing but a cold stare.

"Look, I know once you end up on your bad side, it's almost impossible to get back to good, but I'm putting myself so far out there by telling you all of this. Shouldn't that count for something? Jesus, I'm so afraid of--"

"*Of what?* Of feeling like you made me feel after I put myself out there for you? YOU MESSED WITH MY FUCKING HEAD, CHRISSY!"

I'm not sure if it was the heads that snapped in our direction when he yelled or the pure force of his voice that made me grab my purse and run out of the bar and into the now dark and snowy streets of Manhattan.

"Chrissy, wait!"

I whirl around. Half surprised to see him coming toward me, half mad that he's not done making me pay for what I had done to him.

"No, I knew this was gonna happen! It was a mistake to come here!"

He abruptly stops coming toward me. His feet are firmly stuck to the ground right outside of P.J. Clarke's. Neither of us notices the dozen or so curious heads that flock to the window to watch our romantic tragedy play out in front of them.

"I never stopped loving you either."

"You still love me?"

He barks out a noise that sounds like a mix of total frustration, lust, and anger when he admits, "Yeah, but I don't trust you, Chrissy!"

"Then why did you email me? Why did you make me think you still cared?"

"Because I *did* care, but when you never replied, I forced myself not to anymore. I'm so over all of your games."

"I wasn't trying to play games, Leo! I just couldn't understand how one night with you could unravel all of my years with Kurt, and I needed time to figure it out! I didn't know how to protect you, him and me all at the same time, so I lied, and every lie meant another lie! I didn't want to do it, but I didn't know how to put an end to it without something like THIS happening!"

"But you didn't have to protect him! HE NEVER PROTECTED YOU!"

Borderline begging, "I had so much to learn, and I'm sorry that I strung you along in the process. I promise, if I could go back in time and do it all differently, I would, but I can't!"

"You're right, you can't. I love you, Chrissy, and I don't know how to stop loving you, but I'm sorry, I gave you too many chances already. I'd be a fool to go down this road again."

"Or maybe you'd just be a fool in love."

With snow piling on our hair and clothes, we stare at each other forever. My eyes pleading, his agonizing, and the twenty-four or so eyes inside of the bar darting back and forth between us wondering what's going to happen next.

"God knows how much I miss you, but now I'm like you were the entire time we were together. I'm too afraid to put myself out there, even for you."

"Leo, please…"

"I'm sorry about your friend Kelly, it sounds terrible what's happening to her. She's the one you should be with right now, not here with me."

And then he turned and disappeared into the night.

I hear a pair of eyes from the window loudly proclaim, "Damn, that ain't right!"

Once Leo's out of eyesight, I mentally toss my desire-killing force shield onto the snowy street, turn, and walk aimlessly in the opposite direction.

MERCIFUL

FEBRUARY, 2001

A fter Leo told me to take a hike, I checked into a hotel in Greenwich Village, the part of town where I knew I wouldn't run into him, and I spent Christmas and New Year's alone. I missed being at work, but I wasn't ready to go back to Slutty Co-worker's and Megan's hopeful faces and burning questions. I got massages, facials, manicures, and pedicures, and I did yoga twice a day. I shopped my ass off and bought so many new clothes that I had to buy another suitcase. I ate the best dinners at the best restaurants and I watched a new movie every night. If it wasn't for the knife piercing through the middle of my heart, it would've been the best vacation of my life. I checked in with Courtney and Nicole to see how Kelly was doing, and I did it as if I was doing it from home. They didn't need to know about the latest shenanigans of Chrissy Anderson. Well, that and they'd just ask me to bring them goodies back from New York. I was in no mood to play Santa Claus. Neither of them had an update on Kelly's condition, Craig hadn't answered the phone or returned calls for weeks. As my plane took off from JFK nearly two weeks after it landed, I looked down at the World Trade Center buildings and blew Leo a kiss. Then I put in my earphones and fell asleep with nothing but thankful thoughts of knowing such a passionate man.

413

"Okay…that's NOT what I thought was happening this whole time! I thought you guys were like *TOTALLY* doing it all over New York!"

"Me, too! I thought for sure you guys got back together! What the hell happened?"

Staring blankly at Slutty Co-worker and Megan, I think to myself, yep… those are exactly the hopeful faces and burning questions I wanted to avoid.

"Oh, Hunny, I am sooooo sorry I called him!"

"No, it's good that you did…I wouldn't have seen him otherwise. I'd still be dreaming about stuff that's never gonna happen."

"Are you okay?"

"Not really. You should've seen him. He was so handsome. I still love him so much."

"I know you do."

"I blew it, didn't I?"

"Looks like it, Love. But there's gonna be someone else. He'll come around at the most inopportune time and when you least expect it, kinda like Leo did."

This is why I love Slutty Co-worker so much. She tells it like it is and then she lets you cry it out on her shoulder.

"Hey, was that yummy Italian boy with Leo when you saw him?"

And then she makes you laugh.

The rest of January is quiet, and I barely notice when it turns into February. Business is chugging along at a better than expected rate. God Bless all those New Year's resolution idiots who sign up for a six-month membership because "I'm really gonna get in shape this time!" I'm not worried about them dropping out either, because Slutty Co-worker does an excellent job of keeping men engaged, and smarty pants me hired a totally hot yoga master dude to keep all the flighty women from quitting. Yes, we have quite a nice little racket. The only hard part about any of it is keeping the two instructors off of each other!

My lunches and dinners with Courtney and Nicole commenced upon my return from New York. I never mentioned the trip to them; they've had enough of my love life. Every week we reserve a table for four, order the missing friend a drink and do our best to pretend she's with us. We rarely bring up old times because it's too painful, and we don't talk about anything interesting because they don't watch reality TV. The time I spend with my best friends has become the time when I contemplate life. They talk about doctor stuff, and I quietly ask myself, "Am I doing *exactly* what I want to be doing because I could be dead tomorrow."

Aside from *doing* the man I love, the answer is always yes. I'm passionate about my yoga studios and Megan's clothing line is a huge success. It's already in nine department stores nationwide. I'm so busy spending time on projects that I love that I hardly notice the money that rolls in as a result. I suppose I should buy a house, but I can't bear the thought of leaving my cottage. I'm not ready to leave behind the few good memories I have there with Leo. That, and I guess I want him to know exactly where to find me in case he changes his mind about giving me a second chance. I shouldn't hold my breath, though. Megan got word from her friend's ex-boyfriend that I messed him up real bad by going to New York and now he's binge dating to get over me. It hurts like a mother-fucker, and the pain would probably send most candy-asses straight to therapy, but I'm smart enough to know that only time can heal the wounds I opened up on the streets of New York. What I'm going through right now is just a normal girl problem. Confusion and lies are what drove me to seek therapy and I don't have those things in my life anymore. I'd like to see Dr. Maria, but that's only because I miss her, not because I need her. My grandpa's been very quiet, but that could be because I haven't asked him any questions. He'll be back when I need him.

I'm at one of my yoga studios early today because I'm helping Megan prepare for her first solo meeting with a buyer at Macy's New York. She begged me to go with her, but I was like "Hells no, I'm not going back to that city!" We're rolling around in laughter at my imitation of our old Hong King Kong production manager when Slutty Co-worker pokes her head in.

"I hate to interrupt the comedy act but your friend Courtney's on the phone for you."

It took me forty-five minutes to get to Stanford Medical Center and an hour and forty-five minutes to locate Kelly's room. The place is like a labyrinth of sickness, disease, and seriousness. It's dreadful.

Kelly was admitted to the hospital two days ago because of Craig's inability to control her pain and persistent vomiting. He's taken such good care of her for almost a year, but in the last month, the cancer has become more obsessed with her body. No matter how many pills he gave her, he couldn't fight its fury.

"Where is he?"

Courtney and Nicole point to Craig, who's standing with a small group of doctors. He looks ten years older than the last time I saw him.

"Where are you going?"

"To be with him."

"His mom said he wants to be alone."

I snap back, "Jesus, when are the two of you gonna stop listening to directions and start listening to your hearts?"

I walk over and stand by Craig. To be honest, I'm a little nervous to disobey his mom's orders, but when he grabs my hand for support as the doctors finish giving him an update, I'm satisfied with my decision. When the doctors split away, he turns to me.

"She was in so much pain." Then in a whisper, "I thought I had more time." Looking directly at me but talking into space, "They said she had at least three weeks left…they were off by two. I should've done more…said more."

"She knows what you wanted to say, Craig, and you also know Kelly has to do this on her terms. When they said three weeks left, she probably said to herself, 'I'll be the one to decide how much time I have.'"

"The pain was so bad. She wanted to take a bath…thought it might help. She asked me to get in with her and hold her, but I didn't. Goddamn it… Why didn't get in with her? The house was a mess, the baby was fussy, and I was so damn tired, Chrissy. But why did I let those things matter? *Why didn't I get in with her?*"

I always have something to say, a story to tell, a joke to make a bad situation not so bad, but there's nothing you can say or do for someone in Craig's shoes. The only thing you can do is hold them and let them cry out their sorrow for however long it takes. This is what true friends are for. So for two days, Courtney, Nicole, and I camp out in one of the special rooms dedicated for families of people who are about to die. We take turns delivering coffee and making food runs for Craig, his parents, and Kelly's mom. We do our very best to support them while they cry out their sorrow, and when they aren't looking, we hold each other while we cry out our own.

On the eve of day two, after making sure everyone has had enough to eat, I sneak out of the special room and make my way down the hall to Kelly. The hospital staff has been very clear that only Craig and immediate family members are allowed in her room and Kelly couldn't have been clearer the entire time she was sick that she didn't want me to see her in a weakened state. Never one to follow the rules, which Kelly should know better than anyone else, I tip-toe inside.

I'd be a wreck if what I was looking at were something that came close to resembling my best friend, Kelly, but what I'm looking at is only a container for the minuscule amount of organs that wearily pulsate underneath her thin skin. My strong Kelly is no more. *As far as I'm concerned, Kelly is no more.* Looking at her now, I know exactly why she didn't wait three more weeks. She's had enough. She's not hooked up to very many things, just one IV that I assume is morphine. She was always a pale girl, not one to lie in the sun or go to a tanning salon. Probably the only thing we didn't have in common. But she's not what I would call pale anymore. She's yellow, but not sunflower yellow. It's more like yellow watercolor paint has been spread over her translucent body. Some areas painted more than others, but her entire body covered in some shade of yellow. Her hair and eyebrows are completely gone and tiny blood encrusted pinholes are scattered all over her visible skin. One enormously swollen leg is poking out of the blanket, and it doesn't look like it could possibly be connected to her frail face and arms. No, this is not Kelly. My Kelly is already somewhere else. I'm somewhere else, too. Rain is pounding on the window. The sound of it along with Kelly's soft breathing and the rhythmic beat of the machines that are hooked up to her create an almost tranquil feeling within me. There's no doubt in my mind that I'll be with Kelly again one day, and the joyful feeling takes me by total surprise. I put my hand on her hand and through my tears whisper, "Keep in touch, Kel," before I reach into my pocket and place one last letter in her hand.

Over the last two days, I've written about ten different self-serving letters, but ended up scrapping all of them and simply went with:

Hey Mama, Give my grandpa a giant hug when you see him. You'll recognize him, he's the exhausted one. If you don't mind, can you act as my angel for a while? That guy needs a break! He had no idea how high maintenance I was, but you…you know exactly what you're in for, and you're young enough to handle it. Oh, and you know I love you, Kel, but I hope I don't have to see you anytime in the near future. Whatever you can do up there to make sure I stay down here a lot longer would be greatly appreciated. I'm starting to feel whole. I love you, Me

After I kiss her cold forehead, I walk to the hospital chapel and beg my Grandpa to put Kelly out of her misery. Three hours later, she died.

After (preposition) af*ter:

Following in time or place or position

I can hear us laughing
I remember every part
I've got everything we ever did
It's tattooed on my heart...
Until the summer brings you back,
You know you got a piece of my heart

("Piece of My Heart," *Keri Noble*)

FADING

MARCH, 2001

The weeks following Kelly's death were a total blur. There was the funeral, followed by my impromptu healing trip to Mexico with Courtney and Nicole. When I got back from that, I focused all of my time and attention on the two most important things in my life: my job and Kelly's child, my God daughter. For the last month, I've dedicated nearly every night and weekend to that little girl. I take her for long walks in her stroller, to the grocery store to stock up on food, and out for ice cream so that Craig can have some much needed time to himself. It's bittersweet that she's still a baby. She's too young to realize the loss of her mother...and it's a shame that she can't. She'll never know how truly and amazingly, smart, funny and beautiful she was.

I'm grateful for the distraction that my yoga studios and the baby provide to me. Every minute of every day has an important and fulfilling purpose that I spring out of bed to tackle. Since Mexico, there has been no time for tears, and with each new day, things become less and less blurry.

Today is my first day back to how things were *before* Kelly died. I'm pulling into Dr. Maria's parking lot for the last time. We've had several phone conversations, but I haven't sat on her couch since August. I've been too busy applying the things I learned on it to real life. As sad as I am to say good-bye to her, I'm anxious to get on with my new therapy-free life.

Everything at our session is going along exactly how I expected it to, until Dr. Maria invited me to listen to the frantic message I left on her machine three years ago. I thought for a long time before I responded to her invitation. Would it bring back bad memories that I had worked so hard to put behind me, or would I be proud of how far I've come? I bet on my new self that it would be the latter, and opted to listen.

When Dr. Maria got done playing the recording of the voicemail, I buried my head in my hands.

"Holy Moley, what a friggin' mess!"

"You got that right."

"I can't believe you actually agreed to help a nutcase like me."

"It's my honor… well that and I was dying to hear the steamy scoop on the boy who stole your heart."

"Oh, so now the truth comes out!"

We share our next to last laugh before I get serious.

"It's crazy, Dr. Maria."

"What is?"

"How you think your life is one way, so set and moving along exactly like you planned and then something so unexpected, *so unplanned* happens that it turns everything upside down."

"Or like you mentioned a long time ago, turns it right-side up."

"Right…And I can honestly say that things have never felt so right-side up."

"So does that mean you're ready to start dating again?"

She'd probably commit me to an insane asylum if she knew I've been holding my breath since his phone call after the funeral and that my heart's been racing all day wondering if he'll actually show up tonight.

"You know me, if something comes along that feels right, I'll jump on it…literally!"

I stand to say good-bye. I love her so much for everything she's done for me, and I hope my hug tells her so. She tells me to drop by if I ever need her, and I tell her as much as I want to see her again, I hope I never have to and the most she should expect from me is a yearly Christmas card. Three years and thirty minutes later, I close the door to her office for the last time. It certainly has been a year of good-byes.

On the way to my car, I see Sad Frumpy Lady standing beside hers searching for her keys. I feel pulled in her direction, and on my way over to her I mumble up to Kelly, "What are you about to make me do, woman?"

As I get closer, I zero in on what it was that caught my attention from across the parking lot.

"Excuse me, can you tell me where you bought that crocheted bag?"

Startled that someone's actually talking to her, it takes her a few seconds and a couple of throat-clearing coughs before she answers me.

"Oh this…I made this a very long time ago."

"It's beautiful. I think it would make an excellent bag to carry my yoga mat around in."

She looks down at her old handbag in a way that stirs up memories.

"I guess it would."

"Do you still crochet?"

"No. It's been a long time."

"That's too bad, you do wonderful work." Making my way back to my car, I suddenly stop, whirl back around, and ask her, "Hey, if I wanted to buy twenty or so of those bags would you be willing to start crocheting again?"

It's as if I asked her to go to the moon.

"*Are you serious?*"

"As serious as therapy."

"If you don't mind me asking, what do you need that many bags for?"

"I own a couple of yoga studios, and I think the ladies would love them. So…what do you think?"

"I suppose I could make them. I would need some time and some materials but…yes, I think I can do it."

"Perfect! I won't be coming here anymore, gonna try to go it alone for a while, but would you like to come to one of my studios later in the week? I can show you around, even offer you some intro classes if you're interested."

"Yoga? Oh, I don't think so."

"That's exactly what I used to say!"

"Really, what made you finally try it?"

"A magazine article convinced me it would change my life."

"Did it?"

Not wanting to scare her away, but wanting to be as authentic as possible, I walk a little closer to her and say, "I think the combination of this place, yoga, and the loss of my best friend changed my life. Sometimes it takes more than one thing to get us back on course. At least in my case it did."

I can tell I'm making her consider the unfathomable.

" But I haven't exercised in years."

"Then yoga will be perfect for you!"

"And I wouldn't even know what to wear."

"Not a problem, I can set you up."

"I wouldn't know anyone; I'd feel like such a fool."

"Not true, you know me." Extending my hand out to her, "I'm Chrissy Anderson; it's nice to finally meet you."

Taking my hand like she's almost afraid I'll snap it in half, "I'm Barbara Cooper, nice to meet you too."

After giving Sad Frumpy Lady, I mean Barbara, the address to the studio and probably her first smile in almost twelve years, I set off to the cemetery to meet Courtney and Nicole. It's been exactly one month since Kelly died, and we decided to mark the occasion by sitting on top of her and drinking some beer. I'm going to limit myself to two though; I don't want to be bloated in case I have a date.

"After Mexico I never thought I'd drink again!"

"Gimme a break, Nicole! You had three Bloody Marys on the flight home!"

With cold beers in hand, and, of course, one for Kelly that's strategically placed on top of her tombstone, we roll around the grass in laughter. We miss her so much, but we agreed to leave our tears behind in Mexico. The last thing Kelly wanted us to do while she was alive was cry for her, and so, out of respect for her and what's left of our own lives, we try to laugh as much as possible.

"Do you think she can see us?"

"Unfortunately for her, yes! Girl can't even get away from us in Heaven! She's our angel, guys."

"Come on, Chrissy, you don't really believe that do you?"

"I absolutely believe it! Crap, if it wasn't for her, I'm fairly certain I wouldn't have a date tonight."

"*DATE?*"

"I think the two of you just woke up the dead."

I stand, give Kelly's tombstone a little tap with my booty, blow it a kiss, and as I make my way back to my car reveal, "Yes, a date, and I'm late, so let's get outta here."

Even though the two of them threatened me with my own death if I didn't tell them who my date was with, I didn't cave in. I need to see where this goes before I take them, Dr. Maria, or anyone else down this road again.

He called right after Kelly died. Said he was worried about me and wanted to make sure I was okay. We didn't talk about what happened to us, only about what happened to Kelly. He expressed his concern for Craig and the baby, and we talked for a long time about how their sadness makes any of our own seem insignificant. Then at the end of the conversation, he asked me out on a date. It was the first time in my life that a man formally asked me out to dinner, and even though it felt like it might be the beginning of my real life fairytale, I expressed reservations. I thought he had moved on, and I was trying to, too. Maybe it was best to leave it at that. But he asked me to trust him, *believe in him*, and because it's all I ever wanted to do since the day we met, I agreed to go on a date with him. That was three weeks ago, and I haven't heard from him since. And as I drive down the highway, music blaring, I begin to wonder if he'll even show up. Maybe he changed his mind. Maybe he wants to hurt me, like I hurt him. Not his style, but I really did fuck the guy up.

It's an absolutely beautiful evening, one you wouldn't typically expect in March, and in celebration, I turn the music even louder and open the sunroof. The song on the radio takes me back to times spent with Kelly, then Kurt, then Leo, and then back again. The memories are a beautiful mixed up swirl of the best and worst of what I shared with each of them, and they're bittersweet. I'm glad I have them but also exhausted from holding onto them so tightly for fear of fading. Usually my trip down memory lane makes me cry, but for once, thoughts of the three of them don't have that effect on me. Maybe it's because I want to look fresh for my date, not sure. But what I am sure of is all of the wonderful things my experiences with Kelly, Kurt, and Leo have taught me about myself. Like that I'm stronger, more beautiful, and more courageous than I ever thought I was or gave myself credit for being. And although consciously grueling at times, I put everything my experiences with them taught me to practical use every single day. Whether I'm trying to give my best friend's eulogy, secure a line of credit with my bank to expand my business, or attempt a really challenging yoga pose, there's something that I learned from my time with each of them that gets me through the tough parts of every single day of my life. It's a constant "if I got through that, then I can get through this" conversation with myself. It's a choice to approach life this way. It's that or turn into a Sad Frumpy Lady. And, I admit, some days it's a *very* slippery slope.

At the stoplight next to my cottage, I look up through my sunroof and into the freshly stardusted sky and give a little shout-out to my newest Angel.

"Hey, girl, I know you had *everything* to do with this date tonight. That being the case, can you make sure it's a good one? I've come too far to be back at square one with all the heartache and crap. Kelly, I know you know that I'm still madly in love with him, and I know you know that despite my la-di-da attitude about going on a date with him, I'm praying it's the last first date I ever have in my life. If you have any pull up there, can you make that be the case? Thanks. Oh, and tell my grandpa I said 'hello!'"

As I pull into my parking space, I give the sky one last long look as my sunroof closes. Silently, I thank Kel, Kurt, and Leo for the memories I shared with them, and I make a wish for the new ones I hope to make tonight.

You are my light, you are my star, you are my sunshine and my dark
You are the everything I dreamed about
You are the guy who stole my heart
I am the girl you're always fighting for…
Dream with me, make me believe that this is a real life fairytale!

("Real Life Fairytale," *Plumb*)

FOUND

MARCH, 2001

Showered, perfumed, and nervous as hell, I check the clock every single ticking second, worried that he might not show up. To occupy my time, I sip wine as I flip through the pictures that Kurt gave to me when I met him for coffee right after Kelly died. For a moment, my mind drifts to how relaxed our conversation was that day. No talk of death, divorce, or arguments over eggs and kayaking--just an authentically refreshing chat about the good ol' days. Despite everything bad that happened to us, there's still a lot of good to reminisce about. Done with the pictures, I toss the pile on the coffee table and nervously glance back up at the clock. Then, at the exact moment he said he would arrive, I hear the car. The car I've dreamt about driving around in since the last time I saw it. After the *second* knock (because I don't want to seem too excited), I open the door to what feels like the rest of my life.

"Hey, Stranger."

But there's nothing strange about him or him being here. He's calm and comfortable, like he's finally home. When he called a few weeks ago, I chalked it up as one more silver lining to appear out of Kelly's illness because well…finding silver linings is my coping mechanism for handling the loss of her. Dr. Maria was right when she urged me to focus on the opportunities that present themselves in the midst of tragedy and not just focus on the tragedy itself. For me, it's been the only way to move past a lot of pain. Kelly's *illness* compelled me to finally get a divorce because it made me realize how short life can be, and I needed to free myself up... clear my head...*really* live it. Her illness forced me to open my eyes to opportunity once hidden behind the bullshit minutia and monotony of my fashion career, and it encouraged me to open my yoga studios. Her illness even persuaded me to hop a red eye to the East Coast and search for Leo because I so badly wanted the kind of love she had with her husband. Maybe that trip didn't work out like I wanted it to, but it was worth the shot. It might seem crazy to *always* be on the lookout for the silver linings of Kelly's death, but sometimes it's the only thing that prevents me from crossing over to the dark side, to becoming a Sad Frumpy Lady. But you know what? Looking at the man standing in my doorway right now, I have no doubt that even if Kelly never got sick, he and I would've ultimately ended up in this moment. I guess the silver lining of her death is that it expedited the process. See! I can't help myself! Finding silver linings is my new addiction.

He and I were always meant to be together. No filthy lie I told, no amount of time I forced between us, and no silly fling that we both found ourselves in to take our minds off of the truth could keep us apart. Staring into his eyes, I no longer feel the need to be sorry for all of the horrible things I did to him and I know the only reason he's here is because he doesn't expect me to be. Every piece of my life...every good, bad, and ugly piece of it had to happen to get to this moment and it's impossible to apologize for that. He and I won't work...*I won't work with anyone*, until I forgive myself. And so I do. I'm finally home, too.

After a long synchronized deep breath, I look over his shoulder at the sparkling heap of metal. It catches me by surprise.

"Wow, is that the same car?"

"Yeah, I let my brother borrow it while I was living in New York, and the dumbass washed it. Kinda ruins the whole look, don't you think?"

"Not at all, it looks nice and classy, just like you, Leo."

I take a step back to take him all in. His clothes, while causal and unpretentious, look more expensive than mine.

"Are you ready to do this?"

Scared to death and hands shaking, it's nearly impossible to act composed. All I want to do is jump into his arms. But I restrain myself.

"Yeah, I'm starving."

When I turn around to lock my door, he places his hands on my waist. The drug sends shock waves through my body and my hands begin to shake even more.

"I mean, are you ready to be afraid...*together*?"

The minute I opened the door, I knew I was never going to let him go ever again, but I thought for sure he'd make me pay some kind of price, whether it was making me think he was mulling over his options or disappearing from my life every few weeks to make me suffer like I made him suffer. But then again, why would he do that? *He's* the one who taught me the meaning of vulnerability and showed me through his own words and actions that the faster you expose yourself, the faster you get what you want. There were never any games with Leo.

"Can it be that easy after everything that happened?"

"Unless you want to keep complicating it."

"But you live in New York. I'd say that makes things pretty complicated."

"I told you before...I'll always be where I know you are."

Then he pulls me toward him and touches my hair, then my lips, then the back of my neck. He's saying everything I've wanted to hear for so long. I can barely believe this is all happening.

"So...are you ready?"

"I've been ready. I just needed you to give me another chance."

"Then I don't think I can wait until the end of the night to do this."

It's a kiss that puts to shame all the kisses in all the history of the entire world that have ever taken place before it. It's the perfect combination of wet and dry, of hard and soft, of lust and love. It makes me spin. After he pulls away he asks me if I'm ready for my surprise...*my modified and belated surprise.*

"I'm moving back to California."

"But how can that be? What about your job?"

"I took the wrong one. Everything I ever wanted is right here."

"So everything you said to me in New York…it wasn't true?"

"It was true, I was petrified to put myself out there for you, but when I heard Kelly died…"

"By the way, how *did* you find out that Kelly died? Wait, let me guess."

God bless Slutty Co-worker…my angel on earth.

"Of course. Anyway, when she told me about Kelly, I started thinking about second chances and--"

"Hold on, *did you just say second chances*? That's all Kelly talked about the last time I was with her on her porch."

"I guess she's giving our grandpas a well-deserved rest and working some magic of her own."

"And that's *exactly* what I asked her to do in the letter!"

"What letter?"

"I'll tell you all about it over dinner."

"And I'll tell you about how much I hated New York! The second I got there, I was looking for a way to leave. Now all I need to do is find a place to live."

Without hesitation, I pull him back toward me.

"Oh I know the perfect place. It's charming and quiet, and I think you'll love the roommate."

"Sounds great, where is it?"

"You're parked right in front of it."

He turns to look at the door of my cottage and then back at me. Serious Leo is in full force.

"Just so you know, once I move in, I'm never moving out."

Serious Chrissy is in full force too.

"Just so you know, I won't let you."

"Then maybe I should give this back to you."

He reaches into his pocket, and I recognize my Banana Republic ring the second he pulls it out.

"I love you, Chrissy Anderson. That *is* your name, right?"

"Very funny! Give me that thing!"

Standing about an inch apart, he slips the ring on my finger and whispers, "Promise me this time you won't take it off until I can get you the real deal?"

"Promise."

And that was the beginning of a thousand other promises I made, and kept, with Leo. Sorta.

An excerpt from the forthcoming

THE UNEXPECTED LIST

by Chrissy Anderson

Available Spring 2013

CHAPTER ONE

LISTEN
SEPTEMBER 11, 2002

"What are you gonna get?"

"Thinking we share the usual--buffalo wings and some nachos. Sound good?"

"Duh! But this time make sure you tell them we want ranch dressing with the wings, none of that blue cheese crap!"

Some things never change. Kelly and I have been sharing the same two things at Chili's for like a hundred years. I always give her a lot of shit for dragging me here, but I have to admit, there's something really comforting about our usual table, the bottomless beverages and the never-ending trash talking about our former high school classmates/current servers.

"Look! Look! Look, Kel! Isn't that the guy you went to homecoming with when we were sophomores?"

"Oy vey...would you look at him?" Shaking her head at the now thirty-two year old man-boy. "After all this time, still a waiter. Jesus, to think I let that guy touch my boobs in the back of his mom's Toyota Celica."

This is the way it's always been with us. The greasy food, the ruthless revolting chitchat that makes Courtney and Nicole roll their eyes, it's my very favorite part of the week. I'm secretly glad those two had to work late tonight so we can say whatever we want to without their smug looks and smarty-pants doctor jargon.

"Oh my gosh, Kel, I almost forgot to tell you! I had this horrible dream about you the other night. You had cancer. It was that one that sounds like a pancake or something."

"It's called a pancreas, you moron! It's a good thing Court and Nic aren't here; they would've made fun of you until you ran away in tears."

"Yes, that's it! You had pancreatic cancer! Man, it was brutal Kel. You got all skinny… and mean too! I wanted to help you and stuff, but you completely shut me out."

"Sounds like something I'd do."

"Didn't work though, I sat on your front porch and wrote you a bunch of mushy letters telling you how much I loved you. You totally hated it."

"No doubt. So did I die?"

I tilt my head and say, "Odd, I can't remember now."

Bored with my boring dream, Kelly looks at me over the rim of her Diet Coke and asks, "So, tell me what's been going on with you? I mean, besides the obvious."

I roll my hands down to my belly and give my bump a little rub.

"Is that husband of yours in town or are you alone again this weekend?"

"Alone again. He's working his ass off to get that new division off the ground."

It's sorta the truth. He's in Nevada taking a crash course to get his pilot's license for I have absolutely no idea why. Seriously, where the hell does he plan on flying off to when this thing pops out?

"Let us know when you guys have a free weekend. Craig wants the gang to go camping one last time before the fall."

Lovely. I hated camping enough when I didn't have an extra twenty-five pounds to drag around. But never one to ruin everyone's fun, I enthusiastically nod my head like sleeping on rocks and peeing in the woods is the most super fantastic thing I can possibly think of doing at this stage of my life.

The food arrives, and after yelling at the idiot for bringing us blue cheese dressing, I proceed to tell Kelly the most hilarious story.

"So get this…I'm at a bar a couple of weeks ago-"

"*A bar?* But look at you! And, you can't even drink!"

"I know, right? It was for my co-worker. She was having some sort of mini-meltdown and she begged me to sit with her while she drank her troubles away. I don't know why, but I went."

"And….so?"

"So she bailed on me the second we got there! Yep, ditched me for some little Korean guy. Oh man, he had the funniest name. *What was it again?* Ho-gab…Ho-dog…Ho-Bag! That's it, Ho-Bag! Anyway, when they took off, I started talking to the Korean guy's friend, and you're never gonna believe this…HE HIT ON ME!"

"Was the dude blind?"

"Nah, the countertop on the bar was totally huge." Rubbing my belly again, "This thing was comfortably tucked underneath. Anyway, we actually had a nice conversation. Don't laugh…it was about ghosts."

"Oh, brother…you and your ghost stories."

"Actually he was the one who brought them up."

"Whatever. So what happened with…*what was the dude's name?*"

"Leo."

Saying his name out loud sends chills up the back of my neck and rousing thoughts of that evening begin to flash through my mind. It causes me to pause long enough for Kelly to bug her eyes out at me to continue.

"Oh! We talked until my bladder was about to burst, that's what happened." My voice trails off, "Something about him was…I dunno…special."

"*Hoooold on!* Back the story up, you bar hopping Barbie! Sounds like you're leaving something out."

I'm leaving a lot out. He was mysterious and sexy and *totally* into me. Our conversation was packed full of things we had in common and the way my heart pounded whenever he looked at me…

"Okay, okay…I left out the fact that he was only twenty-two!"

"Holy Hannah! You could almost go to jail for that!"

"Calm down! All we did was talk!" Looking from side to side and lowering my voice to a whisper, "Can I tell you a secret though?"

"I don't even repeat the things you want me to repeat, so what do you think?"

"I kinda can't stop thinking about him, Kel. He had these hypnotic eyes…"

"Wow, this isn't like you. It's freakin' me out."

"Freakin' me out too." And then my voice trails off. "I had so much in common with him. Almost more than anyone I've ever met."

"*Hellooooooo?* What about your husband?"

Snapping back to reality, "Except for him, obviously!"

Wiping sauce from her lower lip, Kelly points to my stomach and says, "So when did he notice that thing?"

"When the bar was about to close I--"

"*You stayed until closing time?*"

"I'm telling you, his eyes were crazy beautiful! Anyway, he suggested we talk outside for a while. I was like, HELLS NO! But I still didn't have the guts to stand up and show him that he wasted his entire evening on me. This bar was crawling with chicks! And, trust me; this guy could've had his pick of the lot."

"You chick-jacked him!"

I'm looking at Kelly like she's an idiot.

"What? You get to say stuff like that and it's cute. But when I do, it's lame?"

"Well…kinda."

"Oh, whatever! So, what the heck happened?"

"I peed my pants."

"You're kidding me, right?"

"Nope, peed all over the fucking floor. You know how it is when you're this far along."

"Oh my God! Did he notice?"

"No. I pretended to spill my water and asked him to hurry and find some towels. When he was gone I made a run for it."

After a laugh so intense that no sound emits from either of our bodies, I catch my breath and say, "I feel bad though."

"About?"

"Bailing on him." She's looking at me like I've lost my mind. "I know, I know…I'm married and…" pointing at my gut, "I have this.

But still, it seemed like he was relieved to meet me. Like I made him feel something he never felt before. Like I saved him. I dunno...I wish..."

"You wish what, Chrissy?"

Catching myself before I say something Kelly can't even comprehend, "I wish that damn waiter would bring the bill. I gotta get home and catch up on my sleep while Kurt's gone. It's like the only time I can get a solid ten hours."

Standing up to flag down the waiter, my pregnant belly bashes into the table, spilling our drinks everywhere.

The commotion jolts me out of my sleep and straight up in bed. My head darts all around to try and figure out what the hell is going on. My hands clutch my stomach and relief washes over me. Flat as a board.

"Thank you, Lord Jesus, who I'm still kinda struggling to believe in."

I'm thankful only until I remember that Kelly's dead and Leo's long gone.

ACKNOWLEDGEMENTS

B ecause I'm extremely committed to my tagline, "the difference between doing something and doing nothing is everything," I feel it's necessary to acknowledge those who have offered me love, genuine encouragement, and selfless guidance while writing *The List Trilogy*.

First and foremost, I want to recognize my husband. The irreplaceable love I have for him is the inspiration behind every word I write. From the moment I met him, I felt compelled to write about our love story. And once I started, I became obsessed with sharing it. I appreciate his understanding when it comes to my commitment to helping others find true love and I pray to God I have honored him in the process of doing that, for his love and respect means everything to me. My daughter, who was four at the time I began writing *Part I of The List Trilogy*, is nine now. My baby has demonstrated a level of patience with my "hobby" that blows my mind and warms my heart. *The List Trilogy* is for her to read with an open mind and a willingness to learn…when she's an adult, of course, because it's filled with cuss words and Ooh-La-La sex!

There were many times over the last five years when I almost chickened out of publishing my work. If it wasn't for my best friend, Eva, who took my panicked phone calls, stressed out texts, and rambling (almost psychotic) emails about how stupid I think I am, and turned them into rejuvenating and motivating therapy sessions, *The List Trilogy* would never exist. Thank you, my dear old friend, for all of your recommendations and for protecting me *once again* from making a total ass of myself. You are the definition of what a true girlfriend is and no matter how many miles separate us, we will always be close. On a local level, it's essential that I acknowledge my pal, Vikki. Vikki's the most amazingly tireless working mother I know. As busy and professional as this woman is, she's the only one of my friends who appeared on my doorstep with tears of delight streaming down her face after she read the last word of *The Life List* (I think I freaked out everyone else I know). To this day she continues to inundate me with marvelous marketing ideas to take my trilogy to the next level. I love you for being you, Vikki, and I'm so incredibly grateful I met you eight years ago. I have to thank my poker group gals, (Lisa H., Lisa S., Nat, and Ang) for the most genuine of genuine laughter and encouragement. The shit that comes out your *almost*-middle-aged mouths after seventeen bottles of wine has inspired my writing more than any of you will ever know. Thank you girls, for my pretty book release party, the weekly laughter, and daily shoulders-to-cry-on. I hope one day we're able to walk some kind of red carpet function together (totally buzzed, of course). Just like I wish every woman had a "Leo" in her life, I wish every woman had the kind of genuine encouragement *all* of my girlfriends have given to me with regard to my work.

I have to acknowledge Peter Baxter (www.blog.designeconomic.com) for the charitable work he's done on my website, www.askchrissy.net. Like me, Peter is one of those freaky left-brain/right-brain people. He's an accomplished author of several works of non-fiction about smart stuff like Africa *and* he's a web developer. Who even thought a species like that existed? Our style of writing could NOT be more different, yet he's offered me subtly valuable advice that's no doubt taken my work to a more polished level.

And speaking of polished level…I'd be a total literary laughing stock if it weren't for Amy Metz of A Blue Million Books (www.abluemillionbooks.blogspot.com), and professional wordsmith and editor, Margie Aston (www.margieaston.weebly.com). Both of these incredibly selfless women picked-up first editions of *The Life List* at random, read it, and loved it. But they could've loved it even more if I knew how the hell to use an ellipsis or how to spell "fuck's sake," so each of them contacted me to offer their professional and much needed support. Words can't express how indebted I am to these two women for their brains, generosity and overall conviction that I had a really great story that could become phenomenal if I knew how to punctuate…and spell, for fuck's sake! (They'd be so proud.) I keep a list of people that I swear to God I will reward for kindness and at the top of it are Amy and Margie. It might take me a while, but it will be done.

I have to slip in a little shout-out to my folks and to my brother--for no other reason than to thank them for putting up with my "chrissygans" for all of these years. Talk about unconditional love! It might've taken a long time, but I found my calling and I know for a fact that no one is more proud of me than you guys.

Lastly, I have to thank all of the mini-Chrissys and forsaken-Francescas out there. While "Leo" was my inspiration for my convoluted and chaotic love story, you were the ultimate courage to tell it. I don't want anyone to ever feel as lonely, scared, or confused as I felt during those years of my life. No matter if you're at the beginning of an arduous relationship, or deep into one that you wish you left a long time ago, I hope I've made you feel sane and supported. I want you to know you have a friend. Maybe those things will be *your* difference between doing something and doing nothing. And if they aren't, well no one knows why better than me.

Xoxo,
Chrissy

Made in the USA
Charleston, SC
25 July 2013